# The Fake Mate

"Lana weaves fantastically the elements we love from a paranormal romance (namely, attractive shifters with extremely interesting drives) with the humor characteristic from the best contemporary rom-com you can get your hands on. This book is addictive, epically smutty, and the breath of fresh air the romance genre didn't know it needed."

—Elena Armas, *New York Times* bestselling author of
*The Fiancé Dilemma*

"An overall delightful experience. . . . Funny, sweet, and very hot, *The Fake Mate* is the ideal venture into mystic romance."  —Shondaland

"Lana Ferguson's *The Fake Mate* is the perfect introduction to the wild world of the omegaverse. . . . Whether you're new to the omegaverse or a longtime fan, the scorching *The Fake Mate* will thrill those in search of a book that turns the heat all the way up."  —*BookPage*

"What begins as a typical fake-relationship story quickly slides into a delightfully endearing study of two people overcoming expectations."  —*Publishers Weekly*

"This fun, steamy romance has interesting, well-drawn characters who happen to be shifters. . . . Fans of fake relationships will appreciate Ferguson's paranormal twist on the trope."  —*Library Journal*

"A steamy, worthwhile romance with plenty of banter, tapping into the popular grumpy-meets-sunshine trope."  —*Kirkus Reviews*

"Charming. Funny. Primal. Ferguson's paranormal romance manages to be sweet and spicy at the same time, with two likable leads who can't ignore their wolfish urges. . . . Readers will tear through this omegaverse novel."
—*Booklist*

"This mash-up of *Grey's Anatomy*, Ali Hazelwood, and high-heat Reylo fan fiction will make even the most seasoned romance readers' hearts beat a little faster."
—Shelf Awareness

PRAISE FOR

## The Nanny

"I need more books like *The Nanny*, stat. A smart, educated heroine (Yes, please!) meets a driven, career-focused single dad. Sparks fly . . . and fly, and fly. Seriously, this book is like if Ali Hazelwood and Tessa Bailey had a smutty baby. I devoured every page and was sad to see it end. This is the spice BookTok wants! Now I need Lana Ferguson to work faster, because I want to see everything she writes."
—Ruby Dixon, *USA Today* bestselling author of *Bull Moon Rising*

"Smart, fun, sexy, and sizzling with romantic tension, *The Nanny* is a mouthwateringly delicious take on second chances, with a healthy dash of steam. I can't wait for more from Lana Ferguson!"
—Sara Desai, author of *'Til Heist Do Us Part*

"Ferguson makes the will-they-won't-they sing with complex emotional shading and a strong sense of inevitability to her protagonists' connection. . . . Rosie Danan fans should snap this up."
—*Publishers Weekly* (starred review)

"This steamy romantic comedy puts a modern spin on traditional tropes, bringing the falling-for-the-nanny and secret-past storylines into the twenty-first century. . . . Readers who enjoyed Julie Murphy and Sierra Simone's *A Merry Little Meet Cute* will adore this positive, upbeat, sex-filled romp." —*Library Journal*

"Everything about *The Nanny* is enjoyable: the plot, the pacing, the compelling characters, and especially Ferguson's wise and funny voice. It's also extremely refreshing to see sex-positive characters who approach intimacy with maturity. . . . If you're a fan of dirty talk and slow-burning chemistry, you'll love *The Nanny*." —*BookPage* (starred review)

# Under Loch *and* Key

## LANA FERGUSON

BERKLEY ROMANCE

NEW YORK

BERKLEY ROMANCE
Published by Berkley
An imprint of Penguin Random House LLC
penguinrandomhouse.com

Illustration by ArtMari/Shutterstock

Library of Congress Cataloging-in-Publication Data

Names: Ferguson, Lana, author.
Title: Under loch and key / Lana Ferguson.
Description: First edition. | New York: Berkley Romance, 2024.
Identifiers: LCCN 2024026828 (print) | LCCN 2024026829 (ebook) |
ISBN 9780593816851 (trade paperback) | ISBN 9780593816868 (ebook)
Subjects: LCGFT: Romance fiction. | Paranormal fiction. | Novels.
Classification: LCC PS3606.E72555 U53 2024 (print) | LCC PS3606.E72555 (ebook) |
DDC 813/.6—dc23/eng/20240621
LC record available at https://lccn.loc.gov/2024026828
LC ebook record available at https://lccn.loc.gov/2024026829

First Edition: December 2024

Printed in the United States of America
1st Printing

To my favorite Scottish lass, Blair, for granting me forgiveness for giving Nessie a penis. My deepest apologies.

# Under Loch and Key

# 1

## KEYANNA

I never imagined that my death would come by way of a sheep avalanche, but as I watch the tumbling mass of floof barreling down the hill toward the stretch of road I am currently stalled on—it occurs to me that it would at least be a *memorable* way to go.

*"Christ."*

I scramble to get the door of my ancient rental open—the door being on the *wrong* side, relatively, I might add, which means it's in direct line of impact for the bleating army currently rushing toward me. I manage to snatch my backpack and duck out of the car and half stumble to a safer area, but the sheep, being less murderous than I'd come to believe, actually start to slow as they spill around the aged blue sedan, voicing their irritation of the impediment it makes by loudly trilling more of the hellishly loud *bah*s.

"Oi!" a voice calls from up the hill. "You all right, lass?"

I bring a hand over my eyes to peer up into the sun, noticing a man with graying hair waving down at me. "Fine," I call back. "They're not carnivorous, are they?"

"Not last I checked," he chuckles, trotting down the hillside. He notices my car in the midst of the sheep-sea, quirking a brow. "Car troubles?"

"I *told* the woman at the rental place I wasn't good with a stick shift, but apparently, it was all they had left."

"You an American?" He doesn't ask it like it's something to be offended by, but he does sound perplexed. "You're a right ways from the tourist spots, aren't you?"

"Oh, I'm here for . . ." I trail off, deciding it's probably a bad idea to vomit my entire complicated pilgrimage to a veritable stranger. "I'm here to visit family."

His eyes crinkle at the corners, a bright, expressive blue among the weathered lines of his face making him seem genuinely interested. "Is that right? And who might you belong to? I know everyone around these parts."

I hesitate, again considering the ramifications of telling a stranger about my spur-of-the-moment reunion with my estranged family before *they* know about it. In the end, I reason that, if nothing else, there's a good chance I will reach my grandmother's house before this man can wade out of his pile of sheep.

"The MacKays," I tell him. "Rhona MacKay?"

"Oh, aye, aye, I know Rhona! Is she your granny, then? Would that make Duncan your da?" He squints as if trying to make the connection. "You've got the look of him. Didn't know he had any weans when he ran off to America."

I try to process all of this; I am deciding to take his stream of consciousness as overt friendliness and not some backhanded comment on my father's complicated history with his family. He must notice my stunned expression, though, because he waves a hand back and forth.

"Listen to me, babbling on. Sorry. Don't get many newcomers in Greerloch." He wipes his hand on the front of his worn flannel shirt, extending it after. "Hamish Campbell. I live over the hill there with this lot." He nods back toward the still-bleating horde. "Pleased to meet you."

I take his hand, still reeling from the influx of conversation. People don't just *chat* like this back in New York. "I'm . . . Key. Key MacKay. Well, Keyanna, actually, but everyone calls me Key."

"Key," he echoes. "I like it. You remind me of Rhona now that I've had a proper look at you. You've got the eyes."

I don't exactly know how to feel about looking like a woman who hasn't wanted anything to do with me for my entire twenty-seven years, but I manage a tight smile regardless. "How nice."

He frowns at his brood, looking sympathetic. "I gather you'd like to be on your way, aye? Your granny is probably expecting you."

I don't correct him, giving a noncommittal shrug instead.

"Might take me a wee bit to get the herd to move along, but I can take a look at your car if you like? I'm right handy when I aim to be."

"That would be amazing actually," I sigh in relief. "If it's really no trouble?"

"No trouble at all." He waves me off. "You just wait right there, and I will have you right as rain within the hour."

I glance across the rolling hills and lush green that spill all around us, biting my lip as I pull out my phone. "You don't happen to know how far"—I squint at the notes on my screen—"Scall-an-jull Cove is, would you?"

Mr. Campbell laughs. "I grant ya, that's a hard one. It's *Skallangal* Cove, love." He says it like: *scall-an-gale,* which sounds much nicer than my butchered attempt. "You're after Nessie, then, aye?"

"I . . . what?"

Another chuckle. "They don't call it 'cove of the fear' for nothing. I've chased many a wean from that cove. Rocks are too rough there, you see? S'not safe."

"Oh, it was just a place my dad mentioned . . ."

"Oh, aye, I reckon he did. Duncan always claimed he saw the beast. Swore on it, if you got him good and steamin'."

"Steaming?"

"That's drunk to you, hen."

*Hen?*

Probably be here all day if I stop him for a slang lesson every time it comes up.

"You saw my dad drunk?"

"A time or two. Before he took off." Mr. Campbell scratches at his jaw. "I was sad to see him go. How's the auld boy getting along, then? He not come with you?"

I feel a twinge of pain in my chest; even after six months, it still hurts to think he can't be here with me. "He . . . passed," I tell him. "In the spring."

"Ah, lass." Hamish sighs, looking truly grieved by the news. "I am sorry to hear that. He was a good man, your da. Can I ask how he went?"

"Pneumonia," I explain. "He was diagnosed with Alzheimer's a few years ago, and he just sort of . . . degenerated. He came down with pneumonia after a bad winter, and he—" I have to clear my throat, feeling it grow thicker. "He didn't recover."

"Oh, hen." Hamish's blue eyes glitter with genuine emotion, which only worsens the pressure I'm feeling in my chest. Hamish reaches into his jacket pocket to retrieve a handkerchief, rubbing at his nose briefly before stowing it away. "I'm sorry, love. And your mum? We all heard the stories about how Duncan ran off with a wily American—is she not here with you?"

*He's determined to pick at all my scabs today, isn't he?*

"My mother died giving birth to me," I manage stiffly.

Hamish blows out a breath. "Aye, I've really stepped innit, haven't I? Forgive me for being a nosy bastard." He shakes his head, clearing his throat as he gestures to my car. "How's about I get to work on this, then? There's some lovely views from the hill there"—he points across the lush green expanse stretching beyond the little knoll his sheep are currently crowding—"and your cove is nigh a mile"—he turns his finger in the other direction—"that way." He winks. "If you're brave enough, mind you."

I chuckle softly. "I'm not afraid."

"Well, mind the rocks, would you? It really is unsafe. Keep to the shore, aye?"

"I will," I assure him. "And thank you for your help."

He waves me off. "Think nothing of it. We're a close-knit group here in Greerloch, and you're family apparently! Don't you worry, I'll have this fixed up in no time."

He turns to shoo away one of the bleating fluff-monsters currently nibbling at his coat hem, pushing his way through the masses toward my poor, pathetic rental car. I watch him for a moment, wondering if it's *actually* wise to leave my car with some stranger, but honestly, what choice do I have? It's not like I can fix it myself, and my only other alternative is to lock myself inside and hope someone else comes along. I let my eyes sweep across the sprawling, endless green of the landscape, not seeing any signs of life outside of Hamish and his horde.

*I guess that's what the rental insurance is for.*

I turn toward the direction he pointed out, which leads to the massive hill that supposedly hides the way to Skallangal Cove, thinking that now is just as good a time as any. I hoist my backpack up

higher onto my shoulders—taking a deep breath and letting it out as
I turn toward the hill.

*Onwards and upwards, I guess.*

I doubt Hamish's "nigh a mile" more and more as I trek across the
grass; the hill itself was a feat, less of a "hill" up close and more of a
small mountain, really. My thighs burn with effort as I walk, and I'm
sure my watch is probably organizing me a pizza party for the over-
abundance of steps I'm getting in today. But when I finally see the
glittering surface of the loch come into view, the sun shining on the
small waves and making them sparkle, I think maybe it was worth
all the steps.

Ever since I set foot in Scotland, I can't seem to get over how beautiful it is. The land itself seems to be alive all around me—almost as
if I can feel the hum of life in the air and beneath my feet. The colors
feel more vibrant, the sights and sounds more lovely, and I can see it,
I think. *Feel* it, even. Why my father was so wistful when he spoke
of his homeland.

There are signs as I get closer—the standard "Keep Out" and
"Danger" posted along the barely there path that leads onto the rocky
shore—but given that there isn't a single soul for miles, it would
seem, I think I'm probably fine to explore a little. I mean, who's going
to tell me I can't? Hamish's sheep?

There *are* a good number of large rocks jutting up at the water's
edge, giving the shore a craggy effect that I can definitely see being
a problem for kids wanting to adventure onto them. For a moment,
I can only stare at the quiet, rolling water that gently ebbs back and
forth against the shore, struck with a sudden memory that isn't

mine—one that *feels* like mine for as many times as I've heard my dad recount it.

*He was just there. Just beyond the shore. I'd slipped on the rocks, see? I thought I'd drown . . . but he saved me. Me! Of all people . . .*

As a kid, the story of my dad's salvation at the hands of some mythical beast had been thrilling. I remember late nights of begging him to hear it "just one more time"—anything to avoid bedtime. Sometimes, I can still hear his voice, soft and comforting, as he lulled me to sleep. Still feel his fingers on my brow, pushing my curls away from my face as my eyes drifted shut.

In the end, his stories were all he had.

I drop my backpack onto the ground and start to dig through it, my hands shaking a little as I pull out the black capsule.

"Hey, Dad," I mutter, rubbing my thumbs across the sleek curve of the urn. "Look where we are." I straighten, holding it close to my chest as I turn back to the water. "I brought you back," I say to the air. "Just like I said I would."

A deep ache settles in my chest and lower in my stomach; I thought I would find more peace here, knowing I was giving him the send-off he wanted. I can't even be sure if this is what he *actually* wanted or if it was just more ramblings brought on by the slow loss of his mind, but it *feels* right, I think. Sure, he never spoke of his family, or of his life here beyond silly childhood stories—but I could tell he missed it. There was a sadness in his voice sometimes that I could hear no matter how hard he tried to hide it.

I realize after a few minutes that I'm just standing here, that I'm stalling, really. It's silly; I quit my job, flew across the ocean, practically uprooted my entire life just to come here, and now that I'm here . . . I'm not sure if I can do it.

The wind picks up, whipping my sun-blazed curls around my face, and I tell myself that it's just the brightness out here that's making my eyes water. I can *do* this, damnit.

I turn to try and scope out a good place; I've never spread someone's ashes before, obviously, but it doesn't feel very special to just walk up to the shoreline and dump my dad out onto the algae. Surely there has to be a better way.

With that in mind, I start pacing along the edge of the water, nearing the expanse of jutting rocks that the signs and Hamish and probably God at this point have warned me about. There's a relatively flat one only a few steps out, just a short climb and a few hops away from shore. Surely I can manage that. I'm not a kid, after all.

I hold my dad tighter as I carefully step out onto the raised stone that leads toward the larger flat rock, hovering with one foot still on the shore as I test my balance. My sneakers aren't the best choice for this, and I'm wishing now that I'd read a few more travel blogs about dressing for Scotland. Not, I think, that any of them would have accounted for rock climbing on the coast of Loch Ness. I curl my fingers to grip my dad's urn as I blow out a breath, readying to step farther onto the rocks and finish this so I can head off to meet the family. Something else I'm not sure I'm looking forward to.

I move to take another step, feeling the soles of my shoes slip against the wet surface as my balance suddenly becomes off-kilter. A surge of panic jolts through me as I start to fall backward—but I'm snatched away before that happens.

"Hey!"

Something thick winds around my waist, hauling me backward, using enough power that I nearly stumble as I'm forced back to both feet on the shore. The thick something—an *arm*, I realize—lingers for only a moment before releasing me, and I whirl around with hot anger flooding my cheeks as I prepare to tell off whoever interfered.

And then, funnily enough, I seem to forget how to use words.

The stranger is . . . beautiful. Not the kind of beautiful that one might attribute to rare works of art or a sunset or anything like that. No. *This* man is the kind of beautiful that makes you think of sex and sweat and all sorts of other filthy things that are currently flitting through my thoughts.

He's taller than me even at my five foot ten—easily by six inches, maybe more. His golden brown hair seems almost highlighted by the sun, but the stubble at his chiseled jaw is darker, adding a rough edge to the prettiness that his high cheekbones and straight nose give him. He's all soft mouth and broad shoulders and *holy hell* his pants can barely contain his thighs—but it's his eyes that hold my attention most. So blue, they almost appear silver, they hold my gaze for more seconds than is probably appropriate as I struggle to think of something, *anything* to say to this ridiculously hot man that might sound halfway coherent.

"I—I'm—"

"Stupid," he finishes for me, his sinfully deep accent—a literal brogue that makes my skin heat—enough to make it take a few seconds for me to fully comprehend what he's said. "That's what you are."

My mouth gapes when it hits me, and I blink at him in a manner that is probably as stupid as he's just accused me of being.

What the *hell*?

## LACHLAN

The momentary surprise in her features quickly morphs into a ruddy sort of anger that pinkens her cheeks and makes her already prominent array of freckles all the more noticeable—her too-red mouth pursing and her titian brows knitting together as she clutches the black vase in her arms tighter.

"Excuse me?"

*Bloody hell*, I think. *Of course.*

"You heard me," I say, crossing my arms over my chest. "Did you not see the signs on the way here? Or maybe you reckoned they didn't apply to you, aye?"

Her mouth parts, her ire briefly flickering with surprise before she straightens her shoulders. "I saw them."

"And you . . . what? You thought you knew better? Typical American."

"Hey! You don't even know me. I was being careful!"

"You were two seconds away from busting your arse on the rocks."

"I wasn't— That's not—"

Her cheeks heat further, and she actually *stomps* her foot at me, which might amuse me in other circumstances, but my eyes are too busy darting past her toward the rippling surface of the water with worry weighing heavily on my chest, looking for signs of movement.

"This isn't a place for clumsy tourists," I tell her. "Best you head back where you came from. There's a nice gift shop in town."

She narrows her eyes at me, and for the first time, I notice the sparkling green color of them, glinting in the sunlight—bright and viridescent—and paired with the fiery, wild curls whipping in the breeze, making her appear as if she was brought up here. She certainly doesn't *look* like an American at first glance.

"I'm not *clumsy*," she huffs, interrupting my study of her. "And I'm not a tourist. I'm here visiting family."

My brows shoot up.

*Family?*

I know everyone within fifty miles of here, and would certainly have remembered her had I met her before.

"Is that right? And who might that be?"

"*Not* that it's any of your business," she tuts, "but I'm here to see my grandmother. Rhona MacKay."

I bristle immediately upon hearing the name. My fists clench against my sides beneath my crossed arms, studying her in a new light. I can see the resemblance now, faintly—Rhona's hair has long turned gray, but there's a similarity in the shape of her eyes, her nose—even the curve of her mouth turned down in a frown is familiar.

I hear my da's words drift through my thoughts like the whispers of an old ghost story, a warning that, until now, held no weight. A shiver runs down my spine, but I don't let my wariness show. My entire life, I have been told to fear this woman, the one I didn't know existed until just now—but she certainly doesn't *look* like the end of the world as I know it.

"Is that right," I mutter, hoping I look composed. "You're a ways from the MacKay farm. You lost?"

"No, I'm not," she huffs. "I was just going to . . ." Her lips squeeze together, and her hands press the black vase in her hands closer to her body. "It's none of your business what I was doing, really."

"Aye, I reckon you're right," I agree, "but again—someone had to keep you from falling on your arse."

"I wasn't going to fall on my—" She makes a frustrated sound, reaching to pinch the bridge of her nose. "Look. I just needed to see the cove, all right? It's personal."

"Personal," I echo. "Right. Well, best move along now. The weather is supposed to turn."

She peers up into the sun with a hand over her eyes, frowning. "It's sunny out."

"Welcome to Scotland," I chuckle. "The weather has a mind of its own."

"I still need to . . ." She looks out at the water, something in her expression that seems almost akin to sadness. "Whatever. I can do it later." She casts a suspicious glance my way. "Is it really going to rain? Or are you just chasing me off?"

I shrug. "You're welcome to sit here and find out." I glance down at her tightly laced gutties, noting that they'd do her no good in the muck of a proper Scottish rain. "But since you aren't even wearing a decent pair of wellies, you'd be more keen on help, I'll bet. Once you're knee-deep in mud, that is."

She follows my gaze to her shoes, looking thrown for a second.

"Wellies are—"

"I know what wellies are," she scoffs.

"Ah, so you're not accidentally ignorant, but purposefully so?"

She tucks the vase into her side, throwing up her other hand. "Who the fuck even are you? The shore police?"

"Something like that," I snort. I give her a mock bow, feeling fully amused now by her disdainful expression. It isn't often I get to vex a MacKay. Especially one I've been taught to fear my entire life. "Lachlan Greer, at your service, princess."

"Don't call me that," she huffs. "My name is Key."

My brow arches. "Key? That's your name?"

"Keyanna," she amends, making a face. "But no one calls me that. Key is fine."

"Key," I try, deciding it suits her, for whatever reason. "Well, today is your lucky day."

"Oh?" She narrows her eyes suspiciously. "Why is that?"

"Because you've just found yourself an escort to the MacKay farm."

"No offense, but I don't need an escort."

I step closer, her long body meaning that she doesn't have to crane her neck *too* much to look up at me, but enough that it feels satisfying if only to get under her skin further.

"No offense," I counter, "but it isn't a request. This is private property, and you're trespassing."

"What," she snorts, "are you going to tell me you own the place?"

My lips curl in a smirk. "Aye, lass. I do."

For once, she remains blessedly quiet.


Key is pouting in the passenger seat of my old Land Rover, clutching that vase of hers tightly.

"I still don't know why I couldn't drive myself."

I roll my eyes. "Did you not hear Hamish? You wore out the clutch on your poor motor. What were you even doing to it?"

"Driving it!" she answers exasperatedly. "I *told* the rental place I wasn't good with a stick shift."

"Well, that's bloody obvious now."

"At this point, I would have rather walked," she mutters.

I chuff a laugh as I point out the windshield to the now-pouring rain beating against the car. "Would have had a bad time with that, I think."

"Whatever."

I sneak a glance at her while I continue down the path, having a hard time not noticing how stunning she is, if not loud and stubborn. She's all long limbs and wild curls, and I try again to see Duncan in her, who I know from Hamish was her da. I was just a boy when he ran off to America, but I remember the story well. Just as I know all the stories of the MacKays.

"Your da," I start. "Hamish said he passed?"

I notice even in my peripheral vision how much she tenses. "He did."

"I'm sorry to hear that," I say, not because I had any particular love for her father, but because it seems polite, at the very least. Plus, know thine enemy, and all that. "I was just a lad when he ran off, but I know your granny was torn up over it."

*And so was my da*, I think bitterly.

She turns in her seat. "You were a kid when my dad left? Just how old are you?"

"Thirty-four," I tell her, frowning. "I was only six when he left."

"So you don't remember him," she says, an air of disappointment in her voice.

"Not really, no. He came back now and again, but I didn't see much of him. Not before he stopped coming altogether."

She turns her eyes down to her lap, frowning. For some reason, it makes me want to keep her talking.

"And how auld are you, then?"

"Twenty-seven," she says.

"Practically a wean," I chuckle.

"Oh, shut up," she grumbles. "You're not some old man."

"I am in my bones, princess," I say with another dry laugh. "Just ask anyone."

It's a joke for her benefit, but there's truth in it too. Some days I feel . . . ancient. But that's not exactly proper conversation between strangers.

"I said don't call me that," she grouses, which only makes me want to keep calling her that.

I point to the road stretching ahead. "The MacKay farm is just at the end of the way there."

"Oh?" She sits up in her seat, and I catch sight of white teeth pressing against the red plush of her lower lip. "That one?"

She gestures to the sprawling white building with several smaller structures littered across the property.

"Aye," I confirm. "That's the one."

She seems . . . nervous. More increasingly so by the second.

"Maybe this was a bad idea," she mumbles.

"A bad idea?"

"What if she won't see me?"

I press on my brakes, turning in my seat with narrowed eyes. "Hold on. She doesn't know you're coming?"

"No," Key tells me with a shake of her head. "It's a . . . surprise."

"Bloody hell," I sigh, scrubbing a hand down my face. "Rhona doesn't like surprises. You could have played this a lot smarter."

"If you don't stop insinuating that I'm stupid," Key says with an icy tone, "then I'm going to punch you."

"Is that right?" I can't help the smirk that forms on my mouth. Now that I've met her, I can't say that I'm all that scared of her, despite my father's warnings. "I'd like to see that." I poke at her arm. "These wee things could do damage, you think?"

"You're an asshole," she seethes. "How do you even know my grandmother doesn't like surprises, huh? Better yet, why even offer to bring me here in the first place?"

"It was on the way," I tell her with a shrug.

"On the way? What? Do you live nearby?"

I chuckle softly, shifting the Rover back in gear and continuing down the lane as the massive farmhouse grows nearer.

"No," I tell her, shooting her a sly grin as I anticipate her flush and her look of shocked outrage. "I live *here*."

I grab one of Key's bags as we come to a stop near the front door, pulling my jacket up over my head and pulling the piece of luggage out of the Rover before she can surely protest my help. The sooner I get her out of this rain, the sooner I can stop freezing my arse off. I hear her muted protests for only a second before I shut the door, and then she's tumbling out the other side with her other bag in hand, shivering a little under the still-steady downpour.

I ignore the fleeting urge to offer her my jacket—the awning is *right there* after all—instead ushering her toward the front door and under the covered overhang that saves us from the worst of the onslaught. I watch her shudder beneath her thin sweater, and I frown despite myself, opening my mouth to say . . . something. What, I'm not sure.

The front door opens before I get the chance, and then Rhona MacKay herself is standing in the doorway, her gray braid hanging over one shoulder and her lined face offering an amused smile as she takes me in.

"There you are," she says. "Thought you might drown in this weather. Look at you. You're completely drookit."

"Aye," I offer, keeping my expression passive. "It's a good one." I gesture beside me at the still-shivering mess of wet red curls, watching Rhona's gaze follow the motion. "Rhona, this is—"

Rhona sucks in a breath, and by the widening of her eyes, it's clear she knows who Key is, although how, I can't say. Her mouth parts in surprise as her hand reaches to press against her chest, and for a moment, there is nothing but the steady thumping of rain against the roof and all around us as no one says anything.

"Rhona," Key tries, her voice sounding small. "I'm—"

"I know who you are," Rhona says, her voice breathless but still carrying a slight edge. "And you shouldn't have come."

It's none of my business, but I don't miss the way Key visibly withers. In fact, it's in my best interest to be involved with whatever is happening as little as possible, and yet . . . I can't deny the fleeting urge to comfort Key as sadness colors her features.

I stamp it down quickly. She's a MacKay, and a stranger at that.

I remind myself that Keyanna MacKay is no business of mine.

## KEYANNA

I hadn't necessarily expected a *warm* welcome when I met my grandmother for the first time, but I can admit that I definitely hadn't anticipated outright hostility. The look in Rhonda MacKay's eyes is cold, the bright emerald color throwing me off guard, given that it's the exact same shade as mine, as my dad's, even.

"I know I probably should have reached out before coming—"

Rhona shakes her head, cutting me off as she holds up her hand to stop me. "Aye, you should have, because I'd have saved you the trip."

Frustration bubbles up in my chest, and I can feel a warm flood of anger creeping under my skin. Surely she can sympathize that I came a *long* fucking way to be here. And we *are* family, after all.

"Look, I know that you and my dad parted on bad terms, but that has nothing to do with me," I point out.

"You're right," Rhona says. "It has nothing to do with you, but still you came."

Anger gives way to rejection, maybe even something that slightly resembles hurt, because with Dad gone, I have no one else. Maybe that's why I reach for her hand.

"Rhona," I stress. "Don't you . . ." I swallow, a thick lump in my throat. "Don't you want to know me at all?"

Her eyes soften, her mouth dipping into a frown as she studies me. I watch her gaze dart down to my hand that's clutching hers, and for a moment I think that maybe she'll jerk it out of my grip, but to my surprise, she just sighs.

"Look, it's not that I don't want to know you, but . . ." She glances up at me, and I notice the weariness in her eyes now, the shimmer of sadness that I know all too well. Her thumb moves minutely to brush against the back of my hand, pausing before it gets too far, as if she forces herself to stop. Her eyes find mine again, holding them as she studies my face. "You look so much like him," she murmurs. "Your da leaving left scars, hen. This auld girl has a hard time forgiving, and I see him when I look at you. I cannot promise that you'll find what you're looking for here."

"I get it," I tell her, fully aware that my pant legs are beginning to soak through from the splashing of rain hitting the ground all around us, but I'm standing firm all the same. "I really do, and I can appreciate how much of a shock this must be, but I . . ." I'm acutely aware of the lumbering presence still looming beside me, Lachlan's towering form making my heartfelt confession even harder to get out, but I refuse to be embarrassed. "I don't have anyone else, Rhona. I just . . . I want to know the parts of my dad that he kept from me. I want to know *you*, if you'll let me."

Rhona stares at me as if considering, and I think to myself that we must make a ridiculous picture—me and two strangers hovering outside a small covered porch while rain beats down all around us. I hold my breath as I watch her expression change, sensing she's come to a decision, and I tell myself that no matter what she decides, I can live with the outcome. That no matter what, I can say that I tried my best.

"All right, then," Rhona says with a weary tone. "You can stay."

She pulls her hand from my grip, pointing a finger at me. "But you'll not laze about. You want to stay at the MacKay farm, you'll pull your weight."

"I can do that," I promise, knowing full well I don't know the first thing about helping around a farm. The closest I've ever come to farm life is a petting zoo Dad took me to two decades ago, but I can wing it, I tell myself. "I'll do whatever I need to do."

"Well, come in, then," she sighs, pulling back finally and opening the door wider to invite me in. "Get out of the rain." She turns her attention to Lachlan. "You coming?"

I finally let myself look at him, turning my head to find him already studying me. His crystalline eyes give no insight to his thoughts, but the slight furrow in his brow makes me think he isn't exactly thrilled at the idea of me staying. Not that I care. I'm not thrilled to be apparently living at the same place as the hot asshole that shooed me off his property.

"I have to meet Hamish at Leo's garage," he tells her.

Her brow lifts. "Your car having troubles?"

"Not mine," he answers, smirking in my direction.

My jaw clenches. "You don't have to do anything. I can handle it."

"Oh?" He sets my bag on the porch and crosses his arms, and I can't help but notice the way it stretches his thin sweater under his jacket, making his already-broad chest seem wider. I don't let myself linger on this. "Were you going to go after it on foot, then?"

I scowl. "It's an option."

"This would be the part where one might say *thank you*."

"I didn't ask for your help," I huff.

He rolls his eyes, shooting Rhona a look. "She's definitely yours."

"I don't know what you mean," Rhona says with an innocent smile.

Lachlan shakes his head, shooting me one last look before he darts back into the rain toward his older Rover. He's tucked inside and backing down the drive in a matter of seconds, and Rhona's impatient tone pulls me out of watching him go.

"Come on, then," she says. "Get inside."

I scrabble for the bag Lachlan dropped and carry my things inside after her, pausing in the entryway to take in my surroundings with mild shock. The space just inside the door spills into a much larger one that seems to be the living room—heavy leather furniture centered around a weathered-looking wood stove that is tucked inside an alcove set in a wall of floor-to-ceiling sandstone that gives me the feeling of going back in time.

"Wow," I murmur.

Rhona points at my shoes. "You can leave those at the door. I just mopped this morning, and I don't want you clodding through the house with your muddy bits."

"Right," I stammer, already toeing out of my shoes. "Of course."

"There's room for you upstairs," she tells me. "Put your things in the second bedroom from the right, and then come back down here so I can introduce you to everyone."

"Everyone?"

"Aye," she says. "They're playing cards in the sunroom."

"And they are . . . ?"

"Well, I suppose he would be your . . . grandpa," she says, struggling a bit with the last word, as if taking herself by surprise. It's good to know I'm not the only one feeling awkward. "And then there's his nephew, Brodie. He's staying with us for the moment. You've already met Lachlan, so I can spare you that, at least."

"Um, yeah . . . he lives here?"

"Not *here*," Rhona corrects. "He's in the guest cottage out back. Just a short walk down the path."

"Am I related to him too?"

Rhona actually *snorts* with her laugh, but I can't say what's so funny. "Certainly not," she huffs. "He works here. Does the odd job, takes care of the cows, things like—"

"There are cows?"

"Of course there are cows," she says with bewilderment, as if it's a ridiculous question. "What do you think we're raising here?"

"Well, I've become well acquainted with the sheep population today."

"Ah, right. Lachlan did mention Hamish. Well, there aren't any sheep on the MacKay farm, but we do have a couple of pigs. They're pets, though, mainly. Finlay would be beside himself if we ate them."

"Finlay?"

"My husband," she says. "Your . . . grandpa."

I can tell that she's really going to struggle with that one. Hell, until this moment, I really hadn't given much thought to the possibility of *more* family outside of Rhona and Finlay. Logically, I knew there most likely would be, but I've been so wrapped up with getting here, so nervous about this bonkers plan of mine, that I hadn't actually taken the time to consider it fully.

"We don't have to do the whole grandma and grandpa thing," I assure her. "I realize how weird this must be."

She eyes me thoughtfully, her lips pressing together in a frown, finally turning as if I haven't said anything as she tosses over her shoulder, "Second bedroom to the right, mind you. Then you can meet them."

I watch her disappear down a long hallway toward a painted red door that creaks when she opens it, taking that as instruction on where to go next after I've dropped off my bags. I eye the narrow staircase in front of me, which is covered in a thin, aged carpet, blow-

ing out a breath as I heave my larger bag up onto my shoulder and
steel myself for what will probably be the most awkward family reunion ever. If I can even call it that. There hasn't exactly been any
union to re-, really.

*This is what you wanted*, I remind myself. *You're here. That's half
the battle.*

I repeat that mantra in my head with every step up the old stairs.

There are voices that carry into the house as I approach the door I
saw Rhona disappear through before I went to put my bags away—a
deep rumble that follows a sharp bark of laughter as commotion
ensues. I linger outside the door for a moment as I listen to the muffled voices on the other side, trying to calm the nerves in my belly as
I realize I'm most likely going to be subjected to the same cold welcome that Rhona gave me all over again.

I take a deep breath and let it out, reaching for the handle and
straightening my spine. I refuse to let these people get to me. I'm going to go in there with my head held high, because I have done nothing wrong.

Right. Yes. That's what I'm going to do.

I turn the knob and step through the door, immediately hit with
a loud shout of, "Gin!"

There is an older man with thinning gray hair looking pleased
with himself as he gestures to a row of cards in front of him, practically bouncing in his wicker chair as he taps a finger on the glass top
of the table. Another man on the other side who looks closer to my
age, if not a little older, frowns at his own cards, his pale complexion
turning pink as he runs a hand through his strawberry blond hair.

"You cheated, Finn, I swear it."

The old man shakes his head. "Och, don't be a sore loser, Brodie. I did no such thing."

"S'not possible to win *every* hand," the other man—Brodie—grumbles.

The older man—Finn—shrugs as he begins picking up the cards. "Seems I can."

Rhona is sitting in a rocking chair in the corner, working a pair of knitting needles, and she clears her throat, drawing the attention of the two men as they both finally notice me, their eyes landing on me at the same time.

Brodie's mouth tilts into a frown, but Finn's lips part as his eyes go wide, his hand coming up to press his palm to his chest. "Losh! Would you look at that?" He turns to Rhona, waving a hand in my direction. "She looks just like you did when we met, Rhonnie."

Rhona doesn't confirm this, just purses her lips and continues working her needles. Finn pushes up from his wicker chair with a grunt, shuffling over to me as fast as his short legs can carry him. He's shorter than me by a good four inches or so, but his shoulders are wide and his chest is barreled, giving the impression that, despite his height, he was once an imposing man.

"Michty me," he murmurs, reaching up to cup my chin. "Haven't seen you since you were not but a wean. Didn't we, Rhonnie? Not since Duncan's last letter."

I can't help the question that tumbles out of my mouth. "He sent letters?"

"Aye, for a bit," Finn says softly. "Until he realized he wouldn't get an answer out of these auld fools."

His voice drips with regret, and his expression looks pained as he stares at my face.

"You've grown into a bonnie thing, haven't you?" he says. "So tall! Must get that from your mother. Certainly didn't get that from us."

"My dad was tall," I mumble, feeling my cheeks flush under Finn's scrutiny.

"Aye," Finn chuckles. "Used to tease my Rhonnie that she must have had a tryst with one of the giants from town."

"That's enough, Finlay," Rhona chides him from the corner. "Don't overwhelm the girl."

"Aye, aye." Finn steps back, pulling his hand away from my face, but his eyes never stop taking me in. "Forgive me, lass. It's like seeing my Duncan come back to me."

"I'm sorry," I blurt out. "For barging in on you all like this. I know I should have called first, but I thought—"

Finn waves me off. "Nonsense. Enough of that. You're family. We're happy to have you. Aren't we, Rhonnie?"

Rhona doesn't look as enthused about Finn's sentiment as he does, quietly watching this exchange take place without saying anything.

"I appreciate that, Finlay," I tell him. "Or Finn? I don't know what you'd prefer."

"Wheesht with that now," he scoffs. "You'll call me Grandpa or nothing at all, girl."

"Oh, I . . ." My eyes dart from his to Rhona's, but she gives me nothing except a cocked brow and a cool expression. "Sure. Grandpa. I can do that."

"Och," he rumbles, his voice sounding rougher. "I dinnae ken this day would ever come."

His accent thickens with the emotion in his tone, and when he opens his arms and approaches me, I can't find it in me to refuse him. I let him embrace me, and the comforting warmth he emanates is admittedly welcome, familiar even. It's enough to make my chest feel tight.

"Aye, but I'm keeping you all to myself," Grandpa says, sniffling slightly as he pulls back. "You've met your granny, but this"—he turns to gesture to the man still hunched in one of the wicker chairs, eyeing me curiously—"is your cousin Brodie. He's not much aulder than you would be, I think?"

Brodie's mouth tightens and relaxes so quickly I wonder if I imagined it altogether, and then he's pushing up from his chair and closing the distance between us to offer me his hand. "Welcome," he says. "Nice to make your acquaintance. Sorry, Rhona didn't give your name."

"Keyanna," I tell him. "But everyone calls me Key."

"Oh, Rhona's great-granny was named Keyanna," Grandpa blubbers, fully crying now. He gestures to his wet eyes. "Forgive this auld boy. Never could hold it in."

"It's fine," I say, feeling awkward as I shuffle from one foot to the other.

Brodie shoves his hands into his pockets. "So how long do we have you, Key? A nice long visit?"

"I . . ." I glance at Rhona, who might as well be Fort Knox, with what she's giving me. I clear my throat. "I'm not sure. I don't want to be in the way."

"Nonsense," Grandpa scoffs, wiping his eyes. "You'll stay as long as you want. It's so good to have you, isn't that right, Rhonnie?"

Rhona seems to realize she's expected to answer this time, pausing her knitting to give a clipped nod. "Of course."

*Yeah, right*, I think.

"Can't show you much of the place in this weather," Finn sighs, "but I can show you around the house, aye?"

"That would be great," I tell him. "But . . . Sorry. Is there any way

I could call the shop Hamish took my car to? Do you have the number? I was hoping to try and find a store where I could grab a few things that I forgot." Heat creeps into my cheeks. "I sort of left in a hurry."

"Leo doesn't have a phone," Grandpa says. "Thinks someone could track him with it. Maybe Brodie could take you by?"

"Lachlan went to check on it," Rhona tells him.

"Ah, well," Grandpa answers with a clap of his hands. "That's settled, then, isn't it? Oh, but you needed a shop, aye?"

"I can take her," Brodie says. "We can check in on the car too."

I fidget. "Are you sure?"

"Oh, aye," Brodie says with a laugh. "We're family, after all."

Grandpa makes a disgruntled noise. "But what about supper? Rhonnie makes a mean shepherd's pie."

I glance at the woman in question, noticing that she doesn't even look up from her knitting. There might as well be frost hanging off her needles, with the icy demeanor emanating from her.

"That's okay," I tell him. I pat my belly. "My stomach is still a little upset from the long plane ride."

Maybe that's not quite the truth, but I can sense Rhona is going to need a bit more time to get used to the idea of me being here.

"Do you need something for it? We've got medicines around here somewhere—oh! Maybe we could get you a warm water bottle. When I was a lad, that always—"

"Leave her be, Finlay," Rhona tuts. "Don't bombard the poor girl with too much at once. She's just arrived."

Finlay looks from Rhona to me, his expression sheepish. "Sorry, hen. Got a wee bit excited is all."

"No, no," I assure him. "It's fine. Really. I'd love a rain check, maybe? Breakfast tomorrow?"

His entire face lights up, and I can see a bit of my dad in his features. It makes my chest feel tight. "Aye, breakfast. That we can do." He reaches to squeeze my shoulder. "Your granny and I turn in pretty early," Grandpa tells me, "so if we're asleep when you get home, I'll expect you for the tour right after breakfast in the morning, aye?"

"That sounds great," I tell him, still feeling slightly overwhelmed.

"Good lass," he says with a grin. He pats my shoulder, squeezing it again for a long moment. "It really is so good to have you, love."

I force a smile. "Thank you."

He wipes his eyes again as he turns to cross the room to where Rhona is sitting, leaning into her space to murmur in her ear. I feel Brodie's hand on my elbow then, turning to give him my attention. He's about my height and just as stocky as Finn, his smile friendly and his eyes a soft hazel that makes him appear kind.

"Come on, then, cousin," he chuckles. "We'll get your things, and maybe we'll stop at the pub, aye? I expect after today, you'll be needing a pint or two."

I blow out a breath, flashing Brodie a more authentic smile as the tension in my shoulders bleeds out. "Or two."

"I've got just the place," he tells me, patting my arm before turning toward the door.

Rhona is still eyeing me warily as I follow after him, but I tell myself not to be too bothered by it. She'll warm up to me eventually. Probably.

I could definitely use that drink.

"So," Brodie says after a long, stilted silence of driving away from the farm. "This must be pretty overwhelming."

I scoff lightly. "Which part? My dad dying? Or my grandma hating me?"

"Both, I imagine," he says with a chuckle. He glances at me with a sympathetic expression. "Although I am sorry to hear about your da."

"Did you know him?"

He nods. "When I was a lad. My mum and dad came down for a spell during the summers when I was younger to visit with Finn and Rhona. He was always kind to me." He chuckles. "And his stories were good."

"His stories?"

"Well, yeah. Most people know about Duncan's tussle with the loch monster."

"They do?"

Brodie lets out another soft laugh. "From what I've been told, he didn't really try too hard to keep it a secret."

"Oh." I avert my gaze to my hands, which are clasped in my lap. "He used to tell me that story all the time."

"Did you believe him?"

"I . . . don't know." When I look up, I notice Brodie's full attention is on me, seeming actually curious. "I think I used to when I was little. But as I got aulder, well . . . I mean, it's sort of impossible, right?"

His eyes linger on the side of my face for another moment, finally flicking back to the road, where his car is creeping along. "Aye, probably. Who knows, though. Living here . . . you hear all sorts of stories."

"Rhona said you were staying with them," I point out, trying to make conversation. "Did you grow up in Greerloch?"

He shakes his head. "Inverness. My mum and dad are still there."

"So are you just visiting, then?"

His lips quirk as if I've said something funny. "Something like that."

"Not cryptic at all," I chuckle.

His fingers drum on the steering wheel, his brow furrowing as he considers. "I'm on a bit of a . . . sabbatical from my job. Needed some time away."

"Where do you work?"

"The Inverness Historical Society."

"Wow. That actually sounds really cool."

He shrugs. "It can be, sure. There's a lot of paperwork and red tape at times."

"I guess I could see that," I say, bobbing my head. "Is that why you're taking a break?"

"Something like that."

I roll my eyes. "Is that your catchphrase or something?"

"Maybe," he laughs, shrugging again. "I just needed some time away from it all. My family is . . ." His mouth turns down in a frown. "Let's just say they've never been quite thrilled with my choice of career."

"What? Why?"

"My da owns a fishing business," he tells me. "One of the largest on the coast. When my brothers were auld enough—"

"You have brothers?"

He nods. "Two. Both good, dutiful sons following in my da's footsteps."

"Ah." I'm starting to get a picture here. "That's tough."

"My da is a hard man. He expects obedience and loyalty above all else. In his eyes . . . I haven't been very good at either."

"I'm sorry," I tell him, meaning it. I can't imagine not growing up with the support I did. "For what it's worth, I think your job sounds really cool."

His lips turn up in a grin. "Appreciate that."

There's another lingering silence that only just begins to feel awkward, and I can't pretend the questions aren't bubbling up inside me.

"Okay, but have you ever found any cool stuff? Old family scandals or something?"

"And what sort of scandals would I be finding, pray tell?"

"I don't know! Do you have some sort of secret proof lying around that the Loch Ness Monster actually exists? Like . . . are you the Scottish equivalent of the FBI guys covering up Area 51?"

A laugh spills out of him. "You have a wild imagination, cousin."

"Sounds pretty evasive, if you ask me," I answer slyly.

"I've found some interesting things," he admits. "Nothing so fantastic as that, unfortunately."

"Bummer."

"Aye, it is."

With every lull in the conversation, the nerves creep back in, the gravity of this day weighing down on me like a tangible thing. I twist my hands in my lap, biting my lip to try and stop the question that's rolling around inside, but it's useless really. I can't help myself.

"Do you think Rhona hates me?"

Brodie lets out a sigh, seeming to consider the question. "Rhona is . . . She can be hard sometimes. Even when I was a lad, she was always sort of . . . stern. My mum used to say she just missed her boy. I imagine it's hard seeing you after she lost him." He nods to himself. "But I don't think she hates you. I just think she's coming to terms with things."

"That's . . . good? I can live with that. Hopefully."

"You'll be all right, mate," Brodie assures me. He flashes me a smile. "Even better after that drink, aye?"

I laugh despite the uneasiness still lingering in my stomach. "Yeah. Definitely."

I *do* let the silence linger then, contenting myself with staring out the window as we creep across the green countryside toward town. I roll Brodie's words around in my head, weighing them, hoping that he's right.

Especially since the alternative is that one of the only real connections I have left to my dad might always hate my guts.

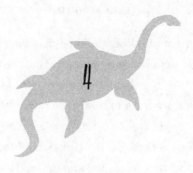

## LACHLAN

The rain is still pelting down on the slate roof of the pub, and I shake off as much of the water clinging to my jacket and hair as I can before stepping through the door of The Clever Pech. It's a bit emptier inside than I thought it would be on a Friday afternoon—no one but auld Fergus doing a crossword in his resident corner booth and the twins chattering behind the bar inside. Blair notices me as I come in, elbowing Rory and gesturing my way just before Rory bellows out a greeting.

"Oi! There he is. Pissin' down out there, is it? You look soaked to the bone, mate."

"Aye," I offer back, shuffling across the old wooden floor to slide onto one of the stools at the bar. "Bloody freezing too."

Blair nods toward the shelf behind her. "You want your usual, then, eh?"

"Please," I answer.

I grew up with Blair and Rory Campbell before moving away after my granny died, and despite the years between then and my move back earlier in the year—the bond between us didn't diminish in the slightest. But that could partly be because the twins are borderline insane, and they adopt people like stray cats. They're both tall, not quite my height but close, and their matching platinum hair is a shade so light, it appears silver under the sun. But their good looks are just a front for the slightly unhinged personalities beneath—personalities that got me into trouble on more than one occasion in my youth.

I run my fingers through the damp strands of my hair as Blair sets about making me a drink, and I tip my head back toward Fergus. "How's your da today?"

"Same as usual," Rory snorts. He raises his voice to shout, "Bloody useless, that's what he is!"

Fergus just raises a middle finger, taking another large gulp of his whiskey.

Rory shakes his head. "Drunken arse. We should ban him from the place."

"His name is still on the deed," Blair pipes up as she finishes pouring me three fingers of Johnny Walker. She slides the glass across the bar, leaning to rest on her elbows. "Maybe we could convince Lach here to . . . you know . . ."

I cock a brow as I bring the glass to my lips. "To what?"

"*You* know," Rory stresses, dragging his index finger across his throat.

I roll my eyes, taking a swig from my glass before setting it back down on the bar. "I'm not killing your da, you numpty." I glance around at the empty bar. "Slow afternoon?"

"Aye," Rory sighs. "People act like they'll drown from a wee bit of rain."

My thoughts flit to the angry expression of one fair American as I threatened her with said rain, and the corner of my mouth tilts up without my permission before I quickly tuck it away.

Blair leans in, lowering her voice. "So how goes the hunt?"

"Not so loud," I hiss, turning around to look behind me out of habit.

Rory scoffs. "Who are you thinking might hear? Fergus? I could plot my da's entire demise right here at this bar and the auld stoater would be none the wiser." He raises his voice again. "He should sign the bar over before he does something useful like keel over!"

"Piss off," Fergus calls back, still focused on his crossword.

"Bastard," Rory mutters before turning his attention back to me. "Come on, mate. You've been living on the MacKay farm for six months now. You really haven't found anything?"

I shake my head, sighing. "Nothing."

"I'll never believe Rhona doesn't know something," Blair hums.

"She's aulder than our da, and he's ancient. That woman knows more than she lets on. It's in the eyes." Rory points his index and middle fingers toward his own eyes for emphasis. "You can tell."

"Well, when I learn how to read eyes, I'll let you know."

"How's it been since that eejit Brodie came to stay?" Rory asks.

"Wanker tried to come on to me a few weeks ago," Blair says with a shudder. "Creepy fucker. Rhona must know he's after the farm, yeah? Why else would he show up out of nowhere after not visiting for years?"

"He's the least of their problems," I mumble as I take another drink.

Not that he hasn't been a thorn in my side ever since I arrived. I've known Brodie MacKay since we were lads, and we never really got on.

Rory cocks his head. "What do you mean?"

"Apparently, the MacKays have some long-lost granddaughter that's just shown up out of the blue," I tell them.

Rory's and Blair's matching brows shoot up.

"Does that—"

"You mean—"

"Aye," I sigh. "A daughter of MacKay."

"Your da always said—"

I shake my head. "My da said a lot of things. It could be nothing."

"Seems a hell of a lot to be nothing," Blair notes.

I eye my drink, shrugging one shoulder as I add quietly, "Duncan was her da."

"Duncan? Bloody hell, he's been gone for, what, three decades?"

"Nearly," I agree. "Keyanna is twenty-seven, she said."

Blair's eyes take on a curious gleam. "Keyanna, aye? So you met her?"

"Found her crawling over the rocks at Skallangal," I say with a scowl. "Came this close to falling right on her arse if I hadn't snatched her back." I shake my head, frowning into my whiskey glass. "Americans, I swear. Signs all over, but of course that means nothing. Traipsing all over the shore like she owns the place, then had the nerve to shout at me for saving her arse!"

Rory whistles. "Oh, boy. The MacKay lass has gotten under our poor Lach's skin."

"Seems that way," Blair agrees.

"She's done no such thing," I huff. "She's just a complication, that's all. One more nose I have to keep out of my business while I look for my answers."

"And what does Rhona think of this long-lost granddaughter? My da told us once about the falling-out between her and Duncan. Said it wasn't pretty."

I think back to Rhona's porch in the rain, remembering the lost look on Key's face and the desperation in her eyes as she pleaded with Rhona to give her a chance. The sympathy I feel is annoying; I have no business feeling anything toward a MacKay besides suspicion. I blame how bonnie she is. Looking at Brodie for the last few months did not give me any sort of inclination that any offspring of the MacKay clan would look like *that*. It's just as annoying as the sympathy I unwillingly feel for her.

"Rhona didn't take to her well," I say finally. "But she did let her stay."

"That's sure to put a kink in your plans," Rory points out.

I snort. "You think?"

"Och," Blair says with a sniff. "You've not found anything in all this time. Maybe there's nothing to be found."

I shoot her a sharp look. "You know why I can't accept that."

She looks properly chastised, lowering her eyes as her mouth turns down. "Right. I'm sorry. You know I talk without thinking."

"Are you okay?" Blair asks.

I cock one eyebrow. "What?"

"I just . . . I know your da and Duncan were close, and I know when he left—"

I wave her off. "I'm fine. S'not like I really knew the man. I can barely remember him."

I bitterly think that the same could be said for my father.

"Maybe you can recruit her," Rory suggests.

My brow wrinkles. "Come off it."

"She's a veritable stranger, aye? But she's got an in with the family. Maybe she'd be willing to help you out if you just—"

"You two knowing my business is more than enough," I cut him off with a slightly bitter tone. "I'm doing good just to keep you two from blathering on about it."

"We wouldn't do that," Blair grumbles.

"Not on purpose," I counter. I hook a thumb at Rory. "Get this one good and steamin', and we both know there's nary a topic he won't yammer on about."

"That's fair," Rory laughs. "But I've done good so far."

"Thank Christ for that," I say with a chuffed laugh. Then my brow knits. "Besides, I can't rule out that her being here is a bad omen."

"You really believe some auld poem?" Rory's nose wrinkles. "Not a very good one at that. How did it go again?"

I heave a sigh, readying myself to repeat the words I'd heard *over* and *over* growing up, but a bell sounding behind us has me turning in my seat, and after the initial frown that touches my lips at the sight of Brodie's familiar and irritating visage, there is a punch of surprise when I see wild red curls bouncing in after him surrounding delicate cheekbones and fair, freckled skin and the greenest eyes I've ever seen.

"Bloody hell," Blair says a bit too loudly. "Who's that?"

"My newest complication," I murmur back.

Blair hums appreciatively. "I'd let her complicate me any day."

"You're no worse than a man," Rory tsks. "You know that?"

"You lot had centuries of being lecherous bastards," she says primly. "It's all about equality now, mate."

They're still bickering behind me, but the sound of it fades away a bit when Key's eyes find mine studying her. Her mouth parts in surprise as she noticeably stops listening to whatever Brodie is saying to her, her body visibly bristling at the sight of me. Which, for some reason, elicits a smile from me, and I raise my glass in her direction in a mock toast.

Brodie must notice then that he's lost her attention, because his eyes follow the line of her sight, frowning when he sees me sitting at the bar. He shuffles inside with Key in tow, giving me a wary look as he offers a threadbare greeting. I can't say what I did to the man, given that we barely speak, but he's made it clear on more than one occasion that he doesn't care for me. Since the feeling is mostly mutual—I'm happy to leave the situation unsorted.

"Lachlan," he says curtly.

I nod my head. "Brodie." I turn my head away, finding Key's eyes again, noticing the wariness there as she regards me, like she's unsure of how I'll be after everything that transpired today. "Leo's fixed your car," I tell her. "He's going to drop it off in the morning."

"I know," she says. "We just came from there."

I quirk a brow. "Didn't trust me to get the job done, princess?"

"I don't even know you," she says irritably.

My mouth tilts at the corners. "And yet you've already decided you don't like me." I clutch at my heart. "You wound me."

"You called me stupid within ten seconds of meeting you."

"Is that what you're so riled about? I was only pointing out how . . . unwise it was to ignore *many* signs warning you to not do exactly what you were doing."

"Well, you didn't have to play the 'I own the place' card just to chase me off."

"You didn't," Blair tuts. "That was an arsehole move, Lach."

Key throws out her hand in triumph. "See?"

"Don't worry," Blair says sweetly, extending her hand. "We're not all a bunch of wankers here in Greerloch."

Key takes it, shaking it lightly and flashing a smile in Blair's direction, and I think to myself that it must be the first time I've seen it. Because I would remember it had she given it before. Hell, it might as well be imprinting itself on my brain in real time. Her smile changes her already pretty face to something breathtaking—straight white teeth with the two front ones just *slightly* longer than the rest and somehow making her smile all the more endearing.

I curse my own train of thought. I do not care about Keyanna MacKay's smile.

"Careful," I warn Key as I finish off my drink. "She's taking your side because she thinks you're bonnie."

"I'm taking her side because you're a right arse," Blair argues. She winks at Key. "Not that I don't think you're bonnie."

Keyanna's fair skin pinkens with a blush, and something sharp pokes at the insides of my chest. My jaw works, not having time to really assess the feeling since Brodie chooses that moment to chime in.

"Key has had a hard day," he says. "I reckon she needs a pint or two to wash it away." He glances at me pointedly. "She's dealt with all sorts of unpleasantness since she arrived."

"Och," Rory scoffs. "And then she had to climb into a car with you? Definitely be needing a pint."

Brodie's cheeks go ruddy, but I catch Key's mouth twitching with a smile before she schools it away. Perhaps she's not as charmed by her new cousin as he'd like her to be, then. I can't say why that pleases me. Probably because sometimes he looks at me like I'm a bug on his shoe.

Brodie takes that moment to excuse himself, saying something about hitting the head. I can't say I hope he makes any hurry to return.

"We heard you made a trip to Nessie's cove today," Blair says, continuing to chat up Key as Rory busies himself making the newcomer's drinks. "You here on the hunt, then?"

I give Blair as surreptitious a glare as I can manage, but she ignores me.

"Oh, well . . ." Key shuffles, rubbing at the back of her neck. "Not exactly."

"Nothing to be ashamed of, love," Blair says sweetly. "We've all climbed over those rocks a time or two around here." She smirks in my direction. "Even before Grandpa here came to spoil the fun."

"S'not safe," I mumble, narrowing my eyes at her.

"Tell me, mate," Blair barrels on, ignoring me. "What had you climbing the rocks? The auld man is right; it's not exactly safe without a good pair of wellies with a strong grip. Even then, you could hurt yourself."

"I . . ." She bites her lip, and for a moment, I find my eyes drawn to the press of her teeth against the soft flesh—something that I quickly shake myself out of. "My dad told me stories." She says this quietly, almost like she's embarrassed. "He died recently, and he asked me before he went to scatter his ashes there."

My brows shoot up in surprise, and a memory pings, one of her clutching that black vase so tightly, and for the first time today, I *do* feel like an arse. Regardless of my feelings about her da and what he might or might not have been to my own father, I know what it feels to mourn the loss of someone so prominent in your life.

"You didn't say," I blurt out, feeling chastened and defensive all at once. "Why not?"

Her mouth forms a tight line. "It's not exactly a conversation for two strangers in which one of the strangers is telling the other one how stupid she is."

Bloody hell. I *did* do that. Knowing what she was there for, it does feel much harsher now. Especially since I can't ignore the current pang of emotion in my chest as my thoughts wander to my own predicament, knowing her grief all too well.

Maybe I really am an arse.

I frown at my feet, which rest against the scuffed wood floor beneath my stool. "It was a much better reason than silly curiosity," I tell her. "I might have been a bit more accommodating had you said."

"Somehow I doubt that," she snorts.

Rory slides two pints across the bar. "She's got your number, Lach." He also shoots her a wink. "He's not so bad. Deep down." He eyes me briefly. "Deep, *deep* down."

This elicits a giggle from Key, and the sound of it sets off another sharp sensation in my chest. The fuck is that about?

"If it's Nessie you're after," Blair says seriously, "I'd suggest you make a trip to Loch Land. It's just a few miles down the road from here."

My brows furrow, wondering what Blair is on about. Surely she knows—

"Loch Land?" Key asks.

"Oh, aye," Blair tells her. "It's the best place for information on Nessie. It's a museum of sorts."

"Really?" Keyanna looks intrigued, and I almost want to tell her the truth. Almost. "And you said it's not far?"

"Not at all," Blair assures her. "I can even get you a map. They left some of those tourist leaflets at some point. I'm sure they're around here somewhere . . ."

"Has this place been around for a while? Do you think my dad went?"

"Oh, definitely," Rory joins in, apparently getting in on Blair's fun. "At some point, I'm sure. We've all been."

Key beams at the pair of them. "That would be great. I'd like to see all the places he might have seen when he lived here."

Fucking hell. Now I really do feel like an arse. I peek over at Rory and Blair, but they show no signs of revealing their little game, and I know doing so myself would give Keyanna the impression that we might be friends of some sort, and that's absolutely not on the table for us. Not when she's a MacKay. It's hard enough playing nice with Rhona as it is.

So I keep silent, telling myself it *doesn't* make me an arsehole. I'm not the one taking the piss with her.

"Here we are," Blair calls, riffling out a leaflet from beneath the bar and slapping it in front of Key. "This will get you there."

The leaflet is pretty innocuous—just a picture of the very misleading front of the building with a small map below it, and I once again have to force myself not to say anything. Let the lass chase her own tail for a day. It'll keep her out of my hair.

"This is great," Key says earnestly. "Thank you. I'll drive out tomorrow if the weather is better."

"You do that," Blair hums. "And best not tell your cousin, yeah?" She leans in conspiratorially. "Not really the adventuring type, Brodie."

Key's cheeks take on that sweet shade of pink again, and she bites her lip as she glances around to make sure the cousin in question isn't in earshot. "He said he works for the Inverness Historical Society, though. He probably knows a lot more than me."

"He's a bloody numpty," Rory chuffs. "I promise you don't want him coming with you. Can't take a joke to save his life, that one."

Brodie appears in the hallway entry to the bathrooms, and the group of us quiets down, but I notice Keyanna tuck the leaflet into her pocket, just as I notice she doesn't say a word about it when Rory starts in on Brodie about something or another.

I cock an eyebrow when she notices I've caught this, rolling her eyes when I smirk, but I have a feeling she won't be saying a word to dear old cousin Brodie about her trip tomorrow.

It almost makes me feel bad for keeping quiet about Rory and Blair's fun.

Almost.

## KEYANNA

Rhona and my grandpa *were* asleep by the time Brodie and I got back from the pub, and I can't be sure if I was disappointed or grateful for it. Rhona has made it no secret how she feels about me being here, and even with Finlay's bright enthusiasm—it's hard not to let that get to me.

I spent a fitful night tossing and turning in the room Rhona set me up in; the bed there has to be older than I am, if not more, and by the time I wake up the next morning to the smell of bacon and coffee, I feel like my back has just as many lumps in it as the mattress. Fitting, really, considering how bumpy a start I've had here.

I crawl out of bed and stretch to try and get the crick out of my neck, tucking my feet into my wool slippers with little mushrooms smattered across them as I reach for my robe. The aroma of cooking food is enticing, and it's enough to give me strength to weather whatever might be waiting for me downstairs. If nothing else, at least Finlay can act as a buffer, since he seems to actually *like* the fact that I'm here.

I find my three other temporary housemates puttering around in the kitchen downstairs—Rhona at the oven and Finlay squinting at a newspaper while Brodie sips at a mug of what smells like very strong coffee on the opposite side of the table. They both look up when they see me, Brodie giving me a tired-looking nod and Finlay offering up a wide smile.

"Morning," he calls brightly, folding the newspaper and setting it on the table. "Och, you look right tired, love. Did you sleep well?"

I don't want to be the one to tell them that their guest mattress is long past its day and due for a good burn, so I force a smile instead. "I slept fine. I think it's just the time change. Jet lag, you know."

"Oh, aye, that makes sense." He nods. "What time would it be in New York?"

I glance at the clock on the wall, which reads just after eight. "Three in the morning."

"That'll do it," Finlay chuckles. He pats the seat next to him. "Come, come. Sit."

I settle into the chair next to him, running my fingers through my wild curls to try and push them out of my eyes. "It smells good in here."

"That'll be your granny," Finlay says. "Best cook in all of Scotland."

Rhona makes a tutting sound from the oven without even looking our way. "Flattery will not get you more bacon," she hmphs. "You know what the doctor said."

"That man is full of shite," Finlay scoffs. He thumps his chest. "I'm healthy as an ox."

Rhona turns then with a steaming plate, setting it in front of her husband. "Stubborn as one too." She finally takes the time to look at me then, her eyes cool as her mouth thins. "You hungry?"

"I—" The iciness of her stare threatens to make me buckle, and I have to force myself a little straighter to answer her, determined not to let her standoffishness deter me. "Yeah, I am. Please."

Rhona nods once, turning back to the oven. "Any particular way you want your eggs?"

"Whatever you're doing for everyone else is fine," I tell her. "Do you need any help?"

She glances at me over her shoulder with slightly narrowed eyes. "You don't think I know my way around my own kitchen?"

"No," I say immediately. "I didn't mean—"

"Oh, hush, Rhonnie," Finlay grouses. "You know she was just being polite."

Her eyes dart to Finlay for only a moment, and then with a small sound that sounds suspiciously like a snort, she goes back to what she was doing.

"So how did you find the pub?" Finlay reaches for the thermos at the center of the table, grabbing a mug and offering it to me. "Coffee?"

I take it, letting him pour me a cup before answering. "It was interesting. The owners are . . . something."

"Oh, aye," Finlay laughs. "The twins are a hoot. I hope they weren't too ornery with you."

I shake my head. "Nothing I can't handle."

I'm opening my mouth to ask about the museum they recommended, but something stops me. I glance at Brodie, remembering what the twins said about bringing him along. It seems unfair, their assessment of him, but still. I think this might be something I want to experience myself.

"My car should be ready today," I say instead. "Leo said he would drop it off here this morning."

"Good man," Finlay says. "I hope Brodie didn't let him charge you tourist prices."

Brodie rolls his eyes, looking sluggish, as if he didn't sleep well either. "He charged her a normal rate."

"Good, good," Finlay says. "Can't have him taking advantage of my granddaughter." He makes a face just after he says it, his lip quivering as his eyes start to shine. "Och, look at me. Sorry, hen. It's just that I never thought I'd be able to say that. Not while you were sitting right there like you are."

I'm gathering that Finlay is an . . . emotional sort. He wipes a stray tear forming at his eye, and I pat his shoulder awkwardly. "I'm really glad to be here," I tell him.

"We're glad to have you," he says. He looks back at Rhona. "Aren't we, Rhonnie?"

Rhona turns with two plates in hand, sliding one in front of Brodie and then holding the other out for me. Her face says anything but her agreement of what Finlay has said, her mouth turned down in a slight frown as her eyes rake over my disheveled state. "Little notice might have been nice."

"Rhonnie!"

I shake my head, keeping my expression passive. "No, no, she's right." I'm determined to win this woman over if it kills me. "I'm really sorry about that. I guess I was just nervous. I went back and forth a hundred times over whether or not I was actually going to come."

"You don't have anyone waiting on you back in America?" Brodie asks as he tucks into his food.

I shake my head. "Not really. My old boss was always really kind to me, and he was very understanding while Dad was—" I swallow thickly, finding it hard to go down that road with Rhona staring at me like she is from her place across the table where she's settled. "Anyway. My friends kind of fell to the wayside with everything. Hard to keep up with people when you're caring for someone around the clock."

"And you had to do it all by yourself," Finlay says quietly, his voice thick with emotion. "Poor lass."

"Might have had help if we'd known," Rhona mutters, stabbing her fork into her eggs.

I nod, still determined to keep my cool. "I wish you had known," I tell her, honestly meaning it. The help would have been nice. "I'm sorry that you didn't."

Rhona stares at me for a beat, then ducks her head to take a bite of her eggs. "S'pose it's not your fault."

There's a ringing silence that hangs in the air after, one that I'm not sure how to pierce.

Thankfully, Finlay does it for me. "Now, I promised you a tour after breakfast, didn't I?"

"You did," I say with a grin. "I'd love to see the farm."

"Well, eat up, my girl," he chuckles. "Because there's a lot of it."

*My girl.* It makes my cheeks heat, but in a good way.

I don't have to ask if Rhona will be joining our little adventure.

I don't know if that's a disappointment or a relief.


"—and over there is the auld barn; it's been there since we first built on this land!" Finlay exclaims with excitement.

We've been walking for over an hour; I didn't anticipate just how *much* there is to the MacKay farm. Rolling hills and creek beds and cow after cow after *cow*—which I am perfectly content to stay far away from—there almost seems to be no end to the place.

The structure he's gesturing to is a massive barn that seems to lean a bit to the left; there is a base of stacked stones that gives way to aged lumber that has seen better days, and yeah, looking at it . . . I can believe it's been there as long as he says it has.

"Now, my great-great-grandpa had to do some restoring, see," Finlay goes on. "But the stone is original."

"That's really cool," I say, meaning it.

It's amazing to think that those same stones have been here for almost a thousand years, to hear Finlay tell it. It makes you think about what sort of place this was that long ago. The people who lived here. The *history*. It's almost overwhelming, going from having only my dad for my entire life to suddenly having so much *connection*.

I press my hand to the weathered wood of the barn, my fingers tingling against the surface, no doubt a precursor to the goose bumps that start to pebble down my arms. It's strange; there's that same feeling of humming life that seems to permeate the very air around me, almost like I can feel the vibration of its current. I rub my thumb over the rusted end of a nail, feeling a sudden zap of static shock.

"Fuck," I mutter.

Finlay rushes to my side. "You all right, lass?"

"I'm fine," I assure him. "Just static." I gesture to my hair, which has started to frizz. "I'm used to it."

Finlay laughs. "Your da had the same problem. Curls for days, he had."

I watch his smile falter as he no doubt falls into some memory of my father, and I reach to squeeze his shoulder, wanting to distract him from it. He's been so happy showing me around the place.

"Show me the inside?"

"Aye, that I can do," he says, discreetly wiping his eye. He peeks up at the sun, which has started to climb much higher in the sky, squinting. "Should be about time to be putting out some hay soon. I imagine that—"

There is a sudden rumbling that sounds from inside the barn, a deafening series of cranking noises before an engine turns over.

"Ah," Finlay says. "Right on time."

My brow furrows as I wonder what he could mean, but before I have time to ask, a faded red tractor starts to putter out of the barn, a bale of hay speared on the end by some sort of attachment. None of this keeps my attention for very long, though, because sitting in the seat of that tractor is the last person I'd like to see while trying to connect with my long-lost family—especially given the fact that said person is, for whatever reason, *shirtless*.

I am momentarily rendered mute by glistening muscles that are bronzed from the sun—large hands covered in gloves gripping the wide steering wheel of the tractor as Lachlan maneuvers it out of the barn.

"Oi!" Finlay calls, waving his hand. "Lachlan!"

*Shit, don't call him over while I'm openly ogling him.*

Too late, Lachlan turns his head to spot us just outside the barn, his worn cap casting shade over his eyes, but not enough to miss the way they narrow slightly when he sees me.

*Well, fuck you too*, I think, followed immediately by, *Actually, don't go there, brain.*

Lachlan looks like he'd rather do anything else but turn the tractor off to chat, but Finlay, being the sunshine of a human he seems to be, is not deterred. He clods across the grass to meet Lachlan at the barn entrance, his broad smile plastered to his face.

Lachlan shuts off the tractor, taking a moment to reach above his head and remove his cap so he can wipe the sweat from his brow. The action makes his biceps bulge and his pectoral muscles pull taut, and if he hadn't already proven himself to be a royal jerk, I might not be able to control my drooling.

*We do not lust after assholes, damnit.*

"Lachlan," Finlay says when the tractor has been shut off. "Everything all right this morning?"

Lachlan's face remains mostly expressionless as he replaces his cap on his head, and it's almost comforting to know that it's not *just* me he seems to be frosty toward.

"All right," he answers. "Had a heifer get out over on the south pasture, but I found her wandering around the creek that way on Hamish's land."

"Was it Girdie? I think she's nearly ready to drop soon. She tends to wander when it's time."

Lachlan shrugs. "It's number two hundred and sixteen."

"Aye, that be Girdie," Finlay says with a nod. "Might want to pen her this evening. Just in case."

"I can do that," Lachlan answers. He glances at me, arching a brow. "Getting the lay of the land, are you?"

"Well, no one has chased me off of it yet," I reply coolly.

I think I notice one corner of his mouth twitching, but I could be imagining it. "Tends not to happen when you don't wander where you're not supposed to."

"Ass," I mutter under my breath, trying not to notice the way his abdomen flexes when he leans over the steering wheel. "What are you doing anyway?"

"Feeding the cows," he says.

My nose scrunches. "They eat that much every day?"

"More or less," Finlay chuckles. "They're big puppies, really."

"Big puppies with massive horns," I point out.

Lachlan's mouth does curl then. "Don't tell me you're afraid of the cows now, are you, princess?"

"I'm not afraid," I grumble. "And stop *calling* me that."

One corner of his mouth hitches up farther. "We'll see."

"All right, all right," Finlay huffs. "Enough with your flirting. There are cows to feed."

"I was *not* flirting," I say, just as Lachlan bites out the same sentiment.

Finlay just laughs. "Aye, aye, of course not. Will we see you for supper, Lachlan?"

Lachlan stiffens, eyeing my grandpa warily. I've noticed that he appears standoffish with my family—me included—and I can only wonder why he would choose to work here in the first place if he doesn't care for his employers.

"Can't," Lachlan says in a clipped tone. "Appreciate the offer."

Finlay shakes his head. "One of these days you'll say yes."

Lachlan technically says nothing, but in his silence he says plenty. I don't think he has any plans of cozying up to my grandparents anytime soon.

My eyes wander to his chest without my consent, and I can't pretend that the sight of glistening sweat sliding over his taut nipples doesn't make my stomach flutter. Unfortunately, Lachlan doesn't seem to miss me looking.

"See something you like?"

I scowl. "Not even a little."

"Mhm." He smirks infuriatingly, reaching for the ignition to the tractor as he glances toward Finlay. "I'll have this wrapped up in a bit, then I'll find Girdie and get her penned."

"Good lad," Finlay says with a grin.

Lachlan only nods, a short, clipped gesture before he cranks up the tractor and starts to idle away. I have to will myself not to watch his back muscles as he goes—because there are *a lot* of them—reminding myself once again that we *do not lust after assholes*.

It's admittedly a hard mantra to cling to when the asshole in question looks like *that*.

"Still want to see the inside of the barn?"

I blink, my head swiveling to meet Finlay's eyes, which are glint-ing with humor, no doubt having caught me ogling the farmhand.

"Is he always so rude to you?"

Finlay waves me off. "Och, he's just a bit stiff is all. He'll warm up eventually. He's been through it, that one."

I'm dying to ask what he means by that, but I know that doing so will only prove that I'm interested, which I am most certainly *not*. So instead, I gesture toward the entrance of the barn.

"Show me inside?"

Finlay's face lights up, and I feel the warmth of it bleeding into my chest, filling me with an urge to bury myself in it and steal some of his brightness. The good feeling is chased away by the pang of disappointment that Rhona hasn't taken to me as much as Finlay has, but there's still time. She'll come around eventually.

Or at least, that's what I keep telling myself.

## LACHLAN

I place the hay bale farther out in the field; the cows are already starting to gather where I drop it even before I've fully set it on the ground. I turn the tractor off and hop down, pulling my shirt from my back pocket and wiping my brow with it. The weather is downright finicky lately; one day we get a regular downpour and the next I'm sweating in September.

I grin to myself, remembering the look on Keyanna's face when she caught sight of me. It was a very obvious case of checking me out, and I find the idea of that satisfying. Even if only because I can assume it will only annoy her further, being attracted to me and not wanting to be.

It also assuages my reaction to her a bit.

I can't pretend that her fiery hair and her freckles and her pouty mouth don't appeal to me; on the contrary, if I weren't so determined to maintain the upper hand when it comes to the newest addition to the MacKay clan, she might catch me having an obvious case of checking *her* out. Which, just as I assume it is for her, is infuriating. Keyanna MacKay is the last person on earth that I should be even remotely interested in, physically or otherwise.

I scratch one of the cows—Bethie, I think, but it's nearly impossible to keep up with the names Finlay gives these overgrown wooly pups—under the chin, grinning at her low *moo* as she chews at a bit of hay. I'll need to track down Girdie after this like I told Finlay I would; it's true that she's due anytime, and we've lost too many calves these last couple of months to mothers dropping in the wrong place at the wrong time.

*Listen to you*, I think bitterly. *Practically one of them, aren't you?*

I remind myself why I'm really here—tending the farm being the furthest from it. In the six months since I arrived, I've searched the property high and low for answers to my predicament, for *anything* that might lead me to answers that might prolong my inevitable fate, but to no avail. After so long, I've started to worry that those answers don't exist, but knowing what's waiting for me if that's true leaves me no choice but to press onward.

I wonder sometimes what my da might think if he knew I was making nice with the enemy; no doubt he'd tan my hide for even giving them a proper hello or the time of day—but I tell myself that if he knew why I had to, if he knew all the secrets and the lies were for *him* as much as they are for me, I have to believe he would forgive me for it. Hopefully.

I pat Bethie's neck, murmuring, "That's a good girl."

There's no sign of Girdie on the horizon, and I worry that I'm in for a long day if she's wandered off the property again. I should have just penned her when I brought her in earlier, but I caught sight of Keyanna and Finlay moving about the backside of the main house, and, well . . . I got distracted.

It's just that it's so *curious*. Her being here. Especially now. I can't help but wonder if it means something. If the *daughter of MacKay* my father warned me about has by chance stumbled into my lap at what might be my darkest hour. And what does it mean if she has?

Too many questions and not enough answers, I think.

*Not yet*, I promise myself.

I pat Bethie again, pulling my now-damp shirt over my head and fixing my cap after. I suppose I have other things to worry about for now. Can't exactly play the part of a farmhand if I don't actually do some farmhanding. The creek I found Girdie at is across the property, and something tells me she's got it in her head that this will be a good place to give birth, as misguided as it is.

I glance up at the sky, noting there are hours of daylight left.

*Good*, I think. *Plenty of time.*

By the time I have Girdie penned up in the barn—I'm an absolute mess. My wellies are caked in mud, which creeps higher up the legs of my jeans, and I'm so drenched with sweat from this very uncharacteristically hot day for this time of year that my shirt clings to me like a second skin.

I latch the lock on the pen where Girdie is currently pacing back and forth, reaching between the bars to pat her snout. "There now, girl," I soothe. "S'for your own good, aye?"

I hear footsteps behind me, and when I turn toward the barn entrance, I spot Brodie shuffling inside, carrying a bucket. He goes still when he sees me, his brow furrowing ever so slightly before giving me a stiff nod.

"Afternoon, Lachlan," he says.

I nod back at him. "Same goes."

"Got some scraps here for Finlay's pig," he says, lifting the bucket in explanation, looking awkward as he does. "Was looking for him to make sure there's nothing he's too finicky about letting the thing eat."

Conversations like this are pretty much the norm for Brodie and me; he goes out of his way to avoid me when he can, and I'm happy to let that habit continue. The guy strikes me as a bit odd, really. Always skulking about the farm.

"Haven't seen Finlay since this morning," I tell Brodie. "He was showing your cousin around."

"Ah." Brodie nods. "Probably drove her off to show her some of his favorite spots, I'd wager."

"Seems a good guess," I answer.

Brodie shifts his weight from one foot to the other, his lips pursing. "Bit odd, isn't it? Her being here. Didn't even know she existed until yesterday."

"Seems that was the case for the rest of the family too."

"You met her da?"

My teeth clench, a flicker of anger simmering in my gut as I think about the man who let my own father down so badly once upon a time, willing my face to stay expressionless. "When I was a lad," I say. "I don't remember much of him."

"Same," Brodie says. "And same." He frowns. "Just strange that she would show up out of nowhere all of a sudden."

I try not to bristle; it would be all too easy to point out that *he* did the exact same thing not but a couple of months ago, and hell, so did I not a few months before that. It's none of my business if he's unhappy with Keyanna's presence here anyway. I don't care if they don't get on. There's no reason to feel defensive on her behalf.

Silence stretches between us, and I can see the gears turning in his head, but what he wants to say, I have no idea.

"Well . . . I'd best be getting cleaned up," I tell him finally.

He doesn't move as I clod past him, only stepping farther into the barn when I've left it.

*Odd one, he is.*

I'm halfway to the little cottage I'm staying in on the grounds when I spot a flash of red in the distance, and if I squint, I can just make out Finlay standing on a hill some ways off with his granddaughter beside him. Her titian curls sway in the breeze, and even from so far away—I don't miss the way she throws her head back in laughter at something Finlay must have said. I can almost imagine the way her cheeks might flush, making her freckles stand out more.

*That'll be enough of that, you arse.*

I scoff at myself, turning away from the sight of them and continuing on toward the cottage. Freckles and red curls are the last things that should be on my mind. And they aren't, really. On my mind. There's no room for them. Not with everything else going on in my life currently. There isn't even a smidge of room for Keyanna MacKay in my thoughts.

It's something I have to remind myself more than once on the walk back to my place.

7

## KEYANNA

It takes me far longer than it should to realize that I've been had.

To be fair, the outside of Loch Land seems legitimate, and I suppose in a sense it *is* legitimate—but not in the way that Rory and Blair led me to believe. I don't fully grasp the weight of my complete and utter foolishness until I'm stepping into the room just beyond the front desk where you purchase tickets, and once I do, it's all too clear why the woman out front gave me an odd look when I told her I just needed one ticket.

*Museum, my ass.*

The walls are adorned with bright-colored childlike murals that depict a cartoon Loch Ness Monster sporting a wide humanlike grin that is objectively terrifying, and littered around the room are miniature interactive exhibits that barely come up to my waist. Because they aren't intended for adults, obviously. Because this is a fucking children's attraction.

I can't decide what would be more embarrassing—wandering around the place by myself or turning around and leaving barely even a minute after buying my ticket, and after a beat, I come to the decision that leaving so soon will just give Rory and Blair more to laugh about.

*And Lachlan*, I think bitterly. Since he had every opportunity at the bar to tell me what was going on, and even again when I saw him during Finlay's tour of the grounds yesterday, but apparently, he was having just as much of a laugh at my expense as the twins were. The thought makes my cheeks heat, and I tell myself that the next time I see him, I'll be sure to let him know *exactly* what I think about that.

There is a family here with their two young children—a little boy and girl who can't be any older than ten giggling over the exhibits, the older boy teasing the smaller girl for seeming afraid of some of the more monstrous depictions. Their dad comes over to break up their tussle, and I feel my stomach clench as he bends to one knee to murmur something to his son. I wonder if my dad *did* ever come here. It looks like it's been around for quite some time, if the aging paint job is any indication, and I make a mental note to ask Finlay about it later.

For now, though, I urge my feet forward, forcing an air of interest about myself as I meander over to one of the exhibits. It's a tiny paper theater of sorts with a wood handle protruding from the front that lets you move the Loch Ness Monster cutout back and forth through the paper waves, and below it there is a wide plaque with block letters that summarizes the legend of the beast itself.

THE LOCH NESS MONSTER:

A LEGENDARY CREATURE OF LARGE SIZE

SAID TO INHABIT THE DEPTHS OF LOCH NESS.

I pull the handle back and forth idly as I continue to consider the fact that my dad might have come here, maybe even as a child. That thought eases some of the irritation at having been duped. Maybe he stood here as a kid at some point, turning this same handle as I am and wondering about the monster that was said to be only a few miles from this very spot.

I shake off my melancholy before shuffling over to another exhibit, a wide, flat map of the entirety of Loch Ness laid into a table and resting under glass. I trace a finger over the top, letting it linger near the little marker that reads SKALLANGAL COVE, frowning when I remember that I will have to make my way back there somehow. I didn't love the sympathy that flashed in Lachlan's eyes when he heard what I was doing on *his property*—but the guilt that followed felt pretty good. Bastard could stand to be taken down a peg.

I frown. I don't even know why I'm wondering about him. He's just an asshole.

The next room has a wall-to-wall collage of what has to be every photo and news article that was ever printed on the monster, all carefully placed into a neat, tight display. I can see the famous "surgeon's photo" from 1934 that started it all, the grainy print just as ambiguous up close as it's always been on a screen. The caption even says that it was later proven that the photo was a hoax, but that doesn't seem to have stopped anyone from pursuing the possibility of some massive beast lurking in the loch.

"S'gonna get ya!"

The little boy growls as he chases his squealing sister, holding a paper Loch Ness Monster attached to a thin wooden rod. Their mother shakes her head from where she leans against the wall, and their father scrubs a hand down his face before sharing a wry look with her; I'm sure that instances like this are commonplace, given how close in age the children seem to be. Their dad once again moves between them to break things up, and the old fluorescents catch on his hair, reflecting the red highlights in it.

I can't help but picture my dad again, younger than I last saw him but not a child—a young man with hair like mine being pulled to shore in the dead of night by *something* that by all means shouldn't exist. I've heard the story so many times in my life, renditions at bedtime when I was sick, over and over again until I could recite it by heart, and now that I'm here . . . I don't know. Looking at this childish little attraction that barely seems to take itself seriously makes me doubt everything.

But I also remember the look in my dad's eyes in those last few days. I remember how he told the story again, how he had forgotten *so much* of his life because of his affliction but still remembered every detail of that one moment. I remember the sincerity in his gaze when he recounted it for what would be the very last time, the way he gripped my arm and asked me to take him back there—something I am fairly certain he didn't even realize he was asking. I would even go so far as to imagine it's something he wouldn't have asked had he been in his right mind. Which means I didn't *have* to honor it. I know he wouldn't have held it against me. And yet here I am, in a fucking children's museum about a damned cryptid, trying to cobble together some connection to the only person who ever loved me.

*I miss him.*

That's the crux of it all. It's why I'm here, if I'm being honest. Because I am terrified of moving forward with my life without him. Maybe I thought that by coming here, I could find some piece of him left behind, something I could cling to so it felt a little less like he was gone forever. Something that won't make me feel so utterly *alone* in this world.

Judging by the awkward dinner last night and the breakfast this morning that wasn't much better—I have a niggling worry that I won't be finding anything like that.

I wander around Loch Land for another half hour just so it

doesn't feel like I completely wasted thirty pounds—which feels like highway robbery now that I've been inside—finding most of the exhibits to be more of the same. There's nothing here that I haven't already read myself online, and there's definitely nothing that would lead me closer to finding any sort of truth in my dad's stories.

The older woman up front gives me that same quirk of her brow when I quietly thank her while walking out, probably wondering what a grown woman is doing playing around with the Loch Ness Monster block puzzle in the back. Which I did, but only because I accidentally knocked it over, and it bothered me to leave it a mess.

It's misty outside—the weather still dreary from the heavy rain the day before—and I pull the hood up on my raincoat in a meager attempt to keep my hair from turning into a frizzy nightmare, blowing a stray curl away from my face as I pass the horrendous statue posted by the front gate that leads out to the street. I had sort of hurried past it on my way in, because it's truly awful; it has a face that resembles more closely a giraffe, and horns that point straight up like an antelope, which even by myth standard, I'm sure isn't accurate. The entire thing is painted in rings of neon colors down to where it ends at the belly that rests in the dirt, and the arms that stick straight out like a Tyrannosaurus rex's are misshapen and slightly crooked, making the thing as a whole appear kind of sad and silly all at once.

I jolt when a car door slamming sounds behind me, feeling my entire body stiffen when I turn to see the person I'd *least* like to catch me here only a few feet away, smirking at me from the driver's side of his Rover. He locks the car behind him before circling to step onto the sidewalk, and I cross my arms over my chest, narrowing my eyes at him as he approaches.

"Are you *following* me?"

Lachlan cocks a brow. "Following you? I've got a lot better things to do than follow you around, princess." My hackles rise at the stupid nickname he won't let go of, but his finger jabbing behind me distracts me from telling him to fuck off, turning to notice the metal building across the street whose sign tells me it's a feed store of some kind. "Your granny sent me after a few things. She had a calf drop this morning whose mum abandoned her. Need bottles and such."

"You're going to feed it?"

"Aye," he says, cocking his head. "Unless you'd like to?" His eyes move to the ugly statue beside us, his lips twitching with amusement. "Och, but you're busy, yeah?"

My lips purse. "Yeah, laugh it up. You guys think you're so fucking funny."

"Ah, don't mind the twins, lass. They meant no harm. They're just nutty, is all. They can't resist."

"I notice *you* didn't say anything either," I point out.

"Well, I reckon Loch Land is a safer bet for your adventuring than climbing over the rocks of Skallangal Cove. At least here you aren't in danger of breaking your legs."

"I told you what I was doing at the cove," I huff.

His eyes soften then, his mouth turning down in a frown. "You did. You might have mentioned that earlier, you know. But it's still dangerous to be out at the cove by yourself."

"I can handle myself just fine," I grumble, rolling my eyes.

"I believe that you believe that," he laughs, letting his eyes sweep across our surroundings with a grin before he adds, "I notice you didn't bring your dear cousin with you. Did he bore you to death on the drive home?"

I don't really want to give Lachlan any kind of ammunition to use against me, because it seems like he might have discovered that he loves to irritate me, so I just shrug nonchalantly. "Brodie is fine," I say. "He was just busy this morning."

*Not that I would know*, I think, *since I snuck out after breakfast before he could spot me.*

Again, it's not that I dislike Brodie; he actually seems like a nice guy, but this is something I wanted to do on my own. Not with someone I just met. Not that I'm going to tell Lachlan that, since it all turned out to be bogus.

"Oh, is that right?" Lachlan's smile widens, turning a bit sly and causing a dimple to pop in his cheek that immediately draws my eye. *Fuck.* That's not fair. He shouldn't be allowed to look like he does *and* have dimples when he's such a dick. "You two fast friends, then?"

I scowl, tearing my eyes away from the offensive dimple that on anyone else would be utterly lickable. "You're such an ass."

"That's what they tell me," he chuckles.

"What's the deal between you and Brodie anyway?"

"What do you mean?"

"You two were glaring at each other the other day at the bar. It was pretty obvious."

"Och. Brodie never really warmed to me when we were kids. Can't really remember when it started. Always had his nose stuck in a book, that one. S'pose he thought he was better than the rest of us."

"Or maybe he just knew you'd grow up to be an asshole."

"Could be," Lachlan chuckles. He eyes the statue again, still looking entirely too amused on my behalf. "So how did you find Loch Land? Learned a lot, did you?"

"It was about as useful as this . . ." I gesture to what might be the world's ugliest statue, trying to find the words. "Whatever this is. I guess I should have known when I passed it what I was in for."

"You don't think this is a fair representation?"

Now it's my turn to quirk an eyebrow. "Seriously?"

"Who knows." He shrugs. "The beast is a mystery."

"*You* believe in Nessie?" I squint at him in disbelief. "Somehow I highly doubt that you believe she exists."

"Oh, it's she, is it?"

"Well, yeah? The Loch Ness Monster is canonically known as being female."

There's a sparkle of . . . something in his eyes, and paired with that maddening smirk he's wearing, I feel my stomach twist with something I can't quite name. I decide it's aggravation.

"Canonically," he echoes. "Well, far be it from me to argue with an expert." He shoves his hands in his pockets, moving to step past me, but not before leaving me with parting words over his shoulder. "I'm sure you learned all sorts of things in there, after all."

I feel my cheeks heat moments before the sensation spreads into my ears, shooting daggers at his retreating figure as I try to spit out some sort of retort. My tongue seems to be tied into a knot if the way I sit there floundering is any indication, and I finally let out a frustrated sound, stomping my foot on the sidewalk moments before realizing what I just did and cursing myself.

What is it about Lachlan Greer that makes me act like a twelve-year-old?

I stomp off in the opposite direction of him toward the place where I parked my car, telling myself he isn't worth my time. I owe the twins a visit at the pub to give them a *thorough* thank-you for the recommendation of such an *educational* trip—deciding then and there that I won't be letting any more Scots poke fun at me while I'm here.

"Don't slip on the curb, Your Grace," Lachlan calls after me.

I give him the finger over my shoulder as I climb back into my car.

The rain is coming down harder now, and I scowl at the pitter-patter of droplets colliding with my windshield, already feeling my hair start to frizz up from the weather. Of course, it's not enough for me to be sent on some pointless wild-goose chase, no, the weather had to be abysmal too. I already know it's going to make the road back to my grandparents' a muddy mess, and I can only hope that my tiny car won't get stuck somewhere along the way. Heaven forbid I need Lachlan to come to my rescue again.

"You could work with me here," I grumble to the air as I crank my car. "Knock it off with the shitty weather."

I blink in surprise when the rain starts to slow at that very moment, my hand still lingering on the key in the ignition as I stare out the window with an open mouth. Did I . . . ?

I shake away the thought, given that it's a ridiculous one.

*It's Scotland,* I remind myself. *The weather is temperamental.*

I cast one last irritated look at the hideous statue outside Loch Land as I pull away from the sidewalk, shaking my head at my own naivete, not knowing what I'm dreading more—another dose of awkward time spent with my "family" or more fruitless searching for some flimsy connection to my dad. Maybe I'm making it harder on myself than it needs to be. Maybe I should be trying harder to connect with my estranged family. Maybe I shouldn't be making enemies of the locals—namely, one very attractive but infuriating farmhand who apparently isn't going anywhere.

Not for the first time, I wonder if coming here was a stupid idea.

*Stupid,* I hear the echo of Lachlan's voice in my head. *That's what you are.*

As I pull away from the curb, I wonder to myself if hitting someone with your car warrants the same punishment here as it does back home.

## LACHLAN

My entire body aches when I roll out of bed, but that's nothing new. I always try to get a few hours of sleep in my actual bed before greeting the day; I do normally sleep through the night, but sleeping outside under the circumstances that I do isn't exactly conducive for actual rest.

The sun is already high in the sky when I sit up from the bed in Rhona's caretaker cottage, which I'm currently living in; my feet hang off the end a little, but the place is so small, I don't know how I would get a bigger bed in here anyway. Besides, it's free. Money might not be an issue for me, but with Granny's old house having been sold, it's not like there are better options in Greerloch even if I *did* want to throw money at the situation. Better to put up with the tiny bed to be closer to the property, given the reason that I'm here.

I scratch at my stomach as I shuffle over to the kitchenette, which is only a few feet from the corner of the cottage that serves as the bedroom, turning on the coffeepot so that I can get some much-needed caffeine in my system. In the six months since I arrived back in Greerloch, I have yet to find what I'm looking for. It would be easier if I could just *ask* Rhona, but with the likelihood that she most likely doesn't know herself, given the secrecy of it all, I imagine it wouldn't do anything but make her think I'm insane.

Lately, I'm starting to wonder if I am.

I hear something buzzing on the counter, and when I reach for the old cell phone I barely use, my mouth immediately turns down. I only *keep* this phone for her, really, but with every conversation, there seems to be only more distance between us. Still.

I swipe my thumb across the screen to answer, putting it on speaker as I fiddle with the coffeepot.

"Hello?"

"Hi," a soft voice answers.

Silence rings for a beat.

I clear my throat. "How are you?"

"Okay," my mother says. "I was just thinking about you."

*That's rare.*

I shake away the bitter thought, reminding myself that I'm not the only one who's suffered from everything that's befallen us.

"How's Auntie?"

"She's good," Mum tells me. "And you? How are you gettin' on?"

"All right," I tell her. "Still working on the MacKay farm."

"You know you don't need to work. Not since your fath—" She cuts herself off, making a choked sound. Like even today it still hurts her to talk about him. "What made you want to do that anyhow?"

"Oh, just . . . missed Greerloch, I s'pose. Seemed wrong not to offer when they're letting me stay in their groundskeeper cottage. Keeps me busy."

*In more ways than one,* I think.

"You're not . . . you know. Are you?"

I pause, my hand against the now-closed lid of the coffeepot. "I don't follow."

"You don't really believe the stories, do you?"

"Those *stories* are kind of my life, so."

She sighs. "I just don't want you to be getting it in your head that there's something out there, son. It'll drive you mad."

"Seems that could happen to me either way, aye? Might as well try."

She goes quiet, no doubt thinking. I wrestle with whether or not to tell her—I can't know if it will upset her or not, knowing.

*Fuck it.*

"The MacKays had a granddaughter show up out of the blue," I say. "Apparently she's Duncan's girl."

My mother sucks in a breath, but says nothing. I don't know why that irritates me. What do I expect her to do—get excited?

"Maybe it means something else," I tell her. "Maybe it means it's not too late for—"

"Don't," she says softly. "Please."

I sigh, scrubbing a hand down my face. "We can't just *never* speak of him, Mum."

"I can't," she practically whispers, and I can hear her shutting down.

"Well . . . I can't not."

More silence. It seems we are, once again, at an impasse.

"Stay away from that girl," my mother says finally, her tone grave. "Please."

I don't tell her that's literally impossible, given our proximity, but I imagine it would do no good anyway. After this call, she'll use whatever newest coping mechanisms she's been reading about to push this entire conversation from her mind anyhow.

"I have to go," I answer. "Work to be done, you know."

I hear her sniff on the other line, and my chest clenches with something like guilt. Which seems insane, given that she's the one who left *me*.

"All right," she says. "We'll talk again soon, aye?"

*No we won't*, I think, knowing her patterns.

"Aye," I say instead.

"I love you, son."

I take a deep breath, releasing it slowly through my nostrils before replying, "I love you too."

I listen as she disconnects the call, feeling a bit wearier than I did a moment ago. A common occurrence when talking to my mother. I try not to blame her for leaving, I really do—but when a mother tells an eight-year-old her running off to cope is "temporary" but then just . . . never comes back . . . Well. It's enough to make anyone a little bitter, I think. Regardless of everything she's been through.

Because haven't I been through the same things?

After the coffee is made, and I've slipped into warmer clothes, I drop down onto one of the kitchen chairs at the small table by the window with a groan to read the paper while I sip from my cup. The window by the table is streaming with sunlight now, and I reach to brush open the aged white curtains to let the light in, wanting to feel the warmth of it while I prepare for the day. I try to push the conversation with my mother out of my mind, knowing that if I let it, it will consume my thoughts for the rest of the day.

But as it turns out, the universe is ready to provide a distraction, because a second later when I peer out the window, I am greeted by the sight of what I *think* is Rhona's granddaughter wrestling a pitchfork from a bale of hay.

I lean onto the sill with my coffee in hand, smirking against the mug as I watch her quietly. She's a good ways away near the barn, her pale face flushed red from exertion and her lips moving fervently with what I imagine are curses, given the way she's tugging on the pitchfork so violently. She braces her booted (because it seems that sometime in the last week while I have been avoiding her, she's managed to find a proper pair of wellies, even if they are a garish pink color) foot against the heavy bale, pulling at the wooden handle with all her might for several seconds before nearly falling backward on her arse. She's not the most graceful woman I've ever met, despite what her long, lean body might suggest.

I would like to say that watching her doesn't make me smile, but the quirk of my lips would make me a damned liar. I tell myself that I am laughing *at* her, which is a perfectly acceptable way to treat the enemy, which is a necessary distinction. I take another swig from my mug as she starts to pace back and forth in front of the hay, glaring at the pitchfork as if it's personally offended her, and I suspect in a way, it has. The entire thing is even more hilarious given that I know she has no chance of pulling that fork out; I stabbed the thing in the bale myself just yesterday, and I have it on good authority that I am much stronger than her. Than most people, really. One of the few perks of being a Greer son.

I contemplate for a few minutes on whether or not I should rescue her while watching her toil on fruitlessly, knowing full well that I absolutely *shouldn't*, but for some reason, having a slight desire to do so anyway. It's because I like to see her angry expression, I think. That's definitely it. It's satisfying in a way that has nothing to do with how it makes her green eyes shine brighter. Nothing at all.

Boots on and decision made, I leave the peace of the cottage and trudge outside; the weather has been better this week, so the ground is relatively dry, but it's still fairly chilly. Keyanna is still muttering to herself as I draw near her, so much so that she doesn't notice me coming up behind her.

Not until I lean in close to murmur, "Having trouble, princess?"

I'm rewarded by her slim frame jolting a good meter into the air, a shrill sound squawking out of her that is not princess-like at all. She whips around and gives me her best glare, her cheeks a ruddy pink and her titian brows knitted tightly between her emerald eyes.

"Don't scare me like that!"

"I didn't do anything but walk over," I tell her. "You didn't hear me, I think. Too busy cursing the poor hay bale here."

She shoots a disdainful look back toward the bale in question. "Rhona asked me to give Girdie some hay, and I am trying to be useful, but I can't even get the stick out of it. How am I supposed to move it?"

There's something almost admirable about her determination to win over her grandmother. If she were anyone else, I might even tell her that. As it is, I think I'll keep it to myself.

"Hm." I rub my fingers along the neat bristle of my bearded jaw, going for a ruminating look. "That is a puzzle, isn't it?"

"Can you get it out?"

"Are you asking me for a favor? That's a surprise."

Her eyes narrow. "What's surprising is I thought maybe you might not be a dick for once."

"Now, that's not fair," I say with a mock-pout. "I haven't seen hide nor hair of ya in days. What could I have done this week to wrong you?"

"Where *have* you been?" She crosses her arms and cocks her head, and the way she asks the question . . .

A grin splits across my face. "Did you miss me, Key? Were you looking for me?"

"Absolutely not," she scoffs. Her cheeks are still pink, and she averts her eyes with a scowl. "But you work here, don't you? How come I never see you, you know, *working*?"

"I'm what you might call . . . part-time help," I tell her. "I have other dealings to handle than just Rhona's cows."

She cocks a brow. "Well, isn't that mysterious of you."

"Nothing mysterious about it, princess," I say sweetly. "Between you and your dear cousin, I reckon I can afford to cut back on my hours a bit, yeah?"

She huffs out a breath. "Are you *ever* going to stop calling me that?"

"I will when it stops making you blush," I counter immediately.

Her mouth gapes and her eyes widen, and her shocked expression fills me with such an intense satisfaction, it feels like a win somehow, and underneath that . . . Well. I don't analyze the feeling underneath all that.

"You don't make me *blush*," she practically hisses. "You're—you're just—you're infuriating! That's what you are."

"Aye, aye, so I've been told." I tilt my head toward the pitchfork still lodged in the hay. "You want me to get that out for you or not?"

"I . . ." She looks like she'd rather eat sand than ask for my help, and I find I like watching her squirm. She's just . . . very fun to annoy. I consider her irritation partial restitution from the MacKay clan. "If you don't mind," she says finally, in a very tight tone.

"Don't mind at all," I answer cheerily. "As long as you say please."

Her flush is immediate, and her mouth opens with what was surely supposed to be a curse or a barb, but then she glances at the pitchfork again, and then back toward the house, and I know she's considering what might be the lesser of two evils—asking for help from *me*, or from one of her estranged family members.

She takes a deep breath, not even looking at me when she mutters, "Please."

"What was that?" I cup my hand to my ear. "I didn't quite hear you."

"I said *please*," she grinds out a little louder.

There's no good reason for me to feel so satisfied by her acquiescence, but watching her pert mouth begrudgingly offer up the word sends a tiny thrill swooping through my stomach.

"Ah, now that wasn't so hard, was it?"

I reach around her and grab the handle of the pitchfork with one hand, giving it a swift tug and watching her mouth fall open when it gives way with ease. She stares at it for a good number of seconds when I offer it to her with that same look that says it might be her new worst enemy, finally snatching it away.

"Thank you," she mumbles before I even have a chance to goad her for it. Pity.

"Just trying to be a good person," I tell her seriously.

She rolls her eyes, and the action is almost . . . cute on her.

Cute?

I recoil at my own thoughts.

Definitely not *cute*.

"I don't know why it had to be cows," she mutters under her breath, more to herself than anything.

"I knew you were afraid of them."

"They're very . . ." She glances at Bethie, who is several paces away and lazily chewing on a wad of grass. "Big."

I consider that. The highland cows are massive animals; their thick fur makes them seem even bulkier than they are, and their horns might look menacing if you didn't know what giant puppies they are.

"They're harmless," I assure her.

She casts another wary look in Bethie's direction. "That's what they *want* you to think."

"You're *really* scared of the cows?"

"I'm not *scared*," she insists. "But before this trip, I barely left New York. I'm not exactly an expert on bovine creatures. They're . . . a new experience."

"Ah, they're practically big weans themselves." I give a short whistle between my teeth, and Bethie's head perks up to notice me before she slowly starts to trot over. "Wouldn't hurt a fly."

"Don't call it over!"

I give her a gentle push between her shoulder blades. "Now, you can't work on the farm and be scared of the livestock. It just won't do. Come on now, I'll show you they're harmless."

"I don't think—*fuck*."

She jumps back when Bethie sidles up right beside her, still chewing slowly as she regards our new farmhand with a bored look. The cow's eyes blink slowly, and her tongue dips out to lick at her own snout before she resumes her chewing.

"Now, the trick is not to show any fear," I tell Key seriously. I'm already forming a solid plan to scare the shite out of her. Shouldn't be too hard to get Bethie to rear up with a well-timed smack on her arse. Maybe it will put the wee princess MacKay on hers. "You don't want them to come after you with their horns."

"What?" Key's eyes widen. "You said they were harmless!"

"As long as you don't spook 'em," I say, completely full of it. These cows wouldn't trample a blade of grass unless they had a mind to eat it. "Now, approach her real gentle like, and give her your hand."

"My hand?"

"Aye. You want to let her smell you. That way she gets your scent. Let her know you're her friend."

Key clenches and unclenches her fist slowly, her hand trembling a bit when she extends it toward Bethie. She looks utterly serious as she stares down the aging old cow, her fingers unwinding one by one and shaking slightly when she brings them near Bethie's snout. She looks so serious, in fact, that I start to feel a bit guilty over my idea to scare her.

"That's good," I tell her quietly, telling myself I am just positioning myself closer to Bethie's rump when I circle around to Key's other side. "That's really good." I don't know what possesses me to curl my fingers under her elbow—am I distracting her before I give her a scare? Then why are my fingers sliding down to circle her wrist? Her hand is so much more delicate than mine, and I can't help but notice how well it fits in my grasp. "Just hold it steady now. Let her come to you."

Any second now, I'm going to give Bethie a slap. Any second now, I'm going to have Keyanna squealing in terror and then surely cursing my name after. It'll be *satisfying*, I remind myself.

But then her green eyes flick up to meet mine, looking so wide and guileless that I damned near forget the whole prank. "She won't bite?"

"I . . ." I try to remember what I was doing, let alone what I'd planned to say, momentarily taken aback by the clenching sensation in my chest when those viridescent eyes meet mine. "No," I say finally, clearing my throat when it sounds too rough. "She won't bite."

Bethie chooses that moment to nudge Key's hand, sniffing at it gently as if looking for a treat before giving it a heavy lick. The resulting peal of laughter that falls from Key's mouth is probably the most unattractive sound I've ever heard—her laugh is high-pitched and more of a shriek than a laugh really—so why do I want to make her do it again?

I release Keyanna immediately, taking a step back from her if for no other reason than to get a handle on my own thoughts. This entire interaction is too friendly for my liking; if there is one thing I have no wish to be, it's friends with a MacKay. Even one as amusing as this one.

"There," I say evenly, keeping my expression flat. "See? You were just being daft."

The mirth in her features evaporates, replaced by a disgruntled frown. "Just when I thought you might not be a total asshole."

"That's what you get for thinking, I reckon," I say blithely.

She rolls her eyes. "Are you this insufferable with everyone or just me?"

"S'pose you're just special," I answer with a smirk. I watch as she drags the pitchfork upright, her eyes darting warily between it and the hay. I cock my head, suddenly curious. "Why are you taking this so seriously anyway?"

Her brow lifts. "What do you mean?"

"Why agree to help with the farm? It's not like you're invested in it, and with Rhona acting like she's counting the days until you piss off back to America . . . I don't get why you're out here sweating to try and impress her."

"I'm not trying to *impress* her," she grumbles.

Now *my* brow lifts. "Are you not?"

"Ugh." She tosses the pitchfork to the ground, frowning. "I don't know. Maybe. I figure it can't hurt."

"Seems like a lot of effort for only a wee bit of reward."

"I've been thinking the same thing," she sighs, her eyes immediately widening when she realizes what she's said. "I mean—why do you care anyway?"

I study the rigid way she holds herself; her spine is straight and her shoulders are damn near up to her ears, and the tension she carries seems to radiate from her in waves, giving away the truth of things, that for whatever reason, she's determined to make this asinine venture of hers work. Again, I can't help but think that it's almost admirable. Almost.

"I don't care," I tell her, the words sounding not quite right even as I say them. "I'm just curious why *you* would care so much about a relative stranger liking you is all."

She runs her fingers through the wild mass of red curls, her lips turning down as a sharp exhale escapes her nostrils. Like this, with the morning sun kissing her skin, her freckles seem to almost sparkle like tiny flecks of gold.

I don't even realize I'm fixated on this until she says quietly, "They're all I have left, you know?"

She doesn't look at me as she says it, but I can hear the vulnerability in her voice. I very much doubt she means to appear that way in front of *me* of all people, but given that her shoulders are sloping now as an air of defeat settles over them like a heavy cloak—I also suspect that she might be desperate for any sort of connection. I distantly think to myself how alone she must feel, here in a new land with a family whose matriarch acts as if she's not wanted.

"Aye," I answer softly, a strange, heavy weight in my chest. "I know what that's like."

Her eyes flick to mine. "You do?"

Something like hope shines in those green depths, and I don't like the way her looking at me makes me feel. Keyanna MacKay is not someone to be friendly with, and I should know better. It's that thought that has me tearing my gaze from hers, clearing my throat as I shrug.

"Aye, well. You'd best be getting to that hay if you're to have any hope of finishing before breakfast. If the cows get too hungry, they might just bite after all."

The soft expression she'd been wearing evaporates, replaced by her familiar scowl. I tell myself it's a good thing. It's safer, her scowling at me. I'm not sure how to deal with anything more than that. She opens her mouth as if she might call me out for the blatant brush-off, but eventually, she just shakes her head and reaches down to grab the pitchfork again.

She turns on her heel, dragging it behind her, moving right past the hay bale toward the barn in a tizzy. Her shoulders are hunched up high again nearly to her ears, and even from here, I can see the red hue of the shell of them, no doubt a color that is all over her face. I watch her go for a moment, reminding myself that I have no reason to go after her.

Thankfully, I have other things to attend to that can keep me from changing my mind.


The attic is cold when I climb up the old pull-down stairs, the one lone lightbulb casting an eerie glow over the wide space. I was deathly quiet as I made my way through the house to the second story; Rhona and Finlay have already left to go into town, and Brodie usually spends most of his days doing . . . whatever he does. Anything to keep him from having to help around the farm. I begrudgingly think to myself that at least Keyanna isn't as useless as her eejit cousin.

Not that it matters.

I know that I'm betraying Rhona's trust right now, but with the arrival of Keyanna, I find myself running out of options. Especially since I don't know what her presence will mean for me. Also, I can't get Blair's words out of my head—about Rhona knowing something. Rhona has been good to me, all things considered, far better than any other MacKay has ever been to a Greer, but she *is* still a MacKay, which means I can't let myself trust her. Not completely. Not that the thought keeps me from feeling guilt at having nicked the key to the attic while I was chatting Rhona up in her kitchen the other day.

I've known where it is for weeks after seeing her return it to a drawer after using it, but I've been able to convince myself not to resort to such measures before this. After months of finding no answers, however, I am not too proud to admit that I'm getting desperate. I recall the night before, even press at the bruises on my ribs that I know will be gone before tomorrow but will still ache with something that isn't just physical long after, and remember why I'm here at all. What I have to lose. What I've *already* lost.

Rhona's attic is full of old trunks and dusty boxes—and just looking at it from the landing, I know there is too much up here to go through in one afternoon. It will take weeks to riffle through it all, and that's not counting the fact that I will have to do so quietly and in secret, lest Rhona's good graces run out should she catch me going behind her back.

I reach for the nearest box and flip it open, frowning when I'm met with dusty baby clothes. The box beneath it yields much of the same, with the exception of a small framed photo wedged between the folded clothes. I almost toss the box aside without looking, but for some reason, my curiosity has me pulling it out, and my eyes meet with the smiling, younger face of Keyanna's father. He can't be out of his teens yet in this photo, his hair the same shade as Key's and his smile like hers too. He has the same slightly noticeable bunny teeth that she has, so slight one might miss it if they weren't paying attention, and I would like to say that looking at the photo doesn't make me recall the strange sensations in my chest upon seeing that same smile in his daughter, but I would be lying.

I shake my head and move to put the picture back.

I have bigger things to worry about.

KEYANNA

My first week at Rhona and Finlay's farm is strained, to put it mildly. My grandpa, as he insists I call him, has determinedly done his best to make me feel welcome, but Rhona has been decidedly less warm. Her icy regard of me is still as frosty as the day she begrudgingly invited me in from her porch, and I am starting to think that no number of attempts at helping around the farm will thaw her reception of me.

Not to mention their infuriating farmhand, who seems to take distinct pleasure in making me feel as stupid as he first assessed that I was.

Just thinking about the interaction with Lachlan today outside the barn has me frowning in the small twin bed in the guestroom I'm occupying, and even hours later, after a full day of work and fruitless attempts at conversation with my would-be grandmother at dinner—I'm still flustered when I think about it. I have never been the type of person to let someone get the best of me, and I can't for the life of me determine why it's *Lachlan* who seems to have found all the right buttons to press to make me mute with irritation. I don't even really *know* the guy. Especially since he's done his best to make himself scarce since that day outside Loch Land. Not that I've been *looking* for him or anything.

I saw him again later coming out of the house, not missing the smirk he shot at me when he took in my frazzled state after I'd finally managed to complete the chores I'd volunteered for. He silently regarded my wild hair, which had turned frizzy after all my sweating, a maddening quirk of his brow that was loaded with all the thinly veiled insults I just knew he wanted to give. I still can't decide if him striding past me without a word was a better or worse outcome.

*Better*, I tell myself. *Definitely better.*

I don't know why I can't sleep tonight; I could blame the slightly uncomfortable mattress that feels like it hasn't hosted a body in years, or the racing thoughts pinging around my skull surrounding my precarious family situation, or even the dick of a farmhand I have to actively not think of—but strangely, the most predominant thing that keeps me from closing my eyes is the all-encompassing feeling of failure. It's been a week now, seven whole days, and I'm not one step closer to learning anything about my dad that I didn't know before.

There have been moments when Finlay has started talking about his son, but every instance earns him a sharp glare from his wife, and he is always quick to fall silent after. It's so frustrating that I don't even know *why* they won't talk about him. Even more so that I had every opportunity to ask my dad when he was alive and yet never did simply because I was afraid of that sad look he got whenever he mentioned his home in Scotland.

What could have possibly happened to make Rhona want to forget she had a son?

After several more minutes of tossing and turning, I can't take it anymore. I swing my feet over the side of the bed, moving to the window to get some air. I try the latch, but it doesn't budge. I notice when I lean closer that the thing is rusted with age—probably hasn't been opened in years. Great. I grab for it again and pull with all my might, doing nothing but working myself up into a warmer state as exertion floods through my limbs.

"Fucking hell," I mutter, glaring at the window.

*Can nothing go my way this week?*

I rattle the window like a toddler having a tantrum, but quietly, still not wanting to wake anyone with my bout of insomnia. I can't imagine how ridiculous I must look right now. I'm sure Lachlan would love to make fun of me for it. I throw up my hands after a few seconds with a frustrated huff, craving water now that I've worked myself into a sweat—maybe even alcohol if I can properly raid the cabinets. I shove my feet into my worn slippers and grab my robe from the old wooden rocking chair in the corner, wrapping it tightly around myself.

I'm still muttering obscenities at the window that hasn't really done anything wrong but is the perfect victim of my misplaced ire, and when I start to shuffle out of my room, I hear a soft *click* followed by an eerie creak, and when I turn back, the window is cracked open slightly, the two panes parted down the middle and pushed outward as chilled air starts to make its way in.

*Huh.*

I move to the window once more, finding the latch just as rusted and stiff as it was before, but now it's pulled all the way back. I stare at it for a moment, my sleep-deprived brain thrown for a loop, finally shaking my head and rationalizing that I must have loosened it with all the frantic tugging. Maybe the universe just decided to throw me a bone. I let the cold air wash over me, breathing it in deep and letting it refresh my mind.

*Okay*, I think. *Drink. Then bed.*

I pull the window closed but don't latch it so as not to risk it getting stuck again, quietly making my way down the stairs. The last thing I need is to wake up Rhona and have to face her while she's tired when she already barely tolerates me.

I'm only a few steps from the kitchen when I hear the voices, momentarily frozen by the hushed tones coming from the open doorway. Almost like my thoughts of my grandmother manifested her presence.

"—been nothing but cold to the lass since she arrived, Rhonnie. She's your blood!"

"She's not a MacKay," I hear my *grandmother* say. "Not really. Duncan gave her the name, but that doesn't make her ours."

Something squeezes in my chest, wrapping around my heart like a vise, and I know I should back away, that this is a conversation I don't want to hear, but I can't seem to make my feet move.

"Are you willing to push away the only part of our Duncan we have left over something so foolish, love? We lost our boy." Finlay's voice is low and mournful. "We don't want to lose her too."

I can't help it; I take that final step that allows me to peer around the doorframe and into the dimly lit kitchen—enough light from the small lamp in the corner to see the harshness in Rhona's features when she answers, "Aye, we lost our boy. We lost Duncan the day he walked out of this house, and I'm not interested in anything he left behind."

Finlay shakes his head, opening his mouth to say more but seeming to think better of it as he stalks toward the back door to escape to the screened-in porch just beyond. Rhona stands resolutely by the counter, a hard set to her jaw and pure, unadulterated anger in her eyes that tells me she meant every word.

The crushing grief swells up in me all at once—grief for my father, for this family, for *me*—and I feel it piling up inside my chest like water, filling my lungs like I'm drowning. The pounding in my head is a living, throbbing thing, and I struggle to take in air, the feelings in my chest needing to get out, to go *somewhere*—needing to *escape*, and I—

The crashing sound of glass breaking startles all three of us, a small pile of shards now on the floor where the remnants of a cup lay in pieces, seeming to have fallen from the counter of its own will. I can't help the quiet gasp that escapes me, and I don't miss the way Rhona's head swivels to meet the sound, her eyes so like mine connecting with my gaze and holding it. Her lips part, genuine surprise in her features, but no remorse, I note. Her eyes flick from the broken cup back to me, her mouth closing as she seems to lose the battle of finding something to say for herself. Maybe there *is* nothing to say for herself. Not in her mind.

And I realize all at once what a mistake this was.

I turn on my heel and rush back up the stairs, gulping in lungfuls of air as I stare at the small, cold room that I'm realizing has nothing for me. It takes me only a second to begin packing my things, to start throwing on clothes. In the entire twenty minutes it takes me to do so, no one comes after me up those stairs.

Not even when I walk out the front door.

It's silly to be here, and I know that. As dangerous as the cove is supposed to be during the day, I can only imagine it's more so at night.

I can practically hear Lachlan's voice in my head telling me how stupid I am, and it's strange how a flicker of disappointment rushes through me at the thought of him, but for what, I can't even pinpoint. I clutch my father's urn in my hands as I watch the gentle lapping of the waves, knowing that I have to do this, regardless of who owns the land or how stupid it might be.

"I'm sorry," I say to the air, imagining that maybe my dad is listening. "I tried. I really did." I take a deep breath in through my nostrils, trying to quell the urge to cry. I can feel the traitorous prickling in my eyes, and I wipe away the lone offender on the back of my hand. "I wish you had told me more," I tell my dad. "I wish I had asked more questions." I tilt my head back to the sky, blinking rapidly. "I wish you hadn't left me *alone*."

The sky is clear and brightly lit with twinkling stars, and sitting in the quiet, I can feel the beauty of this place, and I wonder for the umpteenth time what would have caused my dad to leave it. There's a buzzing energy here, like a presence you can almost touch—almost as if the land itself is listening to my sad little soliloquy.

But maybe that's just my fucking loneliness talking.

I take a deep breath as I strengthen my resolve, because neither rocks nor Lachlan fucking Greer is going to keep me from doing this one thing. I am *going* to finish this, at the very least.

I make my way along the shore with determination in my steps, finding the same wide, flat rock from that first day that marks the start of a path of sorts farther out into the water. I test my brand-new boots against the stone to ensure that they have the grip the store owner promised, inhaling deeply before stepping up onto the rock.

*Stupid*, I hear Lachlan's voice say. *That's what you are.*

I grit my teeth and take another step, moving toward the next rock that's just a little higher.

*She's not a MacKay*, says Rhona's voice in my head. *Not really.*

Another step, and I have to shift my dad's urn under one arm to grasp the largest rock and start to hoist myself up.

*We lost Duncan the day he walked out of this house, and I'm not interested in anything he left behind.*

Standing a few feet higher than the water, I feel a rush of accomplishment, because even if I failed at what I came here for, even if I never know this part of my dad, and in turn this part of myself—I can say that I did this, at the very least. I bring the urn higher to press my forehead against it, closing my eyes for a moment as I quietly tell my dad goodbye for the last time. I know if I drag this out, I'll end up crying myself to sleep right here on this rock, and the last thing I need is for some asshole farmhand to find me out here tomorrow morning with a smug look and a big fat *I told you so.*

I remove the lid from the urn, taking one last deep breath before tipping it down to let the contents flutter in the light breeze, watching as they gently float toward the water below. I watch until the urn is empty in my hands, the weight of it seeming more substantial now. Even empty, it feels heavy in my grip.

"I did it," I whisper. "I did it, Dad."

I smile despite everything, feeling a flicker of triumph.

And it's exactly at that moment that I'm thrown into the water.


It takes me several seconds to orient myself when I break the surface of the loch, gasping for breath as an ache blooms in my legs and my shoulder. Something *hit* me. Something solid and *large.* I felt the weight of it sweep across my legs just before my shoulder collided with the rock, grateful in hindsight that I didn't bash my skull against it on the way down.

I kick my legs under the water as I turn my head to try and determine the culprit, and even as I'm trying to make sense of it, alarm bells are sounding in my head. The rational part of my brain is desperately trying to dismiss the notion, trying to make sense of how I got from point A to point B in a way that is logical and not mythical in the slightest—but a splash a few yards away shuts that little voice right up.

I don't see it at first—maybe because it's dark out. The light of the moon and the stars only offers so much, the glow of them making the water's surface seem almost black. But the distinct shape of *something* rolls with the wave that passes in front of me, and inside it there is an impression, an impossibility, really, because there is *no way*.

First comes the head: wide and flat with eyes that gleam like a cat's in the night. The shape of its neck follows, then the curve of its back as it glides through the water. I'm frozen, unable to do anything but try to stay afloat and gape at what—until this very moment—I had been almost sure didn't actually exist, but proof is right there, coming at me at breakneck speed that doesn't even allow me time to be properly terrified.

*I'm going to be eaten by the fucking Loch Ness Monster.*

It's a hysterical thought, one that in my delirious state almost makes me laugh—and I see teeth now, *sharp* teeth—and this is really it. This is how I'm going to go.

*Stupid. That's what you are.*

He would really get a kick out of this if he—

The force of another wave pushes me farther in as it crashes over me, and I have to kick my legs even harder to try and stay afloat. Water gets in my eyes and my mouth as I come up sputtering, blinking water away and trying to clear my blurred vision as a haunting sound rings out in the night. Like a fucking dinosaur and the screech of a bird rolled into one, the roar of the monster is so loud that it feels impossible that someone might not hear it even from miles away, and it distracts me for a moment so that I don't immediately realize what I'm seeing.

Because not only is the fucking Loch Ness Monster *real*, but apparently—there is more than one.

I watch as a similar monster rushes the first, snapping at it with its teeth and rolling its body against it as if trying to force it in the other direction. The first monster howls, spinning in the water with a ferocity that pushes me below the surface again. I see the new monster rolling its body weight into the first when I manage to sputter topside again, and when it rolls once more to put its body between me and the first beast—an impossible thought occurs to me.

I think it's *protecting* me.

It seems ludicrous, but every move from this second monster seems purposeful, designed to keep the first one away from me, and absolutely nothing about that makes sense. If I weren't cold and terrified and half drowning, I might marvel at that, but as it is—I take the opportunity given by my would-be savior to start swimming in the other direction. Let the monsters duke it out. This is more than I bargained for.

I swim away as best as I can with the throbbing in my legs from where the monster struck me, hearing the commotion of their battle still raging behind me. Another screech pierces the air, one that sounds almost . . . pained this time, and I can't help the way I pause in the water, turning to see who's winning. I feel a pang of sympathy when I realize that my protector has just received a nasty bite from its opponent, the flesh where its long neck meets its body ragged and darker as if coated with blood.

*You can't do anything to help it*, I rationalize. *Get the fuck out of here.*

I float idly for a span of seconds as my protector continues to fight back, my eyes going wide when it surges upward suddenly, its massive body crashing into the other monster with all its might. Another howl of pain, this time from the one that wanted to eat me, and as if by some miracle, it starts to swim in the other direction. I watch it sink lower into the water, its body disappearing more and more by the second—my protector lingering several yards away and seeming to watch it go. It makes another low sound, teetering a bit in the water, and I watch as it slowly turns, its glowing eyes landing on me.

*Oh, shit.*

I take off, not wanting to stick around to find out if the monster just wanted me for his own dinner—kicking my legs as fast as I can as I rush toward the shore. I can hear it behind me, its massive body seeming to create a wind of its own as it slices through the waves, and even when I'm stumbling onto the rocky shore, I think to myself that this might be the end.

So it's a massive—pun intended—surprise when the monster rolls onto the shore behind me, its giant form slumping like a beached whale instead of a fearsome creature of myth. Its head lolls to the sand, and from where I'm standing several feet away, I can hear the harsh puffs of its breath.

I don't know what compels me to move—maybe it's the way it's looking at me, not like it wants to eat me but with what *seems* like weary curiosity, and despite my best judgment, I take a cautious step forward. The monster doesn't move to snap at me, and when I take another step closer, I notice the wound at the base of its neck, ragged and bleeding.

*It's really hurt.*

I bite my lip as I hover, stuck between fear for my own safety and worried that *the Loch Ness Monster* might die because of me—even having a horrible thought that at least there's another one before coming to a decision.

"Okay," I tell the creature, taking another slow step. "I'm going to have a look at that, but if you eat me, I'm going to curse you with the *worst* indigestion you've ever had."

The monster gives a weak chuff, something that might almost sound like a snort on something that wasn't the size of a small charter plane. I imagine it's thinking that my threats aren't much of an incentive not to take a bite out of me, but it's all I've got.

It doesn't move when I finally get closer to its wound, one big, gleaming eye rolling to watch me as I carefully assess the damage. Which is pretty bad, it seems. The bleeding is steady, and given that I know nothing about the beast's anatomy, I have no way of knowing if it's a fatal blow or not.

I rip my jacket off in a flurry of movement; it's not much in the way of first aid, but it's literally all I have. I press the fabric to the gaping bite mark, immediately seeing it start to soak with blood, and I feel a sudden onslaught of sadness for this creature, one that I'm pretty sure saved my life.

"You can't fucking die," I say raggedly, feeling my eyes burn. "Not now."

*I did it*, I think distantly. *I found it, Dad.*

"You're not fucking dying, do you hear me?"

I press harder at the wound, desperation clawing at my insides as I silently pray for the bleeding to slow. I don't know what that will mean for me, and I don't know if what I'm doing will make any difference, but the desire to *try* is so strong, it feels like it's filling me up.

Like earlier, I feel so . . . *full*. So full of emotion that I can't seem to contain it.

My body feels too hot, and my eyes blur with tears as I press harder, as I silently *beg* whoever is listening to *save* this creature that is the only tie I have left to my father—and I feel my head swim with the effort of it. I feel that same sensation from Rhona's house threaten to suffocate me, feel it pouring into my chest like liquid heat.

Heat I can feel in my hands too, weirdly. It's in my chest and my arms and my palms, and my vision is so blurry now that I can barely see, and my head swims, and my lungs burn, and somehow, there is a faint glow, and then . . .

Everything goes dark.

## LACHLAN

I wake up to the sound of screaming.

I blink at the morning sun that streams down, feeling a faint twinge in my shoulder when I instinctively raise a hand to shield my eyes. For a moment everything seems fuzzy, like waking up from a dream you can't quite remember, but when another feral screech sounds from nearby, and paired with the rumpled, irate redhead staring down at me with wild eyes—it doesn't take long for everything to come rushing back.

*The sound of his roaring. The crash of water. The weight of his body slamming into mine.*

"Fuck," I mutter, trying to sit up. "Can you just—" I press the heel of my hand to my forehead, trying to will the throbbing there away. "Can you stop screaming?"

One glance at Keyanna MacKay tells me this was the wrong thing to say.

"Are you fucking kidding me?" She throws up her hands just to let them plop to her sides, still gaping at me with wide eyes and an open mouth. "*You're* the Loch Ness Monster?"

*I could have just let her be eaten*, I think distantly. *But no.*

I squint in her direction, her flaming hair seeming to burn brighter while backlit by the sun. "What makes you say that?"

"What makes me . . . Seriously?" She paces back and forth restlessly, gesturing at me with a wave of her hand. "I passed out last night next to a literal dinosaur, and I woke up and it's *you*, and you're *naked*."

My eyes flick down, and it occurs to me that she's right. "Huh." I bring my knees up and rest my elbows on them, trying to hide the more sensitive parts of my body. She's already blushing enough as it is. "I like to night-swim every now and again."

"You like to night-swim," she echoes blandly.

I stretch my arms above my head and groan at the tightness in my shoulders. "That's right."

"That's what you're going with," she deadpans. "Really?"

"Doesn't that seem like a more probable explanation than you falling asleep next to—what did you say it was again?"

"You're seriously trying to gaslight me right now?"

"Me? I would never."

"You're doing it right now."

"I think maybe you hit your head, lass."

This only makes her angrier, her cheeks growing even pinker, impossibly. "Are you *actually* trying to pull an Edward Cullen on me?"

"I don't know what that means."

"I did not hit my fucking head! I *know* what I saw."

I shift to pull myself up to standing, and her eyes immediately avert so she isn't looking at my naked form, but not before a flush creeps down her neck.

"I saw you floating in the water last night," I tell her, keeping my tone even. "I warned you about the rocks, but it seems you didn't listen. I hear a bump on the head can cause all sorts of trouble with your memory. There's a doctor in town . . . I could drive you there, if you want?"

"So the story you're sticking with is that you saved my dumb ass from drowning after I fell off a rock," she says.

I shrug. "Not a story if it's true."

"And you're naked because . . . ?"

"Didn't want to get my clothes wet, now did I? I must have passed out from the effort. Saving people is hard work."

She peeks back at me, her eyes narrowed. "Really?"

"Really, really," I answer earnestly, trying not to smile at her angry expression.

I can tell how hard she's trying not to look at all of me, and I can't help the way I widen my stance slightly, spreading my legs to plant both feet firmly in the sand as I cross my arms over my chest. It does what I intend; her cheeks flame and her eyes train pointedly on my face, but it only takes a second for them to stray, and when they do, a sly, pleased smile crosses her face.

"If you like the look of me that much," I tease, "you're welcome to take a gander as long as you like."

"You wish," she scoffs. But then she takes a step closer, one delicate brow lifting as her expression turns smug. "So you saved me."

"Aye, I did," I tell her, watching her advance cautiously.

She nods, pressing her lips together as if considering. "And I just imagined the Loch Ness Monster."

"It's not the first time it's happened," I say. "No need to be embarrassed."

"Huh." Her jaw works, and the quirk of her lips spells trouble, but it doesn't hit me how much until she says, "Then what's this?"

Her fingers skirt along my shoulder, her touch eliciting a prickling sensation followed by a rush of warmth that I don't have the time to analyze, because seconds after, a dull ache echoes there.

"Fuck," I hiss.

She pokes at the pinker skin that looks new, like it's just stitched itself back together, but even though it's not nearly as raw as it should be, there is still a clear pattern of a bite, now shrunk to match my smaller frame. I frown at it, both confused by the state of it and irritated that it gives Key more reason to fight me on this, and when I glance back at her, there is triumph in her eyes.

"I *know* what I saw," she says firmly.

I run through a number of excuses, trying to grasp *any* other solution to offer her that doesn't involve me spilling a secret that spans back centuries—but as little as I know this woman, I still think that this is not something she is just going to let go. It seems I have very few choices here.

I take a deep breath, expelling it slowly.

Centuries we've kept this secret, and in an instant, it's undone by one wild, irritating woman. A *MacKay* woman, the last person in the world I'd want to share with and who, if my father is to be believed—could be my ruin.

*Fuck.*

"Wait up!"

I continue to stomp farther down the shoreline in search of my discarded clothes with as much dignity as I can muster in the brisk morning air—Keyanna's crunching footsteps close behind. I reach up to let my fingers press into the tender skin of my shoulder, trying to reason how it possibly could have healed so quickly. Being what I am *does* mean a certain level of resilience, but a wound of this nature should have taken days to heal. There's no reasonable explanation for it already being so much better.

Keyanna's hurried footsteps interrupt my musings. I peek at her over my shoulder, scowling. "Don't you have somewhere to be?"

"You mean somewhere other than the cove where the magic loch monster saved me and then turned back into an asshole farmhand?" She scoffs. "No, I don't have anywhere better to be."

I smirk down at her when she catches up, falling in step beside me. "Admit it," I taunt. "You just like the view."

"Hardly," she answers with a roll of her eyes, but I notice her cheeks are still pink. "I don't need to stare at your ass. You make an ass out of yourself every time I talk to you."

"Cute," I murmur.

The anger in her eyes has dimmed now, and in its place is a terrifying sort of curiosity, one that tells me she is absolutely not going to just keep quiet about this and leave me the fuck alone.

"So have you always been . . ." She waves her hand in a circle as if searching for the word. "A monster?"

"No," I answer dryly. "A witch gave me a magic apple after I pissed in her roses."

Key's eyes widen comically. "Really?"

"No," I say with a smirk.

Key scowls. "See? Total ass."

"So you keep saying."

I spot my clothes a few meters ahead, trying my best to ignore the woman beside me when I manage to scoop them up a minute later to dress. Key, to her credit, stands demurely to the side, her gaze fixed pointedly in the other direction.

"Not like you haven't seen it all," I tease.

Her mouth does this twisting thing, like she's bitten into something sour. "I didn't see anything."

"Sure you didn't."

"So what *did* happen to you?"

"Nothing happened to me."

"You just woke up one morning as the Loch Ness Monster?"

"I hate that term," I huff.

She chuffs out a laugh. "What exactly do you prefer?"

"I *prefer* not to be called anything at all."

I shove my feet into my boots with more aggression than is necessary, cursing my own damned luck for being in this situation. Of all the people who I could have spotted in the loch, of all the people who could have landed themselves in that situation . . . Why did it have to be *her*? Is it some sort of cosmic joke? One last laugh of the MacKay clan at the expense of the Greers?

I pause in dressing, my father's whispered warning flitting through my thoughts.

*For the end only comes—*

I shake that thought away. I'm not about to be swept up in panic by superstition and conjecture. With that in mind, I start dressing again, but faster. I need to get the fuck out of here and regroup.

"Wait," she says suddenly, her voice a sharp outburst in the still air surrounding us. "Nessie is a girl!"

"It would appear that is not the case," I remark.

"But Nessie has always been a girl!"

"I *did* try to hint at the falsity of that, you remember," I remind her. "Outside of Loch Land."

"Yeah, but I just thought you were being a dick."

"No, I was trying to tell you that Nessie *has* a dick."

She instantly flushes red, and I have to admit that some part of me, however small, really loves riling her. She really is very pretty when she blushes.

*Stop thinking about how pretty she is, you arse.*

"So then who is the other monster?"

I go still in the process of putting on my jacket, my jaw clenching as my mouth presses into a firm line. I turn my head to gaze at the water, letting it skim the now-smooth surface fruitlessly. I know that during the day he'll have gone to deeper waters, as if some part of him still remembers the necessity of doing so.

Even if that's all he remembers.

"Never you mind," I tell her.

I keep walking with every intention of finding my car, my mind still racing on how best to handle this situation. If Key starts blabbing about what she saw to everyone in town . . . What will happen? If Rhona knew that it was more than just stories and legends passed down in her clan . . . Would history repeat itself? She is still a MacKay after all. No matter how welcoming she's been. It's in their nature.

"You have to give me *something*," she practically whines.

I spin on my heel, stepping closer to her so quickly that she takes a step back to put distance between us. "I don't have to tell you *anything*," I practically growl. "This isn't a fun party trick, it's my *life*. Do you understand? Can you imagine what would happen to me if people knew? Can you imagine the consequences? Because I can. I've thought of nothing else for years. So no, I don't have to give anyone *anything*." I eye her shocked expression, and I don't know what possesses me to poke her further, but I feel a sudden anger that isn't even meant for her, I think, only her kin. "Least of all you," I grind out. "Least of all a *MacKay*."

I leave her there to stomp in the other direction, my temple throbbing and my chest hot with anger at the entire situation. I know that it's not really aimed at Keyanna—it's not *her* fault specifically, after all, but she's the only one here now. The only receptacle for my rage.

And yet she doesn't seem to be deterred in the slightest.

"But you work for my grandmother," she points out, jogging to catch up with me. "If you don't like my family, why are you living on her land?"

I purse my lips, cursing myself. I definitely set myself up for that question. I rattle off a distracted excuse. "Your line is as auld as mine. I'm just hoping there's something in your family records that might shed some light on my curse."

"Aha!" She stops walking, pointing a finger at me with a grin. "So it's a curse!"

"Fuck's sake," I mumble. "Can't you just let this go?"

She looks *excited*, damn her. Why does she look so bloody excited? Can't she be properly terrified of me? I'm a monster, for fuck's sake. Not a fucking puppy.

"But this is incredible," she exclaims. "My father was right! Was it you that he saw? I mean, you said you were only six when he left . . . How would that even be possible?"

"It wasn't me," I say. "It was . . ." I inhale deeply just to let it out. "It was someone else."

"Wow." She stares at her feet as we walk. "So all this time there have been *more* of you. That's wild. I mean, my dad was always so *convincing* when he told the story, but some part of me always wondered."

"Well," I sigh. "You got what you came for. You proved him right. Can you leave now?"

"What?" Her head snaps up, her eyes finding mine. "I can't leave now. I have so many questions!"

I stop walking again, my car close now, but my fear at what this slight woman could do to me is much closer. "And what will you do with this information?"

"What?" She looks confused now. "What do you mean?"

"Are you going to tell the world? Tell everyone what you saw?"

"I . . ." Her head cocks, her mouth opening and closing just to open again. "No? I'm sensing that would be . . . bad for you. Right?"

I narrow my eyes. "And why would you care about me?"

"I don't *care* about you," she splutters, averting her gaze. "But you did save my life. I owe you one . . . Right?"

I study her, trying to find traces of a lie but finding none in her guileless face. In fact, Keyanna seems to have the affliction of wearing every thought and emotion as a mask for people to read freely. She should work on that, I think.

"Aye," I agree cautiously. "I did. But how do I know I can trust you?"

"I guess you don't?" She reaches to rub at her neck, and a breeze passes between us, stirring her wild curls so that they whip around her face, framing her lovely features that I shouldn't even be noticing. "But I . . . Look. My grandmother hates me. She basically said so last night. I was actually planning on leaving after I . . . finished here."

"So? You still could."

"But . . ." She bites her lip. "You're *real*. Don't you get it? My dad told me stories about you—well, not *you*, obviously—but creatures like you, and I—" She heaves a sigh. "If this is really a curse, I think he would want me to help you."

I raise a brow, cocking my head. "You want to help me."

*Well, that is definitely not what I expected from her.*

"I . . ." Her mouth twists again in that sour-lemon motion, her nose wrinkling. It makes her freckles more prominent. "Yes. I think I do."

I don't know what to make of that. The thought of a MacKay

wanting to help me is laughable, given everything I know, but Key's expression is earnest. Her emerald eyes practically shine with excitement, and I can see it written all over her face, how desperate she is to know more.

*For the end only comes—*

I shake my head to clear the thought, but it's a good reminder that I can't trust her, and it would be stupid of me to even consider doing so.

I'm already turning away from her when I say, "I don't need your help."

"But it can't hurt!" she calls after me.

"Go home, Key," I toss over my shoulder, reaching my Rover and wrenching the door open. "Forget all of it and go home."

"Don't be stubborn, Lachlan," she shouts, still standing where I left her.

I give her one last long look while standing in the open door of my car, a strange, wriggling feeling in my gut as I regard the pure *want* in her eyes for me to give her something, *anything*.

But I just can't.

"Go home."

She does that thing that I'm starting to think she reserves just for me, stomping her foot in anger as she crosses her arms tightly over her chest.

"Pretty sure I saved *your* life too, you know!"

Her voice is muffled since I'm enclosed in the car, but still it makes me flinch.

She's right. I know that. She really did save me—but how, I can't quite figure out. I don't even think *she* knows. I hesitate with my fingers clutching the steering wheel, squeezing it tightly as my teeth grind together.

*Pretty sure I saved* your *life too, you know!*

I shake my head, cranking the ignition and throwing the car into reverse.

*Yeah*, I think. *But someone just like you ruined it once.*

And I can't let myself forget it.

## KEYANNA

I don't go back to my grandparents' house after the encounter with Lachlan. A part of me wanted to chase after him, but realistically, I can't even be sure that he went back himself. Not to mention the fact that I'm not quite ready to face Rhona again after hearing her blatantly say that she didn't want me there. Which leaves me sitting on one of the barstools at Blair and Rory's pub, sipping at a glass of water despite their assurances that eleven in the morning is a perfectly suitable time for a beer and waiting on food that Blair insisted on making for me.

"Here we go," Blair says as she sets a basket in front of me. "That's my grandpa's recipe there. Best fish and chips you'll have in all of Scotland."

"Or at least this side of Inverness," Rory adds.

Blair frowns at him, clucking her tongue. "Never mind him." She nods toward the basket. "Eat up, and tell us what's got you looking all peely-wally."

I glance down at my wrinkled clothes, which have gone stiff with the loch water, and I can't even imagine how bad my hair looks after sleeping on the shore all night. I don't know what *peely-wally* means, but if I had to guess, I'd imagine it's got to be pretty close to "like shit."

"It was . . ." I reach for a fry, nibbling on the end. "It was a rough night."

"Aye, if we weren't the only pub in town, I'd think you got good and steamin' last night," Rory notes.

I shove the rest of the fry—chip, whatever it's called—in my mouth. It really *is* good, or maybe I'm just starving. "Definitely not that," I tell them.

"Well, come on," Blair prods. "Tell us your woes. It's what a bartender is good for, yeah?"

I narrow my eyes. "The last time I opened up to a bartender, they sent me to a bogus kids' attraction."

"Och," Blair tuts. "That was just a bit of harmless fun. You learned something, didn't you?"

"I learned not to trust the bartenders," I grumble.

Rory shoves Blair's shoulder. "It was your idea."

"You went right along with it," Blair argues.

"It's because you're aulder," he says matter-of-factly. "Just respecting my elders."

"I'll show you 'elder,' you damned—"

"Stop fighting," I huff. "I'm not mad at you anymore."

"We're real sorry," they both say in unison, which is downright creepy, truth be told.

"Make it up to me by getting me that beer."

Rory's face lights up. "That's the spirit!"

"You *really* must have had quite the night," Blair says, leaning on her elbows over the top of the bar. "You've got a bit of . . ." She reaches to pluck something from my hair, pulling away what looks to be dried bits of some leafy vine that I'm sure made a home there while

I was swimming for my life last night. "Is this crowfoot?" She cocks her head at me. "Did you go swimming in the loch last night?"

I feel my cheeks heat, turning my face down to my basket of food as I stab a plastic fork into my fish. I try to shrug one shoulder in what I hope is a casual gesture, but I can feel Blair's eyes on me.

"Who went swimming?" Rory sidles up with my tankard, sliding it across the bar toward me. "You didn't go back to the cove, did you?"

"It really isn't safe," Blair grouses, twirling the weed between her fingers. "Especially at night."

Without thinking, I mutter, "You can say that again." I pause with a fry halfway to my mouth, my eyes widening a bit as I try to backpedal. "I mean—I just meant—"

"She knows," Rory says, looking at me as if seeing me properly for the first time. "Do you know?"

I try to keep my tone casual. "Do I know . . . what?"

"Rory," Blair says evenly. "Shut your hole, would you?"

The three of us stare at one another for a long moment, one where the only sound that can be heard is the occasional scraping of Fergus's chair at what seems to be his staple booth behind us. Blair glances at the plant—she called it crowfoot—in her hands, then back to my rumpled outfit and even up to my disheveled hair.

"*Did* you go swimming last night, Key?"

My brow wrinkles, and it occurs to me that I might not be the only one who knows that there is some truth to the legend of Loch Ness. Lachlan said he'd been friends with the twins since childhood, didn't he?

"I . . . might have," I try cautiously. "Why?"

Rory's eyes go wide, his hands slapping to the counter as he practically leans all the way over it. "Did you see anything?"

"What exactly would there be to see?"

I'm trying to be stoic, trying not to show all my cards in case I might be somehow betraying Lachlan, which is a strange thought, given that I still sort of hate him. But I meant it when I said my dad would have wanted me to help him, and if for no other reason than that, I won't hand out his secrets so quickly.

"Skallangal Cove," Blair says pointedly, "is *not* safe. You ought not be going there. Not again. Especially not alone."

I keep my expression as flat as I can manage, deciding to test the waters. "I wasn't alone," I answer. "Lachlan was there."

Now it's Blair who looks rattled, her eyes rounding slightly as her lips part in surprise. Her gaze moves over my face for a second or two, then a wave of understanding seems to pass over her expression.

"You do know. Don't you."

"I can neither confirm nor deny," I tell her.

She nods slowly. "That's a good answer. There are . . . things about that cove we have to protect, see?"

"I would never hurt anyone intentionally," I promise without explaining myself. I have a feeling we're on the same page here. "But something *did* try to hurt me."

Rory sucks in a breath. "You saw him? Not Lachlan, but—"

"Rory," Blair warns, still eyeing me. "S'not your place." She assesses me for another moment, and then, "Lachlan is a good man, Key. I know he might seem like an arsehole upon first meeting, but he's seen a lot in his life. Too much for someone as young as he is. He doesn't deserve the lot he's been cast, and it's made him harder than he should be. Harder than he wants to be, I imagine. Do you understand?"

"Not really," I answer honestly. "He wouldn't exactly talk to me . . . after."

I'm staring at my hands as the memory of last night resurfaces—the details a little hazy but prominent nonetheless. I remember the desperation I felt when I saw that the creature—*Lachlan*—was bleeding, how hopeless I'd felt wanting to save him somehow. In the fog of my memory, I can almost recall a warm glow, a heat in my palms; I'd been so focused on staunching the blood flow, on slowing the bleeding, but have I actually stopped to ponder what happened? Everything went so dark, and his wound had been mostly healed the next morning . . . Was it *he* who made that happen? What could possibly be the alternative? Surely there's no way that I could have—

"Aye, I reckon he wouldn't," Blair sighs, jolting me out of my memories. "He's not an easy man to know. He thinks he has to carry everything on those stupidly big shoulders alone."

That makes my mouth twitch in a smile. "Now, I can totally believe *that* about him."

"Just . . . give him the benefit of the doubt, aye? He has his reasons to be so skittish. Especially with you."

"What does that mean?"

She shakes her head. "That's not my story to tell. You'd have to ask him yourself."

"How can I do that?" I snort. "The stubborn ass won't even—"

"Keyanna!"

I turn on my stool, taking sight of my grandpa standing in the open door of the bar, his chest heaving as if he ran here. His eyes are watery with old or maybe even fresh tears, and his thin frame seems to shake as he crosses the space toward me.

"There you are," he cries. "I thought you'd up and left! When you weren't there this morning, I . . ."

He trails off, looking so forlorn it forces me off my stool, and the minute my feet touch the floor, he's rushing to embrace me. I can rest my temple on top of his thinning hair at my height, inhaling the scent of tobacco and peppermint, which is strangely comforting.

"I'm sorry," I murmur. "I didn't mean to worry you, but I . . ."

"I know you heard what your granny said," he sniffles. "She didn't mean it, hen."

"I kind of think she did," I counter.

My grandpa pulls back, frowning up at me. "I know what my Rhonnie said was hurtful, and I know it doesn't make it right, but she's hurting too. She has been since our Duncan left, but Rhonnie . . ." He shakes his head. "She's stubborn. Thinks she has to bear everyone's problems, but not let anyone bear hers. Seeing you . . . I imagine it is terribly hard, knowing that it was *her* fight with our boy that drove him away."

"It was?"

"Aye. It was a terrible fight. One I think she regrets now, but it's too late, isn't it? But you're here, and you look so much like our boy . . . Aye. I imagine seeing you makes my Rhonnie feel all that pain and regret all over again."

I consider that, trying to see it from her point of view. Something that proves to be difficult, given that I don't know a damned thing about what my dad and my grandmother fought over that was so terrible it had him leaving his country behind.

"I don't understand," I say honestly. "My dad never talked about it. He never told me why he left, so I don't . . . I don't know how to help."

"Just come home with me," he urges. "Talk to your granny. She'll never admit it, but she regrets what you heard. I know she does."

"I don't know, Finlay—"

"Grandpa," he corrects, standing straighter to his full height. He clasps me by the shoulders. "No matter what, I am your *grandpa*, understand?"

Fucking hell. Now *my* eyes feel watery. I nod thickly, trying not to break down as the gravity of last night's events—my grandmother, the cove, the fucking Loch Ness Monster—comes crashing down on me. I take a deep breath just to expel it shakily, nodding again, but surer this time.

"All right," I tell my grandpa. "I'll come back. If you're sure."

"Never been more sure," he says with a blinding smile. It reminds me of Dad's smile at that moment, which makes my chest constrict. "You hop in your car, and we'll sort all of this out back on the farm, aye?"

"Okay." I glance back at the twins, who have been watching this exchange, both of them looking curious but solemn. "I just need to pay for my—"

Blair waves me off. "We're square. I reckon I owe you for Loch Land."

"Deal," I chuckle.

Finlay says something about warming up the truck, and I notice Rory looks sheepish as I gather my stiff jacket from the stool, rolling it up tight to hide the dark blood staining it. "You do forgive us, right?"

"Yeah. I do."

He blows out a breath. "And about . . . the other thing."

I hover for a moment with my jacket in hand, looking between the twins and taking in their serious and slightly worried expressions.

"I don't know what you're talking about," I answer with a shrug. "I didn't see a thing."

They smile in unison, twin versions of the same grin, and I have to suppress a shudder.

That really is so creepy.

⌒

I'm admittedly grateful not to need to share a ride back to the farm with my grandpa; not that he isn't wonderful—because I'm beginning to realize that he is—but I need the time to sort my head out. With everything that happened at the cove last night, I almost forgot the reasons that had driven me there in the first place. At least until Finlay came bursting into the pub.

Now my grandmother's words play on a loop in my head with stunning clarity, and despite agreeing to come back, I don't share my grandpa's confidence that Rhona regrets any of it. Not when I saw her expression as she said it. Like my very presence in her home was an offense.

When I see the sprawling farmhouse come into view, there's a wriggling sensation of nerves in my belly that is quickly followed by that same clenching sensation in my chest. I stall in my car for a few extra seconds while Finlay teeters out of his beat-up old truck, watching as he gives me an encouraging wave from the front of it while waiting for me to join him. I blow out a steadying breath to calm my nerves, telling myself that it will be fine. That no matter what, at least I will get closure.

"You all right?" Finlay asks when I join him.

I nod. "I'm fine." I nibble at the corner of my lip as I glance at the front door. "Are you sure she wants to talk to me?"

"Aye, I'm sure," he urges. "You go on in. I'm going to go help Lachlan with the cows. Give you two some privacy."

I have to shove the reminder of last night down at the mention of Lachlan's name, having—oddly enough—bigger problems at the moment than the existence of a shape-changing water dragon. Hell, Rhona is a dragon all on her own.

*Fuck, don't leave me alone with her*, I want to say, but I can sense that my grandpa is a lot more optimistic about this than I am, and I can't find it in me to squash his optimism. So I just nod again when he says he'll see me at dinner, entirely unsure if that's true. For all I know, I'll be looking for a new place to stay by then.

*Because apparently, even if your family doesn't want you, you're still set on sticking around.*

I mentally scoff at the chiding tone of my own brain. As if someone *wouldn't* stick around if they found the *actual* Loch Ness Monster.

But that's a problem for future me.

I don't knock when I enter the front door, figuring that it would be even more awkward for the pair of us to dance around each other in the entryway. Instead, I quietly shut the door behind me as I step inside, lingering on the mat as I listen for signs of my grandmother. I can hear a clinking coming from the kitchen, the telltale sound of her spoon scraping against her teacup, which I've learned is a bit of a ritual for her. Rhona loves her afternoon tea.

"You might as well come in," she calls, her voice sounding weary. "Stop lurking out there."

I frown as I trudge forward, entering the kitchen and finding Rhona sitting at the head of the table, blowing gently on her steaming cup of tea. She doesn't look at me when I enter the room, doesn't even glance my way as I slowly walk around the table and take a seat near her. She just takes a slow sip, exhaling noisily through her nostrils after she swallows.

"This was Finlay's great-great-granny's china," she tells me absently, her finger tracing the delicate pink filigree painted on the side. "Been in the family for over a century."

"It's pretty," I comment.

She still doesn't look at me. "It's been passed down to the women in this family with every generation. It's a tradition of sorts. Every MacKay matriarch passes along the set when they reach a certain age."

"I . . . see."

"I thought I would have to leave it to your cousin if he ever wrassled up a woman to wed him," she mutters. She eyes me from the side, her expression cautious. "But I suppose I won't now, will I."

Anger and hurt bubble up inside me. "According to you," I remind her, "I'm not really a MacKay. So I don't see why the plan would change now."

"Aye," she answers quietly after a beat, her shoulders slumping and her eyes taking on a haggard look, one that almost seems like regret, but I might be imagining it. "I did say that."

She stares into her cup for several long moments, the silence stretching between us as I wait for her to say more. I'm not going to spoon-feed her an apology, and I'm not going to sit here where I'm not wanted. So she's on her own as far as I'm concerned.

"You have to understand. Dunc—" She swallows thickly. "Your father was my world. My pride and joy, you see? He was . . . He was so smart. Such a kind, sweet boy. From the day he was born, he brought me . . . such joy."

She doesn't seem to be looking for any sort of input from me, so I say nothing, just leaning a little closer to the table as she continues.

"Your mother was here on holiday when they first met," Rhona tells me. "From the first time he brought her around, I was scared. Scared that she would take him away from me. I could see in his eyes that he was over the moon for her, and I knew she had the power to whisk him away, to take him from my life and leave me with nothing but the odd holiday. I couldn't bear the thought of it."

It feels . . . strange. Hearing her talk about my mother this way.

The stories my dad told me painted my mother as a kind, thoughtful woman who loved everyone she met—so I can't reconcile the woman Rhona speaks of with the mother I was told about.

"I don't think she would—"

"Aye, aye," Rhona sighs. "It was the error of an auld fool. I made a right arse of myself when the inevitable happened. When he told me he was marrying her . . . I said many things I wish I could take back."

"And that's why you had a falling-out?"

She shakes her head slowly, the action filled with sorrow. "No. Things were strained between us, but we still spoke. We wrote letters, talked on the phone . . . They even came to visit when they could. It wasn't until he told me they were going to have *you* that I went and ruined it all."

"I—" I rear back, confused. "Me?"

"Aye. Did you know the MacKay clan haven't had a girl born in this family in centuries? You're the very first."

"I didn't know that," I answer, not sure what to do with that information.

"I thought maybe you might bring us back together. I thought that your birth would mean our family would find a reason to reconcile. That maybe, just maybe, we could finally make things right."

My fingers grip the edge of the table, my knuckles turning white with the force of it as answers I've been denied for *years* finally seem within reach. "What happened?"

"It was the last time he ever visited," Rhona says slowly, like each word is difficult. "He called me down to this very table. He seemed . . . frantic, somehow. Not quite himself. He told me that your mother was pregnant, and that they had found out it was to be a little girl. I remember how shocked I was to hear the news, but Duncan . . . Duncan almost seemed upset by it."

This throws me for a loop. My dad *never* gave me any indication that he was unhappy with me. Not once. "Why would he be upset?"

"I don't know. I never got the chance to find out. He started rambling about taking your mother back to America. About raising you there. He started talking about never bringing you back here. He said—" Rhona looks to the ceiling, and I notice her eyes are shining. "He said that he knew I had never approved of his marriage, and he didn't want his bairns growing up around that kind of animosity. I . . . didn't take it well." She flashes me a thin, watery smile. "You might have noticed I have a bit of a temper."

At any other time, I might laugh at that, but even though I've only known Rhona for a short while, seeing her look so fragile is . . . jarring. She's been nothing but the picture of strength since the first day she opened her door to me.

"What happened?"

"I said things . . . He said things . . ." She shakes her head. "I can hardly remember exactly what now. Not but a bunch of bitter, angry words that I suspect neither of us really meant. But that doesn't matter, does it? Once the words are out there . . . the damage is done. Your father packed up his things and your mother, and I—I told him—" Her lip quivers, her wrinkled hands trembling against her cup. "I told him if he walked out that door, he wouldn't be welcome back."

Her eyes close, and I have the strangest urge to reach out and grab her hand. I don't know if she would welcome it, though, so I resist the urge.

"And you just . . . never spoke to each other again?"

She nods, her eyes still closed. "He wrote letters. For a short while. I was not smart enough to swallow my pride and answer them. For your entire life, I clung to that pride. A useless, ugly thing. I lost my boy, the light of my life, and I never told him ever again how much I loved him. I didn't even know he was sick. He didn't tell us. Why would he? It wasn't until he passed that we—"

Her voice cracks, and one solitary tear leaks from the corner of her eye.

"I didn't know," I offer. "I didn't know that he didn't tell you."

"S'not your fault." She chuckles under her breath, a bitter sound. "S'not your fault I've been so cold to you either, I reckon." Her eyes are glassy and wet when she opens them to look at me, a bright, vivid green as she studies my face. "Seeing you . . . it was such a shock. You look so much like your father. When I saw you on that doorstep, looking almost like you'd brought a piece of my boy back with you, I felt . . . angry. So bloody angry."

"I know that I should have—"

"I wasn't angry at you, lass," she cuts in, shaking her head. "Not really. I know that's what I've made you believe, but it's not true." She takes a deep breath, blowing it out through her nostrils. "I was angry at *myself*. Still am, truth be told. I saw you, and it was suddenly so clear how much time I'd wasted, the life that I'd thrown away, the *family* I'd cut from my life because of my stubborn pride. And for what? Absolutely nothing." Her brow furrows, and her eyes gain a faraway look. "That's what I feel every time I look at you, Keyanna, and I don't yet know how not to feel it."

Her confession leaves me stunned. This entire week I have wondered how I might bridge the gap between my grandmother and myself. I've wondered what might have come between her and my father to tear them apart. Finding out that in a roundabout way it was *me* was not on my bingo card.

"I don't know what to say," I tell her honestly. "I'm sorry."

She waves me off. "You've naught to be sorry for. Truly. I just needed you to know what I'm dealing with, and I wanted you to know that I'm going to try harder to do just that. I . . ." She swallows, her eyes flicking to my hand, which rests on the table, as her fingers inch toward it tentatively. She gives me a quick glance as if seeking approval, and with my barely there nod, she brushes her fingers over mine. "I *do* want to know you, Keyanna. I do. Trust me when I say that. If you can forgive your stubborn arse of a grandmother, I'd like a second chance to prove it to you."

I watch as her eyes, so like mine, begin to swim with emotion, feeling almost like a weight has been lifted from my shoulders. Sure, I've still got the whole "there's an actual monster living on the property" thing going on, but to know that my presence might not be actively hated by the last remnants of my family definitely makes it a little easier to breathe.

"I can," I say, offering her a small smile. "I can forgive you."

She nods, on a deep inhale, reaching to wipe her eye with her free hand. "Probably more than I deserve, but that can be said about most things in my life." She pats my hand as she returns my smile, the first one she's sent in my direction since I arrived, and with it, I feel something like hope pouring into my chest. "Now, how's about a cup of tea?"

I can't help the bubble of laughter that spills out of me; the last twenty-four hours might have been the longest of my life, and I have a feeling this is only the beginning.

"Got anything stronger?"

Rhona's eyes crinkle at the corners, and she gives me a wink. "Aye, hen. That I do."

## LACHLAN

I never thought that at thirty-four I would find myself actively avoiding a person as if caught up in some schoolyard drama—and yet for the last week, I've been doing exactly that. It's become all too obvious that Keyanna MacKay is not someone easily ignored, however. She's a constant thorn in my side, hounding me around the farm and trying to corner me at every turn, no doubt doing her best to catch me alone and grill me about what she knows. Because of course she couldn't just make things easy and cart herself back to America. No, now she's dug her heels in as if she's got all the more reason to stick around.

Not that I have the slightest clue as to why.

There's no good reason for her to want to *help* me as she continues to claim. In fact, if my family has learned anything from history, it's that the MacKays are the *last* people to expect help from. Rhona and Finlay might be the right sort, as far as I can tell, but they're surely a fluke in an otherwise ghastly line of folk that I've been taught to avoid since before I knew how to walk. And given what I know about *daughters of MacKay*—I have all the more reason to keep slipping away whenever I find myself in a nearby radius of the determined redhead.

Last night was a doozy, another disappointing venture of trying to make contact and ending up retreating to a secluded bay licking my literal and metaphorical wounds. I don't know why I'm still subjecting myself to this, since I know nothing good can come of it, but I can't seem to make myself give up completely. As long as he's out there, it seems that some part of me will always hold on to the foolish hope that I can get him back.

The sun is high when my eyes open, and I can tell from the way it streams through the curtains that I've already got a late start to the day. I stretch my arms above my head as my jaw cracks with a loud yawn, scratching my stomach as my lashes flutter closed in a last-ditch effort to grab a few more minutes of rest.

I've just started to drift when a loud banging sets off at my front door.

"Lachlan! I know you're in there."

I groan. It's the third time this week she's come pounding on my door. I grab the pillow from under my head and bring it to my face, trying to drown out her voice.

"I'm not leaving," she calls through the wood. "I'll wait out here all day if I have to."

*That's what you said on Tuesday*, I think with a mental smirk.

"I mean it this time! My ass is not leaving this stoop until you talk to me."

I can hear the determination in her voice, and I sigh into the pillow, fearing this might be the end of my streak of luck. It seems that no matter how much I might like this problem to go away, she's stubbornly decided to insert herself into the situation.

*Maybe I really should have just let her be eaten*, I think wistfully.

I chide myself for even thinking it; I definitely wouldn't have let that happen, but I can't help fantasizing about the quiet it would have given me. I swing my legs over the side of the small bed, glaring at the door across the room, where the squalling sounds of The Proclaimers start drifting through the wood, horribly off-key.

"—well I know I'm gonna be, I'm gonna be the man who wakes up next to you!"

*Would have been nothing*, I mentally grumble, shoving off the bed. *Could have just looked the other way.*

I stomp across the short distance.

"And I would walk five hundred miles, and I would walk five hundred more, just to be the man who walks a thousand miles to fall down at your—"

I wrench the door open. "Will you knock it off?"

She's sitting with her back to the door, and she tilts her head back to peer up at me, a triumphant grin spreading across her mouth as her long red curls spill toward her waist. Her green eyes almost glimmer in the midmorning sun, and the light touching her lashes makes them seem to burn a golden red.

I hate how fucking lovely she looks when she's being a pain in my arse.

"You don't like The Proclaimers?"

"Be honest," I huff. "That's the one Scottish song you know, isn't it."

"I plead the fifth," she answers with a shrug. She pushes herself upright, dusting off her jeans and turning to flash that same smug grin my way. "You ready to talk to me like a big boy, Nessie?"

"Keep your damned voice down," I hiss, glancing around as if Rhona's house isn't more than a mile from the guest cottage. "And that is *not* going to be a thing."

"Sure," she says sweetly. "Whatever you say . . . Nessie."

I narrow my eyes. "I really wish you would just let this go, *princess*."

She doesn't reward me with her usual irritation, just clucks her tongue, shrugging one shoulder.

"Yeah, not gonna happen. So can I come in? Or would you like to talk in the doorway?"

I silently fume for a moment, fantasizing about throwing her into the bloody loch myself, finally moving to the side so she can push past me while I mutter under my breath.

"Pain in my arse," I grumble.

She ignores me. "Oh, wow, this is so tiny! Do you even fit on the bed?"

"Ten seconds, and you're already thinking about my bed?"

This does earn me a withering look, and now it's my turn to grin in triumph.

"Cute," she says flatly, just before plopping herself down into one of my kitchen chairs. She gestures to the one across from her like she owns it, cocking an eyebrow expectedly. "Well?"

I release a sigh that I feel down in my bones, closing the door and shuffling after her to drop myself into the empty chair across the table from her. I scrub a hand down my face, letting it hover over my mouth as my eyes drift closed wearily.

"Ask your bloody questions."

"I have so many!" Her voice is bright and animated, full of genuine wonder. "How long has this been going on? How did it happen? Who was that other monster? Can you breathe underwater all the time or just when you change? Do you do any magic?"

I crack open one eye, frowning as I let my hand drop to the table. "That's . . . a lot of questions."

"*Excuse* me," she scoffs. "*You* meet a magical cryptid and see if you don't have a million questions. If Bigfoot walked into your kitchen right now, pretty sure you'd have questions."

"Bigfoot isn't real," I mutter.

Her jaw drops. "Are you kidding? You're out here practically fueling podcasts worldwide and covering tabloid pages, and you're telling me you don't believe that Bigfoot might be real?"

"Is this what you'd like to discuss?"

"No." She scowls. "Answer my questions."

"I still don't see why I should."

"Because I can't help you if I don't know the facts!"

"And what makes you so sure you could help me?"

"I . . ." She looks thrown by the question, pausing with her lips parted as if she'd just been about to speak. She closes them, presses them together, an act that makes them look even fuller, and my eyes dart unwillingly to the soft pink of her mouth briefly before I drag them back to her eyes. "I guess I don't know for sure," she admits. "But I want to at least try. You said it was a curse, right? That doesn't exactly sound like a fun time. That's what you're doing here, isn't it? You said you were looking for answers. Let me help you."

I narrow my eyes, studying her. She looks so . . . earnest. Guileless, even. It's true that she wears every thought in her expression for the world to see, which means that it's painfully obvious that Key truly wants to help me, that she thinks—or maybe just hopes—that she might be able to. I can't make heads or tails of it. It goes against everything I know.

"I don't understand *why* you would want to help me," I tell her honestly. "We're not exactly friends. We don't even like each other."

*Which I don't*, I confirm in my head. *I don't like her. I don't care how bonnie she is.*

"I'll admit we've had . . . a rough start," she ventures, reaching to rub her hand at her nape in a seemingly nervous gesture. "But I just feel like . . ." She huffs out a breath. "I *know* that I'm supposed to help you. It's what my dad would have wanted."

I frown. "You said that before, but it doesn't make sense. Why on earth would Duncan want you to help me with this?"

"Because you saved him!"

I cock my head. "I . . . what?"

"I mean . . . Well. Now that I think about it, it couldn't have been *you*—but someone like you." She rubs her temples. "He told me this story so much growing up that I know it by heart. He was at the cove, and he fell, and he thought it was all over, but then—" Her eyes round as she looks at me earnestly. "*Something* saved him. Something like you. I always wondered . . ." She bites her lip. "When I was a kid, I believed every single word. All of it. As I got older . . . part of me thought that it was just my dad's way of bringing some kind of magic in my life, but . . . near the end . . ." Her hands clasp on the table in front of her, her fingers twisting as her brow furrows. "He was so adamant. So insistent that it was all real. In the end . . . it was the *only* thing he could remember."

"Finlay told me," I murmur, a bubble of discontent in my chest from seeing her so distraught. I reach to rub the spot. "He told me about your da and his illness."

She nods solemnly. "It was just me and him in the end. I took a leave of absence from my job to care for him; I used to work for this small accounting firm back in New York. My boss was old friends with my dad, so he was very good to me as far as assuring me that my job would still be there. I didn't know how much time he'd have before he—" She sucks in a shaky breath, her throat bobbing with a swallow. "After the pneumonia, he just . . . It's like his body couldn't do it anymore. Like he was just tired. He still hung on for four months after he got out of the hospital, though. His memories were a jumbled mess by then; hell, he barely knew who I was most days, always called me by my mom's name."

"I'm sorry," I manage, not sure what else to say. It feels odd, sitting here and commiserating with her this way when I've known nothing but barbs and glares since the moment I met her. "That must have been terrible."

She nods heavily. "It was."

"But you don't think you've already done enough?" I wonder. "Like you said, you already saved me." I frown at my own words. "Do you even know how you did that?"

"I . . ." She bites her lip, and I can't help but be drawn to the sight of her teeth worrying at the soft flesh. "I have no idea. That night is kind of hazy." Her brows raise. "Do you have any idea?"

I do, actually, now that I've had time to think about it, but I'm not sure if she's ready to hear it; if it weren't for my own cursed predicament, I would say that it's too fantastical to even consider.

"Does it matter?" I counter, ignoring the question for now. "My point is, you could argue that you've already paid this debt you've built up in your head. You don't owe me anything."

"You don't understand." Her eyes flash to mine with a determined glint. "My dad forgot almost everything about his life at the end, but he *never* forgot that story. It was all he took with him."

"But I don't see why that would make you want to—"

"You saved him," she says firmly. "Or, well, someone like you did. If you hadn't . . . I never would have known him. I wouldn't even *be* here." She nods again, the motion resolute. "So if I can help you, then I owe it to whoever it was like you that pulled him out of the water that day to try."

I sit across from her in stunned silence for several moments, and for every second that passes, her gaze never leaves mine. Her eyes seem so bright they almost burn, a fire in them that almost rivals the blazing curls framing her face. I realize she means every word of it. That in her mind, helping me is some final homage to the father she lost. Like saving me will somehow ease the pain of it. That it will somehow make it all not have been for nothing.

And knowing that . . . it hits far too close to home.

I don't say anything as I push away from the table, rising from the chair and turning to the kitchenette behind me as I start up the coffeepot. I stare at it for a few more seconds until it starts to sputter with steaming liquid, finally turning my face to cast her a long look.

"How do you take your coffee?"

My banal question has an immediate effect, her pink lips forming an indignant pout and her copper brows pulling together. "That's it? That's all you have to say? How do I take my coffee?"

"Aye," I answer, crossing my arms over my chest and leaning back against the counter. "For the moment."

"Are you purposely trying to infuriate me?"

I shake my head. "No, I'm trying to caffeinate you. You'll need it."

"I'll need it," she echoes, her eyes turning a wee bit suspicious. "And why is that?"

I turn to reach for two mugs from the cabinet, giving her my back as I let out another weary sigh, coming to terms with the fact that, for better or worse, it seems I now have a tentative ally. The last one I ever expected.

"Because I have something to show you."

## KEYANNA

Can you just tell me where we're going?"

"It's not much further," Lachlan tosses over his shoulder.

I push another branch out of the way, trying to follow Lachlan's broad back. His red flannel is a beacon in the sea of green branches we've been maneuvering through for the last half hour, and at this rate, I'm starting to wonder if this is another Loch Land situation. Or maybe something even more nefarious.

"You're not leading me into the woods to kill me, are you?"

I don't see him roll his eyes, but I can feel it. "Lot cleaner ways to get you out of the picture if I wanted to, lass."

"Well, *that's* comforting."

"I have a feeling you'd be just annoying enough to haunt me anyway," he answers with a chuffed laugh.

"Absolutely I would," I assure him. "I'd be singing at you every night while you tried to sleep."

"Aye, that would definitely be terrifying."

I scoff. "It's not *that* bad."

"About as lovely sounding as Bethie was when she had her last calf," he chuckles.

Now I roll *my* eyes. "Seriously, will you just tell me where we're—*oof.*"

I come to halt as I collide with his wide frame, my hands slamming into his back and my cheek squishing between his shoulder blades. I shove myself away as I start sputtering, but then I notice where we are. The ground is covered with dried leaves, the entire area shaded beneath the canopy of trees as filtered light streams down through the foliage. The rows of granite and stone are weathered with age, and I step around Lachlan, cocking a brow up at him as I cross my arms over my chest.

"Well, this is . . . ominous."

He's brought me to what looks to be a massive graveyard, and I frown at the worn headstones that span as far back into the trees as my eyes can see. I've never liked cemeteries, not that I imagine anyone just *loves* them—but something about the idea of bones beneath my feet leaves me unsettled. It makes me grateful that my dad wanted to be cremated. I could never quite come to terms with the idea of burying him in the dirt.

"Our family is buried here," Lachlan tells me.

"*Our* family?"

"Aye, yours and mine." He points to the rows that creep to the east. "See that fence there? The one going right through the rows of graves?"

"Yes."

"That's the property line between your family's land and the Greer land. It goes on for miles, dividing it right down the middle. My family owned *all* of Greerloch once upon a time, but over the last few centuries, it's been broken up into smaller parcels. This spot here, though . . . this is where everything began."

"In a graveyard," I clarify.

"In a manner of speaking," he answers thoughtfully. "It's the first parcel your family bought after mine was cursed."

I turn my head toward the opposite way, hearing Lachlan moving behind me as I close the short distance between myself and a cluster of graves. The tombstones vary between small, stumpy little curves that barely rise from the grass all the way to towering monuments that are as tall as I am—and sure enough, upon closer inspection, I notice the name *MacKay* etched into the whole lot of them.

My eyes come to rest before one in particular that is just a few inches taller than me, drawn by the realistic carving that feels almost *too* real, given that the stone is weather-beaten and decorated with moss. A wide, rectangular base comes all the way to my chest before sprouting into the thick neck of a horse. There's an old, brittle leather strap around the horse's neck, curling around and up to its face as if you could actually grab it and urge the horse to move. A quick glance at the front reveals faded marks in the stone, the name so old you can barely make it out. If I didn't *know* these were MacKay graves, I wouldn't even know the last name, but the first name is illegible. Thomas? Travis? Something with a T. Maybe—

"This way," Lachlan calls, interrupting me from my side quest.

He walks away from me toward the fence line, pressing his foot down on the barbed wire and holding another piece up so I can squeeze between them. He follows me through it, moving past me for a few more yards before coming to a stop in front of a massive grave adorned with a statue of a Celtic cross. His last name is etched into the stone, and I watch as he kneels in front of it, brushing away a pile of leaves.

"This was my ancestor," he tells me. "Some great-grandfather to the umpteenth degree back at the end of the thirteenth century."

"Was he . . . ?"

"Like me? Aye. The first."

Lachlan's elbows rest on his knees as he remains crouched, and I sneak a peek at the furrow in his brow, watching the light breeze blow his dark honey locks around his temples. His plush mouth is pressed together in thought, and I have to tear my eyes away from the picture he paints—brooding Scotsman is not what I'm here for today.

"I come here a lot to think," he admits.

I make a face. "That's kind of creepy."

He doesn't answer, still staring at the ruined tombstone. He opens his mouth to speak again, and his voice comes out in a low whisper when he says:

> *"O Thou, of face so fair an' name so high,*
> *With heart as black as the darkest sky*
> *Thy cursed deeds yield cursed prize*
> *An' prayers nor pleas will spare thy fate*
> *In moonlight change till the sun doth rise*
> *Yer flesh shall bear yer soul's foul weight."*

He lets the words marinate in the air for a moment, and I sense there's something important about them, but I don't really know what. I've never been one for poetry.

"That's . . . pretty?"

He shakes his head, scowling up at me. "It's a curse. It's *the* curse. The one placed on my ancestor almost eight hundred years ago. And *every* son born into my family is cursed to become a monster from sundown to sunrise. *Every* single one."

"But . . ." My mouth opens and closes as my mind reels, trying to make sense of what he's saying. "For eight hundred years? Really?

What in the hell did your ancestor *do?* I mean, to be cursed, you usually have to do something bad, right?"

Lachlan's jaw tics, his eyes narrowing. "He didn't do anything besides put his faith in the wrong person."

"Really?" My nose wrinkles. "But the poem said, 'Thy cursed deeds yield cursed prize,'" I point out. "Doesn't that mean he did something?"

"I can't make sense of the words of a witch," he scoffs, rising to his full height. "My ancestor gave refuge to a kelpie, and in the end, this is what it got him."

"A kelpie?"

"Aye. Fae creatures from the auld ages. They were said to appear as beautiful maidens when they weren't in their horse forms."

"*Horse* forms?"

"Och, because I suppose your American nine-foot-tall ape man is so much more believable?"

"I'm not trying to argue which cryptid is more believable," I say. "I mean, I saw the Loch Ness Monster last week. So . . ."

"*Kelpies*"—he stresses the word, daring me with his eyes to question him—"are known to be tricksters with great magic. Their power lies in their bridles, and it's said that if you can take control of a kelpie's bridle, you can control their magic as well."

"Okay, that's interesting, but what does it have to do with your ancestor?"

"My ancestor struck a deal with a kelpie witch. He promised her safe haven for her and all her kin if she would lend him the power to defeat the clans who sought to claim his land."

"And did she?"

"Aye, she did," he tells me. "But when it was through, she cursed him anyway."

I frown. "But why?"

"And how am I to know?" He throws up his hands in frustration. "It's not as if there's some history book I can leaf through. Everything I know has been passed down in stories from one Greer to the next. It's said they're wicked, selfish creatures. Maybe he was punished for daring to think he could wield her magic in the first place. All I know is that, because of her, every son in my family turns into a beast at night."

I look down at my shoes, considering. It seems too fantastical, everything he's telling me, but then again, I *literally* just found out last week that the Loch Ness Monster was a hot, asshole-ish farmhand during the day, so I know I need to keep an open mind. Besides, magic horse witches seem as good a reason as any for Lachlan to turn into a dinosaur-looking creature every night.

"And that's all the curse said? Was there any more?"

His lips part, and for the briefest moment there is a slight widening of his eyes, but then his mouth drifts closed, and he clears his throat. "Aye, that's all there was. All I have to go on. It's not been much help, I can tell you that."

"So what happened to the rest of your family? Are they . . . are they in the loch too?"

He shakes his head. "We don't live longer than any other human. We don't have any special sort of powers. My grandpa passed away when I was a boy. My mother left when—" His jaw clenches as he goes quiet, and I notice the way his fists tighten at his sides. "My mother left when my da disappeared."

"He disappeared? When?"

"When I was still a boy. Eight or so. My mum couldn't handle it. I lived with my granny after that until she passed."

"I'm sorry," I tell him, meaning it. "Was it—was it something to do with your curse?"

He meets my gaze, his eyes hard and so angry-looking. "Aye, it was."

"He didn't— I mean, that is, is he still . . . ?"

"He's alive."

"How do you know?"

"Well," Lachlan says carefully, his eyes still locked with mine. "For starters, he tried to eat you the other night."

My mouth gapes with the implication. "You mean—you mean he's—"

"Aye." Lachlan nods solemnly. "One night, my da changed into a monster." His brow knits, a glint of sadness in his eyes. "And then he never changed back."

"I . . . Wow."

"He's no more than a beast now," Lachlan says quietly. "He doesn't know me. Not anymore."

His words send a sharp stab of pain through me, and I have the strangest urge to reach out and hug him, but I hold myself back. I have a feeling he wouldn't be very welcoming of the gesture.

"I'm sorry," I say again. "I know how hard that is. Trust me."

"I reckon you do," Lachlan answers just as softly. "Maybe that's why I'm telling you."

"So your dad . . ." My head swims as pieces fall together, the enormity of everything he's saying crashing down on me and making it a little hard to breathe. "Your dad saved my dad."

"He did."

"Did you know?"

"Aye, I did."

His omission sparks a flicker of anger inside me, and I take a step to crowd his space without even realizing I've done it. "Why didn't you tell me?"

"Why should I have? I didn't even know you."

"But you did *after.* You knew after you saved me in the loch—you *knew* about my dad! How could you not say anything?"

"I think a better question would be why didn't your *da* tell you any of this?"

That gives me pause. "What?"

"You really think Duncan didn't know any of this?"

"I don't—what do you mean?"

"Your da knew *exactly* who the monster who saved him was. They were *friends* for a time."

"No," I say immediately. "No. He would have told me if he knew."

"Maybe he didn't want to have to tell you the truth of the matter," Lachlan says with an accusing tone. "Maybe he didn't want to tell you how he *swore* to help my father, just like you are swearing to me now, only to run off to America with the first bonnie lass he laid eyes on!"

"That's not true," I argue. "No. He wouldn't do that."

"Aye, but he did. My father was a fool to believe him in the first place."

"Don't," I warn.

Lachlan's lip curls. "My da should have known better than to trust a MacKay. It's the only thing we've ever been sure of. You can *never* trust a MacKay."

"You keep saying that!" I yell, throwing up my arms. "Ever since I first met you, you've been grumbling about how *awful* my family is, and yet you're living on their land! I don't get it, Lachlan. My dad was a good man. He would never just *abandon* someone if he promised to help them. Why do you keep insisting that my *entire* family is bad?"

Lachlan takes a heavy step, lowering his head so that his eyes are level with mine, and I feel my heart thump harder in my chest with the proximity. I can smell the spicy scent of his cologne blending with the scent of clean detergent and a bit of the greenery we spent the afternoon walking through—and without even realizing I'm doing it, I draw in a deep inhale just as his silvery blue eyes turn hard.

"Because," he says darkly. "It was *your* family that cursed mine."

I rear back as if he's slapped me, trying to reconcile what he's said with everything he's already told me and coming up empty.

"But that's not possible," I scoff. "That would mean that—"

"Aye," he cuts in. "Congratulations, Keyanna. You're the proud descendant of a kelpie."

## LACHLAN

I watch as shock passes across her features; her eyes go round and her lips part, and she's looking at me as if I've grown a second head. My own chest rises and falls too quickly, my breaths coming short as the old wound of my anger bubbles inside. It doesn't seem *fair* that Key got to grow up away from all this, that she's spent her entire life blissfully ignorant of what her family did to mine—but then again, why do I feel so much more strongly about it with *her* than I have with any other MacKay I've met? It's not as if Finlay or Rhona or even Brodie have any idea what happens to the Greer sons at night. So why do I feel so angry that *Keyanna* has gotten to live without this burden?

"I . . ." Her eyes fall to the ground, her lips pressing together and her nose wrinkling in thought, and I can practically see the gears turning in her head. "Are you sure?"

I can't help the harsh laugh that escapes me. "Aye, I'm pretty fucking sure. Not a detail one tends to forget."

"But how can that be possible?"

"My ancestor managed to capture the kelpie after she cursed him. He locked her away. Tried to force her to take it back. She was there for a year, they say, before *someone* set her free. Before someone gave her back her bridle and let her escape into the night, taking with her any chance of fixing what she'd done."

"And that person was . . ."

"Your great-great-something-or-other," he says. "A stable hand, they say. They say he married her. That she gave him a son. Her blood runs through *your* veins."

I expect her to deny it, or at the very least refute the idea of it, so what she does next takes me by the utmost surprise.

"I'm sorry," she says quietly, her voice *actually* full of regret. "That's terrible."

"It is," I manage, almost like a question because I'm still stunned by her reaction.

"God, Lachlan . . . your entire family? And then your dad . . . Wow. I can't even imagine."

I can feel something unwinding in my chest with every word she says, almost like her apology carries the weight of *all* the MacKays, as ridiculous as that notion is. Maybe it just feels good to tell *someone* and have them confirm how fucked up it all is. How terrible a life we've been forced to live. Or maybe it's just the mournful way she says it, like she actually cares.

"I . . ." I feel like a fish with the way my mouth opens and closes while I try to remember how to use words. "Thank you," I manage finally. "I appreciate that."

She looks up at me with that same fire in her eyes that I saw in my kitchen, nodding once as if confirming something to herself before she takes a step closer to me. I startle as she grabs my hand, holding it in her smaller ones and clutching it tight as she regards me seriously.

"All this does is prove to me that I'm supposed to help you. If it really was the MacKays that cursed your family, then maybe it's the MacKays that have to help you undo it."

I almost tell her everything, but something holds me back. Maybe I don't trust her enough yet, or maybe I'm enjoying the look of determination on her face, and I'm not quite ready to snuff it out just yet.

She must realize that she's still holding my hand, a fact that I haven't been able to distract myself from since the moment she reached for it, given how warm her hands are, because suddenly she goes pink in the cheeks and lets me go. She clears her throat and takes a slight step back, averting her eyes.

"Anyway." She shuffles her weight from one foot to the other. "Kelpies, huh?"

I swallow, ignoring the tingling in my hand. "If you believe the legends."

"And I suppose we do, right?"

I cock a brow. "We?"

"Well, yeah," she says in a way that feels more like a question than an assertion. "I mean, we're in this together now, aren't we?"

It seems ridiculous, impossible even, that I would be standing here with a member of the family that thrust mine into ruin and considering accepting her attempts at bullying me into allowing *her* to help *me*—and yet that's exactly what I'm doing, as asinine as it might prove to be. Because for whatever reason, and regardless of how little, I realize at this moment that I *do* trust Keyanna. I can't say why, can't even give a solid reasoning as to why I should even begin to, but I do. I can feel it, how she won't go back on her word. How much she *actually* wants to help.

Maybe that's why I open my stupid mouth.

"Aye," I answer softly. "I reckon we are."

Her answering smile punches through me like an actual blow; it's wide and bright and full of a joy she's *never* directed at *me*. Her wee bunny teeth draw my eye, and I have an insane, fleeting curiosity as to what they might feel like against my tongue.

*Get it together, you numpty.*

I shake the thought away, taking a deep breath and letting it out before glancing between the trees, where the sun still seems to be high in the sky. I wager I have a few more good hours before it starts to sink.

"We should get out of here," I tell her.

"Out of the creepy graveyard?" Her voice is laced with sarcasm. "But I was so enjoying my time here."

I roll my eyes. "Still a pain in my arse, even when you're my ally."

"Only for you, Nessie," she teases.

Nothing about that should make my stomach flutter, and I practically snort at my traitorous body for daring to do so. I shake my head, stomping past her as I toss over my shoulder, "Let's grab a drink at the pub. We can talk more there."

I hear her scurrying behind me, her boots crunching the leaves beneath her feet as she catches up. "Hey, Lachlan?"

"Hm?"

Her voice lowers as if she's uttering an important secret. "Does that mean I'm going to turn into a horse?"

My answering boom of a laugh is worth every bit of her scowling.

"So a pech is like . . . a gnome?"

I chuckle into my glass at Key's confused expression as Rory and Blair try to explain the origins of the name of the pub.

"Aye," Rory tells her. "Wee folk. Tiny things, but incredibly strong, see?"

She leans to prop her chin on her fist. "But why The Clever Pech?"

"That's a good story," Blair says, cleaning another glass. "It's an auld folktale we heard as weans. About this clever wee pech that challenged the strongest man in the village—a giant, they say—to a test of strength in exchange for their firstborn."

"I'm guessing he won," Key notes.

"He did," Blair goes on. "The giant man underestimated him, aye? Got knocked on his arse, which I imagine left him right embarrassed. Threatened to come after the pech with the force of the entire village for tricking him."

Rory slams his hands on the bar excitably. "So the pech gave him a test!"

"Hush." Blair playfully slaps Rory's shoulder with her dish towel. "You don't tell it right."

Key looks thoroughly enraptured now. "What kind of test?"

"The pech told the giant he could keep his babe if he could guess his name," Blair says.

Key's nose scrunches, and I try not to linger on how sweet an expression it is. "Wait. This sounds a lot like Rumpelstiltskin."

"Damn thieving Grimm brothers," Rory mutters.

"So," Key presses. "Did he guess his name?"

"Nope." Blair shakes her head. "Ran off with the babe and raised it as his own. They say the girl grew as tall as her giant father and could be seen stomping through the lands with the pech on her shoulder."

"It was a girl?"

"That's what they say."

Another nose scrunch. "That's not a very good ending."

"Not everything has a happy ending, mate," Blair tells her.

I snort into my drink. "Most don't, in my experience."

Keyanna glances my way with sympathy in her eyes, and I realize that I'm not quite yet used to the idea of her being anything more than my supposed downfall, if my da is to be believed. It's been easy to dislike her when all she was to me was a potential enemy—but the Key who looks at me with compassion shining out from her emerald depths is someone I definitely don't know how to deal with.

"Well," Rory says with a smirk. "Now that you've got some real brains on the operation."

He looks proud of himself as he gestures to Key, and I arch an eyebrow in his direction. "You realize that you just called yourself an eejit more or less, right?"

"I . . ." Rory frowns, then waves his hand in front of his face as if to clear the thought. "Oh, you know what I mean. Surely having a woman on the inside can only help you, aye?"

"And how do you guys know about this anyway?" she asks pointedly.

"This one"—Blair hitches a thumb in my direction—"changed right in front of us."

Key's head swivels toward me. "Really?"

"I was just a lad," I explain. "We knew I would eventually start to change, but there's no set day. I was usually more careful about where I was around sunset, but the three of us got caught in a storm one evening."

"Imagine how terrifying it is to be stuck in an auld barn with a giant lizard," Rory scoffs.

"How old were you?"

"Twelve?" Blair answers her. "Thirteen? Young enough that we about pissed ourselves."

"And you're the only ones who know?"

I nod at Key. "Now that my granny has passed, aye."

"And none of you have ever figured it out?"

All three of us shake our heads.

"I'm not really sure how much help I can actually be," Key admits nervously. "My grandmother *just* decided she doesn't totally hate my guts."

"Och," Blair tsks. "Hadn't thought of that. Still. You're a right ways less suspicious than this lot"—she jerks a thumb in my direction—"if you go digging around the property."

"True," Key agrees, her expression contemplative. "Do we even know what we're *looking* for?"

"The bridle, of course," Rory chimes in.

Key turns her head to look at me with a furrowed brow. "It really exists?"

"For my sake, I hope so," I scoff.

"You mean you don't *know*?"

"How could I possibly know?" I set my glass on the bar top, turning on my stool. "It's not like someone left me a set of instructions. All I know is that the story says the bridle is what got us cursed, so surely the bridle can undo it."

"What about Key?"

Everyone swivels their head toward Rory, staring back at us with his head cocked.

I look at her and find her just as confused as I am. "What about her?"

"You said she saved you," Rory points out. "At the cove. You think she's got a bit of that kelpie witchcraft in her?"

"I—" My mouth closes just as soon as it opens, my lips turning down as I consider. "She doesn't even know how she did that."

"It's true," Key adds. "I'm not sure how I did any of the things that have been happening since I showed up here."

"Right, and she—wait, what?" I lean in closer, narrowing my eyes. "What do you mean 'any of the things'? What else has been happening?"

"Well, I can't be sure"—she rubs at her arm—"but there was this thing with a window opening after I couldn't get it to budge, and of course there's the whole healing thing, and then . . ." She shakes her head. "It sounds insane, but I may have made it stop raining the other day."

"You made it stop raining," I echo.

She shrugs. "I mean, I asked it to stop, and it just . . . did?"

"And that didn't strike you as odd?"

"I thought it was just a coincidence!"

I mull this information over in my head, an inkling of possibility trickling through my thoughts, but then I clear it away with a firm shake of my head. "We can't be counting on whatever is happening to Key. Not without knowing more about it. *Especially* since she can't control it. The bridle is our best bet."

"So," Key says, crossing her arms over her chest. "Where are we supposed to look for it?"

"I've already been through Rhona's attic—"

Key makes an indignant sound. "You went snooping in my grandmother's attic?"

"I think I've more than earned the right, all things considered," I snap.

Key narrows her eyes. "Point taken."

"Regardless, I didn't see anything of note, but there's so much stored up there . . . I could have missed something. Haven't found anything in any of the wee rundown buildings around the farm either."

"What about the auld Greer castle?" Blair asks.

Key perks up. "Castle?"

"Belonged to my ancestor," I tell her. "There's nothing there. I've searched all over that place."

"But not with Key," Rory urges. "Maybe her kelpie magic will pick up on the scent of something."

"She's not a bloody hound," I snort.

"I mean . . . it couldn't hurt," Key says.

I peer at her suspiciously. "Are you sure you're not just wanting to see the place as some sort of tourist excursion?"

"Oh, fuck you," she huffs, rolling her eyes. "Like any of this trip has been at *all* a holiday. I haven't done a single touristy thing since I got here!"

Rory raises a finger. "You *did* visit Loch La—"

Key shoots him a glare.

"Never mind," he finishes.

"We have to start somewhere," Key urges. "I just *know* I'm here for a reason. I can feel it."

"It's a two-hour walk," I tell her. "Land is too rough that way to go by car."

"I can walk," she answers eagerly.

I rub my lower lip, frowning. It feels pointless to visit a place I've already crawled all over a dozen times before, but I can't help wondering if perhaps there *is* something I missed. Something that Key and her strange, burgeoning magic might uncover. The possibility is enough to shoot a tiny thrill through my stomach, but I don't let it show. I don't want her to realize just yet how desperate I am. It would only frighten her.

"S'pose it can't hurt," I sigh. "But it really is a hell of a walk."

She juts out her chin in this petulant, adorable way, and just *thinking* of her as adorable has me reeling, because I should be holding this woman at arm's length. And yet, here I am, signing up to go trekking across the countryside while she most likely complains the entire time. My da would think I was completely mental if he knew.

I ignore the pang in my chest at the thought of my father.

*I'll save him. It can't be too late.*

"All right," I concede wearily. "I guess we're going on a hike, then."

"Right now?"

"In the morning. There's not enough time today. I have to get back and check on the cows."

"Oh."

That look is in her eye again, and I'm not quite sure I like the way it makes me feel. Almost like *I* should be comforting *her*. Mental, I tell you.

"You just be ready for me at sunrise," I tell her. "You can meet me at the cove."

Her sympathetic expression morphs into a smirk. "Will you be clothed this time, at least?"

"I'm sorry," Blair interjects. "Come again?"

I roll my eyes. "Never you mind." To Key, I add, "I'll try to make sure I'm decent." My lip quirks. "I'm sure you'll be very disappointed by it."

The slight pinkening of her cheeks is admittedly lovely, and I wonder if it's possible that I actually *enjoy* making her so irritated. Almost like this odd back-and-forth between us is . . . fun.

Her eyes glitter with amusement. "In your dreams, Nessie."

*On second thought . . .*

## 15

### KEYANNA

think my spleen is rupturing."

I hear a disgruntled sound from ahead, Lachlan not even bothering to turn around for my dozenth complaint since we set out. "Quit your whinging. You wanted to take this trip."

"Yeah, yeah," I grumble. I hoist my backpack higher up on my shoulders, pausing to peer out at the rolling hills of lush green ahead of us. The sky casts a gray light with the promise of another dreary day, and I frown as I continue walking. "Is it supposed to rain?"

"It's always supposed to rain," Lachlan tosses over his shoulder.

"So what do we do if it rains?"

"Walk faster."

I huff out a breath. "You're a real ray of sunshine, you know that?"

"That is what people say about me. Yes."

I scowl even though he can't see me, trudging along in the path of his footsteps as I try to keep up. I swear the man must have some super-monster strength even when he's in human form, because the guy moves like the fucking Terminator.

Still. I can't pretend that the view is . . . all that bad. From my few steps behind, I can't help but notice the way his burgundy-colored wool sweater hugs his shoulders, and if I glance down a little lower (which I wish I could lie and say that I haven't), it's impossible to miss the way his jeans hug his thick thighs and his firm ass, which is actually kind of hypnotizing in the way it moves with his every step.

*Jesus. Get a grip, Key.*

I clear my throat, tearing my eyes away from the ass's ass.

"So what's the castle like?"

I can't see his frown, but I can hear it, I think. "It's a castle."

"Okay, but what is it *like*? Are we talking about collapsing roofs and crumbling walls or . . . ?"

He doesn't say anything for a moment, and from my vantage point I can just make out the way his jaw works. "Roof is still mostly okay. There are definitely some unstable parts in the floor, so you'll want to watch your step, and the walls have begun to crumble in many places. No one has lived there for centuries."

"Why not?"

"Wars," he says. "These lands were invaded by the English not even a decade after my family was cursed." He snorts. "My ancestor was so busy worrying about neighboring clans, he didn't prepare himself for the possibility of anyone else."

"So it's been abandoned that long?"

"Aye. I hear tell of some great-great-something-or-other trying to repair it back in the thirties, but . . . Well. Numpty got his picture taken and everyone had to go into hiding after."

I stop walking, my mouth falling open. "You don't mean the surgeon's photo."

"Mhm." He pauses, turning to take in my shell-shocked expression. "What?"

"You mean the photo was actually real?"

Lachlan makes a face. "What else would it be?"

"But that guy came out and said it was all a hoax?"

Lachlan chuckles. "Alastair? Oh, aye. He was . . . a family friend. Did us a real solid coming out with all that talk of Spurling confessing."

"So the hoax was . . . a hoax?"

"Kelpie magic and monsters, and *that's* the part you're struggling with?"

His quiet laugh drifts back toward me as he continues forward, and I stumble after him, still in a daze. "Okay, but you have to admit that plaster and wood on a toy submarine was pretty believable."

"A toy submarine from the thirties? How on earth do you think they even got it into position? Remote controls?"

"I . . . Hm. I didn't think of that."

"Sometimes, lass . . . things are exactly what they appear to be."

I pick up my pace so I can fall into step beside him. "Have there been other real sightings?"

"A few," he tells me. "It's hard to hide when you're so . . . big."

*And he really is big.*

I shake my head back and forth.

*Stop that. Just because he isn't being a total dick to you doesn't mean you should start appreciating how hot he is.*

I sneak a glance to my left, eyeing the way his neat beard highlights the sharpness of his jaw. The way it makes his mouth look soft and full and—

*Stop. It.*

"So how much further?"

Lachlan shrugs. "We're close to the halfway point. There's an auld barn on the other side of that hill"—he points to the rising slope that seems miles away from this vantage point—"and from there it's less than an hour left, I'd say."

A rumble of thunder sounds above us, and I peek up at the sky warily. "Do you think we'll make it there dry?"

"Don't worry about it," he says confidently. He taps the side of his nose. "I can smell when it's going to rain. We've got hours yet before it starts."

Sounds like bullshit, but what do I know?

"Okay," I answer. "If you're sure."

Lachlan scoffs. "I'm *always* sure."


We're utterly drenched by the time we make it inside the dilapidated old barn that's really more of a leaking, thatched roof over four rotting walls—and I shake off my backpack as I glare at Lachlan, who is shaking the rain out of his hair.

"You can smell the rain, huh?"

He shoots me a glare. *"Haud yer wheesht."*

"English," I groan.

"Be quiet, you arse."

"Wow." I ring out the end of my sweater. "Real nice."

He presses his hands to his hips after he drops his pack, looking around the space. "Least we'll be dry here. I'm sure the rain will pass soon. It always does."

"So what do we do until then?"

"Well, you could ask nicely for it to stop, I s'pose."

I narrow my eyes, but he actually looks sincere. I frown out at the entrance, where it's still coming down in buckets, chewing at the inside of my lip.

"Stop raining," I say to the air, feeling silly.

I hear a snort behind me. "Think you're going to have to be a wee bit more forceful than that."

My hands fall to my sides, and I clench them into fists. "Stop raining!"

There's a stretch of silence before, "Well. Merlin, you are not."

"Shut up," I grumble.

I turn to watch as Lachlan trods over to the remnants of what might have been a hay bale, testing the straw with his foot before appearing satisfied. He drops down onto it with a groan, stretching out his long legs and leaning back on his hands. He lifts one to pat the space beside him, arching a brow.

"Your throne, princess."

I narrow my eyes. "You're a dick, you know that?"

"Aye, aye, I know. Sit down and dry off. Get away from the wind. You'll catch your death over there."

As if on cue, a shiver runs through me, and I wrap my arms around my chest as I eye the spot next to him warily. "No funny business?"

"Who actually says that in real life?" A laugh burbles out of him. "Come sit, Your Highness. Your virtue is safe with me."

"My virtue is the last thing I'm worried about," I grumble, trying not to picture what *that* might entail. I plop down beside him with my arms still wrapped tightly around my chest, trying to urge some warmth back into my limbs. "You really think it will let up soon?"

"Most likely," he says. "At least you have good company while you wait."

"Oh, yeah," I snort. "Absolutely stellar."

We're both quiet for a bit while we watch the rain coming down outside, and after a few moments I notice the warmth radiating off Lachlan's side where he's *almost* touching me.

"Are you a furnace? I can feel you from over here."

He shrugs. "Always ran hot. Side effect of the curse, I s'pose. The loch can get right chilly."

I frown as I hug myself tighter, feeling my teeth begin to chatter as I try to keep my limbs under control. The last thing I need is to appear weak in front of him. He'll have a field day laughing about it.

"You cold?"

*Damn it.*

"No," I huff.

"I s'pose the shivering is just your excitement to be in my company, then, aye?"

"I think I liked you better when you were avoiding me."

He chuckles. "You wanted to be allies, remember? You made your bed."

I continue to shake for another minute before I finally cave, scooting closer until my entire right side is squished against his left. The heat emanating from him is an immediate relief, and I have to physically restrain myself from snuggling closer.

"There now," he teases. "Was that so hard?"

"Debatable." I lean in just a little closer. "You're being awfully . . . agreeable."

He shrugs. "I reckon if you're going to be a stubborn arse about helping me, the least I can do is be a bit more agreeable."

"That's . . . nice. Almost."

He chuckles softly. "Trust me, it's a foreign concept to me too."

I watch the rain falling outside the sagging entry to the barn, oddly content to be quiet for a time. Lachlan says nothing beside me, and I can't help but wonder what he's thinking. I find myself wondering a lot of things about him since learning the truth of his curse. I wonder what it's like to live your life knowing how it will end. It makes my chest feel funny when I think about it.

"Do you remember the last time you spoke with your father?"

He startles at the question, his head whipping toward me. I can feel his eyes on the side of my face, but I continue to stare at the rain.

I'm not sure what prompted me to ask, but I realize I'm curious, now that it's out there. Maybe it's because he knows how I feel, given the things we've both lost.

"Aye," he answers finally, his voice soft. "I remember."

"How old were you?"

He leans to brace his forearms over his bent knees, eyes on the downpour outside. "I was only eight. A wean, really. I still remember the day, though."

"What happened?"

"There were signs," he tells me. "The curse is becoming unstable, see? We saw it in him, my mother and me. When he was angry, when he lost control . . . It was like you could see bits of the beast shining through the man."

"Does that—" I can feel myself leaning in. "Does that happen to you?"

"Not much," he answers. He looks at me then, his eyes moving slowly over the planes of my face as if studying me. "I do my best not to lose control."

I swallow, the weight of his gaze suddenly too much. I avert my own gaze, clearing my throat. "That's . . . good."

"Aye. My da . . . he lost control one day. He . . ." Lachlan's fists clench, and his body tenses, his brow furrowing as he remembers. "He hurt my mother. Not badly, you see, but enough to scare them both. The grief of that, of what he'd done . . . It's like he let himself go to the monster. He went into the loch that night . . . and he never came back out."

My chest clenches in sympathy, and I have the strangest urge to reach out and touch him, to offer him some sort of comfort—but I can't decide if it would be welcome or not.

"I'm sorry," I say softly.

He shakes his head. "I still remember what he said that morning. The last words he ever spoke to me."

"What did he say?"

"He said . . ." Lachlan's voice breaks, and he sucks in a breath just to blow it out. "He said that he was sorry. He said that he—that he tried. He tried to save me. I'm still not sure what he meant by that, but I can't forget the sadness in his eyes when he said it."

"It sounds like he really loved you."

"Aye," Lachlan murmurs. "He did." He's thoughtful for a second before, "My mother left not long after. She told me it would only be for a little while, me staying with my granny, but . . . I think looking at me was too hard. She missed my da too much. It did something to her mind. She's never been . . . quite right since."

"I'm sorry," I tell him, meaning it.

He shrugs. "S'fine."

"Did she know?"

"Hm?"

"Your mother," I clarify. "Did she know about the curse?"

"Aye, from early on."

"Then why did she—"

"She never expected to lose him to it," he tells me. "My da was the first to be consumed by it like he was."

"Oh." I consider that, feeling sympathy for this woman I don't know, but also irritation. "But she abandoned *you* in the process too."

Lachlan is quiet for a moment before admitting, "Aye. She did."

A shudder racks through me before I can say more, making my whole body quake from the lingering chill. Lachlan's arm comes around me in an instant, and I don't know who looks more surprised by the quick action—him or me.

"Sorry," he says quickly. "I wasn't even thinking. I just—"

I lean into him, letting the heat of his arm seep through my still-damp clothes. "It's fine." I take a chance and rest my head on his shoulder, trying not to read too much into it. It's just necessity, after all. Just to keep me warm. "Fucking freezing."

"Far be it from me to let the princess freeze to death," he chuckles.

"Asshole," I grumble.

Silence falls over us once more, and to my surprise, it's not as awkward as it should be. It's almost . . . comfortable. His fingers twitch against my shoulder, like they want to move, and I am all too aware of the warmth and weight of his arm as it drapes over me. I'm dialed into the firmness of his body against mine. How long has it been since someone touched me like this? Am I so touch-starved that I would relish something so simple?

*Apparently so.*

"What about you?"

His question shakes me out of my errant thoughts, and I peek up at him. "Hm?"

"Your da," he says, still studying me with those icy blue eyes that seem to see right through me. "Do you remember the last time you spoke?"

"Oh." My gaze falls to the straw beneath us, my lips pressing together. "Yeah. I do."

"If it's too painful—"

"No, no," I assure him. "It's fine. Fair is fair."

"Key," he says firmly, forcing me to turn up my face and look at him again, something that is becoming harder and harder because he really is sort of beautiful, and without the distraction of, well, *hating* him—it's hard to ignore that fact now. His fingers brush against my chin, tilting up my face even more. "There's no quid pro quo here.

You don't owe me anything, all right? I'm just asking as . . ." His brow knits, like he has to ponder his next words. "As a friend?"

I can't help the way my mouth turns up in a grin. "Wow, that must have been so hard for you."

"Like pulling teeth," he scoffs.

I bite the inside of my lip slightly. "Are we? Friends?"

He's doing it again. *Studying* me. I can't help but wonder what it is that he's thinking when he looks at me. It's strange to think that only a week ago I considered him an enemy, and now . . . Now it's like there is some insatiable urge inside me to help him. To *save* him, if I can. One that I can't even figure out where it comes from. It pulses inside like a seed waiting for water, one that is desperate to grow.

"Aye," he says. "I s'pose we are."

I feel warmth flush at my neck and chest, and I can only pray he doesn't see it. He already thinks I'm a *numpty*, as he likes to say—he'd never let me live it down if he knew I was getting flustered from just this.

"R-right," I manage, tearing my eyes from his. "Yeah. Okay."

He doesn't say more, seeming to sense that I need a moment to collect my thoughts. I let my memories drift to the last days with my father, choosing one as if plucking it from a box, dusting it off and letting it breathe as happiness and sadness course through me all at once.

"His last day," I start, willing my voice not to crack. "It was strange, really. He'd been mostly out of it for the week before, and I knew he would go soon. You just . . . know. At the end. You can sense it. But that day . . ." A smile touches my lips despite everything. "That day it was like he'd come back to me, just a little. It was almost like that day he was my *dad* again. Even if only for a while."

"Maybe he knew too," Lachlan offers. "That he was close."

"Maybe he did." I can feel myself resting more and more against Lachlan, the indelible warmth he gives off like a siren song that I can't resist sinking into. "He looked at me that day and for the first time in ages, I could just . . . I could *tell* that he was really *seeing* me. He put his hand on my cheek"—I reach to press my own palm against my cheek, closing my eyes—"and he said my name. Said it like he hadn't seen me in forever. Like he'd just been away for a long time, and he was finally coming home." A choked sob gets trapped in my chest, and I force it back down. "He said he'd missed me. He asked me where I'd been."

I can feel Lachlan's fingers at my shoulder gripping me tighter, his thumb stroking there. "Key . . ."

"We talked for a bit. Not about what had happened to him or what he'd been through—just about little things. Things that made us laugh. Things that made him smile."

"I'm glad," Lachlan says gently. "That you have that memory."

I nod. "Me too. And then . . . before he went to sleep—for the *last* time—he asked me . . ." I blow out a shaky exhale. "He asked me to take him home."

"Home," Lachlan echoes.

I manage another nod. "He said to take him back to the loch. That he wanted to see it one last time. I'd heard the story a hundred times growing up—I knew exactly which one he meant. Obviously, I never got to bring *him* back, but I just thought . . . I thought he would like knowing that it would be his final resting place."

I catch a glimpse of Lachlan hanging his head beside me, and I can't help but twist mine to take him in. "What?"

"I'm sorry," he says. "I was a real arse that day I found you."

"You didn't know."

"I didn't, but still. I could have been better. I heard who you were, and I just—"

"You didn't trust me."

He shakes his head. "No, I didn't."

I can't help it—the question bubbles up inside without my permission, so violent that I physically *can't* hold it back.

"Do you trust me now?"

He looks up at me, his eyes holding mine, an intensity in them that makes me hot all over in a way that has nothing to do with how he's touching me and yet *everything* to do with how he's touching me. I notice his gaze dip to my mouth, and I feel my lips part, because it's insanity to even entertain it—isn't it?

"Aye," he half whispers. "I think I do, Keyanna."

The rain is still falling outside, but there's a roaring in my ears. I can feel the heaviness of my chest with each rise and fall, feel the thumping of my pulse in my throat, and I notice the second he starts to lean in, looking as hypnotized as I feel. The heat in my skin feels alive, climbing higher and higher, my fingers tingling and my palms *burning*, but he's so *close*. One more second, one more inch, and we'll—

"*Fuckin' hell*," Lachlan shouts suddenly, his accent thicker than usual as he jolts away.

I blink, trying to discern what happened—and then I feel it.

"Shit!"

The straw beneath us has been set aflame, the fire small but growing. I try to pat it out with my hand, beating at the smoking lump incessantly.

"Key," Lachlan says incredulously. "It's *you*."

And that's when I notice.

The fire is coming from my fucking *hand*.

I panic, shooting up and shaking my hand frantically as if I can somehow put it out. "What do I do?" I give it another frenetic shake. "Lachlan, what do I—" I go still even as Lachlan starts to stomp out the crackling straw with his boot. I stare at my palm, where a tiny flicker has formed, resting in the cradle of my hand, and I realize: "It doesn't hurt."

He stops smashing the small flames below with his shoe, peering at the one in my palm with a slack-jawed expression.

"How long have you been able to do that?"

"Um . . ." I roll my hand this way and that, watching the flame roll with it. "Just now?"

"Jesus suffering fuck," he breathes, running a hand through his hair.

I close my fist, astonished when doing so extinguishes the flame. "Wow."

"That's a lot more than blowing open a window," he notes.

"What do you think it means?"

"I think . . ." He blows out a breath. "I think it means we need to hurry and find some fucking answers."

I nod dazedly, agreeing wholeheartedly. I'm still a bit stunned as he starts to gather our things, and I can distantly hear him talking about the rain starting to let up, dictating that we should be going. I hear all of it, but it seems far away because even with everything that just happened—the fire, the magic, all of it—there is another thought that rings louder than all the rest.

Did Lachlan and I almost kiss just now? And what's more . . . am I disappointed that we didn't?

# 16

## LACHLAN

*You almost kissed her.*

*You almost* bloody *kissed her.*

I've been turning over this fact in my mind for the last half hour, quiet as Key and I continue our trek toward the old Greer castle. I can see it now, just over the next hill—and given that she isn't peppering me with questions as I am learning she's prone to do, I can't help but wonder if she might be thinking about the same thing.

I can't say what pushed me to throw away every rational thought in my head and lean into her back in the barn. Maybe it was how vulnerable she was allowing herself to be. Maybe it was the atmosphere, the feeling of her delicate body tucked against mine.

Or maybe it's how fucking beautiful she is, something I wish weren't so bloody obvious.

I don't know when it happened—or maybe I do, but just don't want to admit it—but sometime between Key sitting at my kitchen table begging to help me and leaning against me in a falling-down barn, I seemed to have forgotten all the reasons why I should be keeping her at arm's length. It's like now that I can't drum up proper disdain for her, my brain and body seem to have decided to stage some sort of coup against me, coming to the conclusion that Keyanna

MacKay is actually a sensual but somehow also adorable daydream of a woman who I couldn't have conjured up in my wildest fantasies.

Which, to be fair, has been true since the day I met her—but given that *then* I was able to bury that knowledge under a thick layer of animosity, it was a lot easier to ignore.

I know that there are bigger concerns here than what her mouth might feel like against mine, and I frantically drudge up those reasons as we both traipse along the wet grass, knowing that this drawn-out silence is only making things worse.

"So, back at the barn—"

"Yes?"

The eagerness in her tone gives me pause, and when I turn to look at her, I can see it in her eyes as well. Those emerald depths stare back at me with shining anticipation, and for a moment I'm spellbound, like a sailor caught in a siren's song. Does she *really* have to be so tempting?

"I, uh . . ." I clear my throat. "That trick with the flame." I ignore the way her expression falls; there's nothing to be done for it. "Do you have any idea how you did that?"

"Oh." She glances down at her feet, shrugging. "No idea."

"Can you think of anything that might tell you *how* it happened?"

"I don't know . . . It felt like I was heating up, but I mean . . . You were kind of touching me. And you do run really hot. So I didn't think much of it until—"

"Until you nearly burned the barn down."

She rolls her eyes. "Don't be dramatic."

"I think when a woman nearly sets my arse on fire, I'm allowed a wee bit of dramatics."

"Says the guy that turns into a dinosaur at night."

The bickering is safer territory, and I tell myself I am relieved by it. The softness of the moment in the barn is a dangerous, slippery slope—one I can't afford to traverse.

"Aye, princess," I chuckle. "S'pose you're right." The castle is in full view now that we've crested the hill, and I pause at the top, tilting my head in its direction. "Well, there she is."

Key looks positively beside herself—her lips parting in a sound that can only be described as some sort of birdcall as she squawks her enthusiasm. And why do I find that cute?

"Oh my God. It's amazing!"

I cock my head, trying to see it through her eyes, but given that I've been here a hundred times, all I can see is the same crumbling piece of history that is a reminder of all the things wrong in my life.

"It's just an auld pile of rocks, Key."

She nudges me in the side with her elbow. "Don't take this from me. We don't exactly have thirteenth-century castles just lying around in New York."

"Well," I say, unable to help the way my lips curl into a grin. "That seems a shame, given your royal status."

"Ugh. I'm not even going to let you piss me off." She shakes her head, stomping forward. "Not this time! Let's go explore."

I'm still chuckling as I follow after her, her long legs meaning that she's able to barrel off without me, forcing me to increase my speed just to keep up.

I don't imagine those legs in any other capacity. Especially what they might feel like wrapped around my waist.

That would be utterly mental.


"This is insane." Key runs her hand over the weathered stone wall with an expression of awe. "It's like a fairy tale."

"Like a nightmare is more like it," I mutter, letting my eyes sweep across the wall-to-wall stone. "You want to keep going?"

She turns back, biting her lip. "Is it safe?"

My eyes linger on the press of her white teeth against the softness of her lip for a second too long, remembering how close they'd been to mine. I shake the thought away.

"Just keep close," I tell her.

I've shown her the courtyard and the great hall, even let her poke around for the last hour in some of the smaller rooms connected to it. There's nothing really notable, like I tried to tell her, but it hasn't stopped Key from acting like this is the most thrilling experience of her life. Even now, she's touching the weathered old stone as if it were something precious. I try again to see it through her eyes, remembering how it had felt when I first saw it. Like stepping into another world, almost. Now, it's just a sore reminder.

"Watch your step," I tell her, eyeing the weak spots in the floor as she keeps exploring. "The last thing I need is to be fishing you out of a hole."

I don't see her roll her eyes, but I can practically feel it.

"Yeah, yeah."

I watch her wander into the next room, the one that I believe was the main dining hall—hearing her *ooh*s and *ahh*s when she finds the massive oak table that is still miraculously in one piece.

"Lachlan!" She peeks her head back out, her eyes wide as she waves me over. "Have you seen this?"

I shake my head as I follow after her. "I've seen it all, remember?"

"Oh. Right." She nods absently as she runs her fingers over the dusty surface of the table, her brow furrowed in thought. "When did you first come here?"

I frown, thinking. "I was young. So young, I'm not sure I remember the first time."

"With your dad?"

"Aye."

She nods idly, her head practically on a swivel as she takes in the room. "I bet it was really beautiful once."

"I imagine it was," I note, unable to keep from watching her as she takes it in.

There's a wide-eyed innocence to Key that I might normally find annoying, but paired with what I know of her—her determination, her loyalty, her strength even in suffering—it actually leaves me a wee bit in awe of her. It feels almost wrong to admit it, even to myself, but with how jaded this world has left me . . . seeing Key endure so much in her young life and still have this fresh outlook, this *hunger* for life . . . it does something strange to me.

"What's in there?"

Her voice rouses me from my thoughts as I catch her ducking into the next room—and I hurry after her if only to make sure she doesn't *actually* fall through the floor. The sun that has snuck through the clouds streams in through the holes in the ceiling, casting light on the decrepit state of what I'm sure was once an impressive kitchen. I find her there, putting her hands on everything they can touch as if she might learn something just from handling anything within sight.

"This is so cool," she gushes, holding up a rusted saucepan. "Isn't it?"

"It's a pot," I answer flatly.

She purses her lips. "But think of how old it is! This might have made soup for your great-great-great . . . something-or-other. Isn't that neat?"

"Neat," I echo dumbly, her bright smile slightly dizzying. "Sure."

"You're such a spoilsport," she chuckles. "Show me your favorite room."

"My favorite?"

She closes the distance between us, tugging on my arm. "Yes. Show me."

"I . . ." My mouth closes as I ponder this. "Okay. Come with me."

I turn on my heel and lead her back through the dining room, through the great hall, to the opposite wing that leads deeper in. I can hear her steps echoing behind me, her gait quick and full of that same eagerness she seems to give everything else. It almost makes *me* excited to share this with her. I haven't shared it with anyone in a very long time. Not since I came here with my da.

I pause when we get close to the entrance, turning back. "Close your eyes."

"What? No."

I cock a brow. "What happened to your sense of adventure?"

"I'm not entirely convinced you won't chuck me down an old laundry chute the second I turn my back."

I can't help the way my lips curl, and I take a step closer, pressing a knuckle under her chin. "Now, does that sound like something I would do?"

"I . . ."

I don't miss the way her eyes flick to my mouth, and I know she's thinking about it. That she's remembering how close we came to crossing a line only a short while ago. I tell myself that it's good that we didn't, that it would only complicate things—but that doesn't stop me from wondering how good it might feel.

"Close your eyes, Key," I urge softly.

I watch the delicate line of her throat bob with a swallow, and after only a second, her lashes flutter closed just as I asked. My knuckle still rests against her chin, and with her eyes shut, I can almost imagine leaning in just a bit, closing the gap, it would be so easy . . .

I step back, taking her hand instead.

"Now watch your step," I remind her.

She huffs. "Kind of hard when you told me to close my eyes."

"Don't be an arse."

I lead her carefully into the room, watching the floor as I steer her toward its center. I do my best not to touch her too familiarly, keeping my fingers light against her waist as I turn her where I want her before stepping back. She still looks so eager—her cheeks are flushed and her breathing is just slightly quicker than it should be—and I realize that my excitement over something as simple as this is the most I've felt in a long time. I wonder what I might find if I explore that thought.

"Okay," I tell her, taking another step back. "You can open them."

Her lashes flutter open as she takes in her surroundings, letting out a gasp when she notices what I've brought her to see. The light from the stained-glass window slithers over the old floor, the sunshine streaming through it making the colors seem to dance.

"Wow," she says, stepping closer.

I reach for her wrist, holding her back. "Careful. It's ancient."

"How did it survive this long?"

I shake my head. "No idea. It's been here as long as we can remember."

"What does it mean?"

I tug her a step closer, pointing out the images in the center. "It's my family crest. The tree symbolizes strength. The sword is for power."

"It's so strange," she says quietly. "Isn't it crazy to think that you had ancestors in this room hundreds of years ago?"

"Aye," I answer softly. "I reckon it is." I can still feel the heat of her skin under my fingers, and I could probably let her go, but I don't. "When I was a lad, I would sit in here for hours while my da scoured this place. The lights change with the movement of the sun."

"It's so beautiful," she murmurs. "Do you ever think about taking it out of here?"

"I wouldn't want to risk it," I tell her. "Besides, I'm not sure it would bring me much luck." I chuff out a laugh. "Never did anyone else in this place."

"Lachlan," she starts, her voice full of sympathy. I'm not sure if I like it or not. "I'm—holy shit."

She brushes past me suddenly, leaving me bereft. "What?"

"You don't see that? It's right—"

"Careful, I said!" I move after her. "The floor."

"I heard you, I heard you," she says flippantly, still moving toward the corner of the room. "But look!"

"Key," I say with more force. "I mean it. The floor isn't stable here."

"Oh my God. I heard you, okay? I promise. I'm not going to—"

The sharp *crack* rings through the space, and there is a flash of terror in her eyes only seconds before the floor crumbles beneath her. I feel my heart jump into my throat as I watch her disappear through it, feeling a wave of fear unlike anything I've ever known washing over me as I rush to the hole she's left behind.

"Key? Key! Talk to me. Are you all right?"

There's a cloud of dust billowing upward, and I think I can make out the faint sounds of movement, my panic still ratcheting higher.

"Keyanna!"

"I'm here," she says weakly, and a flood of relief courses through me. "I'm okay."

I blow out a breath, my heart still in my throat. "Bloody hell, Key. I told you to be—"

"Lachlan," she calls out.

"What?"

"Shut up."

My mouth falls open, two seconds away from telling her what an eejit she is, but then—

"Get down here."

Dropping myself down after her is easier than I thought it would be; the room below is hardly eight feet from the floor, leading into a tiny, windowless space. I can't see any doors either by the thin light coming from above.

Key is dusting herself off, and I push down the urge to check her for injuries. I have a feeling she would tell me to piss off if I fussed over her.

"What is this place?"

She gives me an incredulous look. "You mean you don't know?"

"I've never seen this room before," I tell her honestly.

Her eyes widen. "You mean I *did* find something?"

"Aye," I scoff. "It seems your clumsiness has come in handy."

"Shut up," she grouses. "I thought I saw something in the wall upstairs. I couldn't get close enough to tell what it was before I fell through."

I let my eyes sweep around the room, taking in our surroundings. In the corner there is a metal cot of some sort, and beside it, a rotting wooden chair that seems days from falling apart. I can't make out any other remnants of furniture.

"Lachlan," Key says, crouching by the bed. "Look."

Attached to bed posts that are bolted into the floor are thick, iron shackles. Too wide for wrists, I think; no, these seem to be the type that would fit around the ankle.

"The fuck is this?" I mutter.

"Pretty sure it's a dungeon," she says.

"I've seen the dungeon."

"Wait, you didn't show me the dungeon?"

"You were too busy waxing poetic about pots."

"Seriously? How could you not show me the—"

"Key," I interrupt, pointing behind her. "Look."

She turns to see what I'm seeing, both of us staring at the etches in the wall that seems random at first, but upon further inspection, it's clear they're carvings of some kind.

"They're so perfect," Key notes, running her fingers along the grooves. "It's like a machine did this."

If I hadn't lived the life I had, it would almost feel silly to say, "Or magic."

"Oh my God," she gasps, almost sounding excited. "Do you think . . . ?"

"I think the writing is on the fucking wall."

The carvings depict a woman—a beautiful one, one that looks too real to be carved—with wild curls and a willowy frame. There are dozens of eerily perfect etchings of this woman in different scenarios; the highest image shows her offering up something, something that looks suspiciously like the bridle I've been desperately searching for. In another, we see it being held by a large man with shoulder-length hair draped in fur and a kilt.

"Do you think that's your ancestor?"

"It has to be," I murmur, my eyes still scanning the other carvings.

There is a carving of the woman—the *kelpie*, no doubt—weeping in the dark. Another where she looks enraged, baring her teeth. We see more depictions of my ancestor: leading his army, standing on a hill holding the bridle high . . . but it's the very last carving that gives me pause.

"It's them," Key breathes, touching the last image.

The kelpie holds the bridle out to my ancestor, and then he takes it, holding it high above his head. There's triumph etched in his features, and something like anger grips my chest.

*Why did you betray him?*

Even as my heart starts to race, I can hear Key's soft breathing beside me, and oddly, it's soothing. It reminds me I'm not alone. Not right now, at least.

"What do you think it means?"

I rise from the crouched position I'm in, dusting off my pants as she does the same. "I don't know," I tell her. "But it seems like this is where he kept her locked away."

"You did say he locked her up . . . after."

"I did." I stare at the last image, my mind reeling. "I don't know if I blame him. Not after what she did."

From the corner of my eyes, I see Key's eyes avert to the floor, and hear her whispered "I'm sorry."

"Hey." I turn to once again press my knuckle to her chin, forcing her eyes up. "It's not your fault. All right?"

Her eyes, even in this light, are so bright that they seem to cast a glow about the entire room. "It's not?"

"You're no more to blame for the past than I am," I say, surprised to find that I mean it. "You're here now. You're trying to make things right. That's what matters."

Her lip quivers, and suddenly I'm acutely aware of how close we are. I can viscerally recall the memory of her warm breath against my mouth back in that barn, can feel the heat of her skin pressed against mine.

*Would it be so bad?*

I can feel myself leaning, once again caught in her spell. And maybe it *is* a spell. Maybe this gorgeous creature I've been taught to fear has me bewitched.

None of that stops me from continuing to lean in, and it seems the same can be said for Key.

*Crack.*

I only have a second to register the beam from the floor above splitting away from the rest, only a single moment to predict where it will land before I roughly shove Key out of the way. She winds up with her back pressed to the wall just as the beam crashes against my back, and I grunt and tense as it rolls away, already assessing her.

"Are you okay?"

Her lips are parted in surprise, her chest heaving. "You saved me again."

"Aye." I realize my hands are braced on either side of her head, our bodies only a hair's breadth apart. "Seems now you owe me again."

I can make out her pulse fluttering at her throat, and her pink tongue swipes across her lower lip, and her eyes—those eyes are utterly *bewitching*—and I do the last thing I should, most likely.

I crash my mouth against hers.

17

KEYANNA

The surprise that courses through me lasts all of three seconds. Three fucking seconds of *What the hell?* before my body catches up to the situation and has a team meeting with my brain to decide that, yes, we are absolutely on board with Lachlan kissing us senseless.

I feel his hands lift from their place on the stone on either side of my head, his palms finding my cheeks to hold my face as his lips move against mine with an intensity that steals my breath. It's like every second of the frustration I've felt since meeting him has suddenly morphed into this all-consuming *want* that has me grasping at his sweater to pull him closer, has me tilting up my face to seek more.

"Key," he breathes roughly against my mouth. "Is this all right?"

"Don't stop," I manage, my voice sounding all wrong.

He groans, a sound that I feel down in my toes, and then his fingers are in my hair, tugging gently enough not to hurt but with just enough pressure that I *feel* it. I can't remember the last time I've been kissed like this; the last year hasn't really been a great time to date, after all, but honestly, I'm not sure that I've *ever* been kissed like this.

Lachlan kisses like he's trying to consume me; his teeth nip at my bottom lip just before his tongue teases the same spot, and then he's urging me to open for him, something I'm all too happy to do. His tongue touches mine, warm and wet and seeking—the act of it so desperate, it feels a bit like sex. Like his tongue is fucking my mouth, claiming it, eradicating every other kiss that came before it.

"S'not fair," he rumbles against my lips just before his tongue dips back inside.

I suck in a breath, my lids heavy and my limbs feeling like Jell-O. "What's not?"

One of his hands slips from my hair down to my throat, his palm so wide that it covers the entire expanse of my neck, his thumb sweeping back and forth across my pulse. I can feel the way it pounds under his touch, but I'm still dizzy with the way his tongue slides against mine, the way his knee creeps up between my legs to hold me steady, offering a delicious pressure that makes me want to rock back and forth.

"S'not fair that you're so goddamned beautiful," he rasps.

A sound escapes me that sounds suspiciously like a whimper, and I *do* feel my hips tilting as if they have a mind of their own, the friction of my pussy against his thigh eliciting a shower of sparks between my legs even through my clothes.

I've never felt a need like this; I think if he asked me to lie down on the dirty stone right now, I absolutely would. Every moment he's been insufferable, or annoying, or a downright asshole—now it feels like they were just tiny pieces of kindling. Stacked over one another again and again until one tiny spark set it all ablaze. And now I'm fucking burning.

"Lachlan," I whine, shifting my hips again.

His lips tease the corner of my mouth, drifting down my jaw before he leaves a sucking kiss just below it. "Feels good?"

"Mhm."

His hand finds my waist, the other still tangled in my hair, and then I feel him tug at my hips, forcing me to rock back and forth. "So lovely like this," he murmurs. "All flushed and pink from my kisses."

"Is this insane?"

"Mm." I feel the wet heat of his tongue against my throbbing pulse. "I reckon you've done nothing but make me insane since the moment I met you."

I gasp when I feel his teeth scrape along my skin. "Not exactly a glowing endorsement."

"I told you," he says, his deep brogue heavier and his voice sounding gravelly. "I don't lose control." His lips skirt along my throat until he can kiss the sensitive spot beneath my ear. "But you make me fucking want to."

"I don't mind," I assure him, curling my hands up under his shoulders to hold him closer. My lashes flutter open, finding his heavy-lidded gaze on me. My mouth parts in surprise. "Your eyes."

They're glowing faintly—the usual clear blue seeming to burn with some inner source of light. The colors dance and swirl in a way that feels like blue flames, and I can't seem to look away, utterly hypnotized. I almost imagine a sharp prick against my throat, my scalp, but I'm too mesmerized by the way Lachlan bites his lip as he stares hungrily at my mouth.

I don't feel fear, just that all-encompassing *want* that's overriding my ability to think, and I lean in, ready to beg for more—for anything he'll give me, really—and I'm opening my mouth to tell him that. To tell him he can do anything. That he can *have* anything. That he can—

*Crack.*

We both startle as another plank from the floor above crashes against the old bed, Lachlan tugging me closer to shield me with his body. I can feel how fast his chest rises and falls with each breath when he crushes my face there, and I can feel the rapid beating of his heart even through the layers of his sweater and the shirt beneath. It makes me smile softly against the warm fabric, knowing he's just as affected as I am.

"Maybe this isn't the right place to be doing this," I say into his sweater.

I feel his chest move as he chuffs. "Perhaps not."

I pull away as he looks down at me, and I notice that the glow from moments ago has left his eyes, leaving the usual light blue behind. Still beautiful, but definitely less arresting.

"I . . ."

His eyes search my face as if he's trying to think of some way to explain what just happened, looking like he doesn't quite understand himself. Not that I can blame him. Yesterday, I was pretty sure I wanted to trip him with a large branch. Today . . . Well. *Right now* I'm just thinking about the way his mouth tastes.

"I know," I say, saving him. "That was . . . something."

"Mm." He grins wickedly, leaning down to brush his lips against mine in a barely there kiss. "If I'd known this was the way to make you more agreeable, I might have done it sooner."

I smack his chest, rolling my eyes. "Ass."

"You didn't think that would change because of a few kisses, did you?"

His voice is teasing, and it's that fact alone that has me chuckling instead of kicking him in the shins. It's an awkward affair as he starts to untangle himself from me, and I swear, part of me is incredibly disappointed with the sudden distance. Part of me wants to yank him back and demand he kiss me again like he just did.

But this really isn't the right place for it.

Lachlan clears his throat, his fists clenching at his side as he pointedly looks away from me. "How do we get out of here? Should I give you a boost?"

"Yeah, you might have to," I tell him, looking around.

I'm not thrilled at the idea; with my luck, the rest of the floor will give way as soon as I grip the edge of the hole to pull myself out, but I don't see any other options, considering that this room seems to have no exit.

My brow furrows.

*That doesn't make sense . . . Does it?*

I remember what I saw upstairs that led to me falling down here in the first place—a groove of sorts in the wall that, while inconspicuous, didn't seem . . . quite right. With that in mind, I turn toward the wall behind us, running my hands over the stone in a wide arc.

"What are you doing?"

I shake my head. "I'm not sure. It just feels . . . off."

"Off?"

"Yeah. I can't explain it. It's like . . ."

I frown, my hands stilling. Now that my heart rate has slowed and my mind isn't one big chant of *Lachlan Lachlan Lachlan*—I can feel bits of the energy that had surrounded me while we assessed the carvings on the wall. The carvings left by my *magic ancestor*, no less.

It's like . . . a presence, almost. A heaviness in the air. A whisper of . . . *something* that's urging me to do . . . something.

Honestly, this magic business sort of sucks ass so far.

Still, I follow the urge, grasping at the thin thread of an idea as I continue to search the wall. When my fingers skirt over deeper grooves in the stone, they seem to take a familiar shape.

"Lachlan," I call. "I think there might be a door here."

"Maybe you are a bloody hound," Lachlan mutters, coming up behind me.

I probably shouldn't laugh at that, but one tumbles out of me anyway. I shove my shoulder against the wall and push, but absolutely nothing happens.

"Guess it was a long shot," I mumble. I glance at Lachlan over my shoulder. "Can you . . . ?"

"Yeah. Stand back."

He flattens himself against the wall, clenching his jaw as he starts to push. The tendons in his neck pop out when he shoves on the old stone with all his strength, and after a moment, there are creaking sounds from the other side before a *whoosh* of air—and then the wall swings open.

"Seems you're good for something too," I laugh.

He rolls his eyes, something I can make out even in the thin light. He bends at the waist when the hidden door widens to a large enough crack to slip through, gesturing out an arm.

"After you, Your Highness."

Yep, that's still kind of annoying.

There is a staircase on the other side of the door, narrow and curved as it moves upward, and as I step through the stone that hid the opening, I notice rusted, broken chains on the ground that are still looped through thick hooks embedded in the other side of the door.

I bend, picking up a thick iron lock, rubbing my thumb across the keyhole.

"He really didn't want her to get out," I note.

"Aye," Lachlan says. "Seems that way." I feel him bend beside me, crouching. "Look." He points at the broken chain, noting the link that's pulled apart. "The rust on this link is auld. Hasn't been disturbed."

"So?"

"So this chain was broken centuries ago."

"So . . . he really did help her escape. My ancestor."

He stares at the broken link for several seconds. "They say he fell in love with her while she was a prisoner. That he stole back her bridle and used it to set her free."

If it weren't for all the cursing business, I might almost say that was romantic. I don't think Lachlan would agree, so I keep the thought to myself. I'm quiet as he continues to stare at the chain for another long moment, watching as he finally shakes his head and drops it to the ground.

"We should get out of here," he says. "If we want to make it back before sundown."

"Oh. Right."

He brushes past me to climb the stairs, and I hurry to follow, watching as he reaches the landing and tugs on a thick iron handle that is embedded into the wall. I can hear the groaning of some mechanism on the other side, a *clank clank* sound of gears grinding before the door opens and reveals the room I'd fallen through with the beautiful window.

Lachlan helps me around the yawning hole with my hand in his, and I try not to think about his hands on other parts of my body as I carefully step across the rotten wood planks to more stable footing in the center of the room. I watch as Lachlan eyes the window, and then the door, and then the hole—shaking his head incredulously all the while.

"I can't believe this was here the entire time."

"To be fair," I tell him, "it was really well hidden."

"But . . . if I'd found it sooner . . ."

"Then what? We didn't find anything down there but a rusted bed and some old carvings."

He scrubs his hand down his face. "I don't know. Maybe it would have meant something to my da. Maybe he could have—"

"Lachlan." I step closer, lifting my hand to cup his cheek so I can force him to look at me. "There was nothing you could have done differently. You were just a kid, remember?"

He stares at me for a long moment, his bright blue eyes duller somehow. "Aye," he answers quietly. "S'pose you're right."

"Of course I am," I say, trying to sound lighter as I give his cheek a pat. "Now come on, Nessie. We have to get you back to the loch before you go full dinosaur right here in this castle."

He snorts under his breath even as he turns to follow me when I move for the door. "Anything you say, princess."

I grin. Okay, maybe it's not as annoying as I thought.

The sun is getting low when we arrive at the farm—Lachlan walking me back to the barn before stopping. The loch is in the other direction, so I know it would be silly for him to walk me all the way to the farmhouse only to turn around and head a different way.

For a moment we're just standing there awkwardly, and I know that we're both thinking about what happened down in that room. We didn't really talk about it on the hike back; honestly, we didn't talk about much of *anything*—Lachlan was lost in his thoughts, and I was content to let him process things. But now it's impossible to avoid, a thick tension caught between us that refuses to be overlooked.

"I'm sorry that we didn't find more," I say finally, not knowing what else I can offer him.

He shakes his head. "I told you we wouldn't find anything. So what we found already proved me wrong."

"Right," I say, chuckling softly. "Bet that was hard for you to admit."

A ghost of a smile touches his lips. "Like pulling teeth."

There's another stretch of silence, during which Lachlan's features morph into an expression of deep thought, his eyes averting to the ground as he shifts his weight from one foot to the other. Almost like he's nervous, which seems unlike him.

"Key, about what happened . . ."

"Yeah?"

It's embarrassing how eagerly I press for more, but I can't help it.

The thin line his lips make immediately puts me on edge. "Look," he starts, and I bristle because when is that *ever* good news? "I've been thinking . . . I don't know if it's a good idea."

"Not a good idea," I parrot, feeling my stomach twist. "What do you mean?"

Maybe I'm a glutton for punishment . . . or maybe I just want to hear him *say* it.

He gestures vaguely between the two of us, still not looking at me. "This. Us. Whatever that was . . . It can only make things complicated. Nothing good will come of it."

"Oh."

He takes a deep breath, blowing it out. "There's nothing certain about my future, Keyanna. We know that. I don't know how much time I have before . . ."

Part of me aches for him in a way that doesn't involve wanting him to touch me again, but I can't pretend that disappointment isn't there too.

"I see," I say woodenly.

"Don't," he sighs. "Don't act like that."

"Act like what?"

"Don't act like I'm rejecting you."

"Aren't you?"

He throws his hands up exasperatedly. "I'm trying to do the right thing!"

"Or the easy thing," I counter.

"That's not bloody fair," he growls. "You *know* I'm right. If you and I get involved . . . what then? What happens when there's no end to this damned curse, and I end up a monster forever?"

"That won't happen; we can—"

"You don't *know* that, Key," he half shouts. "You don't. Neither of us do. Besides, what if I *hurt* you?"

"You wouldn't," I answer immediately.

"Not on purpose," he scoffs. "I'm sure my da never meant to hurt my mum, but he couldn't control it. What happens when I can't control it either?"

I notice the panic in his eyes, the real fear in them that tells me he's been obsessing over this the entire trek back—no doubt working himself up into a frenzy about possibilities that might never even happen. Maybe I should be more afraid. Maybe I should consider what he's saying, but I can't help it. Something inside me just *knows* he wouldn't allow himself to hurt me. I don't know how I know, but I do.

I square my shoulders, jutting out my chin. "What if I said that I think you're worth the risk?"

"You barely tolerated me a few days ago," he points out.

I frown. "I didn't? Did I really hate you, or was I just trying to pretend I didn't want you as badly as I did?"

Because I suspect the latter is closer to the truth, analyzing it now. Lachlan has possessed my thoughts for weeks—even when I didn't want him to. Even when I was telling myself I couldn't stand him . . . I couldn't get him out of my head. That has to *mean* something.

His eyes soften a bit, his shoulders slumping as he studies my face, looking . . . tired, mostly.

"It's not for you to decide," he tells me softly. "It's not a risk I'm willing to let you take."

I narrow my eyes, disappointment flooding me like hard water, filling me to the brim until I feel heavy with it.

"Okay," I say after a beat. "If that's what you want."

"It's how it has to be."

I stare at him for another moment, finally shaking my head. "Fine." I take a step closer, pointing a finger at him. "But *you're* the one who's afraid here. Not me."

He laughs, but there's no real humor in it. "I'm starting to think you're not afraid of anything, Key."

I have to shove down the elation his praise brings; that's not what he wants, clearly. And can I even be mad at him? This is his life. I can't hold him to the flimsy promise of *one* kiss. It wouldn't be fair. No matter how wrong it feels.

"I'll keep looking," I tell him instead. "Quietly."

He nods. "I appreciate it."

That's how I leave him, stomping off toward the farmhouse without looking back. No matter how badly I want to. I feel unsettled by the entire encounter, and my distracted state means I don't notice a body blocking the path to the stairs inside the house, and I barrel into it with an *oomph* before hands curl around my shoulders to steady me.

"Key?" Brodie takes in my frazzled state with a furrowed brow. "You all right?"

It takes me a second to catch up with my brain still sizzling with irritation, but after a few seconds of staring at my cousin dumbly, I manage to answer. "Oh. Yeah. Sorry. I'm fine. Just had a weird day."

"You want to talk about it?"

He looks sincere, concerned even—his green eyes emanating a soothing energy that makes me wonder why the twins seem to think he's such a *numpty*, as they put it. He's been nothing but nice to me. Still, I know I can't start spilling my guts about everything I've learned this week. It's not exactly my story to tell.

"It's nothing," I tell him instead. "Really. Just a silly argument."

"Rhona says anything can be fixed with a good cup of tea," he informs me with a soft smile. He leans in, lowering his voice conspiratorially. "Now, the jury is still out on whether or not I can manage a *good* cup of tea, but since she and Finlay have already gone off to bed, I reckon between the two of us, we can whip up something decent."

I chuckle, letting some of the tension unwind from inside me. "Tea sounds great, actually."

"Well, come on into the kitchen, and let's see what we can find."


Brodie hums as he riffles through the cabinets in search of honey, and I watch him work from my seat at the table, holding my cup.

"Know it's here somewhere," he mutters.

"It's really okay," I assure him. "This is fine as is."

He peeks at me from over his shoulder. "You sure?"

"Positive." I gesture to the chair opposite me. "Come sit before yours gets cold."

Brodie sinks down into the chair with a sigh, stretching out his legs and reaching for his cup before blowing on the steaming liquid. I notice that he looks pretty weary himself, and I lean to prop my chin against my fist.

"Seems like I'm not the only one who had a long day."

"Hm?" He meets my gaze, blinks, then waves me off. "Och. Nothing too bad. Got caught in the rain out on the property. Had to huddle in one of the auld outbuildings until it passed. Not exactly a comfortable stay."

My mind wanders to sitting on a patch of hay with a particularly infuriating but handsome Scotsman, and I have to shake away the thought, determined not to go there.

"Were you working with the animals?"

He takes a slow sip from his cup, making a satisfied sound afterward. "Not today. I've been indulging in a wee side project of sorts lately."

"Oh? What's that?"

He eyes me with a somewhat sheepish expression, almost as if he's embarrassed to say. "Something like a genealogical report. Been visiting the family cemetery. Tracing back our family tree."

"Isn't that kind of what you do for a living?"

He glances away, the tips of his ears heating to a shade not totally unlike his hair. "I know it's silly," he says. "Given that I'm supposed to be on sabbatical."

"I don't think it's silly," I chuckle, testing my own tea and taking a slow taste when I find it no longer scalding. "I mean, you obviously enjoy it."

"I do," he says with a small smile. "Even if my da doesn't approve."

I frown. "I still think keeping track of all that history is a hell of a lot more interesting than fishing. No offense."

"None taken," he laughs. "Obviously, I agree. It's just . . . I'm the youngest, aye? I never stood a chance of taking over his business. That was always going to be my eldest brother. The most I could hope for is a life of being pushed around by him as an adult as much as I was as a lad. To be fair, he wasn't the only one."

"Your brothers picked on you?"

"Ah, well, I was a wee thing. Didn't quite grow into my limbs until high school. Easy target and all that."

"They sound like jerks," I scoff.

He laughs harder, his eyes crinkling. "They definitely can be."

"Do you like it better here? With Rhona?"

He shrugs. "Rhona has always been good to me. Honestly, I think she liked having me around because it reminded her of—"

His mouth snaps shut, his eyes rounding as he realizes what he's almost just said, and I feel a clenching in my chest.

"My dad," I finish for him. "Right?"

He nods slowly. "It's not something she ever said. Just a suspicion of mine."

"Yeah," I say quietly. "I could see that."

He regards me thoughtfully for a moment, turning his cup this way and that. "It must be difficult," he muses. "Being here."

"It was," I tell him honestly. "At first. Lately . . . it's been a little better."

*Because I've been too distracted by loch monsters and hot farmhands to have time to be sad*, I don't say.

"I noticed you went off with Lachlan today," he offers, not sounding judgmental, merely curious. "Sort of thought you two didn't get on."

"We didn't," I say, chewing at the inside of my lip. "Not until recently. I mean, he's not as big of a dick as I thought he was when I first met him."

*Don't think about his dick, for Christ's sake.*

"Be careful with that one," Brodie says.

"You don't like him, I've gathered."

He shrugs. "Don't care much about him either way. He was always the popular one when we were lads. We didn't mesh. His da and mine were friends, though. Made for a lot of awkward forced playdates that were mostly just him and his friends ignoring me while I read somewhere quiet."

"He didn't . . . bully you or anything, did he?"

Brodie shakes his head. "Nothing so much as that. He wasn't really anything to me. I think my da only wanted me to get on with him in the hopes I might turn out a bit tougher." His mouth turns down, a wrinkle forming in his brow. "I think my da would have loved to swap sons if he'd been able to."

"That's horrible."

He shrugs again. "It is what it is. S'pose that's why it's hard for me not to bristle around the man. Doesn't help that he's so . . . standoffish."

I snort. "You mean an asshole."

"You said it," he chuckles.

"He really can be," I say. "But . . . I don't know. He's not all bad, I guess."

Brodie's grin turns sly. "Does Key have a wee bit of a crush on the farmhand?"

"What? No!"

Even as I say it, I can feel my cheeks heating, remembering the feeling of his lips on mine, the press of his body against my own. I have to quickly bring my cup to my mouth to hide what must surely be a guilty expression.

I huff after I've set it back on the table, scowling at my cousin. "Don't say anything to Rhona. The last thing I need is for her to think I'm only here to chase after a guy."

"Wouldn't dream of it," he says, still grinning.

I toy with my cup as my thoughts drift exactly where I keep trying to pull them back from, remembering what Lachlan said.

*It's not for you to decide. It's not a risk I'm willing to let you take.*

The memory of the defeat in his tone and on his face threatens to gut me, and I desperately wish that I could do more. To help alleviate some of his burden. Which seems fairly ridiculous, given that I barely know him and it was little more than a week ago that I thought I couldn't stand him.

I flick up my gaze to watch as Brodie takes another sip from his cup, letting words roll around on my tongue as I try to decide the best way to let them out.

"So, your job," I try, keeping my voice casual. "You never did tell me if you had insider info on the Loch Ness Monster."

His brow arches. "You're still on about that?"

"Well, I mean . . . you know the stories about my dad. I can't help but be curious."

"I think if the beast existed," Brodie says, "we would have more than some grainy pictures by now."

"So you've never seen anything about it in, like . . . I don't know. Old family documents?"

He cocks his head. "Family documents?"

I consider how to continue carefully, not wanting to give too much away.

"You know . . . I mean. If the monster *did* exist, there would have to be recordings of the sightings, right? What about the Greer history? Didn't they own this whole area once upon a time?"

"Aye, they did," he says with a confused expression. "But most of their family records burnt up in a fire that caught on the main building back in the eighteen hundreds."

My eyebrows shoot up. "Really?"

"Lachlan didn't tell you?"

"It . . . hasn't come up."

*Too busy trying to stick your tongue down his throat to ask the pertinent questions.*

"Aye, it burned half the building down. Lost a lot of records that year."

"Huh." I toy with the handle of my cup absently. "That must suck for Lachlan."

*It also explains why he still has so little to go on after all this time.*

"I imagine," Brodie says with sympathy in his tone. "I actually oversaw the reconstruction of that wing some time back," he says. "There hadn't been funds to do anything with it before then, so it was mostly empty and half destroyed up until that point. It's right as rain now."

"That must have been interesting," I say. "Find anything cool?"

He blinks back at me, sputtering a bit when his tea seems to go down the wrong way. He beats his chest and coughs to try and right himself, finally shaking his head. "Nothing but some burnt-up documents and smoke-damaged books."

"Oh . . . That's too bad."

"Aye," he sighs. "Always hate to see history lost that way. Makes it too easy for people to try to fill in the blanks with nonsense."

"Yeah, makes sense," I say with a small laugh.

Brodie checks the clock on the wall, frowning at the time. "Och, I'd better get off to bed. Early day tomorrow."

"More work for your side project?"

He looks sheepish again. "I know how silly it is."

"I don't think it's silly at all," I say. "Hell, I'm basically here for the same reasons. Maybe we can compare notes sometime."

Brodie beams at me. "Aye, maybe we can."

He bids me good night then, and I think to myself that it seems a lot of people in town might have misjudged him. He's actually very easy to like once you give him the chance. I certainly felt a bit better chatting with him than I did when I stomped into the house.

I scowl. Just the memory of Lachlan's rejection makes my chest sting, creeping back in through the warmth of the tea and leaving me cold and bitter. I try to remind myself again that it's not fair to hold him to any promises, because he certainly didn't make any. Not that it makes me feel any better.

I carry my irritation throughout the process of washing my cup, then up the stairs toward the small bathroom across from my room as I brush my teeth. I stare in the mirror as I work the brush, cataloging the tiny, fading marks on my throat left by Lachlan's teeth that are hidden by my hair. I can tell they won't be there tomorrow, and the thought of that makes me feel even lower than I already do.

*I want Lachlan.*

The realization hits me harder than it should, because you would think it would be obvious, given how hungrily I'd kissed him earlier, how disappointed I'd been when he suddenly declared we wouldn't be doing it again—but it isn't until this very moment that the extent of *how much* I want him makes itself known.

I want to help him. I want him to have a better life than the

Greers before him. I want to kiss him again, and laugh with him, and find out what more there is to the man underneath the shadow of a monster he desperately wants to escape. Once I get the thought in my head, it burrows deep, refusing to be dug out.

Even lying in my bed later, waiting for sleep I fear won't come, I'm still thinking about him. About the absurdity that Lachlan, the man afflicted with a centuries-old curse that could literally steal his life away, would take it upon himself to protect *me*. As if *I'm* the one who needs saving.

And when sleep finally takes me . . . I find that I'm angry as hell about it.

## LACHLAN

Last night was pure shite, to put it mildly.

Not to say that nights spent as a mythical creature, trying to connect with your monster father who doesn't remember what it was to be human are *usually* good—but last night was particularly awful.

All I could think about was the expression on Key's face when I told her it was a bad idea for us to pursue . . . whatever happened back in the castle. Not because I don't want her—because I'm realizing now that, however impractical, I *really* fucking want her—but because she's already suffered so much. She's *lost* so much. I can't in good conscience risk being another thing she loses.

Maybe that's arrogant of me, assuming anything that might happen between us would be so important that she would mourn it once it was gone. But the way I felt touching her, kissing her . . . it feels like the *start* of something important. More than the quick flings I've sought out with strangers just to satisfy an urge, no, touching Key felt almost . . . like I was meant to touch her. Like it was right somehow.

But that's ridiculous, isn't it?

And I haven't even told her everything. I haven't told her what the rest of the curse entails, what that might mean for her. How would that make her feel? And why does the possibility of hurting her with that knowledge make *me* feel terrified? I don't want to hurt her, I've realized. I don't want to give her any more reasons to be sad. Despite what her family has done to mine, despite whatever part she might have to play in my story . . . it feels like she's suffered enough.

These thoughts continue to swirl around in my head as I make the long trek back toward the farm—the sun just beginning to climb higher in the sky as I trudge down the path that leads away from the farmhouse toward my wee groundskeeper's cottage. There is a moment where I stand still and stare at the larger house up the hill, imagining myself pounding on Key's door and telling her I didn't mean any of it. Telling her that I *am* afraid, but that I think she might be worth it.

And how fucking selfish would that be of me?

I eventually shake away the idea of it, continuing on, not stopping until I'm shutting the door to the cottage behind me and shucking off my wellies as fatigue seeps into my very bones. Not physical, really, but mental is more like. Spiritual, maybe, even. Like every awful thing I've endured in my life has culminated into this one giant pile of shite, burying me alive.

Because maybe there isn't an answer out there for me.

Maybe it is simply my destiny to end up just like my da.

I shrug out of my coat and hang it by the door before I shuffle into the kitchen, hoping that coffee will make me feel more human. I grab the filter from the cabinet and reach for the can with the intention of getting it started, but before I can even fill the canister with water—a heavy banging sounds at my door.

My heart starts to thud in my chest as I turn to look, holding my breath until another loud thud rings against the wood.

"Lachlan! Open the door!"

Is it mental that I feel both elation and dread at the sound of her voice? Has she come to yell at me some more? Maybe to tell me off for being a coward? I probably deserve it, truth be told.

"I'm not leaving until you open the door," she calls.

I open my mouth, my voice sounding a bit hoarse. "You've said that before."

"Yeah. I meant it then, and I mean it now too."

I set the coffee can back on the countertop, my heart pounding against my ribs as I take a step toward my door. I should tell her to go. I know that. There's nothing to be said that can change our situation. No good that can come from torturing myself with the sight of her lovely face.

But I still take another step.

"I mean it, Lachlan," she yells. "Don't make me start singing."

I feel my lips curve into a smile without my permission, and then without even realizing I've crossed the rest of the space, I find my hand on the doorknob, pulling it open to reveal Keyanna MacKay in all her wild-haired, emerald-eyes-burning-with-fury glory.

"Anything but that, lass," I murmur.

"You know"—she presses her fists to her hips, glaring up at me—"I think *you're* the stupid one."

My eyebrows shoot up into my hairline. "Do you, now?"

"I do."

She takes a step toward me, arching an eyebrow in silent question as she waits for me to move. She doesn't speak again until I've turned to the side, watching as she stomps past me and plants herself in the middle of the cottage, that same angry look on her face.

I shut the door, crossing my arms over my chest. "And why's that?"

"Where do I start? First: You make me practically twist your arm into letting me help you." She holds up a finger as if to check off my crimes. "Second: You kissed me." That one has my brow furrowing in confusion, but she barrels on. "And third: You have the audacity to think *you* get to decide whether or not I'm allowed to risk doing it some more."

"Doing what, exactly?"

"Kissing you."

I narrow my eyes. "But you said it was stupid."

"It was stupid because you did it thinking you weren't going to do it again."

"Is that right?"

"It is." She steps closer, glaring up at me. "Did you really think you could kiss me like that and then just never do it again?"

"I didn't say it would be easy," I huff. "I just said it was the right thing."

She nods thoughtfully, that same fury in her eyes when she counters, "Just like I said. Stupid."

And then she surges upward, wrapping her arms around my neck as she plants her mouth on mine.

Every good intention I've been clinging to goes flying out the window when I feel her pressed against me; it's not unlike what I felt yesterday, an overwhelming sense of rightness that I've not felt since . . . Well. Ever, really. Somewhere, deep in my mind, I know that I should push her away. That I should stand my ground to protect her from potential heartbreak.

But I physically can't seem to do that.

Instead, I feel my arms winding around her willowy frame, pulling her closer. I feel my lips part to allow her tongue to swipe against mine, groaning at the taste of her toothpaste and the underlying sweetness that is just her. I can't resist letting my hand trail up her spine to shove into her hair, loving the way the springy, silken curls twist around my fingers.

She smells like something soft and sweet, her shampoo maybe—but she tastes like honey and sunshine and every good memory I've ever had, however few. How can I possibly push her away when she's the first thing I've allowed myself to hope for in years?

She makes a surprised sound when I let my hands slide down to curl under her arse, whimpering into my mouth as I hoist her up against my body. Her legs wrap around my waist, the hardening length of my cock pressed against the warmth between her legs and drawing another groan from deep in my throat.

My lips wander, tasting every part of her skin that's been tempting me, even when I thought of her as my enemy—pressing kisses to her cheek, her jaw, along the soft line of her throat until she's gasping with it. I've never felt need like this; the overwhelming heat of her burrows into me and lights me up like crackling electricity, leaving me suspended between wanting to do this, just this, forever, and wanting to take *everything* she's willing to give.

"We shouldn't," I argue feebly.

She just tilts her head, allowing me better access. "If you stop, I'll kill you."

A hoarse chuckle escapes me just before I feel her fingernails scratching at my jaw, brushing the trimmed hair of my beard, quickly moving to toy with the neckline of my shirt before she gives it a curious tug.

"Can you take this off?"

I grin against her mouth. "I knew you liked the view that day."

"Just shut up and take it off," she grumbles.

"Anything for you, princess."

I drop her to her feet before reaching behind me to pull my shirt over my head, and I can't pretend I don't enjoy the flash of heat in her eyes as she ogles me without it. I keep as still as I'm able as her hands run through the dark hair on my chest, sucking in a breath when her thumb flicks across one of my nipples.

"Careful," I warn.

She bites her lip. "Of?"

"I'm all about fair play," I hum, reaching to toy with the hem of her sweater. "And right now we're a wee bit unbalanced."

Her smile is devilish, and she shoves my hands away before tugging her sweater up and off in one fell swoop, letting it dangle from her finger coyly for a moment before dropping it to the floor.

"How about now?"

I let out a shaky breath, my eyes drinking in the gentle swells and slopes of her body, the creamy skin dotted with freckles that beg to be traced with my tongue. "S'really not fair," I mutter.

She beams wider, hooking her finger through my belt loop and tugging me backward until we're falling onto my too-small bed that's barely big enough for me, let alone the two of us. Still, seeing her splayed out on my sheets is . . . something to behold.

I run my fingers through her hair, dipping my head to trace her collarbone with my lips. I feel her shiver against me when I bring my other hand to her waist to tease her hipbone with my thumb, exhaling roughly against her skin.

"What's happening here, Key?"

She makes an amused sound. "I thought that was obvious."

"Hmm." I lift my head, studying her face. "You're going to have to spell it out for me. Stupid as I am."

She lifts her head, her lips feathering against mine as her hand snakes between us, cupping my clothed cock and rubbing me firmly enough that my vision goes white at the edges.

"Take these off too," she murmurs.

I suck in a breath, rolling my hips against her hands before I even realize what I'm doing. "Are you sure?"

"I told you," she says, kissing me gently. "I'm not the one who's afraid."

"Fuck," I grunt, shuddering when she squeezes my denim-clad cock. "You keep doing that, and this'll be over before I can get the damned things off."

The sound of her laugh lights me up; it's still one of the most unattractive noises I've ever heard, and yet, hearing the pealing sound of it, knowing I caused it—it's damned near like music.

It's a flurry of motion as she helps me shove my jeans off, as I help rid her of hers, moments after spent rutting against her, losing it a bit more every time I feel the heat between her legs enveloping my straining length that threatens to escape my boxer briefs.

It feels surreal that we're here, that she's practically naked in my bed, when a week ago I was pretty sure she hated my guts, and I hers—but is that true, really? I think back to what she said yesterday, about how even when she thought that she hated me, she couldn't get me off her mind. I realize the same can be said for me. Was I really so busy hiding behind all the things I thought I *should* be feeling about her that I was blind to what I actually was?

If the desperation I feel for her right now is any indication, I would say the answer to that question is pretty clear.

The way she's tilting her hips is a clear invitation, but still I find the question falling from my mouth, still not convinced this is real. I can see the pink of her nipples through the lacy bra she's wearing—her breasts two perfect handfuls that make my mouth water. "And you're *sure* this is what you want? I don't—" I swallow around the growing lump in my throat. "I don't want to be another regret for you, Keyanna. You've had plenty."

Her eyes soften, as does her smile, and her hands on my face are heavenly, and I go down easily, meeting her mouth for a kiss that's much softer than the ones we've shared so far.

"I'm sure," she tells me between kisses. "Now please touch me."

And even if my brain is having trouble catching up to this turn of events—my body seems to have no such quandaries.

My hands are shaking when they hook into the elastic of her lavender underwear, a soft, simple cotton that would never be called fancy but somehow is the sexiest thing I've ever seen. Or maybe it's just because it's her.

I peel them off slowly, with a reverence I feel deep in my bones—my breath catching at the sight of neat red curls between her legs. I can't stop staring even as I work her underwear down her legs and toss them aside, the color darker than her hair and such a sharp contrast to her fair skin that I'm hypnotized.

My hands look too rough to be touching her when I let them glide over the tops of her thighs—my tanned skin stark against her pale complexion, my calloused fingers abrasive against the softness of her—and yet she makes the quietest, most enticing noises as I touch her. Like she's as hungry for more as I am. Like she wants this as desperately as I do.

"Wanna taste you," I tell her, flicking up my eyes to meet hers. "Want your cunt in my mouth."

Her cheeks go pink and her lips part, her pupils blown wide. "O-oh. Yeah. Fuck, yeah. Please do that."

"Aye," I chuckle, leaning in and simply inhaling the scent of her—intoxicating enough to give me a headrush. "Since you asked so nicely."

She gasps when I shove her thighs apart. I'm feeling feral at the sight of her so soft and wet and pink, like she's *begging* for my tongue. I've never been with a woman who knew me, *really* knew me—and it's freeing to know I don't have to constantly watch what I do or what I say. That I can just enjoy this. Enjoy *her*.

I nuzzle between her legs as I draw in another lungful of her scent, and the sound she makes is almost one of embarrassment, but the soft moan that follows when I lick at her cunt practically makes her melt.

"*Oh*," she sighs. "Do it again."

I hum my assent as I drag my tongue through the crease of her slowly, savoring her taste and her heat and just *her*, really—closing my eyes when I do it again, letting her sounds guide me. I feel her fingers slide into my hair when I circle her clit with my tongue, feel her tug at the strands when I pull it into my mouth, sucking it hard before releasing it with a wet *pop*.

"God, Lachlan, that's—*fuck*, right there."

I love how vocal she is. How she's just as unafraid to voice her thoughts in bed as she is in any other aspect of her life—and every pleasured sound, every gasped word, just spurs me on further. Makes me that much more desperate to take her apart.

"Prettiest cunt I've ever seen," I murmur, holding her open so I can lap at her, letting my thumb press against her entrance, which is slippery and almost begging for me to dip inside. "You want me here?"

"Please," she sighs, one hand still gripping my hair and the other fisting my sheets. "Just—can you—"

"Shh, I've got you," I practically purr. "I'm going to take good care of this."

She cries out when I finally sink my thumb inside her, wrapping my lips around her swollen clit and sucking it deep. I lift her knee and bring it over my shoulder, gripping her thigh to hold her close as I lose myself in the pleasure of tasting her. My thumb is replaced by two fingers, and she moans at the stretch, making needy sounds as I rub at that spot inside that has her bucking against my face.

"Lachlan!"

"So soft," I murmur, pushing my fingers deeper as I swirl my tongue around the sensitive bundle of nerves. "So pretty." I suction my lips to her center, humming against her as I feel her growing wetter around my fingers, softer, somehow. "Wanna feel you come," I groan as I curl my fingers to stroke her inside. "Can you do that for me?" I let my lashes flutter open, peering up her body to find her flushed and panting above me. "Can you come for me, love?"

"Oh—*oh*."

I feel her thighs begin to quake around my ears as her insides follow suit, and her clit throbs against my tongue as her fingers clench at my hair so tightly, my scalp stings, but even that I welcome, because suddenly everything is hot and wet, and I can *feel* her coming against my tongue.

I can't seem to stop tasting her, touching her—licking at her slick cunt that gushes just for me, slick because *I* made her that way. It's intoxicating, and I can't get enough. In fact, it feels like I could spend forever here, between her legs, watching her come over and over again, but her hands are suddenly tugging at my shoulders, her nails clawing at my skin as she urges me upward.

I crawl over her, covering her body with mine as she pulls me down so that my mouth can slant against hers, and it's even headier knowing she must taste herself on my tongue. My cock is so hard that it hurts now, and she presses her knees against my hips so that I slot between her legs, feeling the slick heat of her soaking the front of my underwear.

She's kissing me like she's starved for it, like she can't get enough, and maybe she won't want more than this, maybe this is as much as she'll want this time, and I realize I'm perfectly content with that. If all she wants from me at this moment is to come apart on my tongue, then I'll consider myself incredibly lucky.

But then she falls back against the bed panting, her eyes glazed and her cheeks pink, purposefully tilting her hips up so that she rubs against me.

"More," she whispers, kissing the corner of my mouth. "I want more."

Her lips find mine, her kisses almost desperate, and it occurs to me all at once—there's a good chance that I'd give Keyanna MacKay anything she asked me for.

## KEYANNA

It seems impossible that I could feel this way—skin tingling and flushed from the orgasm he just gave me, chest heaving as I try and catch my breath—and still want more, but I do. I want *so* much more.

I can feel Lachlan against me, his cock throbbing and so hard that it makes me shiver just thinking about how it will feel inside me, and I realize I've never wanted someone as much as I want him at this moment. Maybe it's the sudden shift of all the intense feelings I've been carrying for my would-be nemesis since I met him. Maybe it's the way he's looking at me like he can't believe I'm real. I honestly can't be certain why I suddenly *need* to be as physically close as I'm able to Lachlan Greer, but I fucking need it. Desperately.

He's taking a little too long for my liking, so I push my fingers under the elastic of his boxer briefs to try to roll them down his hips, hearing his quiet chuckle when I huff in frustration at not being able to get them off.

"Are you in a hurry, Key?"

I pinch the side of his ass, frowning when I can barely even get a grip because of how tight it is. Because of course it would be.

"Are you stalling, Lachlan?"

He leans in, letting his lips ghost over my throat as his fingers slip under the strap of my bra. "Just savoring."

"Can you savor faster?"

"Mm." He slips the strap down my shoulder, kissing a path over my collarbone and licking at the swell of my breast. "No."

My breath catches when he finds my nipple and teases it with his tongue, and suddenly I'm a lot more on board with his train of thought. I arch my back so he can snake a hand beneath me, closing my eyes and doing a bit of *savoring* of my own as he sucks me into his mouth while deftly undoing my bra. It takes him an impressively short amount of time to wrestle it off me, and then his hands are joining the fray as he squeezes and kneads, his thumb circling one tight peak as he continues to use his teeth and tongue to drive me crazy.

I'm not sure that I knew before this very moment how sensitive my breasts were; they're a little more than a handful by most people's standards, but under the weight of Lachlan's massive hands—I feel almost small. With Lachlan's hands on my body and his wide shoulders almost blocking out the light—all of me does, really.

"Fucking hell, Key," he grunts against the wet, kiss-bitten bud of my nipple. "I can feel how wet you are." He tilts his hips again as if to accentuate his point, and I shiver at the contact. "It's driving me mad, love."

*Love.*

It's a silly, spur-of-the-moment endearment, and I know that, know that it's fueled by sex hormones and adrenaline, most likely, but it still makes my insides twist with pleasure. Makes my skin almost burn with a satisfying wave of want.

"You're burning hot, darlin'," he hums, nipping at the swell of my breast. "Don't go setting my sheets on fire, yeah?"

I would roll my eyes, but honestly, it's a legitimate concern.

"Lachlan," I whine, actually *whine*, which might mortify me later. "Can you just—" I squirm beneath him, feeling like I'm about to come out of my skin. "Please?"

He pushes up on his hands, suspended above me and studying me with those icy blues, which are almost burning again. Not glowing, but so bright I could get lost in them.

"Not to be killing the mood," he says with a wince. "But I don't . . . have anything."

I snort, running my hand down the tight muscles of his stomach to give him a squeeze through his underwear. "I'd say you have a lot of something."

"Devil woman," he groans, his lashes fluttering. "You know what I mean."

It dawns on me. "Oh. *Oh.* You mean condoms?"

"It's been . . . a while since I've done this. Haven't had the need for them."

I realize I'm stroking him through the thin cotton, unable to resist touching the hot, hard length of him. Needing to feel it against my skin. He grunts when I slip my fingers under the elastic, wrapping them around his cock and squeezing gently.

"I . . . have an IUD," I tell him. "And I was tested three months ago. I was negative." I feel a single drop of precome beading at the head of his cock, and I smear it around as his gaze goes hazy. "You?"

"Six months," he says hoarsely, nodding. "Haven't been with anyone since."

"Neither have I."

His mouth goes slack as his eyes drift closed, thrusting gently into my fist. "I can't promise you I'll last long in that pretty cunt of yours with nothing between us."

I hook my other arm around his neck, pulling him down to me as my hand on his cock is trapped between us. "I have faith in you."

"Makes one of us," he mutters.

But his lips are already finding mine, and his hands are already shoving at the last barrier between us, freeing the hard length of him so that it slides thick and warm across my belly. He thrusts against me as if on instinct, his big body shuddering as I let my legs fall open.

"Want you," I urge, nipping at his bottom lip. "Please."

I feel his hands on my hips, reaching to cup my ass, holding me open as he makes space between my legs. There is a decadent slide of skin as he strokes through the still-wet mess he made of me with his mouth, his breath huffing against my mouth as he *finally* notches against my entrance.

He pulls back, and it's there now, that glow in his eyes, faint but noticeable. "Look at me."

And I do, holding his gaze as he slowly starts to press inside me. I feel all of him, every hard press of his thick cock as he slowly works it deeper—and with every inch gained, his eyes burn a little brighter. Some part of me *delights* in the idea of him losing control. That *I* could make him do that.

When he's as deep as he can be, and I'm so full of him that I feel overwhelmed with it, I see a flicker of something primal in his gaze as he stares down at me, something that sparks and flares when he slowly rotates his hips, *savoring* me again.

"Och, you feel . . ." His throat bobs with a swallow. "Like a dream."

He meets me easily when I curl my hands over his shoulders and pull him flush against me, my lips kissing everywhere I can reach—his jaw, his cheek, the sensitive shell of his ear—my voice husky when I whisper, "Move."

That first thrust makes me feel like I've touched a live wire, sending a current down every inch of me as I gasp in surprise. Lachlan's hands grip me—one burrowing beneath me to hold me tightly against him as the other molds to my hip—and I can feel the warmth of his breath against the hollow of my throat as he buries his face there before doing it again. And again. And *again*.

"Fuck," he growls, his hips finding a steady, rolling rhythm that sets off a tiny shower of sparks every time he bottoms out. "You're practically leaking for me, aren't you, Key?" And he's right, I've never been so wet. I can't seem to muster up a shred of embarrassment. Not with how good he's making me feel. "Aye, you're going to make a mess of my sheets." His voice is harsh and deep, his accent getting thicker. "I ken they'll smell of you for days. I want to sleep with the smell of your pretty cunt and remember how tight you squeezed my cock when I fucked you."

I wrap my legs around his waist, feeling a steady, familiar pressure building inside with every stroke. His teeth sink into my skin, the sting at my shoulder making me only burn hotter as my mouth falls open in surprise. His tongue is there immediately, soothing the mark he's most definitely left behind, and I can feel our bodies growing slick against each other as he starts to move faster.

"That's it, love," he coos. "I can feel you getting wetter. Getting so fucking tight. You gonna come for me?"

"Yeah," I breathe, clinging to him. "Keep going. Right there. Don't—*ah*."

I jolt when I feel a sharp, piercing sting against my hip, and Lachlan immediately goes still—pulling back and blinking as if coming out of a daze. I can feel him throbbing inside me as if desperate to keep going, but once he notices my expression, blinking down at where his hand still clutches my hip, a look of horror passes over his features.

He scrambles away from me so quickly, I barely even have time to register what's happened; one moment he's between my legs and on the cusp of giving me what felt like the most spectacular orgasm I've ever had, and then the next he's pressed against the headboard, looking a little green.

"Key," he says hoarsely. "I'm so sorry. I didn't mean to."

I blink in confusion, following his line of sight and finally noticing the thin cuts along my hip, a slow trickle of blood escaping them.

"Wha—" I sit up, pressing my fingers to them. "The hell?" My head snaps up, my eyes finding his fists clenched at his sides, noticing for the first time the sharp-looking black claws protruding from the ends of his fingers. "Whoa."

Lachlan still looks like he might be sick. "I didn't mean to. I'm so sorry."

"What?" My nose scrunches, glancing back down to the scratches—if they're even worth being called that—and frowning. "It's nothing, Lachlan. It just surprised me."

He shakes his head, his eyes wide. "I hurt you. I lost control. I told you this would happen. I told you that I—"

"Hey, it's okay," I tell him, scooting closer even as he flinches. "I mean it. It's fine."

"I *hurt* you."

I want to sympathize with what he's going through right now, and I do, to some degree, but my body is still very amped up and confused as to why it was robbed of that spectacular orgasm, and frankly, missing out on it because of a few scratches seems ludicrous.

I crawl over to him before he has a chance to slither away, straddling his waist and gripping his hair in my hands so that I can force him to look at me. He still looks like a kicked puppy, so I give his hair a sharp tug, sharp enough that he hisses with it.

"Did that hurt?"

He narrows his eyes. "It's not the same."

"No?" I lean into him, sinking my teeth into his shoulder hard enough to leave a mark. "And that?"

"I see where you're going with this," he huffs, "but it's different. I could really hurt you."

"You won't," I assure him. "I know you won't."

"You don't *know* that."

"No I don't," I tell him, leaving kisses up his throat. "But I trust you."

I feel his fingers tentatively sliding over my hips—clawless now—and despite the sudden stumbling block, I can also feel the stiff length of him against my stomach, and my stomach flutters at the knowledge that he's wet because of *me*. Because he was inside me. Honestly, that thought is way more important to my lizard brain right now than a few scratches.

"You should be more afraid, Key," he sighs, his head falling back against the wood as I tease the spot behind his ear with my tongue. "More cautious."

"Maybe *you* should be *less* cautious," I counter, rolling my hips so that my pussy glides over his erection. "I'm not afraid of you." I press my teeth to his earlobe, nibbling it until he shivers. "Besides," I hum, continuing to tease him with my teeth and tongue. "It's kind of hot."

His fingers grip my ass, pulling me against him until there's no space between us. His head turns so that his mouth can find mine, his tongue plunging inside as he seems to lose himself again, if only a little.

"I never want to hurt you," he mumbles against my mouth.

I kiss him gently, pushing up on my knees and reaching between us to guide him between my legs, hearing his sharp intake of air as I start to sink back down. "Then don't."

"*Fuck*, Key."

His face crushes to my chest; my hands are in his hair and his are gripping my hips tight as he starts to thrust up into me—losing himself to the sizzling energy that seems to surge between us. I close my eyes and give in to it myself, focusing only on the way he fills me, the *heat* of him as he plunges deep inside over and over.

I can feel my orgasm roaring back to life, can feel it cresting higher with every slide of his cock against that sensitive place inside that has my vision blurring and my heart thudding hard inside my chest.

"Come for me," he grates, a command and a plea all at once. "I want to feel that perfect cunt come all over me."

It might be the first time Lachlan has ever told me to do something that I don't immediately feel the urge to contest. Not that I even stand a chance to. It's too late for that. My body lights up, my head falling back and my mouth opening on a wail as I fall over the edge. Lachlan keeps fucking me through it, making it seem to go on forever until my body feels like one giant exposed nerve, like every touch sets me off all over again.

"That's it," he gasps, his hips falling off rhythm. "That's a good lass. Feels so good inside you. You're going to take everything I give you, yeah? Every"—his words come through gritted teeth now—"fucking"—I can feel the way his cock bucks inside me, setting me off anew—"*drop*."

Lachlan grinds me on his cock when he comes, a harsh shout falling from his mouth as he shivers against me, as he twitches inside. I can feel all of it—the heat of his come, the flex of his cock—and I stare at the ceiling without really seeing it, still gasping for breath.

The lights above us start to flicker—the bulbs going out just to spark back to life—almost as if in time with the trembling of my body. I watch it happen in wonder, still struggling to catch my breath. They keep up their flickering, each light returning somehow brighter than before, finally growing so bright, they start to hum. The noise climbs higher and higher, and then a sudden *pop* sounds all over the room—every light in Lachlan's place burning out all at once.

Dazedly, I slowly regain awareness of Lachlan's forehead resting against my neck, my fingers starting to card through his hair as if they have a mind of their own.

"Did you break my house?" he rasps against my skin.

"Mm." I let my lips nuzzle his hair. "I think so."

"I suppose that speaks volumes about my performance," he says with a chuffed laugh.

I tug his hair lightly, clucking my tongue. "Don't let it go to your head."

"Och, it's far too late for that."

I feel myself grinning, so content in this moment that I have no desire to move. We stay like that for a little while, neither of us really seeming to want to go anywhere, and for the life of me, I can't say how long it takes the both of us to come back down from what just happened. I'm not even sure I care to know.

Because two things are glaringly obvious to me at this moment. The first is that I absolutely want to do that again. And the second? Well. Lachlan was right. He was absolutely right.

If I lose him . . . I'm going to fucking regret it.

## LACHLAN

"If you don't stop looking at me like that, I'm going to smother you."

I blink when I notice Key is scowling at me from across the table, realizing I'd been staring at the bandage that is just barely peeking out from the hem of my shirt she's wearing. Honestly, just the sight of her in my clothes would be enough to have me staring—but I can't pretend that I'm not still internally wincing at the thought of hurting her, even when she insists she's fine.

"I should have been more careful," I grumble, taking a sip from my coffee mug.

She waggles her eyebrows as she says, "I like you not being careful, actually."

"Keyanna MacKay," I say with a chuckle. "Are you flirting with me?"

"I'm wearing your shirt and no underwear," she scoffs. "I think the time for flirting has passed."

"Don't remind me," I groan. "I have things to do today that don't involve taking you back to bed."

She blinks prettily back at me. "Are you sure?"

"Devil woman," I mutter, finishing my cup.

It's strange—or rather, it's strange how *not* strange it is—Key in my space. Her looking at me like she's thinking about me touching her again rather than with vague annoyance. I rather like it, truth be told.

"Has it ever happened before?"

I cock my head. "What?"

"Have you ever lost control like that?"

"No." I shake my head fervently. "Never. I'm usually very . . . careful."

Her grin is wide, and truthfully, rather smug. "So it's just me, then."

"Don't let it go to your head," I scoff, echoing her words from earlier.

"Oh, it's *far* too late for that." She giggles prettily, stretching her arms over her head in an enticing move. "So what *is* on the agenda for today?"

I set my cup on the table, leaning back in my chair. "Feed the cows, for one."

"Ugh." She shudders, making a face. "Pass."

"What happened to you being a dutiful wee farmhand for your granny?"

"I have you for that now," she says sweetly.

"Oh, do you now?" I arch a brow at her. "One romp, and you think I'll be at your beck and call?"

"I think I could persuade you to relieve me of any cow-related duties."

I snort, shaking my head. "They're basically giant puppies. They wouldn't hurt a fly."

"You said they might bite!"

"Aye, but that's because you were being vexing."

She narrows her eyes. "Ass. Okay, fine. I'll help . . . from a distance."

I watch as she takes another sip from her mug, drawn to the way her lips shape against the rim and remembering how soft they felt against mine. Which only makes my thoughts tumble down the memories of how she felt against me, how hot she was inside, how fucking desperate I am to touch her again, wondering how soon I *can* drag her back to my bed.

How on earth did I ever think I didn't like this woman?

I might be a wee bit obsessed with her, actually. Not even sure when or how it happened.

"So what else?"

I've apparently zoned out again, blinking back stupidly as she regards me. "Hm?"

"Lachlan Greer," she says sweetly. "Are you distracted?"

"Immensely," I answer, seeing no reason to lie.

Either her laugh is starting to sound attractive—or I really am going mental.

"I have to help Blair and Rory start setting up for the games later," I tell her distractedly, getting up from the table with the intention of stashing my mug in the sink.

She perks up. "Games?"

"They didn't tell you?"

"I've been in the pub like three times," she points out.

"Right, right," I answer, rinsing out my cup. "They have a festival of sorts every year on the anniversary of the pub's opening." I spread my hands out in the air for a bit of flourish. "The Greerloch Highland Games. They model it around the legend where it got its name."

"The one about the gnome and the giant's daughter?"

"Aye. They have all sorts of competitions, but mostly just a lot of folks getting steamin'. It's happening this weekend."

"Are you going to the games?"

"No." I snort. "I've got better things to do with my time than toss logs around and jump through tires."

"Okay, but that sounds fun actually."

I don't like the look in her eyes. "No."

"Could be a good idea," she presses. "Lots of people there, I imagine. Give us an excuse to chat folks up about our family histories."

I cross the distance from the counter to the table, leaning to press my palms to the top of it as I cock an eyebrow at her. "You just expect to waltz up to people and start asking questions?"

"If they're all as 'steamin',' as you say"—she makes air quotes around the word—"I doubt anyone would suspect anything about some harmless small talk from the weird American."

"Why does it feel like you're just trying to trick me into socializing?"

"Because," she says with a grin, reaching to trace a finger across the back of my knuckles, "you're kind of a grumpy asshole, and it would do you some good."

I turn her chair to face me as I drop down to crouch between her legs, giving in to the urge to touch her again as I palm the outside of her thighs. "Is that right?"

"Mhm." Her knees part ever so slightly, and I can hear the way her breath has quickened. "I think so."

"I could think of several things that I would rather be doing than socializing," I tell her.

Her smile is coy. "Why put off for tomorrow what you can do today? Or right fucking now, actually."

"Now you're making sense," I hum, turning my face to press a kiss to the inside of her knee. "Scoot up a wee bit, and I'd be happy to oblige."

The way she rushes to do as I've asked would make me want to tease her any other time, but when she parts her legs, I seem to forget what words are.

"I thought you had to feed the cows," she says breathily as I grasp her by the knees and throw them over my shoulders.

She gasps when my tongue first swipes between the already-slick folds of her cunt, and I shudder at her taste. "After you feed me, I think."

Her groan could be from the bad joke or my touch.

I quickly become too distracted to ask.

Three hours later, I find myself surrounded by dozens of people in the field behind The Clever Pech, watching Key chat with Rory a few meters away from where I've been stacking old whiskey barrels. She did end up helping me feed the cows—although I suspect what I did to her in my kitchen may have made it hard for her to say no— and since she did not, in fact, get mauled by one of the overgrown hairy puppies, she seems up to doing it again. Maybe.

And what's stranger than that is that I *want* her to do it again. I want her to help me every day. Hell, I just want her around. I wonder all over again how my attitude toward the smart-mouthed, beautiful redhead could have done such a one-eighty so quickly.

"If you keep staring at her like that, you're likely to burn a hole in her face."

I shoot a glare at Blair's smirking face, dropping the barrel I had definitely just been standing there holding and trying not to look guilty. "Don't know what you mean."

"Oh, I think you do," she laughs. "I know a moonstruck numpty when I see one." She elbows me in the side. "What exactly happened at Greer castle, eh?"

I grunt, picking up another barrel and moving it to the end of the line where the obstacle course is going up. "Don't you have other people to bother?"

"But you're my favorite person to bother," she says sweetly, fluttering her eyelashes.

"I'll have to let Molly know she's been replaced."

Blair narrows her eyes before turning her head to gaze at the daughter of the feed shop owner with interest, watching Molly tie a ribbon between two trees to mark a finish line.

"Still haven't puzzled whether or not she'd let me toss her around a bit," Blair muses.

I shake my head. "You really are no better than a man."

"Don't be sexist," she tuts. "And stop trying to distract me. You've been making goo-goo eyes at Keyanna since the two of you showed up here. *Together*, I might add. Don't think I didn't notice."

"We do live in the same place," I point out.

Blair stares at me with open disdain for several seconds, finally blowing out an exasperated breath. "All right, then. Keep your secrets."

"You expecting a big turnout this year?" I ask, changing the subject.

She bobs her head. "Oh, aye, aye. Isla says her boys are coming in from uni."

"More twins?" I make a face. "Just what we need."

"They're big and strapping and can throw the tires around. They'll make for good eye candy."

I frown at that, sneaking a glance at Key. Isla's boys aren't that much younger than her. I wonder . . . I shake my head. I'm enough of a beast without working myself into a tizzy about fictional situations regarding the woman I've slept with *once*.

Even if I'm desperate to do it again.

"I saw that," Blair teases.

I turn away from her. "Don't know what you're talking about."

"Maybe I should ask Key to play the prize this year, eh?"

I turn on my heel, narrowing my eyes. "What are you on about?"

"Ha!" She points at me as if she's made some great discovery. "Didn't like that, did you?"

"You're a horrible, horrible friend," I grouse.

She blows me a kiss, looking too smug for my tastes. "I'm an excellent friend. In fact, let me show you." She cups her hand over her mouth, shouting before I have a chance to stop her. "Oi! Keyanna!"

I watch as Key turns our way, seeing Blair waving her over and immediately excusing herself from Rory and his task of setting out folding chairs to make her way toward us.

"Yeah?"

"Key, darling," Blair coos. "Has Lachlan told you about the prize for the games?"

Key's face scrunches. "No?"

"Och, well. I told you the story of how the pub got its name, aye? The maiden and the pech?"

"Yeah, I remember."

"Well, you see, every year we have a maiden pose as the 'prize,' and the winner of the games wins a kiss from her."

Key cocks her head. "That doesn't seem very in line with the story."

"Yeah, well." Blair shrugs. "It gives the gents motivation to work hard, which gets 'em good and thirsty, which means more beer sales for me, aye?"

"I don't think I'm going to like where this is going," Key says.

I cross my arms over my chest, glaring at my friend. "She doesn't need to be ogled for an entire day, Blair."

"Nonsense," Blair hums, reaching to pet Key's hair as if she were a kitten she was trying to persuade to come home with her. "Key wants to help." Blair gives Key her best pout, and I have to stifle a groan at her shady tactics. "Don't you?"

"Oh, well . . ." Key gives her a wry smile. "I guess if it will help . . ."

"That's the spirit!" Blair clasps her on the shoulder, winking at me in triumph. "Everyone will be thrilled to hear it."

Rory calls her name then, and I continue to glare at her as she flounces away, not realizing I'm doing so until Key pokes me in the side.

"Stop making that face," she says. "It'll get stuck that way."

"You didn't have to agree to her shenanigans," I tell her.

She shrugs. "What can it hurt? Doesn't sound like I'll have to do much."

"You'll have to kiss whichever lout wins the games!"

Her grin is Cheshire-like. "Are you jealous, Lachlan?"

"I . . ." My lips press together as I clear my throat. "No."

Key's fingers trail up my forearm, leaving goose bumps behind that I suspect have nothing to do with the chill in the air. "Maybe you should enter. Just to make sure no one else gets the chance."

"Is that right?" I loom over her, feeling my lips twitch. "Remind me . . ." I reach to pluck at a stray curl, twirling it around my finger. "Whose bed were you in this morning?"

Her eyes widen, her pupils dilating slightly, and she opens her pretty pink mouth, only to snap it shut, turning her face toward the sound of an approaching vehicle coming from around the front of the pub.

"That's my grandparents," she notes.

I glance over my shoulder. "Aye, Finlay will be bringing the hay bales, then."

"Hay bales?"

"For the obstacle course."

She smiles again, her wee bunny teeth on full display, and I feel a squeezing sensation in my chest. She's as adorable as she is desirable, and it seems that the combination is a surefire way to leave me dizzy.

"Yeah," she chuckles. "I think I am going to have to insist you enter these games."

"Only because you'd like me to win you, aye?"

Her emerald eyes dance with humor as she lifts one shoulder casually. "Guess you'll have to enter and see, hm?"

I'm cursing the way the sun is already high in the sky—knowing there aren't enough hours left in the day to drag her back to my place and remind her who had her screaming only this morning. Maybe spank her pretty arse for being such a tease.

But Finlay's hand clapping my back quickly yanks me out of thoughts of defiling his granddaughter.

"All right, Lachlan?"

I give the smaller man a thin smile. I like Finlay, and I'm pretty sure he's a genuinely decent person, but he's still a MacKay. Trusting him doesn't feel natural.

I blanch at the thought.

*So why does trusting Keyanna come second nature?*

"All right," I tell him, pushing away the thought. I nod toward Hamish and Malcolm, who are climbing out of the large truck attached to Malcolm's trailer. "I see you managed to put those two to work."

"Oh, aye, aye," Finlay laughs. "Had to drag Hamish away from the herd for a day." He eyes Key standing beside me, moving in close to throw his arms around her. He's so much shorter than her that they land practically around her middle. "And how's my favorite granddaughter this afternoon?"

"I'm your only granddaughter," she reminds him with a laugh.

"Och, we don't know that," he says. "I was quite the catch back in my day. Who knows whether or not I—"

He jolts when Rhona's hand smacks him on the back of his head. "Quit your yapping." She clucks her tongue. "Honestly." She regards Key, her gaze much warmer than it has been in the past. "All right, Keyanna?"

"I'm good," Key answers with a shy sort of smile.

I've gathered that their relationship is still a bit strained, but I can tell the auld gal is making strides to get to know her granddaughter. I can also tell that it seems to bring Key a good deal of peace.

"Key," Finlay says. "Come and meet Malcolm, aye? His father and I were mates back in school." He winds his arm through hers, tugging her along. "Now, don't listen to a word he says about me."

Key flashes me a small smile before she lets herself be dragged away, leaving me half pining after her and trying my best not to let it show. Apparently, I don't do a very good job.

"Don't hurt her," Rhona says beside me, making me startle a bit.

"What?"

Rhona's gaze is assessing and almost cold, looking as if she trusts me as much as I do her. Which is to say not as much as I could. "You heard me. Be good to her."

"I don't know what you're—"

"Och. Save it." She waves me off. "I'm too auld and too tired for games. You just be good to my granddaughter, and everything will be just fine, aye?"

"I . . ." I shut my mouth at the look in her eye, giving her a stiff nod. "Aye."

She offers me a curt nod in return. "Good. Then that's all settled."

"Rhona," a new voice says from behind us. "Where do I take these pies?"

I can't pin what it is about Brodie MacKay that makes my mouth turn down in a frown anytime he's near; sure, we've never really got on, but before coming back here, I hadn't seen the man in nary a decade, and yet still he acts like I kicked his puppy every time we're in the same room together. Even when we were kids, and I would try to include him, he'd always acted like he was just a bit better than everyone else. I remember his father being funny, if not a wee bit too loud at times—but Brodie has always been the opposite. Always quiet, always out of the way. Maybe that's why we never clicked.

Brodie notices me watching him, his face cool and expressionless as he tips up his chin. "Lachlan."

"Brodie," I offer back.

"You can take the pies to the fridge in the back of the pub," Rhona tells him. "Just make sure to hide them under the heads of lettuce so Fergus doesn't get into them before this weekend."

He nods at his aunt, eyeing me again for another moment before stalking off toward the pub. I see him stop to say hello to Finlay and Key, and Key smiling brightly at her cousin makes my stomach twist. Not in any sort of misguided jealous way, because I'm all too aware that they're family—but there's something about seeing them together that still doesn't sit right with me. Maybe it's because he doesn't hide the fact that he doesn't care for me. Maybe it's just that my mistrust of her family and their threat to my future seems to extend to Key now as well. Which, I'm more than aware, makes no sense, because they are *her* family.

It seems Keyanna MacKay is the exception to all of my rules.

Rhona barks something at Blair from across the field and stalks off toward her, seeming to have forgotten that she was threatening me. I find myself standing by Malcolm's truck, catching Key's eye as Malcolm and Finlay guffaw over something one of them has just said. I nod toward the other side of the building once before turning and walking that way, not checking to see if she's following.

This side of the pub faces the woods, nothing back here as I lean against the wall, waiting. It doesn't take her more than a minute to round the corner, and I take her by surprise by throwing my arms around her waist and pulling her against me.

"Someone could see us," she laughs.

I'm distracted by her mouth, but I manage, "Let them."

"Wow, we have sex one time and suddenly you're going all caveman on me."

I arch a brow. "I didn't mean it like that. I just meant—"

Her hand over my mouth followed by her wide grin gives me pause.

"I'm kidding," she says. She pulls her hand away, pressing a kiss to my mouth, which immediately makes me lean in to taste more of her. "I kind of like the idea of you going all caveman."

"That so?"

I hoist her up a wee bit higher by the waist, forcing her up on her toes as I cover my mouth with hers. I take all I can as quickly as I can, trying to memorize the feel and taste of her before I'm forced to leave her for the night.

My lips linger for another second before I pull away, letting my head thump back against the wall. "Things seem to be going better with your family."

"I think so," she says with a small quirk of her lips. "Things have been . . . a lot easier recently."

"Seems even your dear cousin has brought you around."

She barks out a laugh. "What did Brodie ever do to you?"

"Nothing." I sniff indignantly. "Just don't trust him is all."

"You know he works for the historical society," she tells me. "He could probably be a real help. I actually asked him about your family records." She frowns then. "You didn't tell me they were lost in a fire."

"I did tell you they'd been lost," I remind her.

"But I didn't know that they literally burnt up!"

"Does it matter how they went? They're gone. That's all that matters."

"But maybe Brodie could—"

"I don't want his help," I say firmly, more firmly than I intend to.

She presses her palms to my chest, her brow knitting. "I don't think you have the luxury of being stubborn. We don't know how much time you have."

"He's a MacKay," I remind her stubbornly.

She lifts one delicate brow, looking almost amused. "So am I, re-member?"

And there it is again, the reminder that for all intents and purposes—she's my enemy. My da would be furious if he knew I was letting her help me. That I was touching her. That I felt so . . . possessive of her. Key is a MacKay, and that hasn't changed. It's just *me* who seems to have completely disregarded that fact.

"Aye," I answer quietly. "I remember."

"Just think about it, okay?"

"I'll . . . think about it," I concede.

She grins, pressing up on her toes to leave another kiss at my mouth. "Good." She eyes the sun with a wary expression, noticing, just as I have, that it's begun to sink. "You'd better get out of here."

"I know," I sigh.

I tilt my neck until my forehead rests against hers, content to just breathe her in for a second. I know I have to let her go, that it's much too soon to allow anyone to actually come back here and spot us—too many questions to come with that—but still. I feel . . . almost at ease here with her. Like for once there's nothing to worry about in this tiny corner where she's the sole object of my attention.

"Wait for me in my bed," I tell her.

I feel her smile. "Yeah?"

"I'll leave the door unlocked."

"Well, that's just not safe. You'll end up with all kinds of scary things in your place."

I pull back to give her a wolfish grin. "I'm the scariest thing there is, remember?"

I can hear voices not far from us, and I heave out a sigh as I start to untangle myself from her, hating every second of it. She's quietly laughing at what I've said as my hands fall from her waist, and her hand comes to pat my cheek.

"Sure you are, Nessie. Sure you are."

She saunters away from me back toward where the others are still working, and it takes every ounce of my restraint not to follow after her like a lost pup. The only thing that stops me is the sinking sun behind me, a physical reminder of all the reasons why I can't do whatever I want. It feels heavier today, this burden. It presses down on me like a physical weight, and I have a sneaking suspicion I know exactly why that is.

And I think I just watched her walk away from me.

## 21

KEYANNA

I wake up on the morning before the games still exhausted and slightly hungover; last night Finlay roped me into a card tournament with him and Brodie, and whatever I'd let him slip into my tea to "spice it up" had slowly crept up on me, leaving me much tipsier than I meant to get. The resulting headache at the breakfast table is a fair reminder of why I don't drink much. I didn't even sneak into Lachlan's place last night, stumbling upstairs and crashing in my own bed instead.

"You look about as hinging as I feel," Brodie rumbles from the doorway, shuffling into the kitchen and moving to the fridge.

I rub my temples. "Does hinging mean hungover as fuck?"

"Aye, pretty much," he chuckles. "Where's the bloody orange juice?"

"You're drinking *orange* juice after last night?"

"Always did well for an upset stomach," he tells me. "Don't know why, but it's a sure fix for me."

"I'll stick to tea that *isn't* spiked with whatever Grandpa put in it last night."

"That'll be The Famous Grouse," Brodie tells me.

"What?"

"Finlay's favorite whiskey," he explains, pulling a carton of orange juice from the fridge. Just looking at it makes my stomach turn. "He likes to make toddies with it, but they're deadly."

"Obviously," I snort.

The man in question strolls into the kitchen as if summoned, looking entirely too chipper for my tastes. "Morning," Finlay says cordially. "How are we all feeling on this fine day?"

Brodie glares at my grandpa as he drinks straight from the carton, and I have to say that as much as I've come to adore Finlay, I'm tempted to do a bit of glaring myself.

"How are you fine?" I ask him. "I feel like I've been run over by a truck."

"Aye, that'll be your delicate American sensibilities," Finlay laughs.

Brodie makes a disgruntled sound. "That doesn't explain why *my* head is throbbing."

"You've always been a lightweight," Finlay tells him with a wave of his hand.

Rhona enters the kitchen then, clucking her tongue at Brodie, who's still holding his orange juice. "What have I told you about drinking from the carton?"

"Sorry," Brodie offers with a wince. He shoots another withered look toward Finlay. "Your husband tried to poison us last night."

"I told the both of you to go on to bed," Rhona scoffs. "It isn't Finlay's fault you don't listen."

Brodie settles into one of the chairs at the table, groaning softly. He leans in closer to me, lowering his voice. "He got us steamin' so he could win at cards."

"I heard that," Finlay calls from across the kitchen. "Don't need you to be steamin' to beat you at cards." He gives me a pointed look. "Brodie is terrible at cards. No poker face, that one."

"I've got a perfectly good poker face," my cousin grumbles.

I laugh despite the fresh throbbing it sets off in my temples, and graciously accept the cup of tea Rhona offers even though it comes with a disapproving look.

"Drink it slow," she says softly. "Don't upset your stomach."

I give her a shy smile. "Thank you."

Our relationship still isn't flowers and rainbows after the talk we had, but I'm happy to be able to say that it has improved, at least. I can tell with every interaction between my granny and me that she's trying her best, and honestly, that's more than enough for me.

I'll need to find Lachlan after I finish my tea; given that he's found me in his bed every morning for the last three in a row, I'm sure he'll be wondering where I am when he gets back from his night at the loch. It occurs to me that I don't even have his phone number. Hell, I haven't even seen him *with* a phone. It's so strange to be in a position where I haven't found myself checking it consistently, a far cry from life back in New York, to be sure. I actually kind of like it.

I hear a door open and shut from the front of the house just as Rhona is asking me how I like my eggs, and within seconds, the kitchen entry is filled with a very frazzled-looking Lachlan, appearing as if summoned by my thoughts. His hair is windswept and his blue eyes are wide when they land on me, but there is an instant softening in them when they meet mine, like a tension ebbing out of them. Was he worried about me?

"Lachlan," Rhona greets. "Come for breakfast?"

He blinks twice as if coming out of a daze, tearing his gaze from mine and turning to Rhona. "What? Oh. No. I was just . . ." His mouth closes before opening again, struggling to come up with a good reason for being here, no doubt. "I was—"

"Sorry," I offer, saving him. "I know I told you I'd meet you at the barn this morning, but *someone*"—I give my grandpa a scathing look—"got me drunk while playing cards last night."

Lachlan looks confused for only a moment before it seems to dawn on him. "Oh. Right." He shuffles his weight from one foot to the other. "It's no issue. I can teach you how to move the hay another time."

"Well, you're here," Rhona says gruffly. "You might as well stay and eat."

"No, I wouldn't want to impose—"

Rhona furrows her brow, causing Lachlan to let whatever objections he'd been about to offer die on his tongue. He gives her a clipped nod instead, moving farther into the kitchen and taking a seat on the opposite side of the table from me. His eyes furtively seek mine, and I give him a smile that I hope conveys my apology for getting him into this mess. I know he's still uneasy around my family.

Finlay drops into the chair beside Lachlan. "You were going to show Keyanna how to use the tractor, then?"

"Ah . . . Yeah." Lachlan clears his throat. "She was curious."

Finlay beams at me. "Practically an auld hand at this now, aren't ya?"

"Hardly," I scoff. "The cows still sort of terrify me."

Lachlan's lips twitch. "She's convinced they're going to eat her."

"Well, maybe if *someone* hadn't implied that the very first time I saw one . . ."

His mouth curls into a full-blown grin now. "Can't help it that you're so gullible, princess."

I narrow my eyes at him, wanting to chide him about the dumb nickname, but unfortunately, it's started to have the opposite effect on me. Now instead of filling me with flushed irritation, it warms me for a different reason altogether. Reasons we'd probably be exploring right now had he found me in his bed instead of my grandparents' kitchen table.

"I was scared of the cows when I was a lad," Brodie tells me. "Course, I thought they would trample me. I eventually grew out of it."

"I can't tell if you're on my side or not," I say grumpily.

Brodie shrugs. "I'm on no one's side. Just making conversation."

Lachlan is eyeing my cousin with a look that barely contains his wariness, and I remember how he'd said he'd consider it, the idea of letting Brodie help us. We haven't talked about it since that day behind the pub, and I wonder if now is a good time to warm him to the idea.

"Has Brodie told everyone about his side project?"

Rhona turns from the stove to eye us from over her shoulder. "What?"

"He's been researching the MacKay family tree," I clarify.

Brodie blushes slightly, averting his eyes. "S'just a silly way to pass the time."

"I think it's a wonderful idea!" Finlay exclaims, ever the optimist. "There's all sorts of good stories from our family." He nudges Lachlan in the ribs gently, chuckling. "Why, Lachlan's family and ours used to be mortal enemies once upon a time!"

I try to contain my wince as I watch Lachlan's expression go blank, like he's forcing it. This definitely backfired quickly.

Lachlan's voice is flat when he says, "Is that so?"

"Oh, aye," Finlay barrels on. "Don't know the details meself, but my grandpa told me a story once of some skirmish over land. Apparently, the first parcel the MacKays settled on was Greer land at the time!"

Lachlan's jaw ticks, and I know he's doing his best to contain his discomfort, given that it's obvious Finlay has no idea what sort of wound he's poking at, and knowing that makes my stomach clench in sympathy.

"I've heard something similar," Brodie comments.

Trying to save the situation, I chime in, "It's too bad Lachlan's family records burnt up. It would be neat to know the real story." I pause a beat, trying to appear casual as I add, "I wonder if there are MacKay records that would clarify?"

"I haven't seen much mention of the Greers in what I've been able to get my hands on," Brodie admits.

"Could be a fun side quest for your project," I urge. "Maybe we could take a trip to Inverness! Do some digging." I smile in Lachlan's direction, noticing his face is still carefully blank. "Would be very Indiana Jones of us."

Brodie shifts in his chair, clearing his throat. "I don't think there'd be anything there I haven't already sorted through," he says. "Besides, it's a very boring place. Don't know if it would be worth the trip."

"Still, you never know. Maybe there's something you missed? A fresh set of eyes always—"

"Not really up for travel right now," Brodie cuts me off stiffly. "Sorry."

I rear back at the slight harshness of his tone; Brodie has never been anything but friendly with me, so this sudden burst of clear irritation with my prodding comes as a bit of a shock.

Brodie's mouth parts in surprise as if realizing the same thing, frowning right after before rising from the table. "Sorry. Still feeling a bit peely-wally. Think I should probably go lay down for a spell."

We're all quiet as Brodie leaves the room after stowing the carton he'd been nursing back in the fridge, and no one speaks until the sounds of his footsteps climbing up the stairs can be heard.

"Forgive him," Rhona says after a beat. "I think there's been some tension at his job. He's never come out and said, but he never seems keen to talk about it."

"He did say he was on sabbatical," I say.

Rhona nods. "I suspect there's more to that story than he lets on, but I don't want to press him. He's always been a soft boy, Brodie. Clung to his mother's legs like a wee limpet, that one did."

"A limpet?"

"It's like a barnacle," Lachlan snorts.

Rhona shoots him a look. "Finlay's brother wasn't exactly the most supportive of fathers to him. His brothers are carbon copies of Seamus, so that didn't make things easier."

"I should apologize," I tell her.

Rhona shakes her head. "No need, lass. Brodie isn't one to hold a grudge. He'll be right as rain later. He might even come after you with a sorry of his own, knowing him."

I notice then that Lachlan looks perplexed by the entire exchange, his brow furrowed in thought as he stares at the empty seat Brodie had been occupying. Maybe he's seeing him in a different light.

"I do hope he'll still want to talk about his project," I say. "I'd like to know more about our history also. I mean, since my dad never talked about anything."

Rhona chuckles softly, dumping the eggs she's just finished onto a plate. "Duncan was always fascinated by it too. I remember he and Lachlan's father actually took a trip out to Inverness once. They stayed up that way for days looking into our family tree. I think Duncan felt bad for your da"—Rhona nods her head at Lachlan—"since he didn't have any records of his own to sift through."

Lachlan's mouth parts in surprise, and I feel the same emotion mirrored on my face. I know Lachlan mentioned that his dad and mine had been friends, and had even suggested that my dad might have abandoned him when he left for America—but now I realize that there might be more to the story.

"Lachlan mentioned they were friends," I prod.

Rhona flips some bacon in another skillet, bobbing her head. "Aye, they were thick as thieves for a number of years. Always running off together on one adventure or another."

"I have pictures of him," Lachlan mutters. "Holding me as a baby."

Finlay chuckles. "You were a fat wee one. Healthy as an ox, your da used to say."

"It's odd that my dad never mentioned him," I venture. "I mean, I get that things were weird between you guys, but if he and Lachlan's dad were so close . . ."

"That is strange," Rhona answers. "I always assumed they'd kept in touch when he left. At least until Callum up and disap—" Her mouth snaps shut as she peeks over at Lachlan, who visibly tenses. "I'm sorry, lad."

Lachlan shakes his head. "It's fine."

"How is your mum, by the way?" Finlay asks.

Lachlan looks even more tense, if that's possible. "We don't . . . talk much. It's hard for her. I look a lot like my da, after all."

"Och, lad." Finlay pats Lachlan's hand, and unless I imagine it, the action seems to drain some of the tension from Lachlan's shoulders. "I'm sorry to hear that. I'm glad you came back home, then. S'good to be around people that care about you."

Lachlan's eyes meet mine, and I feel warmth blooming in my chest.

"Aye," he says quietly. "I'm starting to think so."

"It's too bad Brodie isn't up for a trip to Inverness," I say, trying to take the focus off Lachlan.

"It's public record," Finlay says with a shrug. "You could technically still go. Although I don't know what you'd find that he hasn't already sorted himself. You'd have an easier time just talking to Brodie himself, I think. He's always had a nose for that sort of thing."

"Too bad we don't have that auld journal anymore," Rhona mentions casually, starting to take bacon from the pan and let it rest on a plate. She eyes Finlay. "You remember the one?"

"Oh, aye!" Finlay's eyes round. "I'd forgotten all about it."

I find myself leaning in. "What journal?"

"Some auld weathered thing," Rhona says. "Duncan found it hidden away in the barn years ago. It was buried in this auld trunk."

I feel my mouth fall open. "Really?"

"Mhm." Rhona nods as she starts putting food onto plates. "Convinced himself it would lead to some sort of treasure for a bit there."

Finlay chuckles. "He said it turned out to be nothing more than some boring day-to-day account."

"You never read it?" Lachlan's voice has an edge to it, like excitement that he's trying to contain.

Finlay shakes his head. "Not much for history, really. I gave it a look-see when he found the thing, but I'm not much of a reader."

"Not that you could ever get him to give it up long enough for anyone else to read it," Rhona snorts. "I'm surprised he never showed it to you." She frowns at me. "Although I suppose if he never spoke of us . . . it makes sense."

Lachlan's eyes find mine, and I can see the same urgency in them that I feel coursing through me. What was in the journal? Where is it now? Is it back in America, or is it here somewhere? Hidden away?

Rhona starts handing out food, breaking the spell as I tear my eyes away to utter a thank-you, taking a plate from her as hunger seems to hit me out of nowhere.

"This smells amazing," I tell her.

She grunts. "It isn't much."

"It's great," Lachlan says, tucking in.

"My Rhona is the best cook in all of Scotland," Finlay sighs.

Rhona rolls her eyes. "Stop with your sweet talk and eat your breakfast."

I watch as Lachlan eats quietly, wanting more than anything to reach across the table and cover his hand with mine, if only to offer him some semblance of comfort. I hold back, not knowing if he's *actually* ready to air . . . whatever this is out in the open, instead extending my leg to rub his ankle with the toe of my sock.

He peeks up at me and I give him a soft smile, one that he returns as he mouths, *It's fine.*

I nod as I dig into my own breakfast, listening to the quiet conversation he makes with my grandpa and granny, feeling an odd warmth settling in my chest at the simplicity of it all. With everything I know about our family history, it seems almost special, for MacKays and a Greer to be doing something as easy as sharing a meal.

I shake off the silly thought.


It takes a bit to extricate ourselves from my grandparents' kitchen table, Lachlan offering up some excuse about needing to get to the cows finally so that we can both sneak away. He tells me he'll wait for me outside, and sure enough, I find him standing not far from the front door after I finish changing clothes, leaning against the house and gazing out at the rolling hills with a contemplative ex-pression.

"I'm sorry," I tell him immediately. "I didn't mean to get you trapped in that situation."

He shakes his head. "S'fine. It wasn't so bad."

"My grandparents . . ." I consider the words before I say them, not wanting to offend him somehow. Not with everything he's endured. "I don't think they're like the MacKays you've heard of. I think you can trust them."

He turns his head to look at me, his eyes roaming over my face. He reaches out to brush an errant curl behind my ear, his lips turning up slightly at the corners. "Maybe I can."

"Lachlan," I say firmly. "I don't think the journal Rhona men-tioned ever made it to America."

His brow furrows. "What makes you say that?"

"Because I went through every single thing my father owned when he died, and I would have seen it."

"Could he have stored it someplace else?"

"I never saw any paperwork suggesting he had anything stored anywhere."

"So where would it be?"

"I think . . ." I nod to myself, convinced more and more that I'm right. "I think it must still be here."

Lachlan looks unsure. "I've combed over this property for months, Key. Don't you think I'd have found it?"

"You'd combed over the castle too, remember?"

He smiles at that. "Bloody hound."

"Face it," I laugh. "I'm your good luck charm."

"Aye," he answers quietly, leaning to press his lips to my cheek. "Maybe you are." He still looks thoughtful when he straightens, his brow knitted and his mouth pursed. "Don't get too excited, though. It could be nothing."

"It's not," I tell him resolutely. "It's not nothing. I can feel it."

He gestures for me to follow him then, no doubt needing the distraction of the morning farm duties, and I can tell that he's still not convinced. That he's not allowing himself to hope that this means something. That we can even find the damned thing if it does. And that's okay, I think.

Maybe I can have enough hope for the both of us.

## LACHLAN

I can't believe I let Blair strong-arm me into this," I grumble.

Key grins down at me as I give her a boost up the ladder to her makeshift "tower." "You mean you don't want to fight for my honor?"

"That's not even how the story goes," I huff. "Blair has manipulated this entire thing to boost beer sales."

"Can't say I blame her," Key calls down.

I watch as she shimmies up onto the wooden platform, finding the carved "throne" that consists of a tree stump carved down into a seat with a backrest, looking like she's enjoying this far too much.

"It's a nice view from up here," she says, adjusting her plastic tiara.

I frown up at her, fists against my hips. "First you make a fuss about me calling you princess; now you're wearing tiaras?"

"I don't know," she says, winking at me. "Maybe it's growing on me. I'm also loving *your* outfit today."

I frown down at the kilt brushing along my knees; it was my da's, and it's utterly ancient, but Blair said it was a requirement to enter. Something about really getting into the spirit of the games. At this point, they barely have anything to do with the story of the pub's name. I'm pretty sure she's just looking for a laugh.

I scoff under my breath, shaking my head as I turn to regard the other contestants. The field behind the pub is crowded with people I've known my entire life as well as new faces of tourists, no doubt enticed in by the discounted beer and promise of sweaty men—all milling about with a brew in hand, laughing and chatting among themselves as they wait for the games to begin. I hadn't planned on participating, I really hadn't, but then I spotted Isla's twins strutting around in their shredded tanks with their bronzed muscles and their matching heartthrob smiles, and well . . . turns out that maybe I am a bit of the jealous sort. Who knew.

"All right, Lachlan?"

I catch sight of Hamish just as his hand slaps the center of my back, his blue eyes twinkling in the midmorning sunlight as he smiles up at me.

"I'd be better if I were in a bloody seat and not out here on the field," I mutter. I arch a brow at him. "Don't tell me you're competing?"

"And why not?" He puffs up a bit. "Don't think I couldn't teach you young pups a thing or two."

I just stare at him until he finally blows out a breath.

"Fine, fine," he relents. "Blair asked me to announce the festivities."

"Lucky you."

"I suspect she only asked me because she knows I'm not much of a drinker."

"Probably. You're the only person here she can trust not to end up passed out on the grass by the end of the day."

Hamish nods before nudging me in the side. "And what's got you itching to compete?" He flashes me a sly smile. "Don't tell me you're after a kiss from the bonnie MacKay girl, aye?"

I don't tell him I know the exact noise the "bonnie MacKay girl" makes when my tongue is between her legs, figuring that giving old Hamish a heart attack wouldn't go over well.

I shrug instead. "I'm just helping out the twins."

"Sure, sure," he laughs. "And my middle name isn't Elsbeth."

My nose wrinkles. "Wait, is it?"

"You've got your secrets," he laughs. "I've got mine."

He gives me another sharp slap between the shoulders, and then he's strutting off to the platform that's been erected beside Key's tower, a speaker in the center that's connected to the mic.

I notice the other contestants starting to make their way closer to the platform, including Isla's twins, whose names I can't exactly recall—one of them might be a Cormac? I also see Malcolm strutting over in a garishly red kilt of his own, his red beard braided like he's marching to battle rather than gearing up to jump through some tires.

"He could have worn a shirt," someone mutters beside me.

I glance at one of the twins—seriously, is it Cormac or Camdan? He's frowning at Malcolm's display as much as I am. Good. At least there's one other person here with some good sense. The other twin saunters up just beside his brother, both of them wearing black shirts with the sleeves ripped off and sporting their tartan kilts of blue and green.

"Aye, he could have," I concur.

One of them makes a face. "And isn't he auld enough to be the lass's da?"

"He is," I grouse. "But I'm pretty sure he's mostly here for the bragging rights anyway."

I don't like the way they both turn to eye Key where she's chatting with Hamish from her tower, and I have to remind myself that, as far as anyone else is concerned, she's fair game. Even if I've started to think of her as mine.

"Ewan," one of them says, sticking out his hand and cutting through my darkening thoughts.

I shake it just as the other brother offers his. "Niall."

*Well, I was completely off, then, wasn't I?*

"Lachlan."

"Aye, we know," Ewan chuckles.

Niall waggles his brows. "Think you can keep up, auld man?"

*All right, so they're both numpties after all.*

"I might ask you the same question," I hmph. "Are either of you even auld enough to drink?"

"We're auld enough for a lot of things," Niall laughs.

I notice him turning his head in the direction of Key's tower, lifting his hand and wiggling his fingers in a wave. "Auld Finlay's granddaughter is a pretty wee thing, aye?"

He shares a fist bump with his brother, and I decide then that I'm going to destroy the both of them.

"You lassies ready to get beaten?" Malcolm calls, taking his place in front of the platform.

I eye his barrel chest and huge arms—reminding myself that I have something none of them have. That I could toss all three of them across the field all at once if I had half a mind to.

My smile feels wild on my mouth as it curls up, showing teeth. "We'll see."


The smugness from my immediate win of the caber toss lasts for all of ten minutes before the twins use some underhanded tactics—

mainly, tripping me—to win the obstacle course, and by two hours in, I'm not only soaked with sweat, but feeling murderous to boot. Ewan is out, thank Christ, but his brother Niall and Malcolm are still in the running.

Every time I glance in Key's direction, I can tell she's enjoying this entirely too much. I'm happy to see her having fun, but I have definitely caught her looking a bit too much like she's laughing *at* me and not with me. I should spank her arse for that.

"You all right, Grandpa?"

I narrow my eyes at Niall, leaning with my hands on my knees as I catch my breath. Damn Blair for making this whole thing so fucking authentic. We couldn't just do a bit of tossing and climbing and be done with it?

"Next up," Hamish calls, "we have the traditional hammer throw! Our lads here will toss a pole with a *heavy* metal ball attached at the end, and we'll be judging them on their distance. The competitor with the shortest throw will be disqualified, and that will leave us with only two left to enter the final task!" Hamish gestures to Key, who does a pretend curtsy even though she's wearing pants. "Remember, a kiss from this bonnie lass is up for grabs, so give it your all, aye?"

*Nothing like the story at all, I swear.*

"You can have the kiss," Malcolm calls, "but I'm still going to kick both your arses."

I notice Niall rolling his eyes, and I have to force myself not to do the same. "Just throw your pole, yeah?"

"With pleasure," Malcolm answers haughtily.

He claps his hands together before strolling over to his pole, lifting the heavy rounded end from the grass to test its weight. I know that normally they can weigh upwards of twelve kilograms, but I also know that Blair likes to make everything "more interesting" so they're probably much heavier than they should be. This is apparent by the way the muscles in Malcolm's arms immediately bulge with effort, his cheeks puffing as he blows out a breath, steadying himself.

Niall and I watch as he starts to spin, dragging the pole through the air as he picks up momentum. His face is red, sweat dripping from his hair as he gathers speed, and in a matter of seconds he's releasing the pole, letting it fly across the field. It lands a good ten meters away, and the crowd begins to clap and cheer as a still-panting Malcolm raises one hand in the air, pumping his fist.

"Age before beauty," Niall says with a bow.

I remind myself that it wouldn't be polite to strangle him in public.

I step up to my pole, adjusting my own blue-and-red tartan so it's settled on my hips, dusting my hands together before reaching to grasp the pole. I plant my feet to get my bearings before I look over in Key's direction, noticing that she's leaning over the railing of her tower. She gives me a wave, and I feel a smile touching my mouth in answer.

I lift the pole, immediately scowling.

Blair absolutely made mine heavier than necessary. The damned thing has to be at least fifty kilograms. There's no way Malcolm could have tossed this, which tells me Blair meddled to make sure it was more of a "challenge" for me.

As much as I love my friend, sometimes I hate her just as much.

I grit my teeth as I start to spin, feeling the weight of the ball at the end of my pole threaten to topple me over as I let it circle around me. I wait until it's gliding through the air smoothly before I start to time my release, finally digging in my heel at the exact moment I let it fly. I watch it sail in an arc before dropping back down, my grin impossibly wide when it drops a good two meters farther than Malcolm's.

I turn to him, breathing hard but no doubt looking smug. "What was that about kicking my arse?"

"Och." He throws up his hand in a dismissive gesture. "You young pups and your bloody ego."

Niall jogs up to his pole, winking at me. "Let me show both of you how it's done."

Niall beats Malcolm by a slim margin, and I suspect if it weren't for the immediate pint of beer offered to him upon losing, he might have a lot more to say about it. As it is, he's grumbling on the sidelines with his second glass, eyeing the field as Niall and I move into position for the final task.

"Our last game is the classic tug-o'-war," Hamish announces, "but with a twist!"

I glare at Blair, sensing she's cooking up something else for my benefit. She just blows me a kiss from the sidelines.

"To make things interesting," Hamish says, "both our lads will be tying their rope around their waist, and instead of your usual pulling their opponent over a line—one of these two will actually need to *bring the other to the ground.*"

*Fuck me.*

"That's right," Hamish goes on. "So it's not just about strength, but cunning also!"

Niall is already stepping into the looped bit of his end of the rope, and once it's secured around his waist, the eejit reaches for the hem of his T-shirt, pulling it over his head and tossing it away so that all his sweat-drenched muscles are on display. He flexes his arms and makes a bit of a show out of it, smiling at me as if in challenge.

*You've nothing to prove to him.*

Then he blows a kiss at Keyanna, and I see red at the edges of my vision.

I grunt as I step into my own loop, settling it around my waist and immediately wrenching off my own shirt. I skip the theatrics; I've nothing to prove to this kid, after all, but given that I'm at least two inches taller than him with a good twenty kilograms on him—I can't help standing a bit straighter. A quick glance in Key's direction reveals her to be laughing behind her hand. She'll no doubt have plenty to say about this after.

Niall grips either side of the looped end of his rope, planting his feet in the grass and steadying himself as I do the same. I can hear Hamish beginning to count down to the start, and by the time the whistle blows—I can barely hear it over the rushing of blood in my ears. I grip the rope tight and force a step back, satisfaction coursing through me as Niall stumbles forward a bit. He doesn't go down, though, surprising me by using all of his body weight to immediately tug me in the opposite direction.

This back-and-forth goes on a lot longer than I'd like; even when I'm able to drag him a meter toward me, I can't seem to get him unstable enough to fall flat on his face. I can feel sweat coating my skin, running down my temples—the sun high in the sky now and burning down on me until my entire body feels hot. It occurs to me that, regardless of my strength, this kid could absolutely outlast me, and with that in mind, I try to think of alternative methods to have him eating the grass.

The frustration of the idea of losing builds up, and the thought of anyone else kissing Keyanna—however innocent—threatens to spark a growing rage inside me that feels physical. I feel it burning under my skin, my fingers prickling as if my claws are seconds from coming out, and I force my eyes shut, knowing they must be burning.

*Bloody hell, you can't lose control. Not here.*

I open my eyes with new determination, because I have to *end* this. Before I lose it and cause a fucking panic. I watch Niall more carefully when he attempts to bring me down again, holding my ground and studying him for any signs of weakness.

On his next tug, I notice him throwing all of his weight backward into the rope as he inches me forward, and a lightbulb goes off above my head. Barely able to contain my smile, I let the rope slacken a bit, trying to appear tired, and I can see it, the look of victory when Niall thinks he has me. I wait for him to start to press all of his weight once more against his rope, watching his feet as they lift from the ground ever so slightly as he digs in his heels.

And that's when I let him have it.

I give a quick and brutal tug at the exact moment Niall starts to lean, the resulting force taking him off guard and throwing him off balance. The look on his face is priceless; shock and disbelief war together just before he comes crashing to the ground, and then he's sprawled on his arse with a dazed expression as I let my rope drop to the grass.

The gathered crowd starts to cheer, but my blood is pulsing in my ears, and I'm already striding over to Key's tower, ignoring the whistles and whoops as I start to climb the ladder. She's waiting for me at the top; her grin wide and her cheeks flushed from the sun, rising from her makeshift throne to meet me as I step onto the platform with her.

"That was something," she says. Her eyes rake down my bare chest. "Wow, I kind of like you all sweaty."

"Do you?"

"Mhm." She plucks at my kilt with her fingers, humming her approval. "And I *really* like this."

I wind an arm around her waist, pulling her against me. "I was promised a prize."

"Well," she hums, throwing her arms around my neck. "Come and get it, then."

I cover her mouth with mine, kissing her in a way that is far from appropriate for the casual prize she was supposed to have given me, but finding I don't care in the slightest. Adrenaline is coursing through me, so much so that I can almost feel myself giving in to my more beastly instincts—almost as if the idea of her touching someone else has the monster inside me needing to remind her who she belongs to.

Because she really does feel like *mine*.

I lick my tongue through her mouth and capture the tiny whimper that results because of it, knowing that after this, people will definitely have things to say. That rumors will be flying all over the place. I decide then that I don't care about that either. Let them talk. As long as I'm the only one who gets to touch her like this. I mean, for fuck's sake, I couldn't even stand the idea of anyone else getting something as innocent as a *kiss* from her. Is that some possessive side effect of the curse? Some latent monsterly instinct that has me wanting to own all of her touches, her kisses, everything she's willing to give?

Or is it just me?

One thing's glaringly obvious. I'm obsessed with Keyanna MacKay. And given that my days could very well be numbered . . . I have no idea what to do with that information.

## 23

### KEYANNA

It just felt like there was something there, you know?"

I lean back in the old metal chair stashed in the corner of the barn, letting my head rest against the inner wall. There's no response, just like there hasn't been for the last ten minutes I've been talking, but it doesn't stop me from word-vomiting all my thoughts.

"I just heard about this journal, and it felt like one of those 'this is it' moments. I *know* my dad didn't have it back at our place in New York. I just *know* it. So it has to be here, right?" More silence. "But..." I huff out a breath. "We've been searching all over the property for the last week, and there's nothing. Not even a fucking stray letter stashed in a drawer. What in the world could he have done with it?"

Two eyes blink back at me lazily, her jaw working subtly as she stares at me with a bored expression. I blow out a breath, rising to my feet and crossing the distance between us so I can scratch at her jaw.

"You're a good listener," I tell Bethie, "but you smell terrible."

She makes a low *moo*ing sound, huffing through her nostrils, which results in a spray of wet air that has me holding back a gag. "Seriously," I groan. "Do you have to be so gross?"

"There you are," I hear from the barn's entrance behind me. I glance over my shoulder, seeing Lachlan pushing off the doorframe and sidling up to where I'm still giving Bethie scritches. "I see you've finally decided the cows aren't going to eat you."

"Jury's still out," I tell him. "But she is weirdly cute. I guess."

"You hear that, Bethie?" He runs his fingers along her cheek, scratching behind her ear as she tilts her head into his touch. "That's a high compliment coming from this one." I try to smile, but it doesn't quite land. Lachlan doesn't miss this. "Are you in here hiding so you can sulk?"

"I'm not . . . sulking," I lie.

"Aye, you are." He steps away from Bethie, wrapping his arm around my shoulders and pulling me in to press a kiss to my hair. "I told you. You can't let this get to you. S'not your responsibility to solve everything."

*Then why does it feel like it is?*

"I just thought we'd find it," I admit, my voice soft. "Like at the castle."

"That was a freak accident, Keyanna," he says gently. "You're not a bloody dowsing rod. And I don't expect you to be, all right?"

I nod stiffly. "I guess."

"Now, have you been practicing?"

"Yeah. Not that I've gotten any better."

Which I guess isn't *entirely* true. A week ago, I couldn't control this weird magic inside me at all—but after another instance of blowing out all of Lachlan's lights and one unfortunate near-setting of his rug on fire . . . we decided I had to try *something*.

"Show me," he says.

I sigh as I step away from him, flexing my palm and trying to grab hold of that feeling that always seems to take me whenever something happens with my magic. It feels almost like a well that's being fed water—so full that it overflows and bursts into a physical manifestation. Like my body simply can't contain it any longer.

I close my eyes and try to poke at that feeling, imagining it as an *actual* well. Imagining that it's *me* filling it with water to the brim. I start to feel that humming warmth under my skin after a moment or so, and there is a lick of excitement in my belly that still hasn't lessened with every instance of this, coaxing that energy higher, stoking it, filling my well.

I imagine that water pouring over the stone edge of the well in my mind, directing it to somewhere more specific. Somewhere small. Somewhere that I can control it. The heat rushes through my body and gathers in my palm, and when I let my eyes drift open, a tiny flame flickers there.

I smile as I watch it, peeking up at Lachlan, looking for acknowledgment of my success.

"That's a fancy party trick," Lachlan chuckles.

I narrow my eyes. "Would you like me to set your ass on fire with my party trick?"

"No, no," he says, grinning. "I take it back. You're definitely all powerful."

"Whatever." I close my palm and make a fist, letting the flame sputter out. "Could be useful someday."

"Aye, it could," he says, more serious now. He pulls me back into him, pressing a kiss to my hair. "You're incredible, Key. You don't need me to tell you that."

I feel a swelling sensation in my chest that is almost painful, clinging to him.

I don't know how to tell him that with every day that passes, every day that I know him a little more—I grow more and more afraid. It seems nonsensical to me that the idea of losing him would feel so detrimental after such a short time, but it's there, regardless of reason. Every passing day with no answers feels like a loss. Even with mornings spent in his bed—the nights spent alone are almost haunting in their loneliness. Like a reminder that the deeper I let myself fall into this thing we're doing, the more painful it will be if I inevitably lose him to his curse.

"How do you do this?"

He pulls away, looking confused. "Do what?"

"Go through every day not knowing what's ahead? Aren't you terrified?"

His brow furrows, a serious frown passing over his features before he looks away altogether, staring at nothing. "Aye, sometimes," he says. "But I can't dwell on it. It would drive me mad. It's better that I keep going as if the answer is out there. Even if some days are harder than others." A smile touches his lips when he looks back at me, his eyes softening. "Lately, it's been a bit more bearable."

I bury my face in his shirt, colliding with him so roughly that he lets out a quiet *oof* as I wrap my arms around his waist. "I'm scared," I admit. "I shouldn't be scared, right? You hated me a few weeks ago."

"Och." He pushes his fingers into my hair, forcing my head back so I have to look up at him. "It's like you said. I don't think I ever hated you, Key. Not really. I think it was just easier to pretend that I did."

I turn my cheek, resting my face in the crook of his neck. "What are we going to do?"

"Tomorrow? We're going to finish searching the attic. Next week? I can't say for sure." I feel the ghost of his lips at my hair, his wide palm cradling my head. "But right now . . . I think we're going to go get a drink."

"It's one in the afternoon," I remind him.

He snorts. "Some of us don't have the luxury of a night out on the town."

"Don't remind me," I grumble into his T-shirt.

"Come on, princess," he chuckles. "Let's get a pint. We'll feel much better after."

"Says you."

"Well, at the very least, maybe it'll get you to stop talking to the cows."

I trudge after him when he leaves me, following him toward the barn entrance and wondering how in the hell he can be so calm. Part of me worries it's an act, that he's projecting this easy attitude to try and bring me some semblance of peace. The thought of that threatens to make me want to yell at him, but then again, I don't want to waste time arguing with him. Not when he's obviously dealing with this in the best way he can.

*Fuck.*

I really do need that drink.

"Okay, but we know that, after the war, your family settled the area where the town is now," I say, poring over an old census book I found in the back of the small library in Greerloch.

Lachlan brings his mug to his lips, taking a long draught before sighing. "Aye. There used to be a manor a few miles from Hamish's property. It burned down in the sixteen hundreds."

"You guys have really bad luck with houses."

He chuckles. "I'd say we have bad luck with a lot of things, love."

My stomach clenches at the word. He doesn't say it often; I'm not even sure it occurs to him that he does, but I collect each one like keepsakes, each one giving me a burst of butterflies.

"But if my family *did* get involved with the kelpie, then it's safe to assume that, at that point, they had the bridle, yeah?"

"Keep your voice down," he hisses, eyeing the lingering bodies in the pub, tourists who are still hanging around after the games. "One would assume."

"So where was *my* family when yours founded Greerloch?"

"As far as I know, your family has lived on the same plot of land since the day they bought it from mine."

"You know, that part has been bugging me."

"Why?"

"Why would your ancestors sell their land to mine if we had a hand in turning you guys into monsters?"

"Well," Lachlan says thoughtfully, frowning down into his beer. "I'd venture to say if they had the bridle, there wasn't anyone that could really tell them no."

"So, what? They use it to bully your family into giving up part of their land, and then they just . . . said fuck it and chucked the thing?"

Lachlan frowns. "I . . . guess?"

"That doesn't seem strange to you?"

"I turn into a fucking dinosaur after dark," he grouses. "Nothing really strikes me as strange anymore."

I wave him off, chewing on my thumbnail as I let possibilities tumble through my thoughts. I can feel something there on the fringe of it all, just out of reach—something I can't quite grasp. If the bridle went to the MacKays, and the Mackays have never left, then surely—

A cheery "Hello, Keyanna," sounds from over my shoulder,

jarring me from my mental tug-of-war. To his credit, Lachlan only stiffens *a little* when he notices my cousin standing behind me, no doubt remembering the conversation he and I had the last time we spoke to Brodie.

I twist in my chair, offering him a smile. "Hey."

"Bit early for a drink, yeah?"

He grins as he says it, letting me know he's just poking fun, and I cock an eyebrow back at him. "Bit of a pot-meet-kettle situation, don't you think?"

"I'll have you know," he protests, "I'm here for the fish and chips."

"Best fish and chips this side of Inverness!" Rory calls from behind the bar.

Lachlan cranes his neck. "What did I tell you about eavesdropping?"

"Aye, but I never listen to you. Why would I start now?"

Lachlan frowns, shaking his head as he settles back into his chair, muttering, "Eejit."

"Oi." Brodie's eyes grow round, and he leans over the table with interest. "What's this?"

I glance down at the census book still open in front of me. "A dead end, that's what."

"Still looking into that history, aye?"

"Trying to," I tell him. I watch Brodie bob his head as a thought strikes me, sitting up a little straighter. "You've been looking into all this too, right?"

"Aye, a bit," he says. "Mostly just for fun. My da used to say we had Vikings in our ancestry." He scoffs. "But he's probably full of shite."

"Yeah," I say with a nervous laugh, trying not to think about magical shape-shifting horses. "Probably."

He glances at the book again. "Anything in particular you're looking for?"

"We're good," Lachlan says tightly, and when I look over at him, I notice his jaw is clenched.

I make a face at him, trying to convey with my eyes that I am prepared to slap the shit out of him if he doesn't tone down the macho bullshit.

"I don't think it would hurt to ask Brodie for a little help," I stress. "It's *just* for fun, after all."

Lachlan gains the look of a scolded child, shifting in his seat. "I guess it couldn't hurt."

"Sit, Brodie." I pat the seat next to me. "Sit here."

Brodie still looks slightly unsure, but takes the offered seat nonetheless. "Sure. I've got time."

"We were actually looking into when the MacKays first settled here," I tell him. "They bought the land from Lachlan's family, right?"

"Oh, aye," Brodie confirms. "The auld farmhouse was actually built right along the border of where the Greer land starts." His face lights up, clearly passionate about the topic. "The Greers already had their dead buried there, aye? That meant their servants and such too, so the MacKays that had worked for the Greers for centuries prior were all there. So, they took what they could as close as they could to the burial grounds to be closer to their family."

"I . . . didn't know that," Lachlan says with genuine surprise. "Is that true?"

Brodie nods, regarding Lachlan warily. "It is. Never could find the original deed, though. Just saw it referenced a lot."

"Did you ever see anything about a journal when you were browsing?"

"You mean the one Duncan supposedly found?"

My brows rise. "Rhona told you?"

"No, not really." He shrugs. "I heard her mention it before, but there's mention of an original record from the first one who settled that land."

My heart flutters. "You know who it was?"

"Sure. His name was Tavish. He was a stable hand for the Greers back at the original keep."

Lachlan leans in. "The castle?"

"Mhm." Even with the way Brodie is clearly unsure about sharing all this so casually with me *and* Lachlan, he looks tickled to have someone interested in his project; it almost makes me feel guilty for not telling him the whole truth. "He married someone else that lived in the keep. Maybe a servant? I'm not sure. Her name is never mentioned. I reckon they're the first MacKays to settle where Rhona and Finlay are now."

My heart is thumping in my chest now; something about this information feels relevant. *Important* even. If Lachlan has always been told that a stable hand named MacKay fell in love with the kelpie, that he helped her escape . . . it *has* to be this Tavish.

It takes all that I have not to jump up from my seat, a frenetic energy building inside as I meet Lachlan's gaze from across the table. I see a similar expression of shock mirrored there, his mouth parted and his blue eyes wide as he digests the same information as I'm hearing.

"What?" Brodie asks, justifiably confused. "What is it?"

"I . . ." I do a spectacular impression of a goldfish as my mouth opens and closes and then opens again—finally swallowing down the thick lump forming in my throat. "Nothing," I say finally. "We just had a bet going. Sounds like I might win."

A muffled laugh escapes Lachlan. "I don't know about that."

"You two are sweet," Brodie sighs. "It's a bloody awful sight for us single folks."

"Word of advice," Lachlan says, lowering his voice. "Maybe move on from Blair, aye? You're barking up the wrong tree. Wrong forest, really."

"You're kidding," Brodie says with genuine surprise on his face.

Lachlan shoots him a sympathetic look. "Afraid not."

"Figures," Brodie snorts. "That's about how my luck runs."

"My da used to say s'better to have loved and lost than to have not loved at all," Lachlan says.

Brodie frowns. "I think Tennyson said that, mate."

"You're kidding." Lachlan's mouth parts. "That auld stoater had me thinking he was a bloody poet!"

Brodie throws his head back and laughs. "Trust me, if that's all you have to be disappointed in your father for, you're doing all right."

"Och." Lachlan shakes his head. "I heard your da is a bit of an arse." He winces when he realizes what he's said. "Sorry."

Brodie seems to remember then that he doesn't actually *like* Lachlan; his smile fades as he shifts in his chair, averting his gaze with a shrug. "Aye, well. That's just the way of it sometimes. I reckon it's my fault for not turning out the way he wanted me to."

"What way is that?" Lachlan asks.

Brodie's eyes are colder when he answers, "To hear him tell it, more like you, I'd wager."

"Me?" Lachlan makes a face. "I help out with the farm. Surely he's prouder to have a smart one like you, aye? With your fancy job back in Inverness."

Brodie bristles even further if possible, and for the life of me, I can't pinpoint where this conversation went off the rails. They had been doing so well.

"Aye, well." Brodie sniffs. "Best be seeing about that fish and chips before I starve, yeah?"

"Thank you for your help," I say, having to hold myself back from asking what just happened.

He nods stiffly. "Good luck with your search."

"You too," I call back. I wait until he's out of earshot before leaning over the table to ask, "What the hell just happened?"

Lachlan shrugs. "Beats me. The guy just doesn't like me, Key. I reckon there's not much I can do about it."

I frown at that, but I guess I don't have time to dwell on it. That's a problem for another day. We have more important things to worry about right now.

"The story. Do you think . . . ?"

"Aye. Definitely," he finishes before I can get the question out.

"What do we do now?"

Lachlan frowns, turning his face toward the window. "Unfortunately, I don't think there's enough time left before dark to do anything today."

"Oh." I wither at the idea of saying goodbye to him for another night; I think because each time I do it, there's a small part of me that worries he won't come back. "Right."

I can see those same fears etched into his features as he studies my forlorn expression, finally reaching across the table to cover my hand with his. "You want to come with me?"

"What?" I rear back. "I don't think it works like that."

He rolls his eyes. "Not like that. I just meant the shore. Just for a while." He looks toward the window again. "There's time yet . . . and I want to show you something."

Given that I'm increasingly desperate these days to spend more time with him, I don't need much persuasion. "Sure," I tell him. "I can go."

"Look at me."

My eyes snap up to his as he rubs his thumb over my knuckles, no doubt trying to ease some of the tension that has to be radiating off me.

"There's still time," he promises. "All right?"

I let out a breath. "Since when did you start being the positive one?"

"Don't know what you mean," he answers indignantly. "I'll have you know I've always been revered for my sunny personality."

I say nothing, simply arching my brow.

"Yeah, yeah. Just get off your arse and come with me, yeah?"

I can't help but grin.

"That's more like it," I chuckle.

I try not to think about the sinking sun as we say goodbye to Rory and Blair and even Brodie—try not to imagine a possibility where it will go down and not bring Lachlan with it when it returns. One of us *has* to keep hoping for a solution.

But it's getting increasingly hard to be the one to do it.

## LACHLAN

A re you *sure* you're not running a long con to murder me?"

I chuckle as she clings tighter to my arm, carefully watching the rocky path under her feet. "I told you. There are a lot cleaner ways to get rid of you."

"Still so comforting," she mutters.

"It's not much farther."

"We couldn't have taken your Rover?"

"It's a shortcut," I tell her. "Where's your sense of adventure?"

She nearly slips on a loose bit of gravel, clutching me tightly as she tries to hold herself upright. "To hell with you," she huffs. "The damn landscape is going to kill me."

"Och, lass. But isn't it beautiful?"

I push a branch out of the way as the setting sun filters through the tree limbs, finally coming into the open air that flutters over the glittering waves of the loch. I hear her breath catch beside me, and seeing the wonder in her eyes—it's almost like seeing my homeland for the first time. This loch, this shore . . . it's often a reminder of everything wrong in my life. It's a rare thing that I can just stand back and admire how beautiful it is.

"The sunsets here are amazing," I murmur. I can't help but laugh softly. "I've seen many of them."

"Lachlan . . ."

I hear the worry in her voice, and I shake my head. "None of that. We're not going to think about any of that." I jostle the blanket that I grabbed from the back of the Rover and is now draped over my other arm. "We're going to have a sit, and enjoy the sunset, and we're going to save everything else for tomorrow, yeah?"

I can tell she wants to argue with me, and funnily enough, that knowledge makes me smile. I let her stew as I lay out the blanket on the sand for us to sit, settling down on top of it and patting the spot beside me. She's still looking at me like she thinks this is silly, like she thinks she should be running off right now to God knows where to try and solve my problems single-handedly—and I think that look in her eyes makes me fall for her, just a bit.

I've known her for barely a month, been touching her for far less than that, and it wasn't very long ago we couldn't share the same space without sniping at each other. But I think the way we started has only solidified the knowledge that Keyanna MacKay is fiercely beautiful in her determination, and it's humbling to be on the receiving end of it.

"Come on," I say, patting the blanket once more. "Sit with me."

She presses her lips together as she sinks down next to me—no doubt holding back her arguments—and I don't give her time to think about it, throwing my arm around her shoulders and pulling her against me as soon as she's close.

"There now," I say. "Was that so hard?"

"Like pulling teeth," she mumbles.

I grin as I press a kiss to her temple, content to just hold her for a bit as the sun continues to sink. "I do this a lot," I tell her.

"What?" I feel her eyes on the side of my face. "Sit out here?"

"Mhm." I nod idly. "The change starts when the sun passes the horizon, so oftentimes, I come here early to sit and wait. Just to be sure."

She's quiet for a moment, her voice soft when she finally asks, "Is it scary?"

"It used to be," I tell her honestly. "The first time I changed . . . I was thirteen." I give her a wry smile. "That'll be the barn incident Blair and Rory told you about." I sober, looking back at the water. "My mum had run off to Glasgow to be with her sister when my da disappeared, and I stayed behind to live with my granny. We knew that I would eventually succumb to the curse, and because of that, it seemed too risky to stray too far from the loch. I left after that, though. Moved up to Inverness. Tried my hand at a normal life for a while." I breathe in deep before letting it out. "I'd tried to connect with my da, but even then he'd forgotten what it was like to be human. He didn't recognize me."

"I'm so sorry."

I shake my head. "It is what it is."

"Did it work?"

I turn my head, arching a brow at her. "Hm?"

"Living a normal life."

"Oh. For a bit, yeah," I say. "My da left me a trust, and since he was presumed dead, it came to me when I turned twenty-one. I didn't *need* to work, technically, but I got a job working for a construction company there. I liked working with my hands, see."

"What about your mom? Did you . . ." She clears her throat. "Do you two still talk?"

"Sometimes. Like I told Rhona . . . I think it's hard for her. She and my da . . . they were the real thing, aye? Loved each other something fierce. Even after he told her the truth of his curse not long after admitting he loved her . . . she never wavered in her feelings. It broke her when he never came home. That he was so close and yet might as well have been dead. Plus, I think seeing so much of him in me hurts her. Not to mention knowing that what could happen to him might happen to me."

"But you're still her kid," Key says indignantly. "She practically abandoned you."

I smile despite everything, hearing that same ferocity in her tone on my behalf. "Aye, you're right. I don't blame her, though. Maybe I did once . . . but not anymore."

"So why did you come back?"

My brow knits, pulling her closer as fear grips me. I've been able to keep it at bay for some time now—but with Keyanna pressed so closely against me, with something to lose literally right here in my arms . . . I feel it even stronger now.

"I didn't turn back one night," I tell her quietly. "I thought the curse had taken me, like it did my da."

I hear her soft gasp, feel her hand clenching my thigh. "What? For how long? Has it happened again?"

"It hasn't," I assure her. "It took two more sunrises for me to come back, and the only reason I didn't lose it completely is because I still kept my mind. I knew from the times I'd tried to connect with my da that if it was truly the end, I'd be nothing more than a monster. That gave me hope."

"Why do you think it happened?"

I shrug. "I can't be sure. It was a stressful time. Work had been grueling, and my mother had an episode . . . She was in a facility for a while. Lost her head for a bit. I think . . . I think maybe the stress of it all made it harder to come back to myself."

She goes deathly quiet, still for so long that I have to shift so I can turn to look at her.

"What is it?"

She doesn't look at me, staring down at her lap instead. "What if I'm just making it harder for you to keep control? What if I'm somehow accelerating the process?"

"Don't be daft, love," I soothe. "You bring me a peace I've not had in a long while."

She tilts up her face then, biting her lower lip. "That's not going to happen to you," she tells me, her eyes blazing. "What happened to your dad. I'm going to make sure of it."

I study her face, reaching to brush my fingers over her cheek. Her lashes flutter with my touch, her lips parting as if in invitation. "Aye," I murmur. "If anyone can . . . it's you."

Her mouth is soft and open when I lean to cover it with mine, a quiet sound escaping from deep inside her throat as my tongue slips past her lips to tease hers. My palm wraps around her jaw to hold her close, reveling in the softness of her, the warmth of her tongue as it tangles with mine.

I've touched her countless times since we first fell into bed together—and with each time I think that maybe this will be the time where the overwhelming feelings she instills in me will settle, where they won't threaten to overtake me completely, but each time I'm proven wrong. Every time I touch Keyanna, it feels *right*— like she's made for me. Like she's *mine*.

I feel her fingers creeping under the hem of my sweater, the tips of them tickling my stomach, which clenches under her touch. She slides her palm up over my abs until it glides across my chest, leaving a trail of warmth blooming in the path it leaves behind. She takes me by surprise when she moves lightning fast to straddle my waist, my hands dropping to her arse to pull her tight against me, still ravaging her mouth.

Like this, I can almost feel the beast lurking inside, like it, too, wants to claim her. Like it recognizes that she's *ours*. It's the closest I've ever felt to the monster that lurks beneath my skin, and maybe that's why it feels so much harder to control it when she touches me like this. It takes all my strength to keep it at bay, to make sure that I don't accidentally hurt her like I did that first time; the thought of hurting her makes me sick to my stomach, actually. It's something I can't allow.

Key begins to rock her hips in my lap, and I feel my cock thicken in my jeans, a Pavlovian response to her nearness. I groan as she grinds down against it, the devil woman, feeling her smile against my lips as her fingers slide into my hair.

She pulls back, her pupils blown. "How much time do we have?"

"A bit longer," I tell her. My mouth quirks. "What . . . right here?"

"Where's *your* sense of adventure?"

I watch with a slack jaw as she tugs her own sweater over her head, dropping it on the blanket beside us and revealing that there is nothing underneath. Her tight, pink nipples are already hard in the chilly air, almost begging for me to taste them.

"You'll catch cold," I murmur, staring as my tongue aches to tease them.

She leans in, pressing a kiss to my jaw. "Then you'll have to keep me warm."

"Aye," I hum, rolling us until she's tucked beneath me on the blanket. "I can do that."

I cover her body with mine, rising only to help her pull off my sweater and add it to the pile with hers. It's a flurry of movement as both of us try to shuck off our clothes as fast as we're able, a thrill coursing between us from being so exposed to the world. It's highly unlikely that anyone would stumble across us, and honestly, the idea of anyone else seeing her like this makes me a wee bit feral, but still . . . the possibility of being caught only amps up the desperation.

"So fucking lovely," I kiss into her skin when she's naked underneath me.

The softness of her body pressed against mine is a revelation—the way her thighs part to make room for me, the way her hands rove over my skin as if she can't get enough of touching me—it culminates into an all-encompassing need to have her, setting off a familiar frenetic energy inside that seems directly linked to her touch.

I glide my hand down her belly to dip it between her legs, groaning when I feel how soaked she is. I slant my mouth over hers as I dip a finger inside her, letting that tight heat wrap around the digit, knowing just how good it will feel when it's my cock.

"Already wet for me, love," I practically purr. "This pretty cunt was made for me."

Her arm winds around my neck, trying to bring me closer. "*Lachlan.*"

"Shh." I add a second finger, twisting them, curling them to touch that place inside that has her bucking her hips. "I wish there was time to taste you. I love the way you come on my tongue. Maybe tomorrow I'll wrap your legs around my shoulders and have your cunt for every meal, aye?"

"Stop teasing me," she huffs.

I pull my fingers free, running them through her slick center in a slow back-and-forth pattern. "Is this not enough for you, princess?" I tease. "You need more than my fingers, aye?"

Her head tilts back and her mouth falls open when I circle her clit with my finger still drenched from being inside her, her lashes fluttering as her breath catches. "Fuck me," she breathes prettily. "I want your cock."

"It's yours, love," I murmur, pulling my hand away and making room between her legs as my cock teases her entrance. I watch her expression as I start to push inside, the wet heat of her enveloping me like a fist, so tight I could come just from this if I weren't careful. "All yours," I sigh.

I feel her nails at my shoulders when she's taken me to the hilt, and I can't help but circle my hips, that sensation of being wrapped up in Key one that never ceases to leave me dizzy.

"Och," I groan, burying my face into her throat. "S'good." My voice slurs with pleasure. "S'always so good."

"Move," she pleads, tilting up her hips as if she might somehow take more of me. "*Move.*"

The breeze makes the air even chillier than usual, and yet I can feel sweat beading at my hairline, can see it collecting at Key's temples, no doubt warmed by my too-hot body. I pull her into me to keep her covered when I start to move, rolling my hips as the snug slide of my cock in and out of her makes me tremble all over.

With every withdrawal I can feel her inner walls clinging to me, and when I ease back in, it's nothing but velvety softness that has me groaning into her throat. I feel her legs wrap around my waist, urging me closer, and I brace my arms against the blanket on either side of her head, rising up so I can watch her face as I start to fuck her steadily. Her emerald eyes are hazy and her pink mouth is parted as sharp breaths puff out of her, and I feel a hot tension licking through my body, almost as if my blood is rushing faster. As if a steady drumming of *mine mine mine* begins to course through me.

I see her eyes widen then, her pupils dilating as she says, "Lachlan . . . your eyes."

Her hand rises so she can run her fingers along my jaw, her thumb brushing back and forth against my cheekbone. I feel my skin grow tighter and my fingers prickle, and when I glance down at my hands, I notice claws starting to sprout from the tips.

I go still, my chest heaving as I struggle to catch my breath. "Key," I rasp. "I need—" I grit my teeth, shutting my eyes as I try to get control back. "Just give me a second."

"Oh. *Oh.*" Her lashes flutter as her head tilts back, a pretty flush spreading up her neck. "I can feel you—*fuck*. I think you're getting bigger."

I clench my fingers as the claws form fully, tearing holes into the blanket beneath us, to watch as I slowly pull out of her. I gape in surprise when I notice my cock has definitely gotten thicker, longer even, maybe—but more noticeable than that . . . there are fucking *ridges* protruding down the length of it.

"What the fuck," I whisper. I snap my gaze back up to meet hers. "Key . . . this has never happened."

She reaches between us, wrapping her slim fingers around my throbbing cock and squeezing from the base to tip. I shudder as pleasure courses through me, watching as she presses her teeth against her lower lip, her eyes roving over my body.

"Wow," she murmurs. "You look . . . pretty."

My brow knits at her choice of words, but when I follow the path of her eyes, I notice shimmering patches of dark green scales cropping up on my skin. On my shoulders, my chest, hips . . . even a line of them running along my pelvis right up to the base of my cock.

"Key, I—" I can do little more than gape, at a loss for words. "I don't know what's happening."

"Do you feel like you're changing?"

I take a quick assessment, feeling nothing of the usual sensations that rack through me when I start to change into the beast. Instead, there is only a thrumming energy that seems to touch every part of me, feeling more *alive* than I ever have.

"I don't . . . think so?"

She presses her hand flat over the top of my cock, forcing it down so that it slides through the wet folds of her cunt. We both moan at the sensation, and just touching her like this makes it that much harder to regain control. To even find the willpower to *want* to.

"I don't want you to stop," she tells me hoarsely. "I want you." She gives my cock another squeeze. "Just like this."

"Key, we shouldn't—"

She's already guiding my cock back to her entrance, rubbing the sensitive head there and forcing a groan to fall out of my mouth.

She does it again, teasing herself with me. "Do you want me?"

"You know I fucking do," I grind out.

I feel her other hand cup my nape, pulling me down for a kiss. "Then take me," she murmurs. "I can handle it."

"Key," I whisper. "What if—"

She covers my mouth with hers, kissing me deep before she says, "You won't hurt me. I trust you."

And when she slicks the head of my cock once more against her drenched opening, I lose any remaining will to protest.

I slide inside her, going as slowly as I'm able even though everything in my entire body is screaming at me to slam into her with everything I have, but she's so much fucking *tighter* now. It's almost unbearable how tight she is. The ridges on my cock press against her inner walls, and her thighs quiver around my hips, a sharp gasp tumbling out of her.

"Oh, *fuck*."

"Key," I groan. "S'like you're fucking stuffed full of me. You're strangling my cock."

"Feels good," she huffs. "Keep going."

Her hand slides across the scales on my shoulder, and the skin there feels more sensitive, sending sparks of pleasure along them. I keep my pace slow at first, letting her get used to me, just a slow withdrawal before an easy press back inside. Even if it's driving me fucking crazy.

"Yeah?" I push deeper, stirring my hips. "You like fucking a monster, Key?"

"It's you," she hums prettily, slanting her mouth over mine. "It's just you."

And maybe it's because I don't have to hide from her, maybe it's because there's nothing about me that makes her afraid—but when she kisses me so sweetly, her heels digging into my ass as if silently begging for *more*—it makes it all too easy to finally *let go*.

I sit back on my heels, grabbing her by the waist to pull her into my lap, and the sight of my black claws against her pale skin is erotic in a way that should be alarming. I'm careful, ever so careful not to hurt her, but I can't stop the way I rub my thumbs back and forth along her hip bones, the viciousness of it so at odds with the wet warmth of her cunt that still hugs me so tightly.

I roll my hips harder, watching her tits bounce with the force of my thrust. "This what you need?" I do it again, my eyes drawn to the sight of those ridges disappearing inside her one by one. "You want me to fuck you like a beast?"

"Keep going," she whines. "Don't stop."

"Och, I can do that," I rumble, sliding my palm along her belly just to marvel at the contrast of my claws along her skin once more. "Gonna fill this pretty cunt until you're bursting with it."

Her back bows when I really start to *move*—the sound of my hips meeting her ass ringing out into the cool, twilight air. The sun has lowered enough to cast a rosy hue along her skin, blending with the all-over flush that's spread over her chest and throat. The sight of my thick cock forcing its way inside her again and again looks almost violent, and yet she takes each thrust with pleas for more. She all but *begs* me for it.

And the monster . . . the monster can't fucking get enough.

"That's it, love," I coo. "Look at you. You're so *good*. Taking everything. You look so bloody good stuffed full of my cock like this."

"Lachlan," she gasps. "I'm— Can you—*ah*. Touch me. I need you to touch me."

And there's a small part of me that wants to remind her of the danger, but it's superseded by the roaring in my ears, the rushing of my blood. I reach between her legs to dip a thumb between the lips of her cunt, circling her swollen clit as carefully as I can while still pounding into her ferociously.

She lights up as soon as I touch her, her belly clenching and thighs going taut as I roll my thumb in a steady circle, as I slip in and out of her again and again and *again*.

"Come for me," I tell her, my voice too rough, too wrong, but falling from my lips as if it's someone else's. "I want you to come on this cock, Keyanna. Want you to come full of a monster."

She trembles all over, as if the words themselves are amping her higher, and I see it, the moment she lets go. I *feel* it; the walls of her cunt ripple along the length of my cock, practically milking my orgasm out of me, forcing me to follow after her.

I let out a roar that sounds every bit as beastly as I feel—throwing my head back and pressing flush against her as I pulse deep inside. She continues to tremble beneath me with aftershocks, and I can't seem to do more than hold her tightly, unable to let her go.

I curl my body, molding myself to her as I nuzzle just below her ear. I can feel her fingers sliding over my shoulders, up into my hair to card through the strands, and I think to myself that at this moment I feel more *right* than I ever have. Keyanna has insisted over and over that everything will be okay, that we'll beat this—but I'm realizing that it's only with her in my arms that I can almost *believe* it.

"I would not object to doing that again before we sort all this out," she says with a breathy laugh, turning to brush her lips along my jaw.

A choked laugh of my own escapes me, and I press my palms on either side of her against the now slightly shredded blanket, cocking a brow at her. I don't miss the way she shivers when the movement stirs my cock, which is now growing soft inside her—things feeling like they might be slowly going back to normal—enjoying the way it makes her eyes go hazy, the way she bites her lip after.

"You really are a devil woman," I chuckle.

Her lips quirk, and she reaches up to glide her palm over the hard planes of my chest. "I think you might like it," she hums.

*I think I might more than like it*, I don't say.

Because as impossible as it may be, as *improbable* even—I might be a bit more than falling for Keyanna MacKay, the woman who should be my enemy but just . . . isn't. The only one who makes me feel like maybe, just maybe . . . things might *actually* turn out all right.

"It's almost dark," I murmur, already mourning the loss of her.

I notice her expression fall. "Oh."

Something squeezes in my chest at the sight of her disappointment, and I can honestly say that I have never felt the weight of the curse more than I do at this moment. I want to walk with her under the starlight, to take her back to my bed and hold her through the night. I want so many things that I've never allowed myself to hope for. Things that make the uncertainty of the future all the more terrifying.

I lean in close, kissing her cheek gently. "We'll fix it, love," I tell her. "We'll find the answer."

She wraps her arms around my neck in lieu of a response, hugging me tightly as if she's afraid to let me go. As if deep down inside, she worries that letting me out of her grip will mean that I won't come back to her. I wish more than anything I could promise her that it isn't a possibility, that it won't happen.

Because in a world where it feels like I've never had much of anything . . . it suddenly feels like I have everything to lose.

## 25

### KEYANNA

I'm righting my clothes when I catch Lachlan peering over at the sinking sun, a frown on his face. "You'd better head back."

"About that," I tell him. "I was thinking . . . I'd like to see it happen."

He stills, his brow furrowing. "You don't want to see it, Key. It's . . . shocking."

"More shocking than claws and a ridged dick?" I ask with an arched brow.

His mouth opens and then closes, his lips pursing. "It's . . . different."

"Hey." I close the distance between us, his chest still bare given the fact that he'd just have to undress in a matter of minutes anyway. I press my hand there, looking up at him. "It's not going to scare me away, okay? It just feels . . . wrong. Not seeing everything. If we break—" I stop myself, shaking my head. "*When* we break this curse, I want to be able to say I saw it all. All of you."

"Technically you already did," he reminds me.

I shake my head. "I didn't see you change."

He gives me a long look as if he's considering, and then he nods stiffly, eyes wary. "All right. But . . . if it's too much, just forget you saw anything, aye?"

"I can handle it," I say, pressing a kiss to his cheek. "Don't worry."

"You'd better stand back, then."

I do as he says, taking several steps back as he glances once more at the sinking sun before grabbing for his pants to undo them. He grins when I waggle my eyebrows, giving a small shake of his head.

"Maybe you just wanted to watch me strip, aye?" he jokes, his voice just barely giving away his nerves.

"It's a bonus," I tell him.

And it is, honestly. As he shucks his pants down his massive thighs, revealing what seems like miles of bronzed skin and an impressive cock even when soft—I mean. It doesn't hurt.

"If you keep looking at me like that," he says, "I'll likely be too hard to get this done."

I laugh. "I don't think it works that way."

"Aye, but I've never been hard as a monster. It's not something I want to learn how to navigate today."

"Now I'm a little curious," I say with another laugh.

"Devil woman," he mutters, pulling his feet free of his pant legs and dropping them to the side.

He casts one more look toward the sun, then starts backing up until he's standing in the shallows of the water. He shivers a little with the cold of it, closing his eyes as the sun creeps lower and lower, until it's only a sliver of light on the horizon.

"Just remember what I said," he reminds me. "And remember . . . I won't hurt you."

I shake my head. "I know you wouldn't. I think it's safe to say, after what we just did, that I trust you."

His mouth breaks out into a smile, but it's short-lived, quickly morphing into a grimace. He all but doubles over, clenching his stomach as his skin starts to ripple with movement and color. It's like moments ago when we had sex, but more violent—a faster change that seems to tear through him all at once. My mouth falls open as his neck elongates, as his features shift into something more monstrous before my very eyes—all the while his skin darkening and forming scales that start to cover all of his rapidly changing body.

He grows and grows, the man standing before me moments ago lost to the quickly forming beast—and after a matter of seconds of watching what looks to me like a very painful shift—the beast I remember saving me floats in the shallows, twisting his neck this way and that as if it's stiff from the change. His gaze settles on me, and I have to remind myself that this is Lachlan, that he would never hurt me. He's just so *big* now.

But then he lowers his head in a submissive gesture, inviting me in, and my feet stumble forward as if they have a mind of their own, bringing me closer to him until they're submerged in the water. I press my hands on either side of his wide face, peering into his plate-size eyes, which are the same piercing blue I often get lost in.

"There you are," I say softly, stroking my hand up one side of his face. "You're still pretty beautiful, you know?"

Lachlan makes a noise that sounds suspiciously like a snort, and I pat his cheek playfully. "You are, you stubborn ass. Different but . . . beautiful."

He shivers in my hold, his eyes going half-mast as he nudges his massive nose against my cheek. I let him nuzzle me there, and there's something so strangely intimate about it all, seeing him in this way no one else can, *knowing* that it's him inside the beast. I turn my face to press a kiss to his snout—closing my eyes.

"Thank you," I tell him. "For showing me."

He makes another noise, a guttural thing that I can only assume is his version of *you're welcome*—and I pat his cheek once more before stepping back just a little. I take in his long neck and his giant body, finding a gracefulness in this form that I doubt he's ever taken the time to appreciate. I doubt anyone has, for that matter.

I give one more kiss to his snout, rubbing my nose back and forth there before telling him, "You'd better go. It's too dangerous for you to be on the shore for too long."

Another rumbling sound, one that must be his agreement, because he starts to swim backward, going deeper into the loch. I watch him go until I can't see him anymore, feeling overwhelmingly grateful that he trusts me like this, especially knowing there are so few in his life he's deemed worthy of that trust.

I vow to myself right there, standing in the shallows of the loch, that I'll do everything in my power to make sure that trust is earned.

A noise behind me makes me jolt, a shaking of the bushes farther up the shore making me spin around as what sounds like the thumping of footsteps makes my heart begin to race.

*Did someone see?*

I rush out of the water toward the sound, only to be met with a rabbit bounding out of the bush, causing a rush of air to expel from my lungs, relieved that it wasn't someone spying. That's the last thing we need right now.

It hits me then that I ran toward the noise without any regard for my own safety, that I was too concerned with Lachlan to even entertain the idea of my own well-being. The realization gives me pause, because while I'm no expert on the matter . . . that feels a lot like what love is.

And given that Lachlan's future is so uncertain despite my fervent proclamations . . . that thought is way more terrifying than the monster I just let nuzzle me.

The walk back to the farmhouse seems longer than usual; I'm still ruminating on this new possibility with regards to my feelings for Lachlan, making it impossible to do more than meander back toward the main path that leads home.

*Home.*

I'm not sure when it started feeling like that to me, but I realize that the farmhouse—my grandparents, the land, Lachlan, even the damned cows—*all* of it makes me feel more at home than I have since the day my dad passed. It makes me wonder about what my future might look like. I think that my grandparents would be thrilled if I stayed here in Scotland, especially now that Rhona and I are finding our footing, but I can't help wondering if Lachlan would feel the same.

I shudder as I recall what happened back on the shore of the loch; maybe it's strange that I didn't feel fear when I noticed that he'd started to shift to some sort of in-between state, but in that moment all I could sense was a burning desire to have more of him. To share parts of him no one else ever had. And *God* had it been good. I'll never tell him this, but I might actually miss the claws if we do find a way to break his curse.

*When*, I correct myself. *When* we break his curse.

Because there's no other option, as far as I'm concerned. Hearing him talk about not turning back . . . it really shook me. I think that's why, in the moment, I needed to touch him, to remind myself that he's still *here*. I needed the tangible proof that we still have time, because I refuse to entertain the possibility that I might lose him after just finding him. He has too much life to live. *We* have too much life to live. Or at least, I hope that's the case.

Fuck, maybe I really am gone for the guy. I think *that* thought scares me more than any monster-y bits he might show me ever could. It's far too soon, far too nonsensical, and yet the thought of walking away from him now, for any reason, makes my breath come shorter and my chest grow tight. I rub the spot thoughtfully, coaxing the muscles to unwind as I tell myself I have nothing to worry about. Willing it to be true.

When I make it back to the farmhouse, I find it fairly quiet, leaving my shoes at the door as I venture inside. I can hear quiet sounds coming from the den, and find Rhona sitting quietly by the fire, knitting while she rocks in one of the chairs.

"Evening," she calls. "You just get in?"

I nod from the doorway. "Mhm. I was . . ." I feel heat flush at my neck as I recall what I was *actually* doing. "I was just out for a walk."

"Good place for it," Rhona chuckles. She gestures to the chair beside her. "Come sit with me a spell before I have to go and start dinner."

I hesitate in the entry for a moment; I don't know if I'll be good company, given that my head is still scrambled with the possibility that *Lachlan might not turn back tomorrow*—but I've had so few moments alone with Rhona since we started trying to make this work, and it's not as if I can *tell* her why my brain is a mess of anxiety.

I shuffle farther into the room and plop down into one of the overstuffed armchairs, sinking into the soft cushion and trying to push some of my muddled thoughts away. I notice that the rest of the house appears to be relatively silent, the only sounds to be heard are the faint clicking of Rhona's needles and the soft crackling of the fire.

"Where is everyone?" I ask.

"Finlay is down at the pub playing cards again with Hamish and a few others," she tells me.

I scoff lightly. "Hopefully he won't stoop to getting them plastered just to win."

"Aye," Rhona laughs. "Your grandpa takes his cards very seriously."

"Is Brodie with him?"

"No, he's . . ." Her brow knits. "Actually, I don't know where that boy has run off to. Been gone most of the day, really." She puffs out a breath. "No doubt working on his little side project."

"It will be cool to see it when it's done," I say. "I'd love to know more about our family."

Rhona hmphs. "Bunch of lovestruck fools, most of them."

"What do you mean?"

"Och. Our name means 'happy,' did you know?"

"Seems kind of ironic, given the last few months," I grumble.

Rhona laughs dryly. "Aye, I suppose so. There are dozens of stories down the line about MacKay men sacrificing something or other for love. Finlay's father used to say it was the MacKay curse. Used to tell this auld story about some auld MacKay *way* down the line who saved a fairy princess or some other from an evil laird." She rolls her eyes. "Finlay used to tell the same story to your da when he was a wee lad."

Something about that makes me pause; it sounds so similar to everything we've been told about the story of Tavish and the kelpie but not quite right. "He saved her from some evil dude?"

"It's just a story," Rhona says with a cluck of her tongue. "But that's how Finlay's father told it. Usually after he regaled us with tales of how he stepped on a weever fish trying to find Finlay's mother's ring after she dropped it in the ocean when he took her to Sutherland one summer."

"What's a weever fish?"

"Nasty wee things," she tells me. "Massive stinger on their back. Hurts like hell."

"So what did Grandpa sacrifice for *you*, then?" I tease.

"Och." She shakes her head, but there's a fond smile on her mouth now. "To hear *him* tell it—he gave up his wily ways to be with me. Popular as he was."

I can't help but laugh. "That does sound like him."

"Truth be told," she says, lowering her voice, "I'm not sure your grandpa has sacrificed a day in his life. He's a lucky bastard, that one." The mirth ebbs from her eyes immediately, as if remembering. "Well . . . save for your father, I suppose."

She goes quiet after that, concentrating on her knitting needles. I can feel pain radiating off her in waves, and it clutches me tight, wishing I knew how to make it better. So much suffering in this family . . . and for what?

I tilt my chin toward the project bundled in her lap—eyeing the soft-looking emerald color of the yarn with interest. "What are you making?"

"I . . ." She pauses her needles as an honest *blush* creeps into her cheeks—making my stoic grandmother appear almost . . . bashful. "Well, if you must know," she says, clearing her throat and trying for her usual hardness. "I was making an extra blanket for your bed. It's getting colder, and I didn't know how long you meant to stay, so I thought—"

"That's for me?"

I can feel the smile creeping across my face, warmed by the

gesture and even more so by the blatant embarrassment coloring Rhona's features. It makes her seem softer, doing something so grandmotherly. It makes my chest hurt all over again but with something more like joy.

"It's nothing much," she mumbles.

I just smile wider. "It's already gorgeous," I tell her honestly. "I can't wait to use it."

"Aye, well." She turns her eyes back to her needles, shrugging softly. "I know Duncan's auld room can get drafty sometimes."

I feel my breath catch. "I'm staying in my dad's old room?"

"Did I not mention that?"

"No, I . . ." My mind whirrs with the information, part awestruck that I'm sleeping in the same place that housed my dad growing up, part reeling with the knowledge that I've barely given the room a second look since I got here—haven't even really *thought* that there might be something hidden in there. "I didn't know," I say finally. "That's . . . interesting."

Rhona pauses her knitting once more, her eyes softening as she stares at her hands. "It's been . . . nice. Having you there. Sometimes it really does feel like a part of my boy came back to me." A small smile touches her mouth, and when she looks over at me, her eyes are full of warmth. "I supposed he did, though, didn't he?"

I feel my eyes sting with the threat of tears, and I have to blink rapidly just to will them away. There have been entirely too many emotional roller coasters today, thank you very much.

"Yeah," I answer thickly. "I hope so."

She clears her throat, blinking furiously, and I suspect she might be fighting back tears of her own, but I won't call her on it.

"Best you go and clean up for supper," she says stiffly. "I'll be done here shortly."

"All right," I tell her.

I push out of the chair, noticing she doesn't look at me as I do so. I'm still buzzing slightly with the new information about staying in my dad's room, but instead of rushing up the stairs like part of me wants to—I hold back. I waver for a moment as I try to determine whether it would be welcome or not, finally deciding to just go for it as I close the distance between my grandmother and me, leaning down to hug her around the shoulders. She goes still in my arms for a moment, maybe two, but then she relaxes into them, and I feel the light pressure of her hand as it pats my forearm gently.

"You're a good lass," she says softly.

I press a barely there kiss to her cheek. "Thank you."

"Now go on, I said," she grunts. "Enough of this silliness."

I leave her be then, knowing she isn't the type to show anything she deems weakness in front of others, but I don't miss the way she smiles gently as she works now. I think maybe she needed the hug a lot more than she would ever let on.

I know I did.

## 26

### LACHLAN

I don't know why I keep doing this. For years, it's been clear that there is nothing left of the man I knew as my da living in the beast that shares the loch with me, and yet every so often, I can't help but try to prove myself wrong. Tonight is no different; in the form of the beast, my senses are higher, so I can feel when he's near. He likes to keep to a shelf in the deeper part of the loch, and I can usually find him resting there when he isn't hunting for fish.

I'm always met with hostility.

We can't speak, not like this, but there's still a line of communication between us. A language that I instinctively understand, but one that he doesn't seem to fully grasp. The voice of the beast is low and mournful, and when I call out to him from a safe distance, projecting everything I'm hoping for in my question—his answering cries are full of disjointed impressions of *STAY AWAY* and *ENEMY*. As if he really is nothing more than a beast defending his territory.

I wonder if it's near time to accept that Callum Greer is really gone.

It's dark tonight, the cloud cover blotting out most of the stars, so I feel safe in going to the surface. Da's territory is in the deepest part of the loch, after all, miles away from shore. It would be almost impossible to spot anything out here even *if* some passersby were walking along the shore tonight. I just need the air. I need to breathe it in and remember that I'm not lost yet.

I can sense my da lurking some distance away, no doubt hovering to see if I'll come any closer. If he needs to defend his home. I have old scars from similar encounters, and knowing that my father has made me bleed on more than one occasion is disheartening to say the least. I often have to remind myself that it's not him, not really.

I truly don't know why I sought him out tonight; I haven't for quite some time. Maybe it's because I feel the weight of it all more heavily tonight. After touching Key earlier, feeling her complete acceptance of me, her ironclad certainty that she'll somehow free me of this—I suppose it got me wondering whether or not freedom for me would mean freedom for my da as well. If the curse can be broken, will he come back to us? Or is it too late for him?

I fear the alternative rings truer, but it's painful to even try to accept. I've been without him for more years than I had him, but something about my growing feelings for Keyanna make it hurt worse somehow. I think about a future where I might live a normal life, where I might make her mine, *really* mine, ring and all—one where we might have weans of our own. Ones he'll never meet.

It's bloody heartbreaking, is what it is.

But I suppose I should be used to that feeling.

Thoughts of Key make things both better and worse; I've been thinking a lot lately about the things I've yet to tell her. Part of me has been too much of a coward, afraid that things will be different if she knows everything, but given the realization that my feelings are far deeper for her than I ever thought they could be—I don't think

I have a choice, really. Curse or no curse, I know that there is no future together that is based on dishonesty. Key has been nothing but open with me, and she deserves the same courtesy.

The clouds part over the loch, revealing a sliver of moonlight, a peek of stars. It hits me then that I haven't seen the stars as a man, not once; I wonder if they might look different. I think if we manage to break the curse—the first thing I'll do is walk under them with Key. It's a good enough start to a to-do list, I think.

*MINE*

*AWAY*

*ATTACK*

I turn just before I feel him approach, my distracted train of thought meaning I hadn't noticed when he got closer. I dart away just as my da lunges from below, his powerful jaws snapping at the air when he emerges from the depths. With the moonlight pouring down on his mossy green skin, his eyes seem to glow with a burning wildness that doesn't look even remotely human. He stays still where he is, drifting on the surface as he projects more violent urgings— mostly of the variety that I leave his territory—and instead of sadness, a creeping numbness seems to take over. One that comes from realizing that there's nothing for me here. That there may never be.

I lower my head in a clear gesture of submission, slowly swimming backward as I maneuver my large body farther away from the area, heading for the channel that leads to the cove where I left my clothes. I feel his presence behind me for a long while, and when it finally fades, I tell myself that it will be all right. That even if it's too late for him, he would be happy knowing that it might not be too late for me. I know my da well enough to know that, at least.

I swim for the shore with new resolve, telling myself that it's not over for me, not yet. Tomorrow, I will tell Keyanna everything that she still doesn't know, and after I've begged her forgiveness for keeping it from her, we'll find the answer together. I allow myself to believe that, sharing in Key's fierce determination and praying it isn't unfounded. Because I think I know now that behind me lies my past, but ahead . . . there might still be a future.

The farm is uncharacteristically quiet when I reach it the next morning; the cows aren't braying their usual morning demands for breakfast, the chickens are silent, and even the main house is dark. I check the cottage to find it empty, frowning while wondering if Key let Finlay get her drunk again. The thought morphs my frown into a slight grin. I'd like to see that someday.

I'm about to knock on the main door of the house when Rhona opens it to my raised fist, pursing her lips at me. "Looking for something?"

"I was . . ." This woman is a foot shorter than me, and somehow still intimidates the hell out of me. "I was just looking for Key."

"Course you were," she answers with a snort. She cocks a brow, looking up at me. "You doing what I said? Are you being good to her?"

I nod immediately, hoping that I am. "As best I can."

"Good." She moves to the side. "She's still in bed. Finlay roped her into another game of cards after dinner."

I have to school my mouth not to lift at the corners. "Thank you."

"No funny business in my house," she calls after me as I move past her.

I raise a hand as if in assent, but truthfully, I can't make any promises.

I find Key sprawled over her tiny bed, her hair a wild mess of curls that cover her face and one of her arms hanging over the side of the mattress. A smile touches my lips; there's a sadness there too, one that comes from knowing I can't wake up with her like I wish I could, but I shove it down, locking her bedroom door instead. Maybe a *little* funny business would go unnoticed.

I sit at the end of her bed, running my hand over one smooth calf as she wiggles in sleep, apparently ticklish. She makes a chuffed sort of sound in her sleep when I trail my fingers up the back of her thigh, smoothing my palm over the round curve of her ass before whispering her name.

"Key?"

"Mm." She presses her ass into my hand, but otherwise doesn't stir. "Lachlan."

I still when I notice her eyes are still closed, realizing that she's *dreaming* of me. It makes the beast in me positively feral, and I feel an itch in my fingertips as my claws threaten to spread. How quickly she pushes me into the monster just by being near me.

"Keyanna," I murmur again, gliding my hand under her shirt to ruck it up, exposing her soft stomach. I lean to press a kiss under her navel, peering up at her all the while. "Wake up."

"That feels nice," she answers breathily, eyes still closed.

"Does it?" My lips quirk as I hook a finger into her shorts, exposing her hip bone and kissing there too. "Wake up, and I'll make you feel better."

I press my nose into the crease of her thigh, finding the scent of her arousal already growing, making me doubly curious as to what she's been dreaming of. I lick at her skin, sucking a kiss there and gripping her thigh tight until I finally hear a gasp above me.

"Lachlan?"

Her pretty green eyes are heavy with sleep, blinking down at me as she tries to make sense of my being here.

"Someone slept in," I tell her.

She groans. "Grandpa cornered me again. Didn't know how to say no."

"How hinging are you?"

She shrugs. "I made sure not to have more than one of those poisonous toddies of his."

"Probably good for your health, that," I chuckle.

She shoots up in bed suddenly. "Oh! Rhona said something last night."

"Did she?"

"She said this is my *father's* old room."

My eyes widen, looking around the space. "Is that right?"

"Don't you know what this means?"

I cock my head, eyeing her curiously. "What?"

"The journal could be *here*." She points at the floor to drive home her point. "It could be hidden in this room somewhere."

My mouth parts, and I let my eyes sweep across the ordinary-looking room once more. "It could be," I tell her. I reach to grab her arm, squeezing gently. "But let's not get our hopes up. I don't want you disappointed if it isn't, aye?"

"It has to be," she urges, looking stricken. "We're running out of time. I can feel it."

"Shh, love," I coo, pulling her into my chest. "Don't fret. It will be all right."

"We don't know that," she mumbles against my shirt. "I feel like shit that we still haven't found it."

I rub her back, hating to see her so stressed.

"Maybe I could make you feel better," I murmur, kissing her hair. I grin then, remembering. "If you tell me what you were dreaming of."

Her cheeks immediately go pink, her mouth parting in surprise. "Dreaming?"

"You said my name, love," I tell her, dipping to kiss her cheek.

"I was—*oh.*" She makes a surprised sound when I push at her chest to urge her back down to the bed, parting her thighs and settling between them. "This," she gasps. "I was dreaming of this."

"You were dreaming about me tasting your pretty cunt?"

She bites her lip, nodding. "Except . . ."

"Except?"

"Well . . . you were . . ."

I run my nose up the center of her underwear, thankful as fuck that she prefers to sleep in just them. "I was?"

"You were kind of like last night."

I go still, peering up at her as I smirk. "Were you dreaming of the beast, Key?"

"Maybe."

The beast in question all but purrs inside me, closer to the surface than it's ever been when Key is around.

"Tell me what you dreamed," I urge.

"Your tongue," she says softly. "It was . . . It got . . . bigger."

My cock twitches in my jeans, and prickling at my fingertips tells me my claws have started to come out. Like knowing that she accepts me like this makes it easier to let go. I scrape them lightly against her skin, earning myself a sharp intake of her breath.

"Your eyes," she breathes. "They're so pretty like this."

I hook one claw into the elastic of her underwear, watching her as I carefully, *carefully* rip at the fabric. I can smell the way she gets wetter, my senses sharper in this in-between state. She *likes* this, I reaffirm. She really does.

"You want me to fuck you with a beast's tongue?"

"It was—*shit*." She hisses when I rip the other side of her underwear, slowly pulling them away and tossing them to the floor. "It was just a dream."

"Maybe it doesn't have to be," I tell her. "But then again . . . your granny said no shenanigans when she let me in."

Her teeth sink into her lower lip. "Did you lock the door?"

"Aye."

"She'll be feeding the chickens for a little while. If you . . . Well. If you wanted to—"

"I told you, love," I remind her. "I could have this pretty cunt for every meal, aye?"

She nods shakily. "You did."

"Spread your legs," I rasp. "Show me what's mine."

She sucks in a breath as she moves to do as I've said, parting her legs to reveal the already-wet crease of her, just begging for my mouth. The sight and scent of her set off a rumble in my chest that sounds barely human, but I force myself to show restraint, turning my head to kiss her thighs instead of diving between her legs to feast on her cunt like my body is urging me to.

"So soft," I tell her between presses of my lips against her skin. "So sweet." I lick up the inside of her thigh, tentatively letting go to the monstrous urges as I feel my incisors elongate and my tongue thicken. I concentrate on that sensation, trying to contain the beastliness to only where I want it, something that is admittedly difficult since I've never attempted it before.

She gasps when I finally let the elongated organ slip between her thighs, licking through the lips of her cunt and letting the tip curl around her already-swollen clit. Fuck, her *taste*. It makes me feel more feral than I no doubt already look.

She whimpers when I let my tongue glide down through her folds to let the tip tease at her entrance, but then something happens that surprises us both.

"Oh!"

I jerk back, glancing down at my too-long tongue with wide eyes as she does the same, eyeing the tip, which has split into two points to make a forked end. I draw as much as I can back into my mouth that will fit, watching her to see if it's too much. When I notice her dilated pupils and the way she subtly wets her bottom lip, I realize that it isn't.

I dip between her legs with renewed fervor, curling my hands around her thighs to keep her open to my mouth as I push the forked tip of my tongue through the crease of her, stopping at her clit to tease the bundle of nerves with both ends. I flick and tug and torment until she's panting, my eyes going half-mast as a satisfied hum resonates in my throat.

When I let the split points of my tongue find her entrance again, her back bows slightly, her mouth falling open as I push them inside, letting the newly stretched length of my tongue fill her in a way I never could as just a man. The wet, soft heat of her inside envelops my tongue, and the forked tip tickles her in the most sensitive places, causing her to buck her hips.

I push my tongue as deep as I can, only to slowly withdraw it, and Key's entire body shivers with its exit, her chest heaving as a small whimper escapes her lips.

"Lachlan," she says tightly. "That feels—"

I can't speak, not like this, so instead I double my efforts, starting to undulate my tongue back and forth, imagining it's my cock pumping into her. The sensation of her softness against my tongue is maddening, and I can feel my cock throbbing against the mattress, begging for relief. But this is about her right now.

I close my eyes as I let my tongue glide in and out of her, her thighs pressing against my hair as her body wiggles in my hold. All I can see and taste and smell is Key, and the beast inside revels in it, *wants more*—it wants to consume all of her, every last bit. My top lip trips against her throbbing clit, and she makes a garbled sound, so I do my best to suck it even hindered as I am.

I draw my tongue all the way out, lapping up her center before murmuring, "Och, love, I could eat you alive."

"Feels good," she breathes. "Don't stop."

"Wouldn't dream of it," I mumble, already tickling her entrance with the forked ends of my tongue before plunging back inside.

I show her no mercy now, giving her a steady in and out and *in* and *out* until she's writhing with it, until her sounds are so loud, I worry about someone coming to see if she's okay. I squeeze her thighs in warning, and I hear a choked sound, like she's trying to hold it back. When I peek up at her, I noticed she's biting the fleshy part of her hand, her lashes fluttering as she tries to keep quiet.

*Fuck, why is that so hot?*

I grip the soft skin of her thighs tighter, holding her firm while I fuck her with my tongue, shutting my eyes tight so I can revel in the scents and sounds of her. The soft, wet noises coming from her warm cunt as my tongue thrusts in and out, the heady scent of her arousal filling my nostrils and the room and my head—all of it a cocktail potent enough to drive me mad.

I can feel my claws pressing into her skin, hard enough to draw blood, and it takes all I have to show restraint, to not pierce her flesh while I lose myself in her. It becomes even more difficult when she starts to shake, her breath coming in short, sharp pants as her back bows and her arms scramble for purchase.

I can feel it—*taste it*—when she comes, and the monster in me keeps going, keeps lapping up every drop, letting it soak my tongue until my head spins. I don't stop until she's whimpering with sensitivity, finally, *finally* drawing my tongue back until only the forked ends remain, cleaning the quivering hole like the greedy beast I apparently am.

I'm still lapping at her gently when she says, "Oh my fucking God."

"Aye," I chuckle. "Lachlan is just fine."

She smacks my shoulder, but it's a weak move. "Pervert."

"Oh?" I nip her inner thigh, willing my heart rate to slow so that I might tempt my body into going back to normal. "And who was dreaming of such a scandalous thing, hm?"

She says nothing, just making a chuffed noise.

"Was it as good as your dream?" I ask.

She blows a puff of air through her lips. "And then some." She rises up on her elbows, looking down at me with glassy eyes. "What about you?"

"S'posed to be helping fix the fence on the western side of the farm," I tell her. "Likely I'll be busy all day."

"So are you saying you don't have time for me to suck you until your eyes cross like you just did me?"

Everything below the belt positively *throbs*, and it takes all my restraint not to pin her to the bed and have my way with her.

"Aye, well . . ." I clear my throat. "I s'pose I have a little time."

She gives me a coy grin. "That's what I thought."

27

KEYANNA

Despite the grand wake-up call Lachlan gave me, it didn't take long after he left to fix the fence for me to remember what had me feeling so urgent last night. Between my grandpa cornering me and the stellar dream and the even more fantastical real-life version of it—I had sort of forgotten about the fact that Rhona had let it slip that I had been sleeping *in my dad's room* this entire time. After telling Lachlan goodbye and having a bit of breakfast, I set to work effectively tearing the place apart.

But after an entire day, a small existential crisis, *and* pretending to have a stomachache so I could skip dinner, I can safely conclude that my dad's old room doesn't seem to be hiding anything extraordinary. I went through bins in the closet that I'm pretty sure weren't opened since before I was born—I did find an old photo of a teenage version of my dad that seemed to capture a particularly bad haircut, making me laugh—I quite possibly broke the chest of drawers trying to find some sort of secret compartment, like this is another installment of *National Treasure*, and currently, I'm sitting in the middle of a pile of shoe boxes I found at the bottom of the wardrobe that contain—surprise—a lot of old shoes.

The room is a mess, but my head is even messier. When Rhona

said that this entire time I've been staying in Dad's old room, it felt *important*. Like the missing piece of a puzzle, almost. I was certain that somewhere within these four walls I would find the journal that I'm still convinced *has* to be on the property. Even if, after this little episode, I can't deny that the doubts are starting to creep in.

Because what if he *did* bring it back to New York with him? What if he simply got rid of it? Lost it during a number of arbitrary moves? What if it simply wasn't as important as my brain seems to have decided that it is? Any of these possibilities threaten to leave me feeling lost, because what else is left when it comes to finding a solution for Lachlan? What if I can't fix things? What if I lose *him* too?

I feel the frustration bubbling up inside my chest, climbing higher into my throat, almost choking me. For the second time tonight I feel the sting of tears, and this time, I don't try to stop them from falling. It feels good to let them out, to allow the physical manifestation of my stress to slide over my cheeks and down into my lap—and I tell myself that after this pity party of mine, I'll pick myself back up. After this, I'll somehow manage to tighten my grip on my own determination.

But for now, it kind of feels good to fucking cry.

I just can't stop thinking about Lachlan just . . . not coming back in the morning. What would I do if he never changed back? I know that I would carry that guilt with me for the rest of my life—that no matter how short a time I've had him, I'd feel the loss of him forever. It makes a squeezing sort of pain grip my chest just thinking about it, making it harder to breathe.

*There has to be something. There just has to be.*

I'm wiping my eyes when I hear a soft knock at my door, and I swipe at my cheeks more frantically before bidding them entry, real-

izing that I probably look like I'm having some sort of breakdown—
which to be fair, I guess I kind of am—sitting here in such a mess
while quietly weeping.

"Key?"

I sniffle, using the heel of my hand to rub the last bit of liquid
from beneath my eyes. "Oh. Hey, Brodie."

"I heard you from the hall . . . You all right?"

I want to laugh, but I'm just too tired. I shake my head instead.
"Just having a bad day."

"Oh." His mouth turns down in a frown, and I can tell that he's
not used to dealing with a crying woman. The poor guy looks like
he's wishing he'd walked past my door now. "I'm sorry."

"It's fine," I tell him, blowing out a breath. "Or it will be. Just
having a little 'woe is me' moment."

He nods, eyeing the open bins and the stacks of papers and random items scattered around the floor. "You . . . looking for something?"

"Looking for something," I echo. I do laugh then, but it sounds
bitter. "You know when you get an idea in your head, like an itch or
something, and you can't think about anything else until you
scratch it?"

"I . . . suppose?"

I gesture my hands around the room. "This is my itch."

"I see." He eyes me warily like I might burst into flames at any
second. "Anything I can help with?"

I chuff out another sardonic laugh. "Not unless you're clairvoyant
and haven't told me."

"Sorry," he chuckles. "Can't say that I am."

I bob my head in a nod. "Figures."

"Rhona said you weren't feeling well," he says.

"Oh, I . . ." I give him a sheepish expression. "Honestly? I just wasn't feeling like socializing this evening."

I consider telling him the truth, that I'm up here destroying my room in search of Dad's old journal, but I can't for the life of me think of one rational reason as to why I would be so desperate for it without hinting at Lachlan's dilemma. And that's just not my place. Especially given that Lachlan has *just* started coming around to the idea of letting Brodie help at all.

"Aye, I get it." He nods idly, letting his eyes sweep around the room again. "Well, if you need anything, you just give me a shout, yeah?"

I offer him a smile. "I will. Thank you."

"None of that," he says, waving me off. "You're family."

*You're family.*

Fucking hell. Between Rhona and Brodie, this family is determined to make me weep all night. Next thing I know, Finlay will be coming up here to give me some family heirloom and read me a bedtime story.

"I know," I tell him, my voice just a *little* thick. "But seriously, thank you."

He nods again, grinning slightly. "Good luck righting all of this"—he gestures to the mess—"before Rhona sees."

"Don't remind me," I groan.

He chuckles. "Too bad there's not a magic button for that, aye?"

"Yeah," I snort.

I heave a sigh when he closes the door behind him, leaving me with my chaos. It occurs to me that I *will* need to get all of this put back where it was if I want to avoid having to make explanations to Rhona, and seeing the mountain of mess before me—it's a daunting task. Especially without the adrenaline of thinking I was seconds away from finding something like I had earlier.

I sigh. It really is too bad there's not a magic button or something.

It takes a few seconds for the thought to settle, and when it does, I go still, my mouth falling open. I look around at the piles and the stacks of things laid about haphazardly, and I wonder to myself if I've been going about this the wrong way.

*Maybe you are a bloody hound.*

*You're not a dowsing rod.*

I can hear Lachlan in my head, but I can't help wondering: *Could I be?*

I rush to my feet, careful to avoid any piles so that I don't trip—the last thing I need is to give Lachlan more ammunition for his assertion that I'm clumsy—closing my eyes and trying to steady my breathing. I can remember that day in the old Greer castle, the way it felt in that secret room. The strange *connection* I felt to something I still can't quite name.

I search for it now, hell, I fucking *beg* for it—chanting nonsense in my head, pleading with whatever force it is that's found me to just give me *something*.

*Come on*, I urge silently. *Where are you? I know you're there. I can feel it. Just give me this one thing. If you never do anything else for me, just let me have this one thing. Come on.* Come on. *Just show me where you—*

I gasp when I feel it, that pulsing thread of energy that calls to me, whispers that I do something. I don't even care that it's vague and doesn't offer any real instruction, too thrilled with the fact that I *found* it, that I'm another tiny step closer to getting a handle on whatever it is that came to me when I came here.

I spin on my heel, feeling something calling to me from . . . the floor? I wrinkle my nose, frowning. There are papers scattered about, sure, but unless they're somehow torn-out journal pages that are written in code . . .

I fall back to my knees, swiping the papers away. Beneath them, there is only the solid wood floor that is scuffed and ancient and has probably been here for more years than I can comprehend—too neatly laid to house any kind of secrets, I think. Too perfect, really, even in its ancientness. There's no way that there's—

Then I see it.

A hole in the wood that's no rounder than a finger, sitting at the corner of one neat plank that's almost tucked completely under the bed. Standing, you wouldn't even notice it. I drop to my belly and crawl under the bed, teasing the hole with the tip of my finger and feeling a rush of excitement when I find empty air beneath.

My heart begins to drum heavily inside my chest as I hook my finger and start to try and work the board loose, the wood fighting back, no doubt having sat untouched for more than two decades. It creaks and groans and tries its best not to give way, but after a minute of tugging and cursing under my breath, the board comes loose, revealing a hollow compartment beneath.

And there it is.

Cracked leather, yellowed paper, and all. It's bound with a frayed strap of separate leather, and I pull it out as gingerly as I can, not wanting to damage it. I sit up and cross my legs as I turn it over to study both sides, seeing nothing particularly special about it, but I can *feel* it, oddly. That same energy, that connection that led me to it. Like whatever strange magic that lives inside me touched this once too.

I carefully unbind the leather strap, knowing I should probably wait for Lachlan but simply too impatient to do so, grinning maniacally the entire time I'm opening the thing until a loose piece of paper falls from inside the cover—old but not nearly as old as the rest of the journal. It's on *notebook* paper, for God's sake. And when I see my dad's handwriting, something I would recognize anywhere even though it feels like it's been forever since I've seen it—the air gets trapped in my lungs.

> Mum,
>
> I don't know if you'll ever find this. I'm not even sure if I want you to. If you read what's inside this journal, you'll know the truth of why I left, and I don't know what's preferable— you being disappointed in me for leaving, or knowing with certainty that I left because I'm a coward.
>
> Maybe one day I'll find my courage, but know that I didn't leave because of you. Not really. I couldn't bring myself to test fate, couldn't make peace with not knowing what was to come—so I left. For her. The story in this journal is entirely true. <u>All of it.</u> Of that much, I'm sure. And that's why I couldn't take a chance. That's why I had to leave while I still could.
>
> But one thing has been, and will always be, certain.
> I love you.
>
> Duncan

I'm sobbing again. It seems like that's just the theme of the evening.

Seeing my dad's words, hearing his voice in them, especially knowing what reading this would mean for Rhona . . . it's too much. I clutch the letter to my chest, not even sure how I would begin to explain it to my granny so that I could share it, but I'm so full of grief at this moment that I can't bring myself to think that far ahead. There are too many questions. Too many things I don't understand.

*So I left. For her.*

What did he mean by that? Did he mean my mother? He had to, right? And what does she even have to do with this? I can't possibly fathom what connection she might have to everything I've learned—about me, about Lachlan, about our history—but I know that the only way to find those answers is to read the journal, whenever my hands stop shaking, that is.

It looks like I won't be getting any sleep tonight.

## LACHLAN

Leaving Keyanna to go and help Finlay was a hardship; while I'm learning to be less wary of the older man, he's no match for his bonnie granddaughter when it comes to preferred company.

"Can you hold this piece there?"

I give my attention to the old man in question, reaching for the wooden piece he's gesturing to, grabbing it and holding on to it so he can hammer it in place. "Got it."

"These wee heifers," Finlay chuckles. "Nothing can stop them when they set their mind to something, aye? Even a fine fence like this one."

"There's nothing 'wee' about your heifers, Finlay."

He flashes me a grin. "Just babies, all of them."

"If you say so," I snort.

I listen to the rhythmic thudding of his hammer as he nails the wood into place, not letting go of the piece I'm holding until he pulls back, wiping the sweat from his brow. "There are at least four more places down like this," he tells me. "It'll take all day at this rate."

"I've got time," I say.

Finlay chuckles again, giving me a wry look. "Time to spare away from my granddaughter, you mean?"

My eyes go wide, my lips parting in surprise at his blatant callout.

"Don't look so shocked, lad," he says. "You think my Rhonnie keeps secrets from me?"

"S'pose she wouldn't," I mumble.

Finlay takes his hammer again, tapping at one of the posts as he eyes me. "Now tell me," he starts. "Are ye jerkin' me granddaughter around?"

"I . . . No. Of course not," I splutter, shocked by the sudden hardness in Finlay's gaze.

I don't think I've ever seen the man frown when he wasn't crying. I shake my head. "I—" *Love her? Am obsessed with her? Want a future with her if I don't lose myself to the beast?* "I care about her," I settle on. "A lot."

"That's real good," Finlay answers with a nod. "Because I know you're bigger than me, lad," he says, "but I know where the sink-holes are."

"We don't have sinkholes," I balk.

Finlay's lips curl up in a grin that is unsettling. "Aye, you keep believing that."

"I don't want to hurt her," I assure him, eyeing his hammer with an uneasiness that isn't like me. "That's the *last* thing I want."

Finlay eyes me for a long moment, his grim expression finally morphing into his usual friendly one as he guffaws a laugh. "Right then," he says cheerily. "That's settled." He waves his hammer at me. "Can't have someone running around breaking my granddaughter's heart when I just got her, aye?"

"Aye," I agree. "And I wouldn't."

"Good." Finlay winks at me, tapping his hammer against the wood post as he eyes farther down the fence line. "Reckon we can get this done before supper, then?" He glances over at me once more. "I'll expect you to be coming to supper soon, by the way. You ken?"

My chest clenches at the knowledge that those promises are ones I can't make, that it's currently out of my hands, but I want to believe in a not-too-distant future where it *will* be something I can agree to.

"Aye," I say, channeling that hope. "I ken."

He pats my shoulder, gesturing to the quad bike. "We'd best get a move on then, aye?"

I follow after him, my head still reeling slightly from the complete shift in Finlay's demeanor I just witnessed. I have a feeling if I were to tell Key, she wouldn't even believe me. Hell, I wouldn't. I doubt I'll see her again today, not with all the work to be done that I'm just hoping we can wrap up long before sunset—but I make a mental note to tell her all about this first thing tomorrow morning.

*Can't have someone running around breaking my granddaughter's heart when I just got her, aye?*

If he only knew how utterly enamored with her I am. It's almost laughable.

Still doesn't keep me from eyeing Finn warily for the rest of the day.


The night is another brutal one; I was exhausted from the long day of fixing fences, and that paired with another night of my father chasing me away from anything he deems his territory—it didn't make for a restful evening. I managed to grab some sleep before sunrise, thankfully, but still my body feels stiff and sore, only partly because of the oddity of changing shape. It's something that I imagine is ghastly to see—experiencing it certainly is—so I'm still a little surprised that Key saw all of it and didn't run away screaming. It actually makes me smile, remembering how she reacted to me. Like I wasn't a monster. Like I was still just . . . me. She makes me feel like that in a lot of ways, really.

The sun is just starting to creep higher in the sky, the gloomy overcast from last night seeming to have dissipated with daybreak, leaving the dew-covered grass glittering in the warm rays of morning. It casts a glow-like backdrop on the farm as I crest over the hill that leads there, and I pause for a moment at the top, taking it all in.

It's not my home, and I know that, but something about knowing that Key is waiting for me down there, that she's missed me during the night . . . it almost makes it feel like it is. It's the first time I've felt close to this feeling since my family fell apart.

I trot down the hill and onto the gravel road that winds up toward the main house, breaking away from it and crossing the grass toward the groundskeeper's cottage instead. It was only yesterday that I last touched Keyanna, and yet all I can think about is burying myself inside her, reveling in her warmth and her touch and letting it make me feel more human. Something about her just *grounds* me in a way nothing ever has.

It means I'm smiling when I open the door in anticipation of her, but when I see her huddled on my bed, dark circles under her reddened eyes as she clutches a thick, leather-bound book that looks positively ancient—the good feelings in me seem to wither and dissipate all at once.

And all at once—I just *know*.

"You found it," I choke out.

She nods solemnly, looking far less excited than I thought she would be. This is it, isn't it? Surely this has to be the answer. It *has* to be.

So why does she look so devastated?

I take quick steps to close the distance between us, coming to the edge of the bed and kneeling as I reach for her cheek, forcing her eyes to mine. "What's wrong?"

"I haven't finished yet," she tells me.

I notice that she's turned somewhere to the three-quarters mark of the journal, and I think to myself that she can't possibly believe that I would be upset that she hadn't, right?

"That's okay," I tell her gently. "We have time, Key. Don't fret."

She shakes her head, pulling her face from my grasp and scooting back to make room for me on the bed. "I think you need to sit down."

I do as she asks, lifting myself from the floor just to take the place beside her on the bed, and she holds the book to her chest as if it's something dangerous, as if at any moment it might explode. She holds it almost like she's *afraid* of it, and that makes me wary too.

"Tell me what's wrong," I all but beg. "You look like you've been crying."

She snuffles out a breath, something between a snort and a scoff. "Yeah, it's been a hell of a night."

"Is it the book?" I feel my stomach sink. "Are there no answers? Is that why you're—"

"There are answers," she says softly, her eyes sad as she regards me. She looks like she's trying to decide how to let me down easy, but for what, I don't know. "I just . . . I don't know how to tell you this."

"You can just tell me," I say stiffly, trying to brace myself for whatever it is that would make her look so desolate. "It'll be all right, Key. I promise."

She nods again slowly, setting the book back on her lap and leafing through it delicately as if looking for something in particular. I watch as she turns the pages one after the other, noticing the way she winces ever so slightly when she seems to find what she's looking for.

"Now, remember," she says. "I haven't finished. There could be something I haven't seen yet. Something that makes more sense? I'm not sure how, but it's *going* to be okay. I just want you to know that this doesn't change things. Do you understand?"

My entire body feels like it's made of stone as dread settles deep. "Keyanna," I manage thickly. "Show me."

"Okay," she practically whispers.

She hands me the journal, open to the page she's found, pointing out a line where I assume she wants me to start. I take one last look at her crestfallen face—remembering what she said.

*It's going to be okay.*

I nod back at her as if in answer, turning my attention to the page. It doesn't take long for me to be absolutely sick.

*Winter, 1297*

*Laird Greer is back. Him and his men stink of blood, but news of their victory over the clans of the North have already made their way across the land. No one will dare challenge him now. He thinks himself to be a king. I watched as he made his way straight to her chambers. He doesn't know her. Not like I do. She's not evil as they believe. She's kept her promise. She waited for his return. No doubt she thought he would keep his. "The bridle in exchange for sanctuary," he vowed. And yet upon his return home he took her. Hid her away somewhere. I have searched the dungeons, but have found naught. He carries her bridle as if it belongs to him, as if it be his right. He <u>betrayed</u> her. He calls her a monster, but Sorcha is no monster. It is the Laird who is the true monster.*

*I cannot let this stand. I cannot let her rot in the dark while he stands in the sun, holding her prisoner. I <u>will</u> save her.*

My voice sounds unlike me when I ask, "Is it all like this?"

"Mostly," she answers softly. "The journal starts just before she comes to the keep. It . . . doesn't paint your ancestor in a very flattering light."

My grip tightens on the journal. "What does it say?"

"Lachlan, that's not important right now."

"What does it *say*?"

I hear her sigh, dropping her head to my shoulder. I can feel the warmth of her breath through the sleeve of my shirt when she speaks again. "It says he was a cruel, war-hungry man. He was unkind to his servants, to his kin . . . It says that he murdered innocent people from neighboring clans in some kind of widespread grab for power." She lets out a shuddering breath, her voice even softer when she adds, "My ancestor—I have to assume this is Tavish—he . . . he mentions a few times that the Laird was a brutally harsh man that was set on conquering the entire area. They say he stole women from villages he overtook and gave them to his men as rewards, that he killed children to end lines that he found threatening, that he—" She clears her throat, looking away from me. "You get the picture."

Every word she says settles over me heavily, threatening to pull me under. I feel everything and yet nothing, trying to make sense of the words now swimming in front of my eyes but coming up short. Everything I have ever known is challenged by this one, short entry— and to consider it to be true means that my entire life, my entire *history*—is a lie.

I can feel Keyanna beside me, waiting for me to say something, to react in some way, but I'm full of that same numbness that took me after seeing my da last night. Only this time, there is no pity, no sorrow. Not for me, and not for the rest of my line.

I touch the name of the creature—the *woman*—who I've always believed was the source of my suffering, wondering now how much pain she endured at the hands of my family. Wondering now if she deserved any of it. Thinking that it's very likely she didn't. Knowing that makes my stomach twist with guilt, replaying every unkind word I've ever thought about her, about her family, about *Key* even, not so long ago. Now . . . every word of it settles on my tongue like ash, leaving a bad taste in my mouth. Because one thing is certain, after reading what's written here.

We aren't the victims in this story.

We're the bloody villains.

### KEYANNA

"You were right," he rasps.

I curl my hand over his forearm, squeezing gently. "What?"

"When you said that we must have done something bad," he clarifies. "We did. We did this to ourselves, didn't we?"

"Lachlan, don't—"

"We *deserve* it," he grits out.

"Stop it, that's not tr—"

"But it is, isn't it?" He turns his face to mine, his ice-blue eyes wet, brimming even. "How far back do you think it goes? At what point did we paint ourselves the victims? Did my grandpa know? My *da*? Am I just a fool they thought to protect with their lies?"

I shake my head fervently, reaching up to grasp his chin. "Look at me. I don't believe that for a second. Look how old this journal is. *Centuries*, Lachlan. If your ancestor was really as bad as they say, doesn't it seem more likely that he started spreading that narrative in his own lifetime? If Tavish *really* married the kelpie—this *Sorcha*—then surely they would have wanted to protect her. Surely what she was would have required secrecy. So it's not as if they could refute rumors like that, right?"

"That sounds wonderful in theory," he huffs. "But honestly, does it matter? *My family did this to themselves.* We've spent all this time searching for some kind of solution, for *redemption*—but we don't even deserve it!"

"Stop it," I tsk. "That's not true."

I can see anger brewing in his eyes now, even underneath the sheen of tears. "It isn't? It sounds like I come from a long line of monsters, Key. It sounds like we were monsters long before this kelpie showed up and made it our reality. It *sounds* like we got what we bloody deserved."

"Look at me." I grab his face with both hands, forcing him to do just that. "Do you remember what you told me? Back in that room where he kept her?"

"Och, and he kept her bloody *prisoner* for no other reason than to siphon off her magic like some sort of leeching bastard. Because it isn't bad enough that he—"

I squeeze his cheeks, making it harder for him to talk. "You told me that I was no more to blame for the past than you were. That I was here now. That I was trying to make it right. You said *that* is what matters." I can see the way he averts his eyes, but I move my head to follow his line of sight, making sure he can't look away from me. "That works in reverse too. Do you hear me? You are *not* to blame for something some evil guy with your last name did almost seven centuries ago. You didn't do those things—*he* did. You are *not* him, do you understand?"

"Am I really so different?" His shoulders droop in defeat, his eyes wrenching shut. "Look at how I treated you when I met you. Like some sort of pariah only because of your last name. Like I was somehow *better* than you because of mine. Am I *really* so different, Keyanna?"

"You are," I stress. "You *are*." I rest my forehead against his, stroking my thumb across his cheek. "Of *course* you acted that way when we met. You've been brought up your entire life thinking that my family was the reason why you lost your father, why you might lose yourself. I don't blame you for how you were in the beginning. I understand it. Hell, I might have done the same if our roles were reversed. I know you're different because you went through life being told one singular thing was true, that it held weight above everything else, and yet when faced with the opportunity to trust me, you weren't afraid to *change your mind*. You. Not your dad, not your dickish old ancestor. *You.* You made those decisions on your own. You dropped all that bullshit about a curse and blame and you *trusted* me based on what *you* knew to be true." I press a gentle kiss to his mouth, letting it linger for a second. "You had the chance to repeat your family's mistakes, and you went your own way. Do you understand? You are *not* who you are because of where you come from; you are who you are because of where *you* choose to go."

A broken sound escapes his chest, and I pull him against me, wrapping my arms around his shoulders as his hands grip my waist, burying his face in my chest. I let my cheek rest against his and breathe him in, a mix of water and air and something inherently him—letting him shudder in my embrace as he no doubt tries to make peace with what I've said. I can't imagine what he must be feeling; to think one way your entire life, to know something to be true spanning across generations, only to have it obliterated in one moment—it's enough to drive someone mad if they let it. But I won't let him fall apart. I'm ready and willing to hold him together, to make sure he doesn't break.

"I don't know if I deserve you," he rasps against my sweater.

I nuzzle his hair. "You do."

"You don't understand," he huffs, pulling back to look at me. "It's not just this, Key. Not that this isn't bloody awful, because it is, but it's not *everything*. I'm starting to think you deserve so much more than me." His face looks pained, and my heart breaks a little. "Than *this*. This bloody headache. Especially since—" He swallows thickly, looking lost again. "I haven't even— I need to tell you—"

He makes a surprised sound when I slant my lips across his, a protest bubbling up for a fraction of a moment before he melts into it. I can feel the tension leave his body with every second that his mouth is under mine, and I think to myself that if he won't listen to me *telling* him how I feel about him, I can damn well show him.

"Key," he sighs dazedly. "Key, I need—"

"You need to shut up," I murmur. "You've talked enough."

He groans when I let my tongue slip past his lips, opening for me without thought. As if it's second nature. And it *feels* like it is. Doesn't he see that? Doesn't he see that this connection between us feels like something *more* than just random chance?

I wind my fingers in his hair, tilting his head back to explore his mouth—keeping my kisses languid, slow, enjoying the feel and taste of him. With every passing moment I can feel him relax just a little more, and crawling into his lap is an easy decision. Molding my body against his is as easy as breathing. It feels like I *belong* there, really.

I feel his hands burrowing under my sweater, his wide palms sliding up my back, searing me with their heat. Our kisses are a slow back-and-forth, a lazy give-and-take—his tongue chasing after mine with every retreat just as mine follows after his.

Usually when he undresses me, it's quick, frantic—but this time, it's slow. He peels my top off as if unwrapping a gift, my hair catching in the neckline for a moment and then cascading down to my shoulders. He eyes my body with a reverence that makes me feel more naked than any lack of clothes could, and I've never been more grateful for boobs small enough to go sans bra than I was before I met Lachlan. Because I've noticed he seems to be *obsessed* with them.

His hands are so large, they cover all of me, his palms kneading the soft mounds before his fingers pluck at my nipples, teasing them into points. He catches my gaze just as he leans in to suck one into his mouth, and my mouth parts on a gasp as his hot tongue swirls around the stiffening peak, sending shivers throughout my body.

*This*, I think. *This is what I needed.*

I needed to see that he still looks at me like I'm everything he wants when he touches me. That everything he learned today hasn't changed the intensity of what he feels for me. That he's as deep in this thing as I am quickly becoming.

I let him tease me for a moment more, enjoying the sensation of his mouth on me, finally shoving him back so I can rob him of his own shirt. I don't stop there, reaching for the button of his jeans and quickly working them down and off, and he lets me do it without protest, watching as I strip him bare. Watching me even more intensely as I get rid of my own clothes.

His eyes are hooded when I urge him to his back, when I crawl over him to straddle his hips, and the way he looks at me . . . I could get addicted to the way Lachlan looks at me. Like I'm some otherworldly creature. At any other time I might find that thought funny, since I suppose that I . . . well. That I am. In a way.

I undulate my hips when I have him beneath me to let his hard cock glide through my wet folds, grinding down on the head of him until he makes a sound that's practically a growl. His hands cover my thighs, squeezing and kneading like he's trying to hold himself back, letting me set the pace, and I grind against him a few times more before I finally decide to put us both out of our misery, reaching between us to grab his cock, notching him against my slick opening.

I hold his gaze as I start to sink down, slowly taking him in inch by inch, feeling each one as they stretch me, as they *fill* me—not stopping until we're flush against each other, his cock as deep as it can be. His hands are making slow circles against my thighs now, stroking a hypnotizing pattern that I'm not even sure he's aware of, his intense gaze roving over every inch of me reverently.

The microscopic changes in his expression when I start to move— the slight flush of his cheeks, the way his lids grow heavier, the barely there part of his mouth—each one makes me feel that much more desirable, that much bolder. I use my knees to pull off him, rising up until only the head of him rests inside me, lingering for a second or more before dropping back down all at once. His wide-eyed expression isn't subtle then, the feral sound he makes even less so.

So I do it again. And again. *And again.*

I don't know when he starts moving with me; one minute I'm setting the pace, controlling the rhythm, and the next—his hands are on my hips to hold me steady, his hips lifting from the bed at a ferocious pace so that I'm practically bouncing on his cock. I throw my head back as he hits deep with every stroke, the thick head of his cock stroking the sensitive inner wall, bumping against that place that has pressure already building low in my belly.

Usually he would be talking right now, spewing words of filth that would make me that much hotter for him—but something about his quiet makes this . . . *more* somehow. Like he doesn't want words to take away from the crackling energy that seems to be sparking between us. One I can feel like a physical thing. Surely he can feel it too. He *has* to.

I don't have to ask him to give me more; his thumb finds my clit and he starts to stroke it with just the right amount of pressure, like he knows what I need without me asking. He swipes back and forth against the sensitive hood, his slow ministrations at direct odds with the still vicious pace of his cock pounding inside me. The dueling sensations have me climbing higher and higher, reaching a peak that feels all too soon.

My thighs start to shake, and my insides begin to tremble, and I feel it; it's *right there*.

And when Lachlan finally opens his mouth, his voice is so soft, so full of awe, that it makes my heart feel fit to bursting with emotion.

"Come for me," he all but whispers. "Come for me, love."

I do, as if my body obeys his command. I fall apart, I shatter— barely even noticing when the lightbulbs spark out, when the windows start to rattle with the force of a sudden wind that has no business here on this very sunny morning.

It's all white noise to the way I quake through my orgasm, vaguely hearing Lachlan grunt after me, feeling his cock pulse deep inside as warmth floods me. I let my hands cover his, which still hold my hips, my mouth still open and panting toward the ceiling, my eyes still shut tight as I savor the feelings still flickering inside.

I don't move until Lachlan physically makes me, pulling me up and off him and down into his arms as he holds me close. He cards his fingers through my wild curls as he kisses my temple, pulling me flush against his body until there isn't a space left between us. His warmth and the calm radiating off him have fatigue settling in after such a long night and what seems like a longer morning, and without either of us seeming to be able to conjure up words for what just happened, I release a long, drawn-out yawn, which makes the sleepless night I had come crashing down on me.

"Sleep," he murmurs, nuzzling my hair. "We'll talk when you wake up."

I nod against his chest, believing him. He'll still be here when I wake up. I know this because I know how he feels about me. I felt it just now. Whether by magic or some deluded sense of intuition, I felt every bit of what Lachlan feels for me, as clear as if he'd told me himself. So I know now more than ever that this thing we're doing . . . it's real.

Because my feelings are exactly the same.

I wake up before Lachlan; I can't be sure how much time has passed since we fell asleep, but the sun is streaming in through the window at full force now, so I would guess it's well after noon. I pretty much stopped carrying my phone most of the time a few weeks ago; it's still a novel thing for me, but with most of my friends back in New York having drifted when my dad got sick . . . there's really no one for me to talk to that I can't just get up and go find now.

A wild concept, really.

I dress quietly, covering Lachlan with a blanket and letting him get what is probably some much-needed sleep—moving to the kitchen table with a cup of coffee I painstakingly made in his ancient coffee maker before resuming my reading of the journal. So far, there have been only a few mentions of the bridle: when Sorcha came to the keep, when Lachlan's ancestor struck their deal, when he betrayed her . . . I'm only just now reading how Tavish reclaimed it and freed her from her prison. This part hurts to read, actually, because another revelation I've stumbled upon has been that Lachlan's ancestor wasn't cursed until *after* Sorcha had been set free. Not as some cruel trick from a fickle creature, but as punishment for almost a *year* of imprisonment under some really horrid circumstances that I hope Lachlan never has to read about. He feels enough guilt as it is for this prick that shares his last name.

The remaining bit of the book grows thinner and thinner after Sorcha's freedom and Tavish's written joy at her having returned his love—after that, there is an account of their wedding, talk of using the bridle to ensure that the Laird never harmed them or their family again, that he even parted with some land that they could start a new life on. After that . . . nothing. Just a day-to-day account of their very sweet—but admittedly rather mundane—lives.

*That's it?* I keep thinking. *All of that, and it's just farm life happily ever after?*

For Sorcha, Tavish definitely fits the "lovestruck fool" moniker Rhona mentioned; the woman could do no wrong in his eyes. Every mention of her is painted through rose-colored glasses, which is sweet, I suppose, but he just . . . never mentions the bridle again. Not after briefly noting that they would do well to use its power sparingly, so as not to gain attention.

I can feel my frustration mounting higher and higher with every turned page, and by the time I've reached the last few, I'm feeling downright morose. Because this can't be another dead end. It *can't*. I can't bear to face Lachlan when he wakes up and tell him I have no more answers. The bridle was *here*, damnit, It was *right* here.

The last page is an ordinary account of an ordinary day—something silly about a broken plow and Tavish feeling his age even though his Sorcha remains as lovely as ever. It would make me smile if not for the fact that it marks absolute failure at being any closer to the bridle's location. At being any closer to *saving* Lachlan.

I'm just about ready to close the book and toss it to the floor, but then I notice the shadow of more writing after the last page. I lift it curiously to the back cover, my eyes rounding when I find more written there that is nothing like Tavish's jagged handwriting, but instead a smooth, almost artful script.

*To you who finds the journal of my beloved,*

*My Tavish has passed in the night, and with him, my heart passes too. In all my years of life, I never thought to love a mortal man. Men have been cruel to my kind, to me, and I have grown knowing not to trust them, to fear them, when necessary.*

*But Tavish changed my mind.*

*I bury this journal on our land, our home, hoping that one day when our story has been lost to the passing of time, our love will live on. That our children's children will find his words and know where they come from. I choose to leave this life with my husband; no world without him is one I want to walk.*

*I leave my bridle with my beloved, for my magic is my heart, and only he can hold it.*

*Remember my curse, O child of MacKay. Remember it, and know that those who gave us suffering now suffer in turn. In my years with Tavish living as a mortal woman, I have come to learn what it is to forgive, but forgiveness cannot be granted from me. Such is the power of words, such is the nature of my curse. For while I can never be a daughter of MacKay, one day one such lass shall walk this world, hold my magic, and be given a chance to forgive. Only should she take it, will my curse be no more.*

*Remember my words:*

*O Thou, of face so fair an' name so high,*
*With heart as black as the darkest sky*
*Thy cursed deeds yield cursed prize*
*An' prayers nor pleas will spare thy fate*
*In moonlight change till the sun doth rise*
*Yer flesh shall bear yer soul's foul weight*

*And all thy sons shall be unwrought*
*A boon in vain forever sought*
*Yer line unravels when sins be forgot*
*An' each son will carry this curse of the Fae*
*Yer monstrous deeds be all for naught*
*For the end only comes with a daughter of MacKay*

The book clatters to the floor, my thoughts of treating it gently forgotten in my shock. Seriously, how many times can a person's world be turned upside down in one day? I hear a stirring behind me, but I don't turn, too lost in my own thoughts.

Then I hear a sleepy-sounding "Key?"

"It's me," I say, feeling thoroughly stunned. I turn in my chair, meeting Lachlan's confused expression. "I'm the daughter of MacKay."

And what's more than the mind-blowing revelation that I have a part to play in this, that everything that's happening to me is apparently *foretold*—what guts me more than *all* of that—is the look in Lachlan's eyes at what I've said. The *recognition* there. That's when it hits me.

He knew all along.

## 30

### LACHLAN

I'm still trying to rouse myself from the dredges of sleep, but even in my drowsy state, it is impossible to miss the way Key's expression morphs from shock to betrayal in only a matter of seconds.

*She knows.*

I don't know what it is she read in that journal, but her eyes tell me everything I need to know. Whatever she found—it's clear that she's aware I haven't told her everything.

"I can explain," I blurt out, swinging my legs over the side of the bed, my body on autopilot as it tries to get closer to her.

She shoves out of my kitchen chair, backing away from me and crossing her arms over her chest as if to guard herself. From *me*. That one small action cuts me like a knife.

"Key," I try again. "I don't know what you found, but I promise it isn't—"

"Isn't what?" she interrupts with a hurt tone. "Isn't true? Isn't what I think? You *didn't* conveniently forget to tell me that your creepy little poem had a second verse?"

I glance down at the fallen journal lying face down on the floor, stooping to gingerly pick it up. I lay it on the table with care, frowning at it. "So you know about the curse. All of it."

"*For the end only comes with a daughter of MacKay*," she recites, and I heave out a sigh. "Why didn't you tell me?"

I scrub my hands down my face, trying to resist the urge to move closer to her. "At first? Because I didn't know you. I didn't know what that part of the curse meant. I *still* don't, I might add. And after . . ." I frown down at my feet, clenching my fists at my sides as guilt racks through me. "I didn't know how to tell you. I thought maybe it would . . . hurt you." I peek up at her, seeing the exact same hurt I'd been so afraid to inflict on her etched on her face. "I didn't want to bring you any more pain, Key. You've had enough."

"So what," she huffs. "You just make my decisions now? You decide whether or not I'm capable of deciding whether you're worth the risk, and now you decide whether or not I'm capable of handling the truth?"

"That's not what I meant. I—"

She throws up her hands, fuming. "What if I'm making everything worse? Did you ever think of that? That damned curse says I'll be the *end*. You don't have any kids, Lachlan. If the curse takes you like it did your dad, the Greer line ends with *you*. What if that's the whole point of all of this?"

"I don't think that's the way of it," I argue. "It doesn't feel right."

"Well, how could I know any better when you *didn't fucking tell me everything*?"

"Key." I reach for her, unable to keep from doing so any longer. "I didn't—"

She backs away, and again I feel the sensation not unlike being sliced by a knife. "Don't," she says, putting more distance between us. "Don't touch me."

The gutting sensation left by her words almost knocks me over, and I have to reach for the table, grasping the edge to hold myself up.

Terror unlike anything I've ever known grips me, wondering if I've fucked this up beyond repair. I've never felt fear like the one that comes from thinking I might lose her.

"I'm sorry," I plead, needing her to believe it. "I was going to tell you."

"But you didn't. I thought you trusted me." She shakes her head. "It makes so much sense now. *A daughter of MacKay.* Did you know Rhona told me that there had been no daughters born to the MacKay clan for centuries? Have you just been *waiting* for me to show up all this time? Or have you been *afraid* that I would?" She crosses her arms tightly over her chest, looking pained. "I feel so fucking stupid, don't you get that? Here I was, thinking that we were in this together, but you didn't even trust me enough to tell me what might be the most crucial bit of information you know. Like I'm some sort of *child.*"

"That's not what I was trying to do," I tell her. "And I *was* going to tell you. *Today.* I swear I was."

Her eyes narrow. "That's convenient."

"I *swear*, Key." I take a cautious step, stilling when I notice her flinch. I hate that after all my yearning to protect her, I still ended up being the cause for more pain. "Please believe me."

She stares back at me for a long while, her green eyes bright with fury and her body rigid with tension. She expels a harsh breath when she finally averts her eyes, her lips pursing as she stares down at the floor, appearing to mull it over.

"I need some time," she says finally, and I feel almost sick from the declaration. "I just . . . I can't think around you. It's hard to stay mad at you when I'm looking right at you, and this is a fucking big deal." She cocks her head, peering up at me. "You get that, right? My entire fucking life has been nothing but secrets. I didn't need any more. Especially not from you."

"I know," I answer with a nod. "I'm so sorry."

Her chest still rises and falls with heavy breaths, and I watch as she seems to struggle with her own thoughts, finally shaking her head roughly back and forth as if to clear it. "I need time," she says again. "I just need some space to think." She holds out her hand. "May I have the journal, please?"

She doesn't move from where she's standing, holding my gaze as she offers her outstretched hand. I want to hold it, to gather it up in my palm and pull her against me so that I can beg her not to leave— because even with her telling me that she needs space, there's nothing I want less with her.

But I did keep secrets from her, and it was my choice to do so. If there's one thing I know all too well—it's consequences. So with that in mind, I gently pick up the journal, placing it in her open palm with the same care. My fingers brush against hers, and I don't miss the way her breath catches slightly with the contact, but after only a moment she snatches the journal back, clutching it to her chest.

"I'll talk to you later," she tells me. "When I've had a chance to calm down. I don't want to say something to you that I'll regret just because I'm mad at you."

I nod solemnly. "I understand."

"I wish . . ." Her expression falls, her eyes sad. "I wish you'd trusted me."

"I trust you with my life," I tell her earnestly, meaning every word. "There's no person alive that I trust more."

Her mouth parts as if she might say something, but then she quickly closes it, seeming to decide against it. She gives me one last long look with that same hurt expression that guts me, and then she spins on her heel toward the door, not looking back as she opens and shuts it behind her, leaving me alone. I stare at the closed door for an indeterminable amount of time, feeling as if the air has gone colder with her absence, like she took all the warmth with her.

*I wish you'd trusted me.*

I know she's right. That regardless of my intentions, I've pulled the rug out from beneath her, leaving her in the dark as if she didn't deserve to know her part in the story. As if she couldn't handle it somehow. She told me only a few hours ago that my trust in her made me different. That it meant I wasn't a monster.

I told her then I wasn't sure if I deserved her.

I hope that this doesn't make her realize that's true.

It takes all that I have not to go after her in the hours following Key's hasty departure from the cottage; I tried earlier to get some work done, but most of my time was spent staring forlornly at her bedroom window. I think even the cows were getting sick of my company after just a short spell with me.

I ended up back in the last place I touched her—face down on my bed and replaying every poor decision I've made lately. There are so many moments where I could have told her the truth: when I first kissed her, when we first made love, hell, even back in that bloody graveyard, where I'd first told her about her history. What had held me back then? I couldn't even claim then that I wanted to protect her.

Or had I felt that need even then, without realizing it?

I suppose it doesn't matter now, because all I can do is wallow here in the shadows—not bothering to change the bulbs after she's gone and blown them out again—content to just lie here until the sun sinks, and I have to trudge back to the loch to spend another awful night away from her. Only now, there will be the added bonus of knowing she won't be waiting for me when I get back.

How in the fuck did I do this before her?

I roll onto my back to stare blankly at the ceiling, mentally checking off ways that I could apologize to her. I have nothing to offer her, not really, but it doesn't stop me from orchestrating half a dozen grand gestures in my head that might get her to hear me out. A more rational part of my mind says that she will come to me when she calms down, but it's drowned out by the part of me that's terrified she won't.

A bitter laugh escapes me.

*When did I lose all my sense for this woman?*

I try to pinpoint an exact moment, but there are too many to choose from. Maybe it's when she first stubbornly asserted that she was going to help me, that she was *meant to.* Maybe it was when I held her in that run-down old barn, her shivering body pressed to mine as she quietly asked me if I trusted her. Maybe it could have even been that moment when she burst into this very cottage—calling me out for being an eejit when it came to making her decisions for her. Not that her outburst seemed to actually teach me a lesson, considering I continued to do just that.

It seems that, ultimately, I can't pick out one single moment when I fell in love with Keyanna MacKay.

Because I did. That much is glaringly obvious. When she walked out of this house, it felt like she took part of me with her. It's inconvenient as hell, but it seems that's not enough to keep me from being head over heels in love with the stubborn, beautiful redhead that might still be my mortal enemy, if the stories are to be believed.

Which, maybe they are. Maybe her very existence will spell my downfall. I can't rule that out. But oddly enough . . . I don't bloody care. I'd rather spend a short time with her than have even *decades* without her.

I shoot up in bed, realizing how much I need to tell her that. How much I need her to *know* that I don't *care* if she means the end of me, of my line. Perhaps that's even part of why I didn't tell her everything—because it simply doesn't matter to me. Whether she's the boon forever sought or the end of it all . . . she's all I want.

And suddenly, I can't go another minute without letting her know.

There is another hour or so yet until sundown—plenty of time to stand outside her bedroom door and beg her to hear me out. And if that doesn't work, I think, then I'll just repeat it tomorrow, and the next day, and every day after until there are no more days left for me.

Resolved, I tug on my jacket as I'm shoving my feet into my boots, and I've barely got the laces tied on just one of them when there's a soft knock at my door. My mouth parts in surprise because, *Could it be her?* I stumble toward the door like a lovesick fool, my jacket barely on straight and my laces trailing behind me. I wrench open the door with a pounding heart, elation ballooning for mere moments before it seeps right back out . . . because there's no one there.

"Key?" I step outside the door, looking around but finding no one. "Key!"

I run to the edge of the house, thinking that maybe she changed her mind halfway through and turned back. I get to the very edge to round the corner, and several things happen all at once.

The sinking sun blazes a fiery light that is near-blinding for a second or more, and I raise my hand to shield my eyes from it. I notice immediately that Keyanna is nowhere to be seen, that it appears that she didn't come at all, something that is obvious given who is *actually* standing there waiting for me.

Before I even have time to react, the sun is blotted out by something massive and solid, something coming down on my head at full speed, giving me no time to even ascertain with complete certainty what it is before I feel a shooting pain that blossoms in my skull but soon spreads outward, leaving blackness in its wake as darkness consumes me. My consciousness fades as I feel my body sink to the ground like a stone, and the last thing I remember is the sight of worn boots resting in my line of sight, that heavy something that might be some sort of club clunking to the ground beside them.

"I'm sorry, mate," a familiar voice murmurs. "This will all be over soon."

## KEYANNA

The door to my bedroom—or rather my *dad's* bedroom—rattles on its hinges when I slam it behind me, and I'm grateful that Finlay's truck was missing from the front yard, that they've apparently gone into town. I need to be by myself for a bit.

I swipe at my eyes, wondering how I could have any more tears to shed after the last twenty-four hours; it hurt me to leave Lachlan like that, and part of me might even understand why he kept these things from me. I know he carries the weight of the world on his shoulders, and that despite his gruff demeanor, he's always willing to add more if it means protecting someone he cares about. I see it in the way he doesn't blame his mother for leaving him, in the way he still tries to reach his father, despite all the evidence pointing to him being lost.

I *know* deep down that he didn't mean to hurt me, but that doesn't change the fact that he did.

I think I just feel stupid more than anything. Here I am, having just given him this grand speech about how it felt to know that he trusted me, and he was still holding on to secrets. *Important* secrets. I mean, you don't just *forget* to tell someone that their entire existence was fucking *foretold* in some insane curse passed down through the generations. I mean, it *has* to be me . . . doesn't it?

I drop down to the floor, crossing my legs as I hold the journal in my lap. I rub my thumb over the leather cover, thinking about everything I learned moments before Lachlan had woken up and rocked my shit all over again. I didn't even tell him what Sorcha wrote about the bridle. Not that I'm even sure what it means. Maybe that was selfish of me, putting my own feelings before his when he's already suffered so much. I'd just been so angry, so *hurt*—I reacted without thinking.

And now here I am, sitting alone and sulking. Great.

God, what am I supposed to do? I don't even know how to begin to process the fact that some magical being hundreds of years ago literally *wrote me into existence*. It makes my brain hurt just thinking about it. And supposedly I'm going to bring about the *end*? What does that even mean? I've done nothing but promise Lachlan that we would find answers, that we would *fix* this—but what if I'm destined to do the exact opposite? What if by simply being near him, I only make things *worse*?

I couldn't bear it.

It's moments like these when I feel the loss of my dad the hardest; these are the moments when I would run to ask him for advice. I don't even think I had a boyfriend long enough to introduce him to before he got sick. I spent most of my twenties taking care of him. What would *Dad* think of all this? I close my eyes, trying to picture his eyes, trying to hear his laugh. What would he tell me right now?

*Och, lass. Don't cry. What do we do when we take a tumble?*

I picture his soft smile as he fusses over my skinned knee, a pink bike only a few feet away, turned on its side. I can see him drying my tears, his fingers tucking under my chin to force my eyes up.

*We get back up again.*

Well, fuck. Definitely not helping with the crying.

A thought occurs to me then, and I crawl closer to the bed to sift through the scattered papers there, pulling out one in particular that had fallen in all the excitement of finding the journal. I settle back in to reread my dad's words in the letter he left for Rhona, feeling a slight comfort at being so close to something he actually touched.

> *Mum,*
>
> *I don't know if you'll ever find this. I'm not even sure if I want you to. If you read what's inside this journal, you'll know the truth of why I left, and I don't know what's preferable—you being disappointed in me for leaving, or knowing with certainty that I left because I'm a coward.*
>
> *Maybe one day I'll find my courage, but know that I didn't leave because of you. Not really. I couldn't bring myself to test fate, couldn't make peace with not knowing what was to come—so I left. For her. The story in this journal is entirely true. <u>All of it.</u> Of that much, I'm sure. And that's why I couldn't take a chance. That's why I had to leave while I still could.*
>
> *But one thing has been, and will always be, certain.*
> *I love you.*
>
>
> *Duncan*

I read it again, snagging the part where he says that he left *for her*, seeing it with new eyes. Bits and pieces of conversation with Rhona flit through my thoughts, and I frown at the memory, trying to remember it more clearly.

*He called me down to this very table,* she'd said. *He seemed . . . frantic. Somehow. Not quite himself. He told me that your mother was pregnant, and that they had found out it was to be a girl. I remember how shocked I was to hear the news, but Duncan . . . Duncan almost seemed upset by it.*

For a moment, I just sit there, staring at the wall as pieces start to fall in place, realizing that my father read this journal. That he saw this curse. That when he found out that I was coming . . . he knew what it meant.

He didn't leave for my mother . . . *He left for me.*

My head buzzes with so many memories—of Rhona telling me that mine and Lachlan's dads had taken trips to Inverness after finding the journal. Lachlan telling me that Duncan abandoned his father after promising to help him. My father refusing to tell me anything about his homeland.

*He abandoned Lachlan's father to protect me. Because he didn't know what he would do when he found out about me.*

It makes my head hurt thinking about how all of this, all of *us* have just been circling around one another our entire lives—bound by fate. I think of all the things that had to happen to get me here, all the pain and the suffering and the loss, not just mine but Lachlan's . . . my grandparents' . . . my *dad's*—and that's exactly what it feels like is happening here. Fate. Like whatever comes next was meant to happen.

I feel that energy in the air, that crackling presence that urges me upward, that tells me to *go*—and even if I still don't fully understand it, it feels as if there is a name to it now. One that was long forgotten.

One that I almost feel a connection to. Like she's there, quietly encouraging me to move.

Because Sorcha also gave everything for love. She gave up her freedom, then her magic, and even her life in the end—all to be with her beloved, as she called him.

*I leave my bridle with my beloved—*

I gasp, shooting to my feet. Like the last puzzle piece fitting into a slot—the answers come to me all at once. I see the picture clearly now, the solutions laid out neatly in a row, just waiting for me to shine a light on them. There are still tear tracks on my cheeks, and yet I find myself smiling.

Because there's only one person I want to tell all of this to.

*—for my magic is my heart, and only he can hold it.*

I smile a little wider, already moving out the door.

I fly down the stairs and out the front door, my legs burning with effort as I sprint across the grass toward the groundskeeper's cottage. I think of everything I have to tell him, every step that brings me closer making me feel that much lighter.

*It's going to be okay. I'm going to save him. It's going to be okay.*

I don't bother knocking, wrenching open the door to the cottage and bursting inside to find—

Nothing.

It's completely empty.

For a second, I'm just confused; there's still more than an hour to sunset, so it seems unlikely that he'd already be at the shore, but maybe he went there to think? I frown, feeling a pang of guilt for how I left things, but I quickly brush it away. There will be time for that later. I step farther into the kitchen as if he might somehow magically appear, but it's clear that the place is definitely empty. I set the journal on his kitchen table, worried now that maybe he *did* go to the shore. Do I still have time to catch him?

I rush back out the door, taking two steps at a time as I move around the cottage with the intent of checking the barn before I go running off to the loch, but when I round the corner of the tiny house, a bright red smear on the grass makes me pause.

It takes me several seconds to make sense of what I'm seeing; it only clicks when I notice the heavy-looking piece of wood—maybe an old table leg? It's just lying there on the ground, that same red splash coating the end as if . . . No.

I crouch, pressing my fingers to the red stain even as dread settles low in my gut. I bring the sticky liquid to my nose, assaulted by the scent of iron. I try to reason with the panic ratcheting higher inside me— maybe an animal got a stray chicken or something—but the same certainty that hit me back in my room whispers to me once more, telling me that isn't the case. Somehow, without having any conclusive proof . . . I know that this is Lachlan's blood. The knowledge fills me with terror, and if it weren't for the surging energy inside me that feels supernatural in origin—I might give in to that terror.

But I know I can't do that. Not if he needs my help.

Instead, I take a calming breath—breathing in a slow inhale before letting it out, trying to center myself. I reach for that thread of energy, the one that seems to pulse in the air around me, grabbing hold of it, urging it to guide me, to take me *to* him. When it takes hold, I can almost see the trail of it, like a shimmering in the air that stretches out in front of me, winding across the property and falling onto a familiar path. One that is faint, but one that I'm sure of.

And without ever being able to ascertain how it is that I know— I know exactly where to find him. I push away any fear that lingers;

there's no time for it, no use for it. I don't know who hurt Lachlan, can't fathom who might have a reason to . . . but when I find them?

I'm going to make sure they regret it.

The path to the graveyard feels longer when I'm walking it alone, but I can feel with every step a growing certainty that I'm headed in the right direction, the shimmering air that guides my way growing clearer the farther I go down the trail. I should probably be a little stealthier in my approach as I stomp on dry leaves, snapping twigs under my feet and pushing through branches without thought. The air in my lungs burns with the pace I'm setting, but I can't seem to slow down. I feel like I'm tied to the end of a thread, someone at the other end pulling me along.

I spot a marker I recognize from when I came here with Lachlan, and I pick up the pace even more as I hurry toward the end. That last thick patch of branches gives way when I push through them, and then I burst into the clearing—dying sunlight trying its best to filter through the canopy overhead. It doesn't take me any time at all to spot them. Lachlan isn't alone here, currently sitting slumped against a giant tombstone, his eyes shut and his mouth slack. It takes me a lot longer than it probably should to clock who is crouching next to him with a wheelbarrow on his other side, which he no doubt used to carry Lachlan here, seeming to be chaining Lachlan's wrists.

I search my memory for any indication of this, for any hints that would have led me to believe that he would be capable of this, that he would have any *reason* for this—but I come up empty. I can do little more than gape, my brain going offline for a good ten seconds before it all comes rushing back, and I finally remember how to use my words.

". . . Brodie?"

He dusts his hands on his jeans before rising to his full height, turning to face me with an expression that hints he's surprised to see me here, but isn't at all apologetic to be here in the first place. And then I notice the large knife in his hand, a chill shooting down my spine.

"Hello, Key. I . . . didn't expect you."

*Well*, I think dazedly. *That makes two of us.*

## 32

### LACHLAN

At first, I can't place where I am. Let alone what's happening.

I come to in pieces—muffled voices filtering in just before my eyelids stop being so heavy that I can actually begin to open them. I blink slowly, assessing my surroundings; my head is throbbing and my wrists ache from the chains I can feel wound around them.

*What the fuck?*

My head is lolled to the side, resting against my shoulder, and when I try to lift it, another burst of pain blooms in my head, blurring my vision. I focus on breathing, on drawing air into my lungs as I cling to consciousness, only just starting to place the voices still drifting from nearby.

"What the fuck is this?" I hear someone ask, a woman, definitely. "What did you do to him?"

*I know that voice.*

I crack open one eye, catching the blurry shape of wild, red curls attached to a very tense-looking Keyanna.

*Keyanna.*

We'd fought. She'd asked for space. I remember that I was going to go after her. I remember making it outside before—

I blink rapidly, my vision just starting to clear. Brodie fucking

MacKay stands only a few meters away from me, his hands out-stretched in a placating gesture as he approaches Key slowly, as one might a wild animal. Something that is admittedly a feat, given that he's carrying what appears to be a wicked-looking bowie knife.

"Now, Key," he says in a calm, even tone. "I can explain." He points back at me. "He's not what you think he is."

If my head wasn't throbbing so much, that might actually make me laugh. He has no fucking idea. I try to tug at the chain binding my wrists, feeling it give just a tad, but not enough to wiggle my hands free.

"He's hurt!" Key practically hisses. "Did you do that to him? What the hell, Brodie?"

Brodie sighs, resting his fists against his hips, knife still carefully tucked in one hand. "I was hoping to handle this without involving you, but I guess there's no choice now." He points at me again. "Lach-lan Greer is a monster."

"Really," Key snorts. "That's rich, given that you're the one hold-ing a small machete."

Brodie shakes his head. "No, you don't understand. He's an *actual* monster. I've seen it. He's *cursed*, Key, and he's been using you to find a way to break it."

I open my mouth to say something, but my tongue feels heavy and like it's made of cotton. I watch as Key goes still, cocking her head to the side, confusion etched all over her face. No doubt she's thinking the same thing that I am.

*How the fuck does he know about me?*

"What . . ." Key's brow knits; I assume she's trying to gauge what all Brodie knows without giving too much away herself. "What do you mean?"

Brodie moves to a nearby headstone, grabbing a thick leather book from the top of it that I'm only just now noticing. By the look of surprise on Key's face, she must only just be noticing it as well.

Brodie holds up the book, shaking it gently. "This journal belonged to Lachlan's ancestor. I found it when we did the renovations for the auld wing. It was inside a false bit of a wall that hadn't burned."

Key looks at me then, noticing that I'm conscious, her eyes rounding. I try to convey with my eyes not to do anything hasty, giving a barely there shake of my head. She rips her gaze from mine to look back to Brodie.

"You had that all this time?"

Brodie nods. "That's why I came here." He walks over to me, giving me a disgusted look as he crouches down next to me. He tips the massive knife up until it rests underneath my chin, ignoring Key's sharp sound of protest. "This book explains everything that his awful family did to ours. It talks about how they finally got theirs—cursed by a kelpie witch they'd taken advantage of. She made them into the monsters they've always been."

"Brodie," Key says placatingly. "That sounds insane."

"Doesn't it?" Brodie smiles, but it's a cruel caricature of one. "I thought maybe it was too . . . but then I saw it for myself."

"You're . . . mental," I manage, my tongue still feeling too thick.

Brodie shakes his head. "And you aren't as careful as you think you are. What? Did you think you'd use my family again? Take advantage of my cousin? I bet you thought she'd lead you right to the bridle. Didn't you."

My mouth parts in surprise, and Brodie laughs.

"See? I have you all figured out. I knew what you were up to the minute you started cozying up to Keyanna. You took advantage of her desperation to know more about her family."

"Brodie," Key protests. "That isn't—"

"Key," Brodie sighs, standing once more. "I know you care about him, but you have to understand . . . He doesn't give a damn about you. He's *using* you."

"No, that's not—"

She catches my eye again, and I give her another subtle shake of my head. I don't want her to reveal any more than she has to. We don't know how Brodie will react if he finds out that Keyanna knows a lot more than he seems to think that she does. Especially since we still don't know exactly what he wants.

"Why're you doing this?" I ask hoarsely, feeling a bit stronger with every passing second, but not enough that I can break free.

"Why?" Brodie laughs again, but there's no humor in it. "Because if I get my hands on that bridle, then everything changes." He glares at me then. "You know, it feels a bit like poetic justice that *you're* the bastard using my family again. My da always thought you were the perfect son, did you know? Used to tell your da over and *over* again that he wished I was more like you." He lets out another bitter laugh. "But he didn't stop there, no, he came home and told *me* the same things. 'Why can't you be more like Callum's boy?' he'd say, or 'If you were a bit more like Lachlan, maybe you wouldn't act so daft all the time.'" He shakes his head. "My personal favorite, however, is when he came home one night after drinking with your da, telling me *all* about how he wishes he could just trade us out. How much *easier* it would have been if you were his instead of me." Brodie takes a shuddering breath, his fists clenching as his neck flushes with anger. "Once I have the bridle, my da won't treat me like a nobody anymore, and my brothers will respect me too." He turns back to Key. "I can be whatever I want to be! I'll make those bastards at the historical society pay for letting me go—" I meet Key's gaze, and her wide eyes say this is news to her too. "Money . . . power . . . respect . . . I can have *all* of it. *No one* will make me feel like I'm worthless *ever* again."

"What do you mean the society let you go?"

He scowls. "I saw the monster once before. Earlier this year. I couldn't be sure it was *him*"—he casts an irritated look my way—"but I *saw* it. I wrote a paper on my findings, using the journal as a way to validate things, but they *laughed* at me. Said I was losing touch. That I was confusing fiction with reality. Can you believe that?"

He's waving the knife around wildly now, and when Key's eyes meet mine, I give still another shake of my head, trying to convey to her that she needs to be careful. At least until I can get free.

"That must have been . . . hard," Key says. "I'm sorry."

"It was *bollocks* is what it was," Brodie seethes. "I saw it with my own eyes, and they *laughed*. So I did what anyone would do—I tried to go over their heads. Took my findings to the papers. But, as it turns out, the editor there is a personal friend of my boss, and all it took was one worried phone call for my sanity to have the entire board decide I needed to be on *administrative leave* while they *deliberate* on what to do with me." He spits at his feet. "Fancy way of saying they were kicking me to the curb."

"So you're here for proof," she ventures.

Brodie nods. "Aye. And I'll have it. Once I get the bridle *and* have photo evidence of Lachlan changing? They'll *have* to believe me."

"Brodie," Key says gently. "This isn't the way. This isn't you. You're actually *hurting* people."

"He's not people," Brodie practically spits. "He's been using our entire family. Rhona, Finlay, *you*—all just a means to an end. All just part of his own selfish agenda. He's no better than the long line of bastards he came from. He's just like my da. People are only as good as what they can *do* for him."

I wince. Clearly this is a case of daddy issues that might get me killed. I start working my wrists behind my back, trying to ease my hands out of my restraints subtly as Brodie continues to rant.

"I know you found Tavish's journal, Key," he says. "I saw you leave Lachlan's place with it. So I know you both know where the bridle is. I really wanted to keep you out of this, but that's not an option now. Tell me where it is."

"Brodie, this isn't—"

"Don't be daft, Key," he grinds out. "You're being dense all because this arsehole has wooed you. Think about it. With the bridle, we could do *anything*. Maybe . . . maybe we could even bring back your da."

I hear her breath catch, her lips parting and her brows shooting up into her hair. Everything inside me says that there's no way that's true—there's no magic in the world powerful enough to bring back the long-dead. But still I see the flash of yearning in her eyes, and I can't say that I blame her.

"Key," I call out. "He's insane. Don't—"

A sharp kick to my side knocks the air from my lungs, and I fall over, my face smashing into the ground as I groan. *Fuck.*

"Don't fucking talk," Brodie growls.

My lashes flutter open even as my body continues to throb, and I can see from my vantage point that Key no longer looks shocked. No, right now? Right now she looks pissed as hell.

"Don't touch him," she says darkly.

Brodie rolls his eyes. "Key, you're being—"

"I said, don't fucking touch him," she repeats louder. "Listen, I don't know what sort of sick power grab you're going for here, but Lachlan is *not* using me. I knew what he was all along. I've been helping him because I *want* to."

Brodie's expression morphs with disgust. "Och. You're not naive, then; you're bloody stupid. I thought you were smarter than that."

"And I thought *you* weren't a miserable prick, so I guess we're both surprised."

I notice Brodie's fist clench around the knife, and he bristles for a moment before turning on his heel and stomping over to me. He grabs for my hair roughly, yanking up my head, and then I feel the tip of the knife kissing against my throat.

"Fine," he says. "Tell me where the bridle is. I know the journal must have said."

"It didn't," she protests. "It didn't say where they put it."

Brodie scoffs. "You're lying. You're a terrible liar, did you know?"

*He's not wrong, unfortunately.*

It's one of the things I love about her, but it's definitely not doing her any favors right now. Even I can see that she knows something, and I'm pretty sure blood is currently dripping into my eyes.

"Tell me where it is," Brodie urges as he presses the knife closer to my throat, "or I'm going to use this."

"If you touch him," she says with a menacing tone I didn't even know she had in her, "I'll fucking kill you myself."

"As if you could," Brodie laughs.

Key clenches her fists, jutting out her chin. "I'm not scared of you. You're just a fucking coward. You're not going to do a damned thing."

Brodie is quiet for a moment, his thick body tense with a quiet sort of anger. He finally releases his hold on my hair and stands back up. "Really," he says coldly. "Let's see about that."

*Holy fuck, he really is mental.*

He's walking toward a wide-eyed Key with that nasty blade pointed straight at her, and suddenly, I'm seeing red for an entirely different reason. The thought of him hurting her fills me with a burning rage that seems to course through my blood, flooding me with renewed energy, and I pull at the chains on my wrists with everything I can, watching Brodie stalk closer to Key even as she tries to back away.

I roll to my stomach to get a better angle, and then I'm tugging my wrists apart with all my might, closing my eyes and gritting my teeth as I feel the links starting to give way. I'm on my feet and off the ground mere seconds after they snap, rushing Brodie at full speed even with dizziness still assaulting my senses.

He makes a surprised sound when we collide; Brodie falls to the ground near Key, still struggling against my weight and shouting curses all the while. I try to get my hands on his wrist in an attempt to force the knife from his hand, but he lifts his knee into my stomach, and I double over with a groan. He takes advantage of my momentary weakness by rolling away, but before he can completely escape, I grab his ankle and yank him back.

I can feel the unchecked anger ramping up inside me, searing my blood as a roaring sounds in my ears. My fingers prick with the almost painful sensation of my claws forcing their way out, and with the way my skin grows tight, I know that the beast is trying to make its way out.

"Get the fuck away from me, you monster!"

I make another play for Brodie's knife, and I can hear Key shouting my name from somewhere, but I can't tear my focus away from this fucker who thought he could threaten her, that he could *hurt* her. It makes my focus singular as we grapple, and I notice only a second before he jabs the knife up and toward me when I manage to straddle him, grabbing his forearm with both hands as the knife gets caught between him and my belly.

Brodie puts all his strength behind the attempt, and our proximity makes it difficult for me to divert the trajectory of the massive blade. It's so close that it would slice me across the gut were I to simply jerk it out of his grip, making the possibility of simply using my strength against him less feasible. I can feel it tear my shirt, only inches from my stomach as I grit my teeth, gripping his wrist so tight that it might snap with any more force. There's a wildness in Brodie's eyes that seems unhinged, like he has nothing to lose, like he doesn't care if he walks away from this—as long as he takes me with him.

Part of me feels almost bad for him, because I can't imagine growing up in a world where my father didn't love me like he did. I can't imagine feeling mental because no one believed what I'd seen with my own two eyes. Maybe in better circumstances, Brodie wouldn't be like this. Maybe we could have even been friends. Maybe he's just the product of years of bullying and neglect, desperately reaching for what he thinks is his only solution.

But none of that fucking matters, because he tried to *hurt* Keyanna.

"Look at you," Brodie spits. "You really are a monster."

I imagine I must look hellish. *Good*, I think. He wanted a monster, and now he's fucking got one.

I lean in closer, still holding his now-trembling wrist, keeping it suspended in place where it sits aimed straight for my stomach. I hear Key shouting my name again, but it's lost to the rushing of blood thumping in my ears, the roar of the monster that wants to see this man bleed.

"Aye, I'm a monster," I growl. My lips curve into a smirk, and I bend even farther, allowing the tip of his knife to touch my skin. "And I've got you right where I want you."

## 33

### KEYANNA

I watch in horror as Brodie and Lachlan reach a standoff—Brodie's knife is so close to Lachlan's stomach that it would take only the tiniest movement for it to run him through. Panic claws at my chest as I try to think of what to do, how to help, but I'm frozen in place, having seemed to have forgotten how to move.

I call for Lachlan again and again, but he ignores me as he continues to grip Brodie by the wrist, keeping him from stabbing him but also not actually removing himself from harm's way. They say something to each other, something I don't make out, and I see Lachlan lean in closer, the knife at his belly practically touching him now.

I let out a scream when Brodie bucks up suddenly, taking Lachlan off guard and managing to flip him so that *Lachlan* is now the one pinned down, and my limbs remember how to work as the fear of actually seeing Lachlan run through with that wicked-looking knife courses through me.

I spin on my heel and sprint in the other direction, trying to find something familiar to let me know what I'm looking for. At first, all the headstones look the same, but once I find the barbed wire fence that Lachlan helped me under only a few weeks ago, I'm able to backtrack from there, finally standing in front of what we've all been searching for. All this time.

And it's been right here under our noses.

I don't have time to take in the intricately carved bust of a horse, the detailing in the headstone obvious even in its weathered state—but I can't help running my fingers over the name that's nearly rubbed off, remembering it from the last time I was here.

The *T* is clearly visible, and even though the rest of the name is still almost impossible to read—I know it now. He'd been here all along.

*Tavish MacKay.*

I reach for the ancient-looking leather strap that rests on the horse head, properly adorned as if you could urge the animal to get up and go even now. I'm gentle as I remove it, knowing it now for what it is, and even holding it in my hands—it's kind of hard to believe. It looks so worn, so plain . . . it looks nothing at all like some all-powerful artifact.

But I don't have time to dwell on that.

I hold it up high over my head as I run back to the clearing where Lachlan is still snarling under Brodie's weight, fighting back against the gravity of Brodie's knife as he tries to drive it downward right into Lachlan's *chest*. The organ in *my* chest lurches at the sight. I watch in horror as he puts all his body weight into it, Lachlan only *just* managing to shove Brodie's hand away so that the knife pierces Lachlan in the shoulder instead of through the heart.

Lachlan's cry of pain guts me, the immediate blooming of red on his sweater forcing my mouth open.

"Brodie!" I yell, holding the bridle higher. "Stop it! This is what you want!"

He blinks at me when he notices what I'm holding; his arms relax a fraction even as his knife remains lodged in Lachlan's shoulder, and I hold out the bridle in offering.

"Don't hurt him anymore," I tell Brodie, "and you can have it."

Brodie's eyes narrow as if this is some sort of trick, but with Lachlan still hissing in pain beneath him, his sweater becoming more and more drenched with his blood by the second—he seems to let down his guard. He tugs the knife free without any finesse, earning another pained grunt from Lachlan, who he ignores as he rises to his feet, stepping away from him.

"S'good choice," Brodie tells me, pointing the knife my way defensively. I have to actively not look at it, the sight of Lachlan's blood making me feel sick. "Now hand it over, Key. I don't want to hurt you. You did nothing wrong. You're a *victim* here, don't you see?" He gestures back at Lachlan's prone form. "*He's* the monster."

I nod slowly, not daring to answer; the crazed look in Brodie's eyes doesn't spark the desire to try and reason with him. I hold out the bridle with only slightly shaking hands, my gut twisting as he takes it gingerly. His lips curl in a maniacal grin as he stares down at it, his hand that holds the knife dropping to his side as he appraises the leather with his thumb.

I'm already moving around him to go to Lachlan, desperate to try and heal his wound, but am taken off guard when Brodie kicks out his leg, tripping me and forcing me down to the ground. I grunt in pain as I collide with the solid earth, hearing Brodie tsk above me.

"You're still choosing to be ignorant, then?" He grips the bridle in one hand, shaking his head disappointedly. "I really did like you, you know. It's a shame."

He wipes Lachlan's blood on the leg of his pants unceremoniously, turning back to Lachlan with a murderous intent in his eyes. I don't even let him make it a step before I reach out and grab for his ankle, holding it as tightly as I can to try to stop him from going.

He looks down at me, amusement playing out over his features. "You don't know when to give up. Do you?"

I close my eyes, blocking out his voice, trying to concentrate. He says something else, something with that same condescending tone, but I keep my hands around his ankle, drawing on that energy, filling that well inside as I give all my focus to *one single purpose*. I feel it when it happens, the heat rushing down my arms and through my hands until the burning is a physical thing, and then I smile to myself even as Brodie continues to bluster above me.

And that's when his pant leg bursts into flames.

He starts to scream as the fire quickly climbs higher up his leg, beating it with both hands in an attempt to put it out. I roll away from him to avoid the flames, his cries echoing around the clearing as he thrashes about in a panic, still smacking at his pant leg. He stumbles backward, teetering off-balance as his feet snag on fallen branches and thick piles of leaves, and he doesn't see it coming, I think—but I do.

His heels catch on an old log as he tumbles backward, everything seeming to happen in slow motion. His body drops like deadweight, his head cracking against one of the tombstones even as his pants continue to burn. He immediately goes still, and in this moment, I have no idea if he's alive or dead. I'm honestly not sure if I care, after everything that's just happened—but then I notice what he's still holding.

More importantly, I notice that it's on fire.

*The bridle!*

I rush to my feet, sprinting toward Brodie's prone body, stomping out the last of the flames that consume the old leather, then shucking off my jacket and starting to beat the fire that still eats at Brodie's pants. When it's all out, and I'm sweating and out of breath and coughing from the smoke—only then do I notice the tragedy of what's happened.

The bridle is ruined.

I kneel down to try to carefully pry it from Brodie's grip, watching as it crumbles in several places where the flames have eaten away at the ancient material. I begrudgingly check Brodie for a pulse, finding that the bastard is just knocked out, not dead, and I resist the urge to kick him in the gut for good measure, knowing I have more important things to deal with.

I make quick work of crossing the clearing to fall at Lachlan's side, blood now fully soaking the sleeve of his sweater. His face is contorted in pain, and I immediately shove my hands under his neckline, not caring about the blood in the slightest as I press my fingers to his wound.

That same warmth from the night on the loch—the night I first found out what he was—collects in my palms, and I can see it clearly now, the glow that comes with it. It comes almost easily. Like a thought made real. It takes several moments for the bleeding to slow, for Lachlan's face to smooth out and his eyes to flutter open, and when I see those icy blues looking up at me with pure awe and adoration, I do the one thing that seems to be a habit, at this point.

I burst into tears.

Lachlan sits up with a grunt to gather me in his arms, holding me to his chest as he frantically touches me all over, his voice a panicked coo.

"Oi," he says lowly. "What is it? Are you hurt? Did he get you? I swear, if he hurt you, I'll—"

I shake my head against his chest, sobs racking my body. "I'm fine. I'm *fine*. But it doesn't matter. I *ruined* it. I didn't mean to, I just wanted to save you, but I—"

My words break off into unintelligible babblings as I continue to weep in a way that *has* to be appalling to watch, but still Lachlan cradles my face in his hands, forcing it up so that I have to look at him.

"Come now," he murmurs. "Shh. Don't cry. We can figure it out. You did so good, love. So good."

This only makes my lip quiver harder, hearing his praise while knowing that I've robbed us of any chance to save him, and I sniffle loudly as I offer up the tattered remains of the bridle, holding it out so that he can see the damage done.

"He was holding it," I choke out. "When he was trying to put the fire out. I didn't think—I just—"

Lachlan stares down at the ruined scraps of leather in my hand, his mouth parting in surprise as he reaches out to run his fingers over it. I can see the flicker of disappointment there, and I'm seconds away from falling into a fresh wave of tears when he shakes his head, grabbing the bridle from me and tossing it away.

"We don't need it," he says resolutely.

I rear back, my brow furrowing even as tears continue to leak from my eyes. "What do you mean we *don't need it*? It's what we've been searching for all this time! How are we supposed to save you without the bridle's magic?"

He shakes his head again, his palms cradling my cheeks as he drops his head to level his gaze with mine. "We don't need it," he says again. "You can do it yourself."

I balk, my mouth falling open even as confusion racks me.

"What? What the hell are you talking about? I can't do anything. Anything real, that is. They're just fancy party tricks, remember?"

"Aye, that's what I said," he agrees. "But look at all you've done! You knew where to find me. You came after me. You *saved* me." He snorts. "Hell, it was *you* who found the journal to begin with. *You* who figured things out when no one in my family could for *centuries*. Don't you get it, Key?"

I frown, sniffling again. "Get what?"

"It's you," he says quietly, his smile soft and his eyes softer. "The magic is *you*."

He looks so sure when he says it, so goddamned certain that he's not spouting nonsense as my brain tries to tell me he is, and for a moment, I can only gape at him.

"No," I splutter finally. "No, I can't—"

He shuts me up by pressing his mouth to mine.

"You can," he murmurs against my lips. "I know you can."

I whip my head to the edge of the clearing, where I can just see the sun starting to sink, and that same panic tries to climb higher into my throat. "We don't have time," I exclaim. "It's almost sundown. We have to get you to the loch. We have to—"

"No," he says firmly. "I'm not going anywhere, because I *know* you can finish this. Right here."

I feel tears gathering again at my eyes, blurring my vision, and fear grips my chest, making me feel cold. "What if I can't?' I whisper. "What if I can't save you? What if I *fail*?"

"It doesn't matter," he hums, kissing me again gently.

"How can you say that?"

"Because," he tells me. "It won't change how much I love you."

A tiny gasp escapes me, the terror rattling around in my rib cage morphing into a hot pressure that seems to fill me up like water in a bowl, so quickly and so *much* that I feel overflowing with it.

"You do?"

"Aye," he chuckles. "Even your awful singing."

A watery laugh escapes me, and I reach out to hold his wrists even as his hands still cradle my face.

"I love you too."

I know with certainty at that moment that I absolutely mean it. Of course I love him. What better explanation is there for this all-consuming need I feel to be near him, to make sure that I'm able to for years to come?

"You can do it, love," he encourages. "I know you can."

I nod heavily as I lift my hands from his wrists, bringing them to his cheeks to hold him in the same way he's still holding me. I rest my forehead against his as I will my breathing to slow, taking deep, heavy breaths and blowing them out as I shut my eyes tight.

At first, I don't know where to begin. I can feel the energy still humming around me, like it knows it's not done with me yet. I gather it closer like a cloak, pulling it until it covers and surrounds us. I let my mind fill with thoughts of Sorcha, of my family, of all the things that led us here, remembering what she wrote in Tavish's journal.

*—one day one such lass shall walk this world, hold my magic, and be given a chance to forgive. Only should she take it, will my curse be no more.*

"You lied to me," I whisper, remembering what drove me from him in the first place, what caused me to leave him all alone.

He nods slowly, his thumb brushing across my cheek. "Aye, I did," he answers. "And if you'll let me, I'll spend the rest of my life making it right."

I feel a pulsing in the air, a thrumming that I can almost hear—

and reach for it in my mind, almost able to imagine the warmth of it under my fingertips. The light continues to die with every second, and yet when I open my eyes, the space around us seems to glow with an otherworldly luminescence.

I imagine a hand resting gently against the crown of my head, a warm, encouraging touch that feels like one I know, even if it isn't actually there.

*Sorcha*.

I can feel her here, and emotion swells inside me as a strange melancholy seizes me, realizing I can never know her. That I can never thank her for what she's given me.

Oddly enough, it almost feels like she might know.

I bring my mouth to Lachlan's in a barely there kiss, urging that warmth, that light, to pour into him, to rush through every part of him, casting its glow on all the darkest parts of him and leaving only him in their wake.

I smile as a swelling sense of calm rises up in me, and I can feel it, all that's left to do.

"I forgive you," I tell him.

He meets me with equal fervor when I kiss him more deeply, his strong arms wrapping around me and molding me to him as that humming energy builds and builds and *builds* before finally—all is quiet.

It takes me several seconds to stop kissing him, just so happy that he's here, that he's okay, but when we finally break apart—I just know. I can feel it.

The curse is no more.

We both turn to watch the last light of the sun sink below the horizon, and when it's completely gone, leaving us in nothing but the dim rays of the moonlight—I see Lachlan's eyes swim with tears. A sob escapes him as he crushes me against him once more, burying his face in my throat as his shoulders shake with the weight of his emotion.

"Thank you," he whispers. "*Thank you.*"

I laugh, the sound of it broken up by my own thick emotion still lodged in my throat. "I guess that party trick came in handy, hm?"

"Aye," he chuckles brokenly. "I'm glad you decided to save my arse this time instead of setting it on fire."

I pull back, unable to wipe the beaming grin from my face, but since Lachlan's is a perfect match for it, I think it's fine. "I did save you, didn't I? *Again.*"

"Aye, you did."

"Who's the princess now, huh?"

"Och. I'll never live that down, will I?"

I lean in, pressing my lips to his cheek. "Not a chance."

"What do we do about that bastard over there?"

I turn back to glance at Brodie's still-prone form. "Tie him up?"

"With pleasure," Lachlan says with a smile.

"And your ancestor's journal?"

Lachlan grimaces, almost a sneer. "Burn the bloody thing for all I care."

I don't know if I agree with that choice, but I guess I understand it.

"This is going to be"—I glance around at the mess of the clearing—"hard to explain."

"Aye, but we have all night to come up with a story," Lachlan says, pushing to his feet and offering his hand to help me do the same. "Now that I won't turn, we have plenty of time to—"

I watch as he goes still, his eyes rounding and his mouth hanging agape.

"What?" I ask. "What is it?"

His wide eyes find mine. "My da. Do you think . . . ?"

"Oh." My heart rate picks up. "Well. There's only one way to find out, right?"

He nods, lacing his fingers through mine, and I send up a silent plea.

I squeeze Lachlan's hand. "He'll be there," I tell him. "I can feel it."

Maybe if I speak it into existence . . . it will have to come true.

## 34

### LACHLAN

I'm almost certain that Key and I run the entire way across the property—her hand gripped tightly within mine as she follows after me, never asking to slow. It feels almost like flying, running under the stars with her, the weight I've carried for so long seeming to dissipate into the night air. My legs burn and my heart pounds as we cross the fields and the sloping terrain to press on toward the loch, and by the time the water comes into view, glittering under the moonlight, it feels almost like my chest might burst with the force of the heavy *thump thump* rattling away inside it.

I can hear her panting breath beside me, but when I turn to look at her, her eyes are bright and her face is lit up with a radiating joy—her lips curving in a smile as if everything is already as it should be, as if she has no doubt that everything will be just fine. I wish I could say I had her confidence.

My steps to the shore are slower then, cautious even, my eyes searching the water for signs of movement, signs of *him*. I know that the chances of him being here in the cove are slim whether he's changed or not—but Key squeezes my hand when she catches me frowning, looking up at me with an encouraging expression.

"It worked," she tells me.

I squeeze her hand back. "How do you know?"

"I can feel it," she says confidently.

I want to share in her surety; I've already seen her do so many amazing things, after all, but a lifetime of disappointment can't be forgotten in only a moment. It will take time even for me to reconcile that, as far as it seems, the worst is behind me. That I can finally start moving *forward*.

The rolling water stirs in the slight breeze as it sways over the surface of the loch, ever still, ever silent. It feels almost like a bad omen, how quiet it is. Like an answer to a question I'm too afraid to ask.

"He could be anywhere," Key says. "Could have changed anywhere. It could take time to find him."

"I know," I answer. "Maybe we should have gotten the Rover."

"There's still time. We could go back for it and start searching. We have all night."

My voice sounds too small for me when I say, "What if he's not out there?"

"He will be," she assures me.

I shake my head, frowning down at her. "But what if he isn't?"

"Then we'll deal with it," she says. "If there was a solution for you, then there is a solution for him. And we'll find it. *Together*."

"I can't ask any more from you."

"You don't have to," she tells me, reaching out to cup my cheek. "You never have to ask me for help. I'll always be here to give it."

My eyes sting as I draw in a shaky breath, bending slightly so that I can rest my forehead against hers. Once again I think to myself that it's possible I don't deserve her. That it feels almost unreal that she would not only stumble into my life, but want to be *a part* of it. For as long as I live, no matter what happens after this moment, I will always be grateful for it.

"Come on," she says. "Let's go get the Rover, and then we can—"

"Oi! Don't s'pose I could ask for a wee bit of help, if you'd be so kind?"

My limbs freeze, my brain stuttering at the sound of his voice. For a moment, it feels like maybe I imagine it, like maybe it was only me who heard it, but when Key pulls back, a wide smile on her face—I know that isn't the case.

We both turn to take in an approaching figure half stumbling down the shore, his legs shaky. Almost as if he isn't used to using them. At first, I can't move. I stare at the man getting closer and closer, frozen in place as my mouth parts and my eyes round. Words fail me, and I all but forget how to breathe, and it is only Keyanna's touch that brings me back to the moment, that makes me remember how to use my feet.

I take a cautious step, taking in the longer hair, the same barreled chest, the smile that sometimes haunts my dreams. "Da?"

He slows only a few paces away, cocking his head as he looks me up and down, his brow knitting. I see the moment it clicks for him, his breath catching as his eyes go wide.

"It can't be . . ."

I take another step, and then another, and then suddenly, he's right there. Standing before me as if he never left. Even in the moonlight I can see the gray in his hair now, can see wrinkles around his eyes and mouth, but underneath that—he's the same man who walked into the loch all those years ago and never came out.

"It's me," I choke out. "It's Lachlan."

His hands reach out as he clasps my shoulders, still appraising me as if he'll be able to make sense of it. The last time he saw me, I was still a wean, after all. I can't imagine the shock he must be feeling to come out and see me as a man.

He pulls me against his chest suddenly, his arms coming around my shoulders to hold me tight. I feel years melting off me in his embrace, and again my eyes sting traitorously as I return it, holding him tightly in the way I've wanted to for so many years. I close my eyes to fight against the sudden sting of tears as I revel in the moment; for so long I thought I would never have this, that it just wasn't in the cards for us, but he's here now. He's *here*.

"Michty me," he murmurs, pulling away to look at me again. "Look at you. How . . ." His eyes snap up to meet mine. "How long has it been?"

I feel an ache in my chest, and I wish I didn't have to give him this news, preparing myself for what it might do to him. "It's been twenty-six years."

"Twenty-six . . ." His eyes drop to our feet, his lips moving wordlessly as he processes that information. "It feels like I just saw you yesterday."

"I'm sorry," I manage. "I'm sorry it took me so long."

My da shakes his head. "None of that. You're here. That's what matters. Although you'll have to tell me how you worked this out, because I sure couldn't make heads or tails of it."

"Well . . ." I glance behind me. "It wasn't really me, if I'm being honest."

My dad leans to peer behind me, and I turn in place as Key gives him a tiny wave. "Hello," she says. "It's nice to meet you."

I notice she's very carefully averting her gaze, and that's when it dawns on me.

My da is completely naked.

I shrug out of my jacket, holding it out to him as he blusters a bit, wrapping it around his waist.

"Thought I felt a chill," he chuckles.

I shiver in the cold air without my jacket, realizing that my usual overly warm body temperature is no more—another sign of the curse finally being over.

"Not exactly how I pictured you two meeting for the first time," I say back, laughing softly.

"This wee thing broke our curse?" My da sounds awestruck, brushing past me to drink in the sight of her. "You must be something special, lass."

"I don't know about that—"

"She is," I interrupt her. "She's very special."

My da beams. "What's your name, hen?"

"My name is . . ." She flicks her gaze to mine, and I nod in encouragement. "My name is Keyanna," she tells him. "Keyanna MacKay."

He rears back a bit, his head swiveling so that he can lock eyes with me as confusion floods his features. "MacKay?"

"Aye," I tell him. "The very same."

"A daughter of MacKay," my da whispers. He turns back to Key. "Then that would make you . . ."

"Duncan's daughter," she finishes.

My da's eyes move over her face, no doubt seeing the truth of it, his throat bobbing with a swallow as he nods heavily. "Aye, you have the look of him."

"I'm very sorry," she tells him. "For everything you went through."

"He left for you," my da says, still looking a bit dazed. "Didn't he?"

Key stiffens a bit, but nods back at him. "Yes, I think so."

"Och." Da's voice sounds thick as he nods again, sniffling a bit. "S'pose that would do it."

"I don't think he ever wanted to abandon you," she says quietly. "If it weren't for me—"

"No," I cut in. "None of that. I won't have you shouldering any blame."

My da looks between the two of us curiously, giving his attention back to Key. "I'd have done the same, lass. We parents . . . we would do anything for our children, aye?" He pats her shoulder. "And your da? Is he here with you?"

Key averts her gaze. "He passed away back in the spring."

"I see," my da answers, his arm circling around her shoulder as he gives it an encouraging squeeze. "He was . . . a good man. It seems he raised a fine daughter." He nods, sniffling again. "I thank you, lass. For everything."

"I was happy to help," she says.

"And your mum . . . ?" my da asks me. "Is she . . . ?"

"She's alive," I tell him. "But she's . . . moved away. She didn't take it well when you left."

His face crumples, but he nods through it. "Aye. I suppose that'll be another wrong to right." He glances down at my jacket haphazardly wrapped around his waist. "Perhaps after I find some clothes."

Keyanna laughs beside me, and I beam down at her, feeling so full in this moment.

I don't say any more about my mum; I have no idea how she would handle this news, but I know that tonight isn't the night to discuss it. Not when I just got him back. There will be plenty of time after this to figure everything out. That's what Key has given us. *Time.*

I look at her now—her wild curls fluttering in the breeze, the emerald of her eyes harder to make out in the moonlight, but still they appear to shine under the stars, her lips curling subtly as I keep my gaze fixed on her, unable to look away. It hits me with full force just how *much* she's given me; I have no idea how I can ever repay her. I will never know how to give her back even a *fraction* of all she's handed over to me, for no other reason than she's just that sort. As if she's some sort of angel personified, sent to me when I needed her most.

I take a step closer and grab her hand, holding it in mine as my face splits into a wide grin, one that she returns instantly. If it weren't for my da standing a few short feet away, I'd be pulling her into my arms, kissing her senseless if only to try to express some tiny part of what I'm feeling. Instead, I tug her into my side, pressing a kiss to her hair and breathing in the soft scent of her, letting the knowledge that I will be able to whenever I like in the years to come wash over me.

"Oi, what's this?" I hear my da's soft chuckle, and when I look at him, his arms are crossed over his chest as he eyes the pair of us. "It seems you have *a lot* to tell me, aye?"

Key is still smiling when I look down at her, and I can feel the weight of it mirrored in my own face, my cheeks almost hurting with the force of it. I can't remember ever smiling like this before I met her. My life has been a never-ending parade of disappointment, of fear, of uncertainty—but there is nothing uncertain about the way I feel when I look at her.

There will always be things in this world that remain unknown to me, but one thing I can know for sure is the way I feel about her. And I know that whenever I'm unable to find my way, she'll be there with an outstretched hand, ready to show me.

That, I think, is a love most people search for—and yet hers came right to my door.

"Aye," I finally manage to answer, my voice thick now as well. I smile a wee bit wider, unable to tear my gaze away from this woman who gave me everything without ever needing to be asked, and I feel, for the first time, that everything really will be all right. As long as she's with me. "Aye, we really do."

35

KEYANNA

He's still sleeping when I come to; I stretch my arms up over my head before rolling onto my side, tucking my hands under my cheek as I watch him. His dark golden hair falls loosely over his brow, his soft mouth parted slightly as he snores quietly. I smile to myself as I snuggle closer; it's still a novelty to be able to wake up with him like this, even after two weeks of doing so. His bed is still too small, and he hogs most of it in the night, but I don't care about any of that because he's warm and solid and *here*—and I'm finally starting to settle into the belief that he won't suddenly be gone when I wake up one morning.

"You're being a creeper again, aren't you."

My grin widens, and I shift up on my elbow, leaning to press my mouth to his. "I was just thinking about the easiest way to strangle you with the sheets you keep stealing."

"Devil woman," he chuckles. He cracks open one eye, his lip curling in a smirk as he appraises me sleepily. "You were doing no such thing."

"No, I wasn't," I admit. "Even if you *do* hog the sheets."

He rolls, his palm covering my bare hip as he hums softly. "That's more intentional than you might think."

I nuzzle into him, allowing my eyes to drift shut as I inhale his warm, sleepy scent. It calms me just a little, tension I hadn't even realized I'd been holding ebbing slightly.

"Trouble sleeping again?" he asks.

I nod into his chest. "I keep thinking I'll wake up and you won't be here."

"Och, love. Don't be daft. You'll not get rid of me so easily."

I take another lungful of his soft scent, letting it out on a slow exhale. "They'll be moving Brodie today."

"Aye," he says. "I know. Over to Glasgow."

"Is it bad that I feel . . . sorry for him?"

"You wouldn't be you if you didn't," he hums thoughtfully. "But it's not your fault, what happened to him. If anything, it's more mine."

"You're not the one who set him on fire," I mumble.

"Aye, true," he says. "But he wasn't hurt seriously, and I reckon I have a lot to do with him being carted away to a psych ward for shouting about monsters to everyone who would listen." His body shakes a bit with his laugh. "Although . . . it was a wee bit funny when he started demanding I strip to prove something to the policeman."

I smack his chest. "He was obviously ill. Like he just . . . cracked or something."

"And now he'll get the help he needs," Lachlan reasons. "But as far as I'm concerned . . . he lost my sympathy when he turned that knife on you."

I feel a white-hot flash of anger pulse inside me, and I huff out a breath. "And the bastard stabbed you."

"Was just a scratch."

I roll my eyes. "You forget I *saw* it."

"Aye, aye, I know."

I wrap my arms around his stomach, pulling him closer. "Did you talk to your dad yesterday?"

"I did," he sighs. "Things are still . . . strained with him and Mum. But she's talking to him now, at least."

"I mean, it has to be a shock for her."

"I s'pose so."

I kiss his shoulder. "Do you think you can fix things between you and your mom? Eventually?"

"I imagine so," he says. "Maybe after things have settled." I feel his finger poke into my side, and I shriek and squirm as he maneuvers onto his side, propping his fist up on his elbow. "And what about you, eh, princess? Have you decided what you'll be doing next?"

My brow wrinkles. "What do you mean?"

"Well, not that I don't enjoy your company, but we can't exactly live in this wee shack forever."

"Are you already kicking me out?"

"More asking what I might have to do to get you to settle somewhere more permanent . . . here. In Scotland."

My pulse quickens as my lips quirk. "Settle, huh?"

"The way I see it," he says seriously, "you've got everything you need right here."

"Oh, do I?"

He nods. "Oh, aye." He holds up one finger. "You've got your granny and grandpa, for starters."

"True."

"There's the pub," he goes on, holding up another finger.

My mouth twitches as I try to hold back a smile. "Rory and Blair would probably miss me, yes."

"And Bethie," he adds. "She's grown rather fond of you."

I can't help it now, my lips tilting into a grin. "Just Bethie?"

"Hm." He taps a finger against his lips, his brows knitting in thought. "There might be someone else."

"Really."

His lips twitch. "S'pose I might like you. Just a little."

"Ass," I laugh.

He smiles at me. "You didn't think that would change because of a few kisses, did you?"

"Apparently not," I hmph.

I feel his lips at my hair, his hand curling around my shoulder, stroking it gently.

"Someone might want you to stay very much," he tells me softly. "Someone might even think about giving you a proper home here, if you wanted."

My eyes prick with tears, not sad or frustrated like they have been so often of late, but happy for once.

"I'm already home," I tell him. "And I'm not going anywhere."

His voice is soft when he answers, "Someone is very glad to hear it."

I feel . . . full, at this moment, like everything is settling into place, my life finally calming after I've felt so adrift in the months since my dad passed. Maybe it's reckless, entertaining the idea of a future with a man I've known for only a few months, but even from our first rocky meeting, I can't deny the pull I've felt for this stubborn man who still drives me a little crazy sometimes. Like maybe we were inevitable. And who is to say we weren't? So much about our story feels foretold, and even if the ending to that story is unwritten—I find myself unafraid of the unknown for once in my life. Like for once, it just feels like everything will work out as it's supposed to.

"You know you should do it today," Lachlan murmurs, popping my cozy bubble of calm. "You've put it off for weeks now."

I groan against his chest. "I know. I'm just afraid of how she'll react. She's already had such a hard time with Brodie's 'breakdown.' If I make that leap, I'll have to tell her *everything*."

"She's a tough auld bird," Lachlan says. "She can handle it."

That much is true, at least. Even though Brodie's situation was a shock for Finlay and Rhona, my granny has been stoic about the whole thing. I can tell that it wounds her to think Brodie might have been suffering without her knowing, and I can't help but feel a tinge of guilt at the idea of being the one to tell her just how much he'd lost his way in the end. But Lachlan is right. If anyone can handle it, she can, and she deserves the truth.

"I'll do it today," I promise. "After breakfast. No more dragging my feet."

"That's a good lass," he says, kissing my hair. When I look up at him, he's sporting a sly grin. "And speaking of breakfast . . ."

I roll my eyes. "You know that's a gross misuse of things."

"But it's so much fun," he counters.

I heave out a sigh, sitting up against the headboard so I can concentrate. Lachlan props up on his side eagerly, looking almost like a child as he watches me scrunch up my face, focusing. The bulb in the ceiling fixture flickers half-heartedly a few times before coming on fully, and then there is the sharp beeping of the coffeepot—waking up at my command as the liquid starts to drip into the filter.

"Don't know how I'll ever go back to making my own coffee with you around," Lachlan laughs. He hugs his arms around my waist, letting his cheek rest against my stomach. "You're getting very good at controlling it."

"It's almost like just knowing it's there makes it easier to tap into. Like it's just been waiting for me to find it. Like, now that I know what to look for . . . I can't *not* see it. Is that weird?"

"I'll remind you again that up until a few weeks ago, I turned into a fucking dinosaur at night. You could sprout wings and fly through the window at this point, and I might not question it." He makes a face. "Although maybe warn me first if you feel it coming on."

I shake my head. "Don't hold your breath."

"Mm." He rubs his cheek against my bare stomach, and the coarse hair of his beard tickles my skin, sending a faint throb of arousal through me. "I'll go with you. If you want."

"I'd like that," I tell him. I card my fingers through his hair, squirming a bit as another wave of want courses through me, as it so often does when he touches me for any extended period of time. "But maybe after."

He turns up his face, his brow furrowed. "After?"

"Mhm." I press my palms to his cheeks, urging him up until he's leaning on his hands, my lips finding his to coax a kiss from him. Within seconds it escalates to something needier, which is another habit we seem to be forming, but I find I don't mind in the slightest. "After."

His lips curl against mine. "I'm at your service, princess."

When he starts to kiss me more thoroughly, his body covering mine . . . I can't even find it in me to be annoyed by the silly nickname anymore.

I'm beyond nervous when I enter the main house a while later after breakfast with the journal tucked under my arm, but Lachlan following close behind me quells the anxiety just a bit, reminding me that regardless of what happens here, everything *will* be okay. He keeps his hand against my lower back in a supportive gesture as we move through the entryway, following the sounds of Rhona puttering around in the kitchen. She's furiously scrubbing at a massive stockpot when we round the wide entry to the kitchen, pausing only to look up at us after letting out a string of curses.

"Och, you startled me," she grunts. "Didn't hear you come in."

"Sorry," I tell her. "Didn't mean to."

She waves me off, reaching for the dish towel she hangs on the oven handle and drying her hands. "None of that. Are you hungry then? I could heat up something."

"No, no," I assure her. "We already had breakfast."

Rhona's mouth forms a thin line, cocking a brow at Lachlan. "If I knew you'd be stealing my only granddaughter only a couple of months after I got her, I might have chased you off the property much sooner."

"I'm open to discussion regarding visitation rights," he deadpans.

Rhona rolls her eyes. "Don't be an arse, boy. It doesn't suit you."

"I have a lot of anecdotal evidence that suggests otherwise," I laugh, slipping into one of the kitchen chairs.

Lachlan scoffs as he takes the one next to me. "Nothing but rotten slander."

"Mhm." I keep the journal stowed in my lap as Rhona pours herself a cup of tea, arching an eyebrow at me. "You want a cuppa?"

"No thanks." I shake my head. "I had coffee already."

"Aye, aye."

There's a quiet that settles as Lachlan and I let her finish her cup, waiting until she's seated on the other side of the table, blowing at her tea, before either of us speaks again.

"Where's Finlay?" Lachlan asks.

Rhona grunts softly. "Stubborn arse is still looking for the calf Harriet dropped yesterday."

"He should have told me," Lachlan humphs. "I'd have gone with him."

"I think he wants the quiet time," she tells him. Her eyes gain a weary look. "He's still a wee bit out of sorts with . . . everything that's happened."

A feeling of sympathy squeezes my chest, knowing that as difficult as Brodie being carted away must be for her, finding out the truth about . . . well, *everything* . . . might be all the more so. Still, I know that Lachlan is right. She can get through this.

"I'd really hoped to give you this together," I start carefully, pulling the book from my lap and letting it rest on the table. "But maybe it's better if you have some time with it first." I think of the worn letter resting just inside the cover. "Considering."

Rhona eyes the aged leather curiously, cocking her head. "And what's this?"

"This is . . ." My mouth closes, and I stare down at the journal, my thoughts buzzing as I try to find the words that capture *everything* that this book is. What it means. "It's something I think you should see."

I let out a shuddered breath as nerves once again wash over me, and Lachlan, noticing my struggle, lifts his hand to place it over mine, giving me a reassuring squeeze. I turn my head to meet his gaze, seeing a faith in me waiting there, shining out clear as day, which gives me courage.

"You're not afraid of anything, love," he tells me.

And I'm not, I realize. Not really. Not anymore. Even with everything I've lost . . . I've somehow found so much more.

"I wanted to tell you that I've decided to stay," I tell Rhona, meeting her gaze. "If that's all right with you."

Her mouth parts in surprise, but there's no hiding the sudden shine of her eyes, the wrinkled corners gathering as she drags in an unsteady breath. "Is that what you want, hen? What about everything you left behind?"

I consider that—thinking of my dad's place that is now sold off, his things that are stored away, the friends that fell to the wayside . . . and yes. There are memories there. But . . .

"When my dad died," I tell her, my voice soft as I watch my fingers twisting, "I thought that was the end of everything as I knew it. I felt . . . so alone. Like I had absolutely nothing left, that I had no one. I left everything behind and came here, hoping to find something that I wasn't sure I could ever have again." I turn up my face to find her eyes again, a smile touching my lips. "But I did find it. With you, and with Grandpa, and with . . ." I bite my lip, glancing at Lachlan, who winks at me smugly. "I never thought I would have a family again. Not without my dad . . . but that's what it feels like I have here with all of you. I don't want to leave that behind. I want to stay and know you better, to put down roots here that I can pass to my own children. I want to make sure that they'll never have to wonder where they came from like I did, because I—and hopefully you—will be there to tell them."

Rhona's eyes are full-on shimmering now, her lip trembling as one single tear escapes her eye, tracking down her cheek. She makes no move to wipe it away, instead reaching across the table to take my hands in hers.

"Sweet lass," she says thickly. "I will forever regret the way I acted when you first came to us. I can't ever take that back. But having you here . . . seeing my Duncan in you, but also seeing the wonderful person that *you* are all on your own . . . I wouldn't trade it for anything." She sniffles softly, nodding as another tear slips from her eye. "I only wish your father were here so I could tell him how sorry I was for failing him. I wish I could tell him that I'll do better with you. That I'll never make those mistakes ever again. I wish . . ." She swallows thickly. "I wish he hadn't left this world with any darkness that we gave him."

My face splits in a grin, my own eyes glossing over as I try to blink away the tears that seem to be just part of my life now. I can't ever remember crying so much as I have since I came here. I nod back at her, giving her hands a squeeze before pulling them away to pat the cover of the journal.

"About that . . ."

I take a deep breath, looking at Lachlan again and finding strength in his encouraging nod, returning it before pulling the crinkled letter from the cover of the journal. I slide it gingerly across the table, letting it rest just in front of Rhona before slowly pulling my hand back.

She looks at it with a downturned mouth and a knitted brow. "What's this?"

"It's for you," I tell her. "You should read it."

She picks it up with care, pulling it closer and squinting a bit as her mouth moves ever so slightly with each word she reads. There's no missing when it dawns on her, her eyes going wide and her hand coming to cover her mouth as the tears fall more freely. I watch her consume each word voraciously, reaching out to press her fingers to the page delicately, almost with reverence.

She looks up at me, tears streaming down her cheeks. "I don't—I don't understand. What does this mean?"

"Well . . ."

I turn to hold Lachlan's gaze for a moment more, silently seeking confirmation once again that this is okay, that he's *okay* with sharing absolutely everything.

"The story isn't just mine, love," he tells me gently. "It's ours."

I flash him a grin, my love for him seeming older than the short amount of time I've had the joy of feeling it. It feels like home to me. It feels like *forever*.

I turn back to my granny, meeting her eyes that are so like mine with renewed determination as I slide the journal her way. "Well . . ." I start again, "We have *quite* the story for you."

And not for the first time, I feel that overwhelming sense of calm touch my heart, like the caress of a gentle hand, like the whisper of a voice from long ago, longer than I can imagine—telling me that everything will be just fine.

Because Lachlan is absolutely right. It's not just a story.

It's *ours*.

# Epilogue

## LACHLAN

Now, now," I say, holding back her chubby little fist when she reaches for the colored glass. "Don't be touching it yet. It's drying, see?"

"Pwetty cuwers," she answers in her adorable wee voice.

"Aye, it's very pretty, love," I agree, bending to grab her by the waist so I can hoist her against my side. "But also very, *very* auld."

"Owed," she parrots, looking serious. "No touch."

I beam at her, reaching to tap my finger against the tip of her pert nose, which is covered in freckles. I ruffle my hand over her wild red curls, the giggle she lets out the sweetest sound in the world. Sometimes I can't help but stare at her, this little life with her mother's curls and my blue eyes and a fiery spirit that might be from the devil himself—so full of gratitude to have her after so many years of thinking it wasn't in the cards for me.

"Dada?"

I shake my head, clearing away my drifting thoughts as I give her a grin. "Sorry, princess," I tell her. "You're just so bonnie, I can't help but look at you for a spell sometimes."

She giggles again, letting her face fall against my shoulder as her little arms wind around my neck. I close my eyes to breathe in the soft scent of her shampoo, feeling the fluttering of her heart against mine and wondering how I got so lucky.

"There you are," the exasperated voice of my wife calls. "What are you doing? People will be showing up soon."

"I was showing this wee tottie her new room," I answer, pointing to the window that just went in yesterday. "I think she's given it the seal of approval."

"She'd better, since it practically took an act of God to get it out in one piece." Key laughs, leaning in to nuzzle her nose against our daughter's. "It will be nice for her to look at in her new big-girl bed."

"Your mother is a stubborn thing," I tell my wee one. "That's where you get it from."

"Mummy," she calls, reaching out her chubby little arms.

"Come here, gorgeous," Key coos, taking her from me. "Are you ready for cake?"

She claps her hands, her face lighting up. "Cake!"

"Well, she knows *that* word perfectly," I chuckle.

"Because she's a genius," Key says sweetly. "She gets it from me."

"Oh, does she now?"

"Obviously." She presses a kiss to one round cheek. "Someone is two years old today," she says. "Do you know who?"

Another peal of laughter, followed by a repeated round of clapping. "Sorcha!"

I watch Key's eyes soften, watch as she meets mine with a grin full of emotion as she no doubt marvels over the same things I find myself marveling over. That we have this, even against all odds. That we're *here*.

"That's right," Key says quietly. "Sweet Sorcha."

"Oi! Anyone home?"

"That'll be your grandpa," I tell Sorcha at the sound of Finlay's entry.

Sorcha immediately starts wiggling to be put down, toddling away on her tiny feet to meet Finlay in the doorway. "Granpa!"

"Och, would you look at that," Finn practically chokes, crouching to sweep the little girl into his arms. "Have you gotten bigger, lass? You're practically grown!"

"I *two*, Granpa," Sorcha says in an almost scolding tone.

"Not too auld to be *tickled*, then, aye?"

His fingers dig into the adorable little rolls of her side, and Sorcha starts to wiggle and squeal in his hold, her screams of laughter echoing in the empty room as she turns this way and that to escape Finlay's grasp. I open my mouth to warn him, but then Sorcha positively *shrieks* with her giggling, and with a soft *pop*—we're standing in a much darker room.

Finlay goes still, holding Sorcha out with a surprised expression. "Well, that's new."

"Yeah," Key says with an amused expression. "At least she didn't bust it. You should see what happens when she *cries*."

Finlay's eyes swim, his voice thicker when he says, "Och, she'll be grown before we know it."

Rhona appears then, squeezing in next to her husband, frowning. "Don't be rushing her life away, Finlay. Let the lass be a wean for a while yet." Her usually stoic face crumples into an expression of utter delight when Sorcha reaches for her, plucking her from her husband and pressing a rain of kisses to her full cheeks as the little girl squeals. "My sweet girl," Rhona says sweetly. "Look at how special you are! I've missed you."

"You saw her yesterday," I point out.

Rhona clucks her tongue, not even bothering to look at me. "*Haud yer wheesht.*"

Key flicks her eyes up to the light fixture, staring at it for a moment before it blinks back to life.

"Adain!" Sorcha begs delightedly. "Mummy, adain!"

Key grins impishly as she winks at Sorcha, the light flickering back out just to come right back on when she sticks out her tongue.

"All right, all right," Rhona huffs. "Enough showing off. Some of us have to lift our auld bones out of chairs when we want to turn the lights on and off."

"It's truly a struggle," I sigh, earning myself a pinch in the side from my wife.

"Hello! Is someone going to help me bring in this bloody thing? It's fucking huge!"

Key rolls her eyes, already bounding off to no doubt scold Rory for not heeding her "no cursing around Sorcha" rule.

"The house is coming along," Finlay notes. "Almost done, then?"

"Aye," I tell him. "My da and I just finished the window for Sorcha's room yesterday."

Finlay chuckles. "I'd say you'll be happy to get this wee thing out of your bed, but something tells me you'll miss her."

"We might need to ease her into sleeping in her own bed," I answer. "So she isn't overwhelmed."

"Oh, aye," Rhona laughs. "Purely for her sake."

Finlay looks up from tickling Sorcha in the side. "How is your da?"

"He's all right," I tell him. "He and Mum should be here soon."

"S'bout time he convinced her to move back," Rhona tuts. She eyes me curiously. "And how are you two getting on?"

"We're . . . good," I settle on, surprised to find that I mean it.

It's taken a long time for me and my mother to find our way back to a relationship, but the return of my da has really paved the way of things. It's been a hard road for her, I'll admit; she lost a part of herself when he went into the loch so long ago, and I believe she might just now be finding it. We might never be what we were, but I have too much good in my life to complain about things that I *don't* have.

Rhona nods. "Good. Wouldn't want to have to knock some sense into the auld gal."

"Probably for the best," I laugh.

Two identical blond heads peek around the doorway, both shoving at each other to try to fight for space. "Are we having the party in this empty room? We've got cake and stuffs waiting."

"And B-E-E-R," Rory whispers, glancing at Sorcha.

Key appears then, smacking him on the back of the head. "You did not bring alcohol to my daughter's *second* birthday."

"It's a special occasion!" he argues.

Key just glares at him, and Blair shoos him away, flashing Key an apologetic grin. "We'll just save the, ah, *refreshments* for after the wean goes to bed, aye?"

"I'd better go see to it that they don't break something," Rhona sighs as she passes Sorcha back to Key. "Finlay, go and fetch the presents from the car."

I cock a brow. "Presents?"

"I'll not hear a word on how many," Rhona calls back, her voice disappearing back through the house.

Finlay leans in, lowering his voice. "She'll be trying to blame the number on me, but believe you me—it was all your granny."

"Finlay!"

He presses his fingers to his lips in a *shh* gesture, following Rhona back toward their car, leaving me alone with Key and Sorcha.

Key's eyes sweep around the space, smiling. "It finally looks all done."

"Aye, it does," I answer. "I'll be adding her furniture tomorrow."

"I don't know if I'm ready to move her to her own bed."

"Aye, love, I know," I sigh, stepping closer to press a kiss to her forehead. "But that's the way of weans, I fear. They always grow up when we aren't looking." I duck my head to give Sorcha a similar peck at her forehead, lingering for a moment more to once again breathe in the sweet scent of her. "But you'll always be our wee princess, aye?"

"Can't believe I let *that* happen," Key mutters.

A laugh tumbles out of me. "Now, darlin'. Don't be jealous. You're still the princess of my heart."

"Mummy pwincess," Sorcha announces. "I pwincess too."

"Aye," I tell her. "That's right."

"Tan I haff cake now?"

"Well, it's not quite time . . ." Key starts, trailing off when we hear footsteps clodding inside behind us.

"Lachlan," my father says with a slap on my shoulder. "Oh, och, that looks michty fine. Doesn't it, love?"

My mother's small frame appears beside him in the doorway; her features are still somewhat alien to me after having gone so long without seeing them. Her pale blonde hair is pulled up into a bun, her clear blue eyes that are just like mine sweeping over the room.

"Oh, aye, it looks wonderful, son." She turns to me, a wariness to her eyes that hasn't quite dissipated even in the years since we first started reconciling. Like she's afraid I might reject her at any moment. "Was it terribly hard to remove from the auld castle?"

"A right pain in the arse," my da snorts.

Key elbows him. "Language."

"Oh, sorry, lass," he says sheepishly. He notices Sorcha in her arms, his face lighting up. "And there's the wee tottie of the hour! Come here, hen."

My da takes a wiggling Sorcha, nuzzling her nose with his. It still makes my chest tight, seeing them together—it's something I thought I would never have.

"And here's Granny Greer too," Da says, turning toward my mother. My mother's usually tense features soften considerably at the sight of Sorcha, a magic our daughter has all her own. It's impossible not to be enamored with her.

"Hello, love," my mother says. "Happy birthday."

"I two!"

My mother's face splits into a grin. "Aye, that's right. You sure are."

"Right then," my da pipes up. "Why don't we go see if we can find you a sweet, aye?"

"Don't let her fill up on junk before cake," Key scolds.

I chuckle. "Technically, cake is also junk, love."

"No one asked you," she tuts.

My father scuttles off with my daughter, leaving the three of us behind. My mother looks around the room once more with emotion in her eyes, and I can see it, I think, how much healing she still has to do. I know that years of grief can't be undone so easily. Still, it warms me to see her trying so hard.

She places a hand on my shoulder, squeezing gently. "This looks amazing, son."

"Thank you," I tell her, reaching to squeeze her hand back.

She pulls her hand away, only to press one palm against Key's cheek and the other against mine, smiling softly. "I'm so proud of the both of you. Thank you for letting us be a part of Sorcha's special day."

"We're happy you're here," Key tells her, and I feel my love for this woman grow impossibly.

My mother gives a slow nod, grinning at us once more before saying something about finding my father, leaving Key and me alone in Sorcha's room.

"I'd better go and change her clothes," Key says with a frown. "I have something that we can just toss after she inevitably gets filthy." She turns her eyes to me. "Can you get the ice cream out so it can thaw a little?"

"Aye, I will," I answer. "Be there in a bit."

She closes the distance between us, lifting her mouth to mine, and even after so much time with her—the press of her lips feels no less life-changing than it did the first time. Her kisses mean as much and yet *more* than they did when we first shared them; now they are for skinned knees and bedtime and stolen moments on the couch and every blissfully normal thing in between that I wouldn't have if not for her.

And I haven't, for one moment, ever stopped being in awe of her.

"See you in a minute," she says against my mouth.

My lips curve against hers. "Aye, you will."

I watch Key leave the room in search of our daughter, that same sensation of feeling like my entire heart goes with them whenever they stray too far clenching my chest tight. I take another turn about Sorcha's finished room, thinking of the memories she'll make here, that *we'll* make here—our new home resting on Greer land that sat long abandoned. The window was the final piece; I wasn't sure about the painstaking process of moving it when Key first mentioned it, but with the help of her magic and a lot of careful work, it's here now, watching over my daughter in the same way it watched over me as a child. I hope that, as she grows, it will remind her where she comes from, and when she's old enough to hear the entire story of how she came to be—it will be a reminder that where she goes is entirely in her hands.

*You are* not *who you are because of where you come from; you are who you are because of where* you *choose to go.*

Key's words still stay rooted deep in my heart, just as much a comfort today as they were the first time she uttered them to me when I needed them most.

Maybe it's the occasion of celebrating Sorcha's birth that has me feeling so sentimental, or maybe it's just that I'm so bloody *grateful* for what I have—but I can't help sending out a silent thank-you to another Sorcha, hoping that wherever she is, she knows that even though a Greer almost took her life once, she ultimately gave life back to one. I hope that somewhere she knows that I will take care of her family, that I will never take them for granted.

Because they're mine now too.

## Acknowledgments

My friends, I remember the exact moment when this book was conceptualized. My agent asked me what I might do next for a bout in paranormal, and I remember pitching vampires. When she told me we needed something "more fresh," I jokingly said: "What if the Loch Ness Monster was a cursed human, not just a monster?" I was surprised at first when she said, "Now wait a minute—" and even more so when the people of Berkley liked the idea. All this time later, I can't believe this is what we ended up with—something I had so much fun writing, something I'm really *proud* of.

Sure, it's a silly book that explores the possibility of the Loch Ness Monster being a hot, cursed man—but it also challenged me in new ways, pushed my creative boundaries, and even inspired me to keep going in this direction, in a way. (But more on that later. *wink*)

As always, there was a lot of hand-holding involved when it came to the fruition of this cryptid concept, so in no particular order, I would like to thank:

Cindy Hwang, my fabulous editor and (known by me as) my publishing mama—I could ask for no better person to push me in the best of ways (and to encourage me to include more monster smut). Truly, she is one of a kind, and I am so grateful for her.

To my amazing agency and my agent, Jessica Watterson, who makes up a good chunk of the aforementioned hand-holding with all the incessant text messages she has to put up with from one neurotic author (read: me). She may regret giving me her phone number, but I will never regret signing on for her particularly wonderful brand of comfort and understanding and all-around support. (Plus, always a special shout-out to "Money Daddy," aka Jennifer Kim, for sending my favorite emails.)

My Bejeweled Babes™, Jessica Mangicaro and Kristin Cipolla (and a special shout-out to the newest BB, little Cipollina, who I am sure will grow up to be as wonderful as her mother), who let me ask the silly questions, who pump me up when I need it most, and who are just honestly fucking rock stars at their jobs—I adore you, ladies.

The fantastic art team for always creating bangers, and for that matter, the *entire* Berkley team for being so amazing at what they do—I know from experience that it isn't easy putting a book out into the world, but you folks are so good that you make it almost look like it is. Shout-out to Rita Frangie Batour, who gave me the tartan spine of my dreams (friends, did you see that little heart lock? A GENIUS, I tell you), and Monika Roe for what might be my favorite cover to date (do I say that every time?).

To Blair, the Scottish lass I referenced in my dedication, who not only beta'd this book and made sure the Scotticisms were on point but also, as mentioned, forgave me for giving Nessie a penis. (Is this a good time to say I'm aware that's not considered to be correct? I took liberties.) So grateful for you, mate.

And then there are the people who I am lucky enough to call not only cheerleaders but also friends, in no particular order:

Kristen (Daddy), who, as always, has a constant metaphorical grip on my hand and a hand on my brow holding my head as I cry about whatever silly bitch (which she affectionately calls me when I am being one—e.g., downing myself) thing I've done that day—the universe knew I needed you and delivered accordingly in bringing you into my life.

Ruby Dixon for always checking in on me to make sure I'm not losing my mind and for also letting me pester her incessantly for her new material the second she finishes writing it (I am a fan first and a friend second, let's be clear)—I'm forever grateful that Cindy pushed us together like two kids at a playdate.

Elena Armas for the twenty-minute voice note about how much she loved this book and for being such an angel in general, really. It's special when you become friends with your favorite authors, and I have made so many of those friends that I feel especially blessed. (Elena, I will get Jack's book to you, and as a thank-you, he IS yours.)

Kate (Golden (wife)), who not only made a romantasy reader out of me but then proceeded to become one of my very best friends—blurbing your book was one of the best things I ever did, because it brought me you (and Jack, who deserves a shout-out, because it never hurts to have a stephusband).

Keri, my sibling of choice, thank you for always being there to tell me when I am being silly and to share even sillier memes with, and for literally any of the thousands of things you do for me on a weekly basis (even if it's googling something because I am too lazy to do it). You're my favorite.

To Sophie, for telling me what a *limpet* was and making it one of my new favorite words, so much so that I had to rush back and add it somewhere in this book. (And for always being so lovely.)

To the betas and cream chat (don't ask) as a whole: Kristen, Kate, Keri, Vanessa, Amber—sure, I forced you all to be friends with one another as well as with me, but look at us. Who would have thought? You are not only my betas but also my friends, and that's a very beautiful and rare thing, in my opinion. (Special shout-out to Vanessa for always having an air mattress at the ready for me and for always being down to put up with following me around while I buy anime figurines I don't need.)

To Dan, who miraculously didn't need coaxing to read this monster smut like she did with *The Fake Mate*—after fifteen-plus years of friendship, I am happy that you are finally learning I am always right. (I love you, even if you're as stubborn as I am.)

A special shout-out to all the fantastic bookstagrammers, bloggers, journalists, BookTokers, librarians, and reviewers who continue to make this a reality—I am grateful for every comment, every article mention, every TikTok, every post. You all make it possible to see love for my books in real time, and that is such a special thing.

On that note: to the READERS—you continue to make my dream a reality. YOU did that. Without you, none of this would be possible, and I can never express my gratitude.

And last but certainly not least, my husband, who is never afraid to tell me when I am being a neurotic silly goose, who hypes me up when I need it, and holds me when it's needed even more—I love you. It's easy to write about love when you've already found your forever.

bjection. Leading the witness."

I bite my tongue, quietly seething as I resist the urge to look back at the owner of the deep, honeyed voice calling out in a bored tone.

"Let me rephrase," I say as evenly as I can manage, keeping my attention on the man in front of me. "You said in your statement that you would often see a visitor coming to the house while Mrs. Johanson was home alone. Is that correct, Mr. Crane?"

The man nods, peeking warily at the woman in question. "That's correct."

"And during those visits, where was Mr. Johanson?"

"He was usually at work, ma'am."

"And this visitor, was it a man or a woman?"

"It was a man."

I bite back a grin. "I see. How long would this man stay?"

Mr. Crane reaches to scratch at his thinning hair, shifting in his seat. It had taken me a hell of a lot to get him on the stand; in the end it was only the promise from Mr. Johanson that he would keep his gardening job regardless of the outcome of this trial that he finally agreed.

"It varied," Mr. Crane said. "Sometimes an hour. Sometimes more."

"So it's safe to assume that Mrs. Johanson knew this man . . . well, correct?"

"Objection." I hear a sigh behind me. "Speculation."

"Rephrase," I say tightly, still refusing to look at him. "Did you ever see Mrs. Johanson and the man interacting when he would visit, Mr. Crane?"

Mr. Crane shakes his head. "No, ma'am. He always went straight inside the house."

"But it was always the same man?"

"Yes, ma'am. As far as I could tell."

"Thank you, Mr. Crane." I give my attention to Judge Hoffstein. "No further questions, Your Honor."

I try not to look at him when I return to my table, I really do—but that pull is there, the one I so desperately wish didn't plague me anytime we're in the same room together. I can feel his eyes linger on me when I'm finally able to avert my gaze, feel it like the weight of his fingers along my skin as I retake my seat.

He stands slowly, one hand reaching to fasten the button of his suit—a deft, practiced motion that makes the tendons in his too-large hands flex—and I can't help the way my eyes are drawn there, remembering the warmth of them on my body hardly even a week ago. I catch a hint of a smirk when I turn my face to meet his eyes, feeling warmth creep up my neck as I clench my teeth.

*Fucking Ezra Hart.*

I train my eyes forward, keeping them on the nervous older man on the stand, in quiet support.

"Mr. Crane," Ezra starts. "Did you know Mrs. Johanson's visitor?"

"No, sir," Mr. Crane answers. "I was told that—"

"That's hearsay," Ezra cuts him off. "What you *heard* is irrelevant." He shoves his hands in his pockets, strolling casually to the side and flicking his gaze to mine for the briefest of moments. "I'm asking if you ever actually *met* Mrs. Johanson's visitor."

Mr. Crane's eyes dart to mine, looking unsure. "Well, no, I didn't."

"So there's no possible way for you to know the purpose of that man's visits. Correct?"

Mr. Crane is quiet for a moment, and my heart thuds in my ribs. There's no way that Ezra can possibly suggest—

"No, sir," Mr. Crane answers. "I could not."

"I see." Ezra's mouth turns up in the ghost of a smile. "Just as you couldn't know of Mrs. Johanson's recent interests in spiritual direction?"

"I . . ." Mr. Crane blinks with confusion, and I can feel the same emotion playing on Mr. Johanson's and my faces. "No? I didn't know that."

"Of course you didn't," Ezra practically coos. "It's not something she advertised. The only people who knew this were her close friends. Well, and her husband, of course." Ezra looks back at our table. "Although I very much doubt Mr. Johanson would recall this, given that he rarely took note of Mrs. Johanson's interests."

"Objection," I call. "Speculation."

"Withdrawn," Ezra says with a grin. "Mr. Crane, did you know that the man you saw coming in and out of Mrs. Johanson's house was her spiritual advisor?"

*Oh, what a load of horseshit.*

"Objection, Your Honor," I almost laugh. "This is irrelevant."

Ezra directs his attention to the judge. "This is completely relevant, Your Honor, I assure you."

Judge Hoffstein nods minutely. "Overruled."

"Thank you." Ezra inclines his head. "You see, Mrs. Johanson's visitor, a Mr. Jacobs, had been hired several weeks prior by Mrs. Johanson to oversee her spiritual direction. There was nothing nefarious about their encounters. If you'll be so kind as to take a look at Exhibit 13—you'll note the credentials I've provided to prove Mr. Jacobs's employment at a company offering such services."

*Son of a bitch. How did we miss that?*

Ezra looks smug as the judge peruses the bit of evidence in question; to an outsider he would simply look contemplative, but I've seen that look on his face too many times. In *and* out of the courtroom.

"Mrs. Johanson was simply exploring her new faith," Ezra continues. "There is no evidence to suggest that she and Mr. Jacobs were meeting under false pretenses, and she paid him for his time. Therefore, this line of questioning isn't relevant to this alimony hearing."

Ezra waits until the exhibit has been passed to the bailiff before he turns back to the witness. "Thank you for your time, Mr. Crane." He looks to the judge. "No further questions, Your Honor."

Ezra takes his seat on his side of the courtroom, a small smile on his lips, practically laughing at the way I'm shooting daggers right now. I feel Mr. Johanson lean into me, whispering, "She can't seriously pull this shit, can she?"

I want to tell him no, that cheating spouses get what they deserve—that *doesn't* include an overly fat alimony check—but I know that without any concrete evidence of infidelity, which we haven't been able to unearth no matter how hard we've looked, it's likely Mrs. Johanson will be milking her soon-to-be-ex-husband dry for years to come.

*Fucking Ezra Hart.*

—

I pinch the bridge of my nose as I wait for the elevator to open, trying to stave off the headache forming behind my eyes. It had taken weeks to find out about Mrs. Johanson's little *spiritual advisor* who came twice a week like clockwork, unbeknownst to her husband while he was at work, and it had felt like an ace in the hole. Until Ezra swooped in and plugged it right up, that is.

They call him "the heartbreak prince" in the papers; it's a stupid fucking moniker that he absolutely eats up, I'm sure. His win record is astounding, and every time I have to be in the same courtroom with him, I know I'm in for a world of bullshit. Not to say I haven't won against him, because I have—but not nearly as much as I'd like, today included.

The elevator dings, and I climb inside, grateful to find it empty as I settle against the back wall to let my head thunk against the cool metal. I close my eyes as I wait for the doors to close, only snapping them back open when I hear something nudging between them to force them back open.

"Room for one more?"

I narrow my eyes at him. "You could always take the stairs. Get a workout in."

Ezra laughs as he strolls into the elevator, leaning against the bar at the back wall as I scoot away from him. "You've never had any complaints about my body."

I glare up at him as the elevator doors slide closed, trapping us inside. He always knows exactly what to say to push my buttons, just like he knows that his stupid face and body are lethal distractions when it comes to remembering how much I dislike him. It's not the dark blond hair that always looks like someone just ran their fingers through it, not the full mouth or the piercing green eyes or the amazing bone structure that makes his face look carved—it's all of it, really. The broad shoulders that fill out his tailored suits a little too well, his long fingers that stir up wicked memories, even his stupid cologne makes you want to lean in closer to get a better whiff.

At least he only has four to five inches on me—I've always been on the taller side, and not having to crane my neck up to his six foot three from my five foot nine gives me an ounce of satisfaction. Especially in my heels.

"Yeah, well, that's just about the only good thing you have going for you," I mumble back, facing my eyes forward to watch the numbers tick by and mentally urging them to go faster.

There's a contrast between us in the reflection of the shiny metal doors—my inky black hair to his golden brown, my pale skin to his bronzed, his brawn to my lithe figure—looking at us side by side, one would never think to put us together.

*Which we aren't*, I mentally correct. Together. Because we aren't. Except . . .

"Really?" He inches a little closer. "I'm told I'm pretty charming."

"Are those people on your payroll?"

"I can think of a few times when *you've* found me charming, Dani."

I roll my eyes. I'm used to people calling me Dani; when you have a name like Danica, I guess it's easy to jump to the nickname—but something about the way Ezra says it always makes my stomach do something funny. I'm sure I'm not the only one Ezra amuses himself with. There's no doubt in my mind that his easy playboy act comes from vast amounts of real-life experience—yet I can't help but wonder if anyone else in what is surely a very wide net of his sexual conquests succumbs to his annoyingly effective charms quite as often (albeit begrudgingly) as I do.

"I can assure you I have never found you charming," I toss back dryly. "Maybe mildly amusing. Your dick, at least."

He clutches his hand to his chest, and I try not to notice how large it looks against his tie. "Only mildly? That isn't what you said when you were screaming my—"

The elevator doors slide open as we come to a halt, and I immediately bolt out of it, trying to put distance between Ezra and me before he notices how flushed my neck most likely is. Not that he lets me escape that easily, since I hear his footsteps, heavy and quick as he catches up to me.

"I'm free tonight, you know," he says casually.

I keep my expression blank, hoping the people milling around in the lobby don't notice how close he's walking beside me. "Good for you. Sounds like an excellent time to take up a hobby."

"Oh, but I would much rather enjoy the one I've already got."

I glance at him from the side, frowning. "What's that?"

"See, there's this certain opposing counsel who makes the most delicious noises when my fingers are—"

I spin on my heel, hissing under my breath as we come to a stop in front of the large glass doors that lead outside of the courthouse. "I told you," I grit out. "Last time was the last time."

"Right." He flashes me his white, perfect teeth—stark against the deep pink of his lips, and I have to force myself to keep my eyes on his. "But you said that the time before that." He leans in a little closer, practically looming over me as he lowers his voice. "And the time before that . . . and the time before that . . ."

"I mean it this time," I argue, trying to convince him or me, I'm not sure. "It was stupid to begin with. You're an asshole, and I was . . ." *Hard up? Horny? Out of my mind?* "It was a lapse of judgment on my part."

"Eight lapses of judgment," Ezra says with a low whistle. "I think they call that a bad habit, Dani. Maybe *you* need a hobby. You know, besides me."

I clench my fists at my sides; I know he's teasing me, but it hits a little too close to home. Especially because I *know* that constantly sleeping with Ezra—someone I barely tolerate outside of what we do behind closed doors—is the stupidest thing I've ever done. After everything with Grant . . . you'd think I would make smarter decisions when it comes to the opposite sex.

*It's just sex*, I soothe myself. *Just scratching an itch.*

Even if I've scratched this particular itch more times than I'd like.

I make a frustrated sound, shoving him away and pushing through the doors as I stalk off quickly. He doesn't follow me this time, but I can hear his stupid laugh even from halfway down the steps.

*Fucking. Ezra. Hart.*


I feel a little less out of sorts when I'm back at the firm; I'm not thrilled to tell my boss how miserably today went with the Johansons, but at least here I can put the headache of Ezra and my antagonistic . . . whatever we have . . . at the back of my mind for a little bit. I drop my case files in my office, noticing on my way out that Nate's and Vera's are empty; I guess they've already headed home for the day.

The door to Manuel's office is cracked at the other end of the hall, however, and I step toward it to update him on everything before I finish up for the day myself. I find him sitting behind his desk poring over a stack of papers, his neat salt-and-pepper hair swept into his usual perfect style. I don't think I've ever seen Manuel Moreno with a single hair out of place, and since Chicago is known as the Windy City, that is a feat.

"Danica," he greets as I knock lightly against the open door. "Come in, come in. How did it go today?"

I purse my lips. "Not as well as I would have liked. The guy she was seeing was apparently her 'spiritual advisor.'"

The deep wrinkle that lives permanently between Manuel's brow worsens. "That's the horseshit they're spinning?"

"Well, horseshit does happen to be a specialty of Ezra's."

"I want to hate the bastard," Manuel snorts, "but he's damn good."

*I refuse to even acknowledge how "good" Ezra is.*

"I've got a lead on a housekeeper who quit a couple of months ago," I tell him. "I'm trying to get in touch with her. Maybe she saw something between them of a more *physical* nature."

"Great. Let me know."

I'm about to return to my desk when he stops me.

"I actually wanted to talk to you," he calls.

I turn back. "Yes?"

"We had a potential client call today. A Mrs. Vassiliev."

I frown. "Why does that sound familiar?"

"Her husband owns Vassiliev Development."

"Shit." My mouth parts in surprise. "The real estate mogul?"

"He owns half the city, practically. God knows how many others."

"They're divorcing?"

"It appears so. A friend of mine recommended us."

"That's great." I wince. "Well, not for *her*, but . . ."

"I was thinking that you should take it."

I blink back at him. "What?"

"You've been here for six years now. You mentioned last year that you were interested in a junior partner position, and with Hinata retiring . . ."

"Wait, are you saying . . . ?"

"I'm saying that Mrs. Vassiliev stands to make this firm an enormous amount of money if she comes out on top in her divorce. She claims to have all sorts of evidence of his infidelity."

"Holy shit."

"But there's a catch."

"There always is."

"She signed a prenup."

I groan. "Of course she did. How solid is her evidence?"

"I guess that's for you to find out."

"Not making this easy for me, huh?"

"High risk, high reward," he chuckles before his expression turns serious. "I think winning this case would be the perfect thing to bring to the other partners and prove you're ready to step up."

"You'd be willing to go to bat for me?"

Manuel rolls his eyes. "I've known you since you were seven. As many T-ball games as I went to with you and your parents, I have 'gone to bat' for you plenty of times in your life."

"That's corny, but I'll take it," I laugh. "I just . . . You already stuck your neck out giving me this job, and I don't want anyone to think I'm getting special treatment just because you and Dad are old friends."

"You graduated top of your class at Harvard Law. It was hardly a burden to offer you a position here. Just like it won't be when you win this case, and I show the other partners what an asset you are."

"I . . . Wow. Yes. Of course. This is . . . Wow."

"You have a meeting with Mrs. Vassiliev at the end of the week," he informs me. "She's a character, but I think you can handle her."

I nod aimlessly. "Yes. I . . . Thank you, Manny."

"Don't mention it." He waves me off. "Feel free to loop Nate and Vera in. I'm sure they'll be foaming at the mouth to be a part of it regardless."

I grin. He isn't wrong about that. This is one of the biggest cases we've had since I started. I can already hear Nate squealing. "I will."

"Don't stay up at your desk all night," he chides. "You have to sleep sometime."

I roll my eyes. "Yeah, yeah."

He gives me a dismissive gesture as he turns his attention back to his paperwork, and I leave his office with a wide smile on my face and a fluttering in my stomach. I've been waiting for this opportunity for the last year or more, and now with it so close—I can feel a bubbling excitement humming under my skin.

A buzzing in the pocket of my slacks distracts me as I walk back to my desk, and all the elated feelings simmer out into annoyance as I take note of the message.

> **ASSHOLE:** I'll be home all night if you change your mind
> about . . . coming.

I grimace. That was terrible, even for him. Which makes the little flicker of warmth in my gut all the more infuriating. Sleeping with Ezra Hart had been a bad idea the *first* time it happened, something I blame on temporary insanity and thinking with my vagina— and the next seven times definitely didn't help things.

If only he wasn't so *good* at it. Bastard.

I tap out a quick response, shoving down the urges that bubble up in spite of his stupid fucking text.

**ME:** Sorry. Better things to do.

I feel smug for about three seconds before my phone pings again.

**ASSHOLE:** I highly doubt there's better than me, but keep telling yourself that. 😏

I scowl, shoving my phone in my pocket.
*Fucking Ezra Hart.*

# About the Author

Illustration by Jessica Patrick

**Lana Ferguson** is a *USA Today* bestselling author and sex-positive nerd whose works never shy from spice or sass. A faded Fabio cover found its way into her hands at fifteen, and she's never been the same since. When she isn't writing, you can find her randomly singing show tunes, arguing over which Batman is superior, and subjecting her friends to the extended editions of *The Lord of the Rings*. Lana lives mostly in her own head but can sometimes be found chasing her corgi through the coppice of the great American outdoors.

VISIT LANA FERGUSON ONLINE

LanaFerguson.com
 Lana-Ferguson-104378392171803
 LanaFergusonWrites

Ready to find
your next great read?

Let us help.

**Visit prh.com/nextread**

Penguin
Random
House